"A DIFFICULT B
DOWN."

San Francisco Chronicle

"Barbara Neil captures quirks of human behavior that bring her characters to life and paints a moving, complex portrait."

The New York Times Book Review

"If Blanche Dubois were to come back as a contemporary Londoner with a big, healthy trust fund to finance her every whim, she would probably resemble Grace Teape, the heroine's dear, flighty, self-destructive aunt in SOMEONE WONDERFUL, a bittersweet, oddly entertaining novel."

Chicago Tribune

"She does what Charles Dickens excelled in—creating characters who are both absurd and touchingly human. . . . Ms. Neil pulls everything together into an explosive and hopeful ending."

Richmond Times-Dispatch

"Something wonderful indeed is this story of a young English woman's growth into love and maturity. . . . Neil writes with grace and heart, and not a whit of sentimentality."

Publishers Weekly

Also by Barbara Neil:

AS WE FORGIVE

SOMEONE WONDERFUL

Barbara Neil

BALLANTINE BOOKS • NEW YORK

Library of Congress Catalog Card Number: 88-43016

ISBN 0-345-36655-7

This edition published by arrangement with Harper & Row, Publishers, Inc.

Manufactured in the United States of America

First Ballantine Books Edition: July 1990

FOR ANDREW, ALWAYS,
AND MY DEAR FRIEND CICI MARSHAM

Book
One

Chapter 1

LILY TEAPE KNELT STRAW-HATTED IN HER PREPOSTEROUS rose garden, pulling weeds from the caked and tumbled earth, wondering again how long it was since he had died. Years, months or weeks? She had lost track in the timelessness of grief, while all around her, beyond the dilapidated walls of the garden, beyond the olive grove with its statues knee-deep in grass, was the hazed and muted view of the Tuscan hills.

They had come there together: she fugitive from life; life fugitive from him. They knew he was dying before they came and that they would not have long to live out their love; they had even wondered whether that circumscription had helped them to make it so right, so thorough.

Raising herself with her hands on the small of her back (the primeval gesture of a woman heavy with child), she turned to look toward a stout olive tree beneath the shade of which Grace Teape sat in a wicker chair, face hidden by hair drained of color (drained in that complete way peculiar to redheads, leaving it not gray but a dusty white). Intent on sewing, she was almost still, almost serene, and when Lily Teape went over to her, knelt before her placing a hand upon her knee, it was a kind, lined face without artifice that smiled back at her.

"All right?" Lily Teape asked.

"All right," Grace Teape assured, holding up the oyster-silk panel she was smocking. "Look, I've nearly finished," and, with surprise, "Who'd have thought I could do that, that I have a talent? It is all right, isn't it?"

"It's really beautiful. You're an artist."

"An artist. Fancy." A twitch on the side of her face, brow

3

gathering, troubling, smoothing once more, something remembered and gone but Lily Teape saw.

"All right?"

"All right."

Lily Teape was kneeling at her own work again when, from the stone steps that led left and right to the first floor of the ancient villa, the housekeeper called, "Signora?" The muscly little woman stepped from the cool of indoors, bringing one hand to her hip where a red check teacloth was tied as apron, flicking flies from her black hair with the other while she used her forearm as shield against the glare.

"Signora?"

Lily Teape raised her head. "Anna, I was just wondering: how long has it been now?"

Anna dropped both arms in a mild gesture of impatience; this question had come frequently since the death, as though he were expected to return at any minute. She looked solicitously at her watch. A present from her son, it had the month, day, date and all sorts of other features she neither understood nor required, because her life was regulated simply; so it was nice for her to be able to use it. Lifting it close between finger and thumb, she scrutinized its face, then calculated, head back, fingers upon lips. "Is two month, three week and five day, Signora."

"Is that all?" Lily Teape pondered, went back to her work.

"Signora, there's a gentleman to see you."

"No thank you, Anna," declining as though she had been offered tea.

Anna shook her head and left the warm stone for the maroon shadow of the house.

Death should not feel sudden when you have been hanging around waiting for it, and his infirmity had so disabled him that his death demanded to be accepted and waited upon. But it was sudden to Lily Teape because he was there one moment, the self he had become, then she left the room for hardly more than half an hour and he died while she was gone. He was only forty-two, seventeen years older than Lily.

She had been kneeling beside him as he lay tidy-limbed under a tartan rug on one of the two sofas in the first-floor room, approached by those stone steps. It was a low-ceilinged room stretching the width of the house; the sofas were set by a large central fireplace where black-barked olive logs burnt; a table between the sofas was littered with newspapers and magazines: a fire-dim isle of Englishness from which the room spread away to the long windows at each end where a filigree light encroached upon the slate floor.

"I'm not ready," Lily Teape had said to him, kneeling beside him laying her head on his breast, her pale hair spreading on the denim of his shirt, a platinum quality about her imbuing her with an endless childhood. "There are things I forgot to say, so much more to talk about."

His eyes were closed, though sleeplessness was betrayed by his expression: rigid deep stamped lines about his mouth, a frown using all the wrinkles of his forehead, his whole face clutched into a premature old age by disability. His face had always been gaunt but now, folded and shaded, it was like some Highland coastline with its promontories, coves and caves. He had been a big man until he was struck by the shaking which brought all manner of unwonted movement. In the last days his body had lived without him, he had in all sanity absented himself. He was like a great medieval castle drawing up, shuttering, closing against the fray: life went on inside but deep, deep through the walls, beyond the sound and bother of it all. His large head with its weary curls had nodded in an endless, almost angry affirmative.

"I know you're awake," she had said. "It won't be yet, will it? Don't go yet."

"Sorry, Lily, no choice." He brought his hand with difficulty from beneath the rug, placing it heavily upon her face. "Time for you to grow up, eh?"

"I'm too old to grow up." She felt the convulsive movement of his hand, brought it round and pressed her mouth to the strained tendons of his wrist, murmuring into his flesh, "Traitor, you said you'd never leave me." She lifted her head to see the effect of her words, waited. Suddenly he opened both eyes wide, showing the complete circles of troubled gray iris, like two windows revealing sky on the inside of a house, then one lid slowly descended in a mannered wink, a single, determined movement among the rest.

"It's not funny," she said, and his hand moved within hers with some definition. She drew back and watched that hand as if it had spoken until, overcome by all the other tiny movements there, she lay her head upon it to press them away with her weight.

It was then she got up and went into her rose garden for half an hour. When she returned he had not moved at all but he had left.

If that had been the only exchange of its kind, it could have been considered a farewell of sorts, but it happened most days and they spoke of little else. He was too tired, too sealed away in the distress his body caused him, to want to talk. He never mentioned the baby although he knew, saw her growing. Sometimes he would put his hand against where it lay inside her, pull her to him, place his head there too. There was nothing to say, despite her claim that there was more; they had in fact said it all. They had discussed his death so frequently in brief sentences that it had lost its dread and become like a tedious trip they both knew he had to take, like going to visit a respected relative, the kind of trip you try to talk yourself out of but know you will make in the end because there is a duty there.

Anna returned to the steps. Again sheltering her eyes from the glare, she focused on the bending figure in the garden, drew her breath to call, thought better of it and descended, traversing the dry earthy paths marked out by bricks diagonally set. On her way, from a habit of tidiness, she gathered the branches and dead wood cut out and left around by Lily Teape. She knelt beside her. "Signora," her voice placatory, "please you come. I cannot make 'im go. 'E is someone you know."

"I know him?" Lily Teape grasped Anna's wrist, who looked down at the trembling hand and back to the questioning, excited eyes, "You say I know him? Anna? Him?" Each word on a higher note of expectation.

Anna covered the hand with her own callused one, shaking her head. "Dear Signora, no, no, it is not that one. You know it cannot be him anymore." She knew Lily Teape was still at the stage of grief where lunatic hopes sometimes assert themselves. She understood because her lover, the father of her son, had been a partisan during the Second World War, had been captured, tortured, killed; there had never been anyone else. "It is 'im of Signora Grace: Cochrane, Johnny Cochrane."

Confusion vanished instantly. Lily Teape looked sharply toward the villa, then across to where Grace Teape remained engrossed in her sewing and saw her as she had come to know her, as something frangible, vulnerable. Nothing must hurt her anymore.

"He shan't see her, Anna. I'll deal with him, but whatever happens he shan't see her."

Chapter 2

GRACE TEAPE WAS LILY TEAPE'S AUNT. A BEAUTY AND A socialite, she was widowed by the same accident that orphaned Lily: Grace's husband and Lily's mother, brother and sister (Michael and Meriel), were spectacularly smashed to pieces when a powerboat he was driving overturned at full speed in a race off Cowes in the Isle of Wight. Grace might have been with them too had she not twisted her ankle the day before. Lily was not there; no one knew where she was exactly: she was six years old and for a while lost to any world that cared. Strictly speaking, she should not have been orphaned by the accident except that Meriel was unmarried and had never named the father. Whether this was because she was ashamed of the liaison, liked intrigue or simply did not know, no one could tell: there had been a time when she was rich enough to indulge whichever tendency; until she became addicted to cocaine, heroin and confused politics. She had got through much of her own money when her trustees shut off funds.

When Lily was born somewhere, some time, Meriel's family were hardly aware of the event; she asked them for nothing. Only her dear brother, an officer in the Blues, cared enough to seek Meriel out to put her from time to time through expensive cures. But she always returned to the man she loved: a failed, smalltime terrorist who brought her down again and again. It was at the end of one of these cures that her brother took her with him and Grace to the Isle of Wight, to set her up with fresh air and some good life. Although the rich man's sport of powerboat racing was against what she felt she believed in, she could not resist the thrill.

7

Mr. and Mrs. Teape were devastated by the death of their only son, but of the death of their only daughter (if the two deaths had not been so bound) they would have said, "It's for the best." It was a relief not to have anymore the threat of her ugly life hanging over their tranquility. They were elderly people fairly tired of any life beyond their own, steeped in class, prejudice and disapproval. It was too late for anything more to grow from their weary lives, and they settled to wall themselves with their sorrow in their bleak, isolated house in Norfolk, until it was pointed out that there was the little girl to be found. Of course there was, they'd known that all the time, but there must be a father, somewhere, his turn now, surely. . . . They couldn't be expected . . . They couldn't.

Lily was found by a private detective (hired by her mother's trustees) in a squat in North London, six months after the accident. She was grubby, undernourished but cared for in a haphazard, communal way. Although she was not destitute—because of the remains of her mother's inheritance, which had been well invested—she was quite alone, save for the elderly Teapes.

They were prevailed upon. "Oh well," they said, "if you say fostering's the only alternative, then we'll have to have her for now. It's all too bad, it really is."

It was to be only a visit with the Teapes: a very temporary measure until something could be sorted out and because of that they did nothing to organize Lily's time with them; there was no point in slipping her into the village school only to remove her again, more disruption for the child. Fearing any emotional involvement, Mrs. Teape treated her like an adult guest, a friend of a friend that is foisted upon one for the night of a local dance. A sense of duty would occasionally come over her and she set upon Lily, plucking at her new clothes, vigorously plaiting her hair, rubbing her face with a flannel with such force as to rub her out altogether. Lily did not feel them to be like the hands and arms of the strangers that had held her during her six months alone, the ones that had pulled blankets about her shoulders at night, that had let her share their love. The Teapes could not, just could not, accept that this common-voiced, ill-mannered child was their granddaughter. She was a different breed from them and, after all, they only had the word of layabouts. The trustees had been satisfied but the Teapes still felt someone, somewhere was pulling a fast one on them . . . and yet . . . and yet . . .

So for two months they kept her, two months that were for Lily a lacuna of sadness and confusion. Where had all the people gone? She was used to an ever changing, on the whole friendly, group about her. She missed wherever it was she had been and she missed her mother.

"When's Mum coming? Where's she gone?"

"Mummy, not Mum. She's gone to live with Jesus. D'you see?" (The "D'you see?" was a habit with old Prudence Teape; sounding more like "juicy" it was drawn out into a patronizing interrogative doubting any understanding in the listener.)

"Who's Jesus? Can I go?"

That explained to Lily why these two old people seemed to be waiting for something, killing time; they were waiting to visit Jesus and she sensed they were looking forward to it. So did she.

Lily did not grasp that the Teapes were her grandparents: that this remote, gaunt-cheeked, set-haired lady was her mother's mother. She believed they were just more itinerants in her life (which they proved to be). She did not know about relations.

Lily spent hours of those days in a tall, dead nursery at the top of the house. Her lonely tinkering and shuffling there never disturbed the reigning desuetude: like her grandparents, the nursery seemed to have done with little children. The fire there was never lit. Alone she would struggle up upon the great painted rocking horse, its ponderous creaking intensifying the quiet all around. She would pull out toy soldiers and dolls and wonder about the little boy and girl depicted in pastels on either side of the mantelpiece, wonder if they would come to play with her upon the scabrous green linoleum that looked and felt like a survivor of smallpox. She asked her grandmother (whom she had been directed to call Prudence) if these children would come. The question produced an intriguing softening, trembling in her face. Head to one side, mouth parted, Lily watched as a tear, broken and flat, worked its way from the corner of one eye. Hardly a tear at all, it was as withered as its host. "Come along, come along" (voice matching that tear), "Henry wants you for Whist before tea" ("Lays the foundation of Bridge, young lady, social asset, y'know"). She found Whist hard to follow but enjoyed it as well as being beside the fire downstairs. After tea it would be bed at five o'clock. They did not expect her to sleep right away but to stay in the nursery which her room adjoined, with her frosty bathroom across the passage.

On one such afternoon during tea, picking her nose ("Don't *do* it, Lily, d'you hear?"), sucking butter from a crumpet ("Chew, don't suck, d'you see?"), Lily began, "When my mum's . . ."

"Mummy, not Mum."

". . . when my mummy's nicely settled wiv Jesus I expect she'll want me."

She had only meant it as a warning that she would not be around indefinitely and it gave her a sense of importance, a sense of elsewhere to say it; besides, she believed it. And she was pleased with the looks and sighs they exchanged.

Then Prudence said, "Lily, we have a guest tomorrow. Your Aunt Grace is coming to lunch. She wants to see you very much. Your poor Uncle Michael's wife. Do you remember him?"

"Was he the Michael who'd give me presents before he took my mum away?"

"Yes . . . well . . . a kind, good man . . ." (the trembling, the softening). "Go to bed now, Lily, and shut the door behind you."

Before she had quite done that, Lily heard Prudence say, "She's not one of us, I'll swear it."

No one came to say goodnight, but then no one ever had.

For those senior Teapes, Grace was one who had cast long shadows across the dunes of their disapproval: she was older than Michael, just to begin; she might now even be as much as thirty-five. She did not look that but the very sophistication of her youthfulness was suspicious. And there were her eyes ("Surely, Henry, you can see it?"), a worldliness there. Her father had been the owner of a chain of Steak Houses, gone expatriate. Why Michael had not picked someone from a nice secure army background, like his and their own, was beyond them.

And she had never given him children in ten years of marriage. There had been plenty of gossip about her thrown at one from all around, reasons why she could not.

Still, she was coming now, full of interest in Lily. How were they coping, she had wanted to know, and they told her it was all most inconvenient. Maybe she could help, she had said. Maybe she could.

Lily was in the nursery. The snow outside caused a pewter light to lean a short way through the windowpanes into the unlit room. A line of dolls was propped into a glandular cretonne sofa, a book before each one. In an uncanny imitation of her grand-mother's voice Lily addressed the dolls, "Can't read? Can't even begin to? This is all too much." Holding up templates for the glass eyes to gaze upon, "This is an 'A,' d'you hear-ah? This is a 'B,' d'you see-ah?" She knew her alphabet. Someone had taught her once; she remembered the face, she did not know the name; she remembered the place, she did not know where.

"Lily?" Prudence called from somewhere far.

"Lilegh," Lily said to herself, with no impertinence, only a distracted pleasure in imitation, a spontaneous sound mirror of what her ear received, adding in her own voice to the dolls, "An' I want you lot readin' by the time I get back."

Slowly she passed from the nursery to the stairwell where she stalked the banister looking down to ascertain the nature of the guest called Aunt Grace.

Lily was not shy, to her grandparents' dismay, but she had learnt to approach people warily; there had been times when she had been inexplicably cuffed. Finding nothing was to be gained by listening at the top of the stairs, because the drawing-room was two floors below with its door shut (like every other door in this house of drafts), she descended.

Lily turned the uncomfortably embellished brass knob, large in her little hand, and entered the drawing-room. Right away the enveloping warmth made her nose run. In there it was light and golden with coal-fire, secure, comfortable, hemmed, letting winter do its own thing outside, melting it at the windows when it dared approach. Erect like two gray flagpoles, their flags flaccid about them, her grandparents stood before the fire, holding small glasses in similar protective gestures across their breasts. There was a wonderful scent in the room that had never been there before but Lily saw no Grace, Aunt Grace. And even then, Lily remembered years later, she had felt disappointment.

"Now then," her grandmother said, with an air of something to be got on with, as though there had been silence before she entered, "here she is."

There was gentle disturbance on the high sofa with its back to Lily, then the top of a pale face with green eyes, a cloud of light red hair, emerged above the line of the sofa back; on either side of the half-face, red fingernails pressed into the chinz. As the movement was made, that dream of scent oscillated in the firewarm air, approaching, greeting Lily before a word was spoken. The eyebrows raised, eyes creased to a smile and the un-seen mouth uttered, "Helloooo. But look at you: *really*, *really* pretty.'' The lovely spectre swung away from Lily's sight toward the Teapes by the fire. They could view Lily without turning. The voice continued, ''You never told me she was so like Meriel.''

''Meriel had black hair.'' The tone implied: Meriel was human.

''But her face. Her face. That lovely little face.''

The Teapes looked embarrassed (an effect enthusiasm had always produced upon them).

The eyes and brows, the breeze of red hair, turned back again to Lily. ''Come in, come round and sit by me.''

Lily walked around the sofa to see before her the smear of rainbow color, a softness, an ethereal vibrance; like a great dragonfly landed in an earthbound room, this beautiful woman seemed to be aflutter. Even when she was quite still, with long arms outstretched in patient greeting to Lily, there was a hum of animation coming from within her.

Lily was unable to move into those arms for a million reasons, like dirty shoes and runny nose, like saying ''Mum'' instead of ''Mummy,'' like not knowing where anyone had gone or who anyone was, like dolls who could not read. For a reason like being Lily at all, she could not move until, arms still wide, the woman put her head to one side, smiling so sadly, so sweetly. ''Come on, darling, come to Grace.'' And Lily went to her, went to her and cried all over the rainbow silk and cashmere.

The arms wrapped her, the jaw caressed her head. Unseen, but felt by Lily, Grace Teape removed one hand, looked at it, presented it to the Teapes, mouthing the words, ''S-h-e-'-s w-e-t.''

With no concession to Lily's presence, Prudence Teape answered in her sculpted voice, ''That's right: wet. Day and night. Knows no shame, knows no better.''

But the arm came back and held Lily again, just where it had been.

Even when you are six you know when something's up. Lily had sensed it when they mentioned Aunt Grace's visit beforehand and in the conversation that now fell fragmented upon her understanding she knew that a move was ahead; she felt herself aligned with Grace from the start. They'd be off to Jesus's soon. The Teapes spoke as though Lily were not present and only when Grace brought the conversation back to Lily did she speak at all.

". . . and she never goes out. Total lack of interest in things bucolic."

"But there's snow outside. It's cold," Grace said.

"She has warm clothes. Children don't mind the cold. What about snowmen?"

"Do you like snowmen, Lily?" Grace turned her luminousness on Lily.

"I don't know any."

"No, you build them with snow. Like little people. Would you like to try?"

Lily stared at Grace with suspicion, then went to the window, looking at the flat whiteness, the humps of besnowed bushes, the nothing, the nowhere, and forgot to answer.

"D'you see?" she heard Prudence say.

"Lily?" Grace came behind her, kneeling quickly with a sneeze of hidden silk, putting her arm around Lily's back. "Don't you like it outside?"

"Too much air."

The calm acquiescence of Grace's reply, cradled in a sigh, "Yes, it's quite true, there's a lot of that," implied Lily had hit upon a shared grievance and this encouraged her to ask about something that troubled her.

"Where have all the houses gone?"

"We're in the country. There aren't many houses." Grace looked over to the Teapes, then back to Lily with a frown. "Have you ever been to the country before?"

Lily did not answer. She did not understand.

Giving Lily a little squeeze, Grace rose to join the flagpoles. "Any chance of another drink?" While the Teapes had little glasses, Grace had a big one with something different in it.

"So you see why I say she's odd," Prudence said while Henry fussed in a cupboard wherein glasses and bottles shone. "Not like one of us at all. No knowledge, no curiosity. Lethargic, inert."

"I think she's seen all sorts of things we'd never dream of. I think she's sad, she's handling unhappiness in her own way. Homesick, too, possibly."

"Homesick indeed. For a squat? With the comfort here? And so much understanding from you. You with no children?"

"Oh don't, Prudence. Not after all we've been through."

"It's all very well, but one would have liked grandchildren."

"But . . . but what about . . ." Grace curtailed her exasperation by turning her back on Lily (who was watching Henry and thinking how much she would like a drink from the cupboard), and continued in a lower voice, ''You *have* one, for goodness' sake.''

''I'm sorry, Grace, but with each day that passes I'm less convinced. Surer, indeed, that there's been an error. My instinct tells me she's not one of us. And other people's children, like other people's dogs, have never interested me.''

''Shhh . . .'' Grace implored.

''She's not listening. She doesn't. In a world of her own.''

There was a pause in the talk during which Grace resumed her place on the sofa looking strangely shaken and Lily decided she could ask her something. ''Do you know Jesus?''

Grace looked up, and with that same voice that understood there was an awful lot to be talked about in this world, she said, ''Not as well as I should. Do you?''

''No, only Prudence says Mum's there and I thought if you went first I could come with you.''

''I see,'' to Lily, and ''. . . so you haven't explained?'' to Prudence.

''I thought I had.''

''When we do the snowman, which we will because I think you'll like it, I'll tell you all about Mummy living with Jesus.''

Throughout the lunch that followed Grace spoke ever more to Lily, ever less to the Teapes, who began to talk about other things between themselves. The only point at which Grace's attention faltered from Lily was when Prudence said to Henry, ''They do it in the shed. I've heard them.''

''Who?'' Grace became charged with delighted amusement.

''We were talking about the gardening couple and didn't think you were listening.''

''You mean those old things actually boff in the potting shed . . . It's too wonderful.''

''They *cook*, blast you, they cook on a primus stove when they should be working. My goodness, you don't change, do you? One might have hoped that grief would bring something about.''

''Come on, Lily, snowmen.''

Bearing a carrot, some coal and two dustpans, Grace, having swaddled Lily in boots and warm clothing, took her outdoors.

Holding one dustpan, Lily stood still while Grace lunged about wearing a fur coat itself the color of old snow. She watched Grace pushing the pan along the surface of the snow, creating a heap. "C'mon, Lily, copy me." So she did and liked the feeling of the chastening cold upon her warm face. Grace deftly turned it into a race that Lily could win: who could put more snow on to the pile in the shortest time? And Grace fell over and Lily laughed, so Grace threw snow at Lily who laughed again and threw some back.

The melody of her laughter suspended in iceblue air brought two putty-colored faces to stare in a blur of heat through drizzled windows. They saw childhood enacted and thought, Yes, that's right . . . That's how it was, how it used to be, and turned their backs on all that play.

When the heap had reached Lily's height Grace said, without stopping her efforts, "Lily, if your mother is with Jesus he's not someone you pop in on. It's not certain she's with him at all; what is certain is she's found Happily Ever After. Do you know about that?" Lily shook her head. "It's what we're all looking for. You too, you know. Mummy couldn't find it here but I'm sure she's found it somewhere else, so she can't come back. You see we can't go until we've all had a good look for Happily Ever After. I'm still looking for mine. I thought I'd found it when I married your Uncle Michael . . ." Grace looked away, idly casting a snowball from hand to hand ". . . but, goodness me, I hadn't." For a moment her radiance chilled, leaving her a flatter image on the whiter scene.

Lily felt this lovely thing was about to fade for good, freeze and break as did the brittle, snowloaded branches of trees all around. So she went to Grace, pulling at her hand, causing the snowball to fall, drawing her back from distraction. Grace looked down at her.

"Lily, would you like to look for your Happily Ever After with me? Live with me?" With the incomparable solemnity of the very young, Lily slowly raised her head up and down. "You would? Lily?" She nodded again. Grace raised Lily from the ground. "Oh, my darling, it's all going to be fine, fine, just fine." She swung Lily in the air and set her down. "Now then, first of all we must finish our snowman. He's going to be the best snowman ever. He's going to be wonderful. So come on, let's not hang about."

They built a figure taller than Grace and she shaped folded arms into the packed snow of its breast and imprinted the division of legs down the column of its body. Together they pushed around a great ball of snow and Grace set it tenderly upon the shoulders, molding a neck with ungloved hands, saying, "Isn't he the best? . . . Isn't he the sweetest?" She held Lily up to place the carrot for his nose, the coal for his eyes.

"Come on now, Lily, we must introduce ourselves formally."

Hand in hand, they walked a little way off, then turned to approach the snowman slowly. "Hello," Grace said, touching a folded arm of snow, "I'm Grace Teape and this is my friend Lily. We're looking for Happily Ever After and we need someone wonderful like you to help us. Will you?"

She placed her ear against the snowball face in the act of learning a confidence, then swivelled back to Lily, arms akimbo. "He said yes, Lily. He said yes."

Lily remained unmoving. Grace dropped her arms. "What is it, Lily?"

"Is Mum dead?"

"Yes, darling, she's dead," and gently, "Come on in, it's getting cold."

Chapter 3

CHILDHOOD ENSUED. WHETHER OR NOT LILY LEFT THE old Teapes that very day or soon after became diffused in memory; she knew only that thenceforward her life was lived within the golden aura of Grace Teape, among houses, in the sound of the city once more.

Grace designed a room for Lily in her penthouse flat north of Regent's Park. The room was Grace's own dream of what every little girl should have, with a narrow, frilled four-poster bed and dressing-table with hangings to match. The wardrobe was full of clothes and still Grace came home with more: a dress, a jacket, a coat ("Do you like it, Lily? It is all right, isn't it?").

She structured Lily's existence with piano lessons, dancing lessons and rituals like taking tea together and reading in the evening; she threw parties for Lily and organized trips to the theater with her friends from school. She took her away to the sunshine and would let her stay up late to mill among others through the evening cool of some village, in what Lily called the ice-cream dark, the time of day when she was allowed to buy with her own money an ice-cream to relish while wandering; watching the foreign crowd, and always her hand safely empalmed in Grace's.

The girls at school were curious and a little envious of Lily's unusual background, of the beautiful woman who fetched her every day and was more like a friend than a mother. Every component was there for the perfectly spoilt child, but Lily never was. She remained a grateful child, a quiet child, not shy, but as though with a wisdom left over from some other life which silenced her a little.

Grace threw parties of her own, parties that would begin as sedate gatherings rising to a bubble of hilarity that vanished all at once through the front door to dispose of high spirits in some other place. At times like this Lily would be in bed watched by the kind, reliable lady who came whenever she was needed. Lily would lie and listen to the silence of the flat after the slamming of the door, to hear again the voices as they emerged in the street below, merry voices going, going away.

Lily was eight when Grace's brother, Oliver Cary, returned to live in the flat below them. "He's been everywhere, Lily: China, India, Africa, think of it, *Africa*. And do you know what my little brother's been doing in Africa, Lily? It's the strangest thing: he's been sleeping. Isn't that odd? A sort of coma. But just like him, to sleep, dream away a few months. He's very sweet. You'll like him, I know." There was something about the phrasing that led Lily to expect a child or at most a small adult. She was amazed when she was brought back from school one day and introduced to a large, quiet man with slow-moving, rangy limbs that appeared to be tacked loosely to his trunk. "This is my little brother, Lily, and Oliver, this is Lily," Grace said with love and pride for them both.

Oliver stood in his still empty flat holding the manner and posture of a question mark: shoulders hunched, elbows bent, hands spread in laconic supplication, contributing, "Hi, Lily. Want a beer?" Then, folding himself to be more in keeping with Lily's size, he said, "Would you like to see some pictures?" He had Grace's tone of irresistible invitation. All over the floor he spread photographs of black babies clinging like frightened bugs to their mothers' backs and breasts; of spindle-legged tribesmen holding spears; of carcasses, calabashes and dust. At twenty-five years old Oliver Cary was already well-known for his photographic records of the wandering, the starving, the embattled all over the world.

His prematurely gray hair was a natural mess of undecided curl, so that if he combed it straight it snaked back on paths of its own. In his casual dress there was an element of acceptable chaos that can only be achieved with some effort. His deckled face was old for his years; he looked far older than Grace. He was weather-beaten and, below his deep brow and lethargic lids, his remarkable eyes were of a disturbing, faraway gray, and Lily thought, Africa . . . Africa . . . He'll go back to Africa.

Oliver Cary became an adjunct to their world, never really part of it; he was the pleasant presence beneath them with the bonding that he was family too. He rarely attended Grace's parties, did not care much for social life. As Lily grew a little older and began to come home from school alone, she would walk up the stairs to pass his door, listen there a moment. For all his terrestrial appearance Lily thought there was something ephemeral about him, that any day she would see a paper pinned to the door, "Gone to Africa." She was too reticent to knock on the door and talk as she would have liked to and anyway he was rarely in.

With Grace here and Oliver there—their friends, their fun—the passage of Lily's childhood was brightly lit. It was all so happy. So it was strange when she awoke one night for no reason other than that some movement or sound had disturbed her unconscious. She sat up and saw bowed on the end of her bed the unmistakable silhouette of Grace. Lily stretched her hand across the cover, touched the reedlike form who snatched that hand and pressed it to her wet face, kissing the fingers and saying, "Lily, Lily, I'll make everything all right for us . . . I'll find someone wonderful some time and Happily Ever After. I really will . . . I promise. Don't worry," then surrendered herself to sobbing.

Another night Lily awoke in the same manner and expected to find Grace once more but was alone. She got out of bed. She was a sound sleeper and could not remember having done such a thing before. Outside her room the flat was dark and quiet but not asleep. It was sinister and watchful, so different from daytime.

She passed down that corridor of erstwhile security, with its familiar things: the letter-table on which lay Grace's keys, the chair where Lily had cast her coat, now only symbols of safety remembered. She stopped at Grace's bedroom door at the far end. From inside she could hear Grace humming, yet not humming, she was moaning without control. Lily feared to open the door for there was something in the sound that made her feel she would see a gloweyed, furskinned wild thing. There came a second sound in curious harmony with the first, then Grace's voice, "I'll die, I'll die . . ."

Panic replaced fear; Lily opened the door. The room bloomed before her in low intimate light. Her eyes focused on movement: Grace's legs hanging white and limp over the side of the bed, her toes brushing the floor. She had no body. Instead, where hers should have been was a glistening black one, and it was from there that the other noise came, a deep one rising from the throat and, finding no utterance there, dying, sinking back inside. ''No . . . Please no . . .'' Grace's voice from behind the massive form.

Lily picked up a stiletto-heeled slipper with a band of pink maribou feathers about its toe, and launched herself upon the back of the black body, felt it undulating beneath her bare legs. She brought the heel of the shoe down and down and the noises changed as she stabbed: she saw little holes the heel made in the mulberry skin; blood spurted from some of them and rubbed into her face and hair. A huge arm reached to pull Lily from her perch on the back and she found herself held to the man's chest.

Her feet, pushing and sliding against him, felt, down below his stomach, another limb: something was growing where no limb should be.

The black man threw his head back, laughing, revealing big teeth in a great pinkness. He pushed Lily on the palms of his hands toward the ceiling and from that giddying height Lily saw down past the pinkness and the blackness the thing her foot had touched, sticking out smoothly away from his body like a short, strong branch, blossoming at the tip pinker still than that throat; and further down, little and cast in a flurry of sheets and pillows, she saw Grace, her nightdress about her neck.

Lily fell to the floor and as Grace screamed, ''Lily . . . Lily,'' she fled. She knew Grace was asking for help but she could not act alone. Tearing the chain from its runner on the front door, she sped to the cold of the stairs outside and down to Oliver Cary. At his door she leant against the bell with both hands, crying to herself and saying, ''Please, please be there . . . Don't be gone yet.''

He opened the door, dressed and wearing heavy-rimmed spectacles, the fatigued air of study about him. Lily only gave him time to say, ''Why . . .''

''There's a black man killing Grace . . . He's killing her . . . Please . . . Please . . .'' She pulled at him.

''Oh, my God.'' He came straight away, raced ahead of her up the stairs, but there was just something about the way he said that: the way he said ''Oh, my God,'' slightly tired, slightly resigned.

When they reached the flat hysterical screaming was coming from Grace's room and the black man was standing in the corridor wearing trousers and unbuttoned shirt, pushing what looked like a multicolored knitted teacozy on to his head. When he saw Oliver he raised his hands, exposing palms to display his terrified and astonished innocence. "Say man, say man. I ain't done nothin'. I's fuckin' the lady an' in comes de child. I ain't hurt no one."

To Lily's horror, all Oliver said was, as he pushed onwards to Grace's room, "OK. OK, I get it. Just go."

For a moment Lily was left with the killer, with the monster she had attacked. He went toward the front door, stopped and faced her before passing through it and said to Lily in a voice wholly without anger, only hurt and sulky, "Shit, little girl. You really hurt me."

Lily went to the open bedroom door, saw Oliver's backview holding up a dressing-gown. "Put it on, for goodness' sake, put it on," he was saying, sounding angry, not the way you should be at all with an attempted murder victim. Lily wanted to go and be kind if he was not going to be. "Stop crying, Grace," he said.

"I can't help it. She saw. She saw."

"She was bound to some time. You're crazy the way you go on. Crazy."

"I can't help it. Don't you see I'm lonely? Don't you understand?"

"You're not lonely, you're sick. Had you ever seen him before tonight?"

"No . . . but he was so . . . so kind. Wonderfully kind."

Lily saw Oliver swipe his face with his hand; he seemed to turn away in despair at Grace's words, then he noticed her. "Oh, Lily," he said with infinite regret, turning back to Grace, "Grace, she's been standing there all the time. Look, I don't know what to do with her, I don't know about little girls."

But Grace was hysterical again. "She saw . . . she saw and now she's heard . . ."

Baffled and frightened, Lily went to Oliver, looked up at him. "I'm sorry. I wanted to help."

Despite what appeared to Lily a calamitous situation, he looked down and grinned at her. "Well, could be you have."

And Lily thought, he's an odd man; first he leaves me with a killer then grins when he shouldn't.

"Come on," he said, "I'll put you to bed if I can."

"What about Grace?"

"She'd rather you were safely in bed, really. I'll come back to her in a minute."

He was amazed by the ritual required to settle her. "Pinocchio there, Grizzly there, Snuzzle beside me here."

"There'll be no room for you."

"There is. Look, I get in here like this . . ."

"Good heavens. You'd be no good in the wild. You need too many trappings."

"Are you going back there?"

"Where?"

"The wild?"

"Not for a bit."

"Don't go."

"You want me to stay?"

"Mmmm."

"I'll see. Light off. Door shut. Night-night."

Just before he closed the door she called, "You've done it wrong."

He put his head back. "I *couldn't* have."

"You didn't kiss me."

"I've got to do that too?"

"I'll show you how." With her arms about his neck, she assailed him with the tight, dry-lipped intensity of her childish kisses, cheeks, brow, lids, lips. "There," she said, "now you do me."

So he did, muttering to himself as he left the room, "All very complicated."

Lily had been made such a secure child that the incident of that night did not disturb her at all; it only confirmed to her that adults were strange. It also gave her a useful step up to maturity: she began to see and accept that she was not the whole of Grace's life, that Grace had needs beyond her. She had not understood them but she had heard those words, "Don't you see I'm lonely?"

Chapter 4

GRACE OF KINDNESS, GRACE OF LIGHT, OF HUMOR AND confidences, of tender goodnights; she was all this and everything to Lily. Gradually Lily became her confidante and accomplice in the search for Happily Ever After, a search with a slow but inexorably gathering momentum.

It was to be many months before Lily encountered again that stranger that dwelt within Grace, the frightened hysteric who spoke of loneliness, and when that stranger did come forth it was the natural wending of Oliver Cary's life that summoned her: "Will you come down this evening, say about seven? There's someone I want you both to meet."

"Who?"

"A great friend. Please come, it's important to me."

Of course they went. Grace prepared herself with care and as she concentrated on her face, grimacing to apply mascara, she said, "Oh, Lily, who can it be? Oliver is so mysterious, so private. We never meet his friends. It'll be a scientist or explorer; someone strange and serious and brave like Oliver."

They descended from the furnished overflow of Grace's flat to the sparse restraint of Oliver's. What had seemed barren to Lily a few years before had become its natural state except that now the floor was dashed here and there with vibrant tousle-edged oriental rugs, some hanging from the walls. There were items of fascination standing about like sentries to Oliver's past: a great tooled saddle with a sheepskin wrapped about it, a life-size figure of a tribesman holding a spear carved in ebony, a massive ochre-colored bowl big enough to sit in; things strange, large and foreign asserting their individuality rather than com-

23

bining for harmony. All about were flowerless ferns and trees
infusing the atmosphere with their green. His armchairs and two
sofas (modern and leather) at first touch took warmth rather than
gave it. But because Oliver Cary kept his home so warm the
place invited and interested; it was like him: remote, individual
and yet approachable.

He was alone when they arrived. "Hi, Lily. Want a beer?"
This had become a standard greeting. Lily longed for the day
she could accept with impunity. Although loathing the sips of
beer she had had, she believed acceptance would confirm their
friendship at a deeper level.

Grace settled, alert, into the reluctant leather of the sofa, semi-
whispering, "Where is he?"

"Who?"

Oliver frowned.

"Your friend."

He smiled curiously at Grace and said, "My friend's a bit
late. A meeting, I think. Home any minute, I expect."

"Home?"

"Yeah, home."

"He's living here?"

Oliver Cary crouched in front of Grace, handing her the drink
he had prepared. Linking his fingers loosely between his knees,
he looked sideways at her and the curious smile turned to an
affectionate one.

"Why do you assume it's a 'he,' Grace?"

"Well . . . Well I thought it was a scientist friend of yours,
someone like that."

"A journalist, actually. A very clever journalist."

"A 'she'?"

"Yes."

"Living here?"

His smile changed its nature once more to surprise sistered
with impatience. "Grace, why are you so surprised? You even
seem a little shocked. You shouldn't be."

Grace's hand fluttered to her neck. "No . . . no, not shocked.
I thought I was going to meet a man, that's all. I was ready for
a man and now it's going to be someone you're living with . . .
a woman . . . I'm just . . . just . . ."

"It's the woman I'm going to marry." Grace gasped. "I
thought the way I asked you down you'd guess. Aren't you
pleased?"

"You're so young."

"I'm twenty-eight."

"Are you? Are you that already?" She turned her face away. "It's all going too fast. Much too fast."

Lily went to Grace, took her hand and said to Oliver, "We're very glad for you, aren't we, Grace?"

"Glad . . . yes, glad," Grace brought out without looking at either of them.

Lily was not glad really. She was feeling what she knew she would have felt had she seen the notice on the door, "Gone to Africa." He had gone his own way without them. She did not know why she felt betrayed, unless it was because she was so accustomed to living in the light of Grace's prevailing mood; and yet she did have her own sense of his getting on, his going away, of being left behind.

"Her name's Melissa Coulson," Oliver offered to break the tension.

"Melissa Coulson?" It worked; Grace was interested. "Melissa Coulson with the column in the *Observer*? She's very well-known."

"That's right. I've known her some time. Met her in Africa when she was doing voluntary work and I was moving with the Sahel tribesmen. I'd been trying to make some sort of photographic report on their starvation. No one knew about it then, not even the voluntary services out there. The Sahel were the subject of my book. Do you remember"

"Of course." Grace was indignant.

"Well, it was Melissa I spoke to and she joined me to travel with them. They were even heading for cities. Think of it: Nomadic pastoral tribesmen driven to cities in the desperation to live. It was bad. Melissa was appalled at their plight. I guess she stayed moving with us a month or so, until I got ill."

"She went when you got ill?"

"It wasn't like that. She had to go and tell the world about these people. They were dying by the thousand. I, with my ridiculous coma, was the least of it. The perspective out there on life, illness, death is different, Grace; but maybe you have to be there to understand.

"Anyway, she came back to England and the BBC didn't believe her about the starvation. Not enough evidence, they said. So she went to America and went public on ABC television. She was big news over there for a while and that of course made her reputation here. She's a wonderful woman, Grace; all her time and energy is spent for the good of others."

But any comment after high praise sounds grudging. "How marvelous."

The front door slammed. Oliver rose with a look toward Grace, not of appeal but of mystification, and his eyes swept past Lily, dismissing her as appendage to Grace.

A dark-haired young woman came to stand in the doorway. Her innate vitality was such that although she was motionless, smiling, watching, taking them in, she seemed to quiver. She was without makeup: her pale skin, red mouth, heavy-lashed eyes announcing themselves easily without accentuation. She wore tight blue jeans and a long jacket. Sliding her shoulder bag onto a chair, she strode into the room with a masculine gait, at odds with her delicate-looking form. She held out a forthright hand to Grace, to Lily.

"Hello you two, I'm Melissa. I've been longing to meet you but life's so stupidly full. Isn't it, Oliver?" kissing his cheek. He nodded and was about to speak when Melissa suddenly struck a pose containing the same vital inertia she had had by the door: her right index finger pointing to Oliver, her left to Lily and Grace, she smiled broadly. "I know what: he's told you, hasn't he?"

Grace withdrew the warmth of her hand from Lily and stood up. "Darlings, darlings," she drew Oliver to Melissa, "I'm so thrilled for you both. So very happy."

Dissembling her shock and reticence, Grace glowed for them. Grace could do it: she understood social ways and means, she would always be right for the moment, she would never let anyone down. Tall, pretty Grace of parties, Grace of fun, embraced Melissa the intellectual, the journalist, the woman with a cause; Melissa the pert, astute graduate of Somerville, Oxford. They embraced, while instantly knowing, accepting and ignoring what the other was.

Grace said, "Will there be a big wedding? Can Lily be a bridesmaid?"

Oliver looked at Melissa then Grace, embarrassed. "Oh seriously, Grace . . ."

"No, no, of course there won't. How silly of me. Who wants a big wedding, anyway?"

"We'll go quietly to a Register Office quite soon. No fuss at all."

"Just like you, Oliver. Eh, Lily? Isn't it just like him?"

Even after knowing him for three years, Lily was shy to claim any certainty of his nature, was not even sure that he would want it to be just like him. So she said nothing but smiled enough not to leave Grace out on a conversational limb.

Grace became animated, asked a lot of questions. She was fluent, bright, effervescent. Oliver and Melissa answered pleasantly, but increasingly briefly, drawing together, touching hands, dropping them, touching again, confirming the other's presence, as though there was something in Grace that threatened, as though they saw something about her they feared for themselves.

Grace stood before the fireplace which contained a piece of marble sculpture among ferns. ". . . in love . . ." she was saying, "what could be more wonderful? It's what we all seek, the security of knowing there's another in this world just for you . . ."

When Grace turned to place her empty glass on the mantelpiece Lily saw her hand was shaking, and before Grace could return to her theme (her head was already bent in momentary concentration tracing her thoughts, hands clasped as if in prayer) Lily said, "It's getting late, Grace, and I have to do my homework."

Grace gave the sharp gasp of one suddenly awoken from a brief, sound sleep. "Oh, my goodness, yes. It's late, very late. How I do go on. I'm so sorry . . . so very sorry."

Collecting the fur coat Grace had flung over her shoulders to descend one flight, Oliver placed it about her, kissed her and said kindly, "Here we are, old thing, keep warm. See you very soon."

"Old thing?" Grace repeated with timid amazement. "I suppose I am to you. Old thing. Fancy."

"Come on, it's only an expression and you know it. You look younger than me by far."

"Do I? Honestly?"

"Absolutely," Oliver said.

" 'Course you do," Lily added. They were both earnest in their words of reassurance.

"Doesn't she, Melissa?" Oliver turned to Melissa who had remained seated, watching the scene but seeming to find difficulty entering into it.

"Well, certainly she does. I mean it's obvious." It was clear she believed what she said but it irritated her to have to state something so trivial.

A vagueness came over Grace as she moved to the front door, through it and up the stairs. Lily walked behind and before he shut the door Oliver touched her shoulder. She looked round.

He jerked his head toward Grace's departing figure. "All right?" he whispered in the way one does to another who is precariously loaded.

Lily looked at Grace who had nearly turned the corner of the stairs. "Mmmm," she confirmed then, "I *am* very pleased for you, really."

He smiled. "You know what? You're terrific."

"Well, I am . . . pleased, I mean." Funny though: now she meant it.

Lily found Grace in the flat by following the sound of her voice. She had not gone to the drawing-room or the kitchen but straight to her bedroom and through that to the bathroom beyond.

Lily stood in the doorway of the bedroom looking across to where she could see Grace leaning against the basin, her face flooded by the light from the bulbs around the mirror. "Oh my God . . . Oh my God," she was saying to herself. Lily went closer. The taps were running. Grace splashed her face, then looked at it again. "It's no good anymore."

"Why are you so upset, Grace?"

She swung round to Lily as though they had been engaged discussing this point for some time already and Lily was being obtuse. "Because don't you see? Look at me, forty and alone. It's not happening for me, Lily. It happens for everyone else but not for me. Now it's happened for Oliver and I am glad . . . I am." She looked at Lily quickly. "I was all right, wasn't I? I mean, they did know I was happy for them, didn't they? I wasn't . . . silly or anything?"

"No, you were like you always are, really nice, charming."

"Oh Lily, why don't I find someone wonderful like he has?"

Lily dared something. Carefully, she said, "Was Michael wonderful?"

Grace sniffed, turned off the taps, looked down at her hands gripping the basin. "At first, you know. At first. He was very handsome, gallant, young. Younger than me. He became very busy with his career in the army; left me alone so very much. I don't like to be alone. You know that. And now the only thing I have, my only currency—my looks—are running short. Nothing else to go to market with, you see, Lily? Look at Melissa: she's clever. Doesn't even try to make something of herself because she has a career, opinions, and she's young. I'm uneducated and fading. What can there be for me except the arms of a man, someone understanding? The only value I ever had has been scattered away with many men and it's left me nothing but alone, desperately alone. Don't understand anymore.''

Lily fixed her eyes on Grace, willing her to hear the words in her head, I'm here for you. I'll always be here for you.

It seemed then that Lily's thoughts had reached her, for Grace said in a voice surprised, refreshed, as if Lily had just entered and she was pleased to see her, ''Oh Lily . . . darling Lily. Your homework, for goodness' sake. And after that we'll plan a party, shall we? Find something to celebrate?''

Chapter 5

T HE FOLLOWING YEAR, WHEN SHE WAS TWELVE, AN IN-
cident finally extinguished any remaining passenger status
Lily had had in her life with Grace. It gave one final twist
to the prism through which she viewed that life and made her
see herself as Grace's Protector, her Improver of the Truth.

There was a night, hot, blue-shadowed, starcrazed: the kind
of night that hangs ectoplasmic in memory. They were staying
at a small hotel in the hills behind Marbella and with them,
unusually, were Oliver and Melissa Cary; but, more important
than the Carys and the shadows and the stars, Jaime was there.
Jaime de Caberro was Grace's new friend. Their three rooms
formed a row on the first floor joined on the outside by a semicircular balcony, a pouting lip on the face of the house; the Carys
were on the floor above.

Lily was changing for dinner. Already tall for her age, she
was depressed by the succulence of puberty about her body.
Grace entered through the glass doors leading from the balcony.
She came, arms raised behind her neck working at the clasp of
her necklace, in a swirl of excitement and red silk which stopped
at her knees to show her thin, brown legs and, in high-heeled
sandals, the feet that Lily particularly admired. Although there
was still so much else she found to wonder at in her aunt (the
way her topaz hair grew so thick and waving, her slanting eyes,
celadon like a Burmese cat), above all it seemed the crowning
of perfection to have beautiful feet, those ever-used and func-
tional things so rarely seen bare; to be beautiful in private places,
that was the real thing.

"Oh pretty, Lily. Really pretty. But what do you think about those trousers? A little tight, maybe? Look, why not put this on?'' From the muddle of Lily's clothing she flicked out a fine lawn dress, broderie anglaise at the hem, and Lily put it on. Grace was always right about clothing. She reached forward. The small, gold St. Christopher hanging on a chain at Lily's neck was caught up, and she released it, leaving her hand an instant upon it. ''There you are, darling: you're beautiful. I'm proud as anything.'' There was an intensity in her words as though she wished for far more to be understood from them, and Lily said, ''I'm proud too,'' fraught with similar unspoken feeling.

Grace then crossed to the mirror and bent to scrutinize her own reflection. Pulling her face gently taut, she began.

''Lily, tell me honestly . . .'' Lily inwardly subsided. The ''Tell me honestlys'' had become her heaviest burden. ''Tell me honestly, can you see any fat at the top of my thighs?'' ''Tell me honestly, do I look much older than Melissa?'' ''Tell me honestly, do you think people still wonder whether you're my daughter or not, could we possibly be sisters now you're older? I mean, is it obvious we're not?''

Honesty was the last thing required; amazement was essential. ''*You*, Grace, *fat*? Oh, come on.'' That was easy.

''You and Melissa could be the same age, really.'' This was harder because Lily was still too young to see the subtleties of years in a face: Grace's face was Grace's face, and Melissa's was Melissa's; and, as for being her daughter, that she could answer.

''I'm sure they don't think I'm your daughter anymore. I bet they think you're my older sister, older and more fun.'' (This Lily believed.)

Lily paused to marshal her spontaneous amazement.

''Tell me honestly, Lily, could I pass for thirty?''

''Oh, *easily*.''

''Darling, you'd say anything to please me,'' but she was credulous for now. She swung away from the mirror and held Lily by the shoulders, shimmering and childlike in her excitement. ''Lily?''

''What?'' She had caught her mood; something wonderful was going to happen.

''How would you like to live in Brazil?'' Hands clasped low in front of her, Grace leant back to get a fuller frame on Lily's response.

Lily drew her smile and breath simultaneously, then touched

her hand. "Do you mean Jaime has asked you to marry him? It's marvelous."

"No, no, shhh . . ." Glancing to the glass doors, Grace knelt and whispered, "But I wouldn't tell this to anyone but you: I really think he's going to, maybe even tonight. But not a word, eh? Our secret."

"Oh yes, our secret, but I'm so glad. He's so nice and kind, and handsome, and . . ."

"I know, I know, but it hasn't quite happened yet."

"No, but it will, I really feel it this time."

"I think so too. So dress, darling, I'll see you downstairs."

Grace turned when she reached the windows through which she had come. "Remember, our secret."

Lily went down to the garden where Oliver and Melissa were already seated at a table beneath an ancient fig tree.

Melissa, who raised her arms in greeting to Lily, was fully, flamboyantly pregnant and, or so it seemed to Lily, used every opportunity to display it. Melissa had it all: the brains, the career, the husband, and now the baby, and she was entering into this with all the self-conscious enthusiasm of the older intellectual first-time mother. There would be none of the nonchalance of young motherhood for her; she ate the right food, did the right exercises and of course the baby was going to be perfect ("If it's not right, Oliver, it must go. You do see that, don't you? It'll have to go"), just perfect, because she had had the test, so she knew.

Lily had met the kind of pregnant woman who grabs any nearby hand, guiding it bellywards saying, "Can you feel it? No, no, now. There. It moved." She had found that indecent enough, but the way Melissa now sat, massive and proud, while the interned anarchist rearranged itself was wholly repellent to her.

"Lily," Melissa reached both hands toward her. "How lovely you look." The gesture invited a token kiss, but Lily could not face leaning across the bump and blew a kiss to Melissa, who smiled knowingly. That was irritating too: she exuded a new omniscient understanding of human nature.

Oliver Cary smiled lethargically at the undercurrents passing between the two women. "The time will come, Lily, when you'll be having a baby of your own and you'll feel just the way Melissa does now and you won't be at all embarrassed."

"Yuk," was all she said, but smiled too, to show it was nothing personal.

There was an eddy of familiar scent and Lily heard, coming from behind, Grace's step, the murmur of her silk dress. (It was a sound Lily would always associate with Grace: even on the grayest day when she was swaddled in fur and wool there would be the sighing of silk, the hush-hush of expense.) When her voice called in greeting Lily felt the quality of the night alter; even that prosaic pregnancy was lifted on to a more supernal plain.

"Darlings, have we kept you waiting? Isn't it a perfect night?"

With Grace came Jaime de Caberro, a man seeming to be formed from some unique fleshly metal, for there was a glinting about him: his slicked, black hair, his teeth, his treacle-dark eyes, the chain hanging at his neck, nestling in the hairs of his chest, even a gloss to his bistre skin. He was impressively quiet; when he did speak the resonance of his voice silenced others without him having to raise it. "Tonight we drink champagne and only champagne. It is my birthday."

"Jaime, how lovely. How old are you?"

"I am thirty-three, Melissa."

"Good heavens, I thought you were at least . . ." She faltered, laughing nervously.

"I know I'm a cradle-snatcher, Melissa," Grace said, sliding her arms possessively around Jaime's body. "What of it?"

"Leely, you look very beautiful tonight."

"Thank you, Jaime." She accepted the compliment a little perfunctorily for she had become entirely used to attentions from Grace's lovers, knowing herself to be considered a path to her aunt's heart that had for a while to be delicately trodden. She remained reticent while considering what might be required from her by a man who was about to propose to Grace. She wanted to get it right.

There was quiet, easy laughter from Oliver, a different, brighter kind from Melissa and, of course, glittering effusion from Grace; not a lot from Jaime, but jollity was not his manner. Every time she caught Grace's eye there was a flutter of conspiracy; hardly a wink, just a faintly perceptible wait-and-see raising of the eyebrows.

Lily drank champagne. She had drunk it before but never quite with such relish. After all, wasn't it all very exciting? Brazil, Brazil and who knows what? She began to enjoy herself with the others. Very soon the still night seemed to sway just for her. Toward the end of dinner talk began about going into town, perhaps some dancing, and Lily knew the moment had come to withdraw.

"I want to go to my room, if you don't mind. I'm dying to finish my book."

"Well, darling, if that's what you want . . ."

"No, no, Leely." Jaime brought his hand to her arm, stroking the fine, fair hairs on her sunny skin. "You must come too, you must not be alone. This would be sad."

"It's not sad. I like to be. I don't want to come dancing or anything."

"Are you sure, darling, honestly?" Grace smiled at Lily and Lily smiled back. They were confident in each other; Grace knew she would not go and Lily knew she could not go.

"Well, I'll go up now. Goodnight everyone." When she turned to say "Goodnight" once more, and "Have a *really, really* lovely time" (all she could manage without actually saying "Good luck"), Grace took her wrist, pulling her down to place a kiss upon her cheek, then turning to the others, presenting Lily to them by holding out her arm, she said, "Isn't she the best? Isn't she the sweetest?"

They made kind sounds of agreement and Oliver said, "She certainly is, you're a lucky girl, Grace."

Still holding Lily's arm, Grace slipped her other hand around Jaime, embracing him into her fortune. "Oh, yes I am, I certainly am."

Lily did not read for long. When she heard the Carys above return briefly to their room before leaving for the club; when she heard their laughter caught up with that of Grace once more from the garden below; when she heard all their merriment being carried down through the garden to the road, to the night, she switched off her lamp and turned to sleep: tomorrow was going to be Happily Ever After.

She did not know how long she had been sleeping when something caused her to wake. It was a noise; at first she thought a creature must have entered her room, and wounded, judging by the constricted, broken nature of the sound it made. She lay a little afraid of putting her feet to the floor, sat up and looked carefully toward the darker corners of the room. There by the dressing-table Grace's red dress glowed where she crouched, and shuddered when she did.

Lily crouched before her, making herself lower than Grace, looking up to the face hidden by hair and hands.

"Grace? Grace, what's happened?"

She put out one hand to Lily, still covering her face with the other. Lily took that hand and it grasped like one drowning. "Oh, Lily, Lily. I've got it all wrong."

"But why?" she asked, though not even sure of what.

"Because . . . he doesn't care about me at all." She withdrew her hand better to cover the fresh distress the statement brought.

"Of course he does. He loves you, Grace; anyone can see that. What's happened?" Lily reached without rising to switch on the light and saw that Grace's feet were bare and cut, her dress was torn. "Please tell me, has there been an accident?"

Grace Teape put her head back, her long neck arched. She drew her lips from her teeth, letting out a ghastly laugh. "Oh yes, there's been an accident all right and I'm the casualty. Like always, I'm the casualty."

"Please . . ."

Grace put out her hand again to be saved from going under. Lily held it tight. "We were there. All there in the club. I think I thought on the way back he'd ask me . . . you know . . . or later, here at the hotel maybe. But a girl came up. Don't ask me what like. I don't know what like, but young . . . yes, young and dark. They knew each other, she and Jaime. She joined us, drank champagne with us. They danced and then . . . and then they weren't there anymore. I went outside to get some air but I suppose looking, you know, looking. He was there kissing her, with his hand all in her hair and then all over her back, her waist. Just like he does with me. The same." She dropped her head on to her arms. "So I ran away. Left my bag in the club. Just ran back here."

"All the way from Marbella?"

"A car stopped, took me in. He thought I was a whore and he . . ."

"Oh Grace . . ." Grace fell into Lily's arms, still yet the arms of a girl barely able to sustain the combined weight of body and anguish. After some moments Lily helped her to her feet, led her to her own room, lay her on the bed.

Lily was still sitting beside her, stroking her hand, saying, "It's all right. He was probably drunk, you'll see . . ." when Jaime came into the room.

Grace sat up on her elbows, "Lily, Lily, my powder, over there."

Lily passed the powder to her and saw as she left for her own room Jaime shaking his head at the tattered, shattered woman patting ineffectually at her swollen face.

Lily sat once more at her dressing-table, an almost tangible ghost of Grace leaning past her (''Tell me honestly, darling''); the strings on the balloons of possibility had slipped from their fingers. Now there was fury in blazed words from next door, followed by silence.

Jaime entered, with moths, from the balcony. He stood lighting a small cigar, the only sounds the click, click of his lighter, the scraping of the moths' wings against the rough, whitewashed wall as they sought the lights set in there and intermittent sobs from next door. He did not go near her.

''Leely, this is all something for nothing. Do you understand me?'' Lily looked at him through the mirror and shook her head.

''I mean to say, Grace running like she did. I just kiss a girl, this is all. The girl, she was an old friend of mine. Leely, I have friends, I am young, I like to kiss them sometimes. Grace should not be so offended. She makes a terrible scene. No sense.''

Lily continued to watch him through the mirror as he snapped impatiently at the yellow plastic lighter with no success, then he cast it on the bed and drew another from his pocket. This time he lit the cigar. ''Well, Leely, tell me at least that you understand?''

Lily pulled her breath, lowered her eyes to speak. ''The thing is, you see, she's awfully proud and, worst of all, I don't think . . . I don't think she'll marry you now.'' Lily felt him staring at her, so faced again his reflection in the mirror. He was peculiarly still, small cigar burning in his fingers, forming a half-completed arc between waist and mouth. Lily sat round on the stool, turned her face upon him and down again to her hands. She was wondering if it was a breach of confidence even to mention it, but he had to know, he had to understand that you could not marry Grace and kiss girls too; it seemed something that had to be sorted out.

At least he said, ''Say it again, Leely?''

''I said, 'I'm frightened she won't marry you now.' ''

He remained shocked into the same rigid position, the glow of the cigar approaching the skin of his finger; a minute shudder as a worm of ash fell to the floor.

''Listen to me.'' There was a long pause before he went on very slowly. ''You have made me understand why there is all this fuss for something so small, so innocent. Never, never, Leely, was I going to marry Grace. She is beautiful and fun but not serious. I like her very much. But for a wife . . . Leely, to only begin: she is more than seven years older than I am. Don't you know that? Did you both really think . . . ? This I can't believe. No, no, no, Leely. Grace, she always go with someone younger. You know that. And this is nice for me to be with a woman like . . . well, a woman. Not a girl. But I say again, Leely, to marry, no. She forget her age. She is a woman with a child not young anymore.'' He left the room muttering to himself, ''No, no, no, nunca.''

At first Lily did not go to Grace, partly because no sound issued from her room: it was possible, though unlikely, that she slept; mostly because she felt herself to be incandescent with Jaime's words. Grace would see in her very body: ''Not serious, not young. Marry? . . . never.''

As the minutes passed, however, she felt bound to go. Even then Lily had an unformed fear about the degree of despair that could engulf Grace. She went on to the balcony, was about to move toward her aunt's window which stood a little open, like lips parted in anticipation, when a movement of dim light attracted her in the shadowed stillness of the dark garden. She half-expected some huge firefly, except there was no longer light to attract such a thing. It seemed to have gone. She made to move and it was there again, somewhere off to the left. It had a certain familiarity. She stood, hands resting upon the balustrade, beginning to know what it was, that cinderous dot of fire etching a crescent: it was Jaime standing looking up toward their rooms. He stepped forward to let himself be seen by Lily, as though he would speak. She leant forward posturing, Yes? Yes, without a word. It would be all right, he'd thought about it. She wanted to say, ''Wait, I'll get her,'' to rush into Grace's room, wake her and say, ''Get ready, get ready, he's been out there, he's coming back.''

Then Jaime de Caberro—young, handsome, noble—words beyond him, raised his arm, held it aloft one second then thrust it at Lily with deadly dismissal. The force of the gesture, its import, caused her to stand back as though struck. She and Grace and all they represented were out of existence, finished.

Returning to her room, Lily lay on her bed thinking about other wonderful someones whom Grace had fixed upon, how these, too, had vanished, snuffing all the luminous possibilities Grace had confided. She thought how often she had sat on her aunt's bed the morning after some anticipated event, sharing coffee, and how at these times there did seem to be an invisible cloth of melancholy trying to smother Grace. She kept it away with laughs and shrugs but if for an instant she was still, reflective, it floated down, tightened, but she would not have it settle, that sadness, no matter what.

The image of Grace she knew, the beautiful, sophisticated lady, desirable, vivacious, melded with another of a woman diminished, pathetic, facile ("Tell me honestly, darling"). Lily Teape faced into the pillow in order to cry as quietly as possible.

Further into the dark heat and despair of that night, Lily heard a cry of pain, and another; then Oliver Cary's voice downstairs at reception raised in urgent command; hurried footsteps along the corridor.

That blasted baby was getting itself born.

Chapter 6

THERE, THEN, IS THE FRAME WHENCE LILY TEAPE GREW from child to young woman; the incidents related being those that caused the lesions, gave the complexion to her point of view. There was one thing more, however, which, had she been asked, would have made her stare distant and say, "Ah, yes . . . well . . . and there was that too . . ."

No one grazed Lily's affections easily; she was good at friendship and keeping it that way. She was sexually incurious, perhaps it had been around her enough in a kind of shadow-play throughout her life with Grace. She did not giggle at it and probe like other girls of her age. Then in the summer of her seventeenth year she fell into gauche, agonizing love with a beautiful French boy, Philippe, two years older than she. He was shy, intense, inexperienced and seemed to love her quite as much in return.

Grace had rented a villa in the South of France where they would pass two summer months with a fluctuating, though similar, crowd of friends: noisy, exuberant, day-sleepers, night-livers. Lily was studying for her A levels, there was no one of her age, she was out of step with the party. She breakfasted alone on the terrace while the household slept, worked through the mornings, lunched in pleasant camaraderie with Grace and the others, then, unlike them, unable to sleep through the heat of the afternoon, she went down to the beach. That was where she met Philippe; their two villas stood in isolation linked by a shared drugget of private sand. Afternoon by afternoon they met alone and talked of A levels, the baccalaureate, art, love and death, while hand crept to hand, knee to knee, secret in the surface of the sand. Now and then they would bathe to cool away their disastrous heat, only to return, talk and touch again until their adolescent philosophizing subsided into suffocating caresses and their passion silenced their talk altogether. Beneath the shadow of the mimosa trees they would try to do away with the pain of desire their young bodies caused them, until one day, haltingly, uncomfortably, with exquisite tenderness, they made love.

"And now," he said, gently brushing away the sand clinging to her hot, damp skin, "there will not be a going back. We will be together always. You will meet my parents and they will love you as I do."

Philippe was staying alone with his parents, fine-looking, serious people, intellectual, aristocratic. The three would dine by candlelight on the terrace of their villa in quiet dignity every evening, while next door light blazed and the air pulsed with music and the whoops and hollers of the fun. Later on the three of them would be woken into the twilight of dawn by more sound: that of Grace and her friends on a riotous return from a nightclub; only occasionally would Lily be with that crowd.

At lunch a few days after Lily and Philippe had become lovers, Grace leant back in her chair and said, "Later today, you know what I'm going to do? I'm going next door to invite them over to dinner." She pushed her hands into her hair, raising it from her head a moment to let it fall in luxurious chaos. "It's only neighborly after all this time. Someone told me he's a Vicomte, so she's obviously a Vicomtesse. Apparently they have a glorious château in Alsace and another in the Médoc, where they have a vineyard, and this place here. What's more, Lily, they have a son of nineteen. Did you know that, Lily? Have you seen him?"

Lily blushed hopelessly and stammered, "I . . . I think so. Yes. Sort of . . ." but it was useless. Already the others (among them the Carys who had come for just two days) were filling the relative cool beneath the striped awning with "Aye aye's," "I says" and "What's this?" The Carys were not quite so vulgar, but Melissa patted Lily's arm knowingly, "Good, Lily, good." Oliver smiled kindly at her with his head on one side.

This had been why she had said nothing at all, even to Grace, and now she felt hideously exposed, like a shell creature unhoused, singed by the air all around.

Grace leant across with bridled exultation; she took Lily's hand. "Darling, is he . . . wonderful?"

It was intolerable. Clumsily, tearfully, Lily lurched from the

terrace to her room. Moments later Grace tapped with her nail
upon the door and entered; she seated herself beside Lily, who
was prostrate, face down upon the bed.

"I'm so sorry, darling, forgive me. So crude, so cruel. One
forgets so much, you know. It was a long time ago that I first
loved. Now I see that you do." She stroked Lily's sun-silvered
hair. "Anything, Lily, anything for your happiness. Anything
never to have you hurt. What can I do? Shall I go and invite, do
you think? Would that be nice? You say."

Lily raised herself, roughly rubbing her face. "Sorry to be so
silly."

"No, no you're not. I'm the silly one; I know it, you know.
One does. I know that I, rather than think too hard, understand
too much, will laugh and have a little drink. I do, you see, it's
the way I am, it's easier for me. Sorry if sometimes I don't get
it right."

"Don't, Grace, please don't. You're perfect. I love you."

"There, there. Shall I then, invite?"

"I suppose. Don't know really." An intangible doubt assailed
Lily, too abstruse to handle. She could tell that Grace was doubting too, so she could sort it out, get it right, couldn't she?

Grace did go next door that evening while Lily and the others
waited in a curious sort of anticipation considering the ordinary
neighborly effort she was making. Nevertheless Grace had
dressed with particular care and carried a small clutch bag as a
token of formality. They did not wait long. Grace's high heels
were very soon tap-tapping across the tiled hall, the tiled lounge
to the terrace where they sipped drinks and tried to make conversation for Lily's sake.

Grace threw herself into a rattan chair, cast aside the clutch
bag, stiffly linked her hands upon her knees and stared fixedly
ahead at nothing, biting her anger into the insides of her cheeks.

"Well?" Melissa said after Grace had completed her en-
trance.

"Drink, Oliver, please." Grace spoke without altering her
demeanor.

"Come on then, Grace," Oliver tried, at the drinks tray with
his back to her palpable fury. "What did she say?"

"She said, 'No thank you, Madame, merci, mais non.' Most
politely, just like that. But well . . . Those bloody French. You
know what they are. There was something in her damnable courtesy that implied I was not good enough." There were general
exclamations of disbelief: "Seriously though's," "Come off

it's.'' ''I mean it. If you'd been there you'd understand. She was utterly cold, utterly downright. No excuses, nothing. And the way she looked at me . . . my God!''

In the efforts to subdue Grace's hurt and fury, Lily's connection in the matter was forgotten and by the time they left for the nightclub Grace was happy once more, or pretended to be. ''Won't you come, Lily darling? Won't you?''

''No thank you. I'm dying to finish my book, really.''

An hour after she had been left alone Lily went through the soft night to the beach, settled near the water and stayed there clutching and releasing the tepid sand. The doubt was now standing like a fogbound vessel, distant in her mind, something she could approach if she chose but was vaguely aware it involved courage. She backed away from it, telling herself she knew Grace was a sensitive woman who in certain moods would read a slight into the most innocuous statement. Lily also knew the French well enough from her life of travel. It was true they were haughty and disdainful, as much to each other as to anyone else. It could not really be that Grace was unacceptable in any way, except that (and here Lily smiled) well, she was a little noisy compared with their temporary neighbors who maintained what sometimes felt like an observant peace, though not necessarily a tranquil one. Anyway Philippe wanted her to meet them, didn't he, the Vicomte and Vicomtesse? She would meet them and make everything all right and they would meet Grace and be charmed by her, just as everybody else was; nearly everybody else. Her mind went on thus, circling ever closer to that moored, crepuscular doubt.

A hand touched her shoulder, hot and dear. She knew without turning it was Philippe; odd she should feel no surprise.

''Can't sleep,'' she said.

''You were thinking?''

''Yes.''

''About us?''

''Well yes. And about those around us. Were you there?''

''When?''

''When Grace came over.''

''Your aunt? Did she come to us?''

''To invite you to dinner. All of you. Your mother refused.''

''She would. My mother, she is very . . .'' (proud of his English and annoyed at not finding the word immediately) ''. . . correct.''

Lily did not mention that Grace had taken offense; she knew

now it was only a misunderstanding. One simply did not trot up the garden path of a Vicomtesse and say, "Pop over for a bite to eat."

"Tomorrow night, Lily, will you dine with us, please? I've told my parents of you, asked them to meet you. I have said it is important to me. I have never before wanted them to meet a girl."

Lily pulled her hands from the sand, held them poised. "What did they say?"

"They are curious."

"Do they know I'm from next door? That I'm . . . I'm Lily Teape?"

He laughed. "Should they? Are you famous?"

"No, but do they know I'm Grace's niece?"

"I've only told them that you are an orphan and that I love you."

It struck her as a silly thing to have said and she was sorry because she loved him and did not want to think him silly. "I suppose you know them, what to say for the best."

"Trust me, Lily."

"I do." She began once more to knead the sand.

"Oh Lily, the pale pink silk, surely, with your hair and your tan. Don't you think?"

"All right, I suppose so." Lily let the dress she was wearing slip to the floor and stepped into the one Grace held out for her.

They were in Lily's bedroom half an hour before she was due next door. "I still don't quite understand . . ." Grace began and before she could finish Lily tackled the equivocation that had been about Grace since that morning when, oh so carefully, Lily had stated that she had been asked to dine next door.

"Grace, they are quiet, shy people, that's all. And it's Philippe who's asked me, not them, so I suppose they felt they had to have me. Like you'd put up with anybody I'd bring back."

"Not just *anybody*, I hope."

"You do understand?"

"Yes, yes, I suppose I do." She went to Lily, inspecting her closely. "Hair up? Yes?"

"Oh no."

"No. No, all right . . . I should have sent a note. I was silly just to go over. The French are so punctilious, aren't they? That's it, you see . . . Look at you, beautiful."

At last Lily got away and walked slowly, not by the way of

the beach but by the road, through the tall double gates and up the drive to the faded pink villa next door.

A maid wearing a black dress and white starched apron opened the front door, ushered her to a large drawing-room. It was stiffly furnished with gilded Louis XVI furniture, pressing ormolu feet into a huge delicately colored Aubusson carpet; five glass doors led on to the deep terrace where could be seen the table laid for dinner, four places set.

Lily stood alone in the room, a clock chipping at the silence together with the sea breathing out, away down there through the closing day. Fearing to seat herself upon the sunshine-yellow silk of one of the fragile, unaccommodating-looking settees, she engrossed herself in the study of a small oil painting (fields, hedges, a lane), until she felt herself being studied from behind. A tall, thin lady, with black hair swept into a chignon, stood in the doorway, one hand loosely resting in the other. She was beautifully uncompromisingly mid-forties; proud, serene and sad. Her almond-shaped gray eyes carried all the expression in her narrow, immobile face, but so complete was her femininity, so polished, it was enough to make one wonder at her womanhood and what had made her so. Was it possible someone so apparently whole, secure, could ever have been the mess of emotions Lily felt herself to be now and knew Grace to be always?

"You are . . . ?" The woman remained quite still; her voice (which was known before she spoke, so well did it match her presence) was deep and carrying.

"I'm Lily . . ." The Vicomtesse nodded slightly as though to indicate that would have been sufficient until Lily added, "Lily Teape."

The Vicomtesse caught her nod on its ascent and left it there for a brief, significant second, her eyes drifting slightly to the left on a calculation before returning and settling upon Lily. She went to the wall, pulled at an embroidered sash.

"You will take a sherry?" The maid entered almost instantly.

"No, thank you."

"Merci, Louise," the Vicomtesse said with her back to the maid, who vanished equally swiftly, leaving Lily wishing she had accepted.

"My 'usband" (the very first trace of an accent) "is talking with my son. They will join us directly."

There was something about the statement that depressed Lily. "I was looking at your Corot. It's lovely."

"You like painting?"

"Yes. More to study than to perform, but after A levels I'm going to art college for a foundation course. It's textiles that interest me most."

The Vicomtesse poised herself on the edge of the yellow silk settee, quite relaxed in the perfection of her posture. Lily attempted the same but somehow had just too many limbs.

"Philippe studies too."

"Yes, I know. We've talked about it and . . ."

" 'E studies 'ard."

"I know . . ."

"It's right that 'e does. 'E must."

"Yes." Lily looked at her lap; she had been driven so hard up to that affirmative she could think of nothing else to say and there seemed nothing else the Vicomtesse wanted to say.

Merciful male voices could be heard in the hall: rattling French from the older, richer one: Philippe's pure tone in monosyllabic response.

The Vicomte entered briskly. He was a long man, immaculate in a pale gray suit as though dressed for an office, hair quite gray and the blandly handsome features of an aging male model: studied, brittle masculinity, perfect and unerotic.

He crossed to Lily (who rose), took her hand and bowed. Although she knew his grace to be innate, it flattered Lily and restored her confidence. She hoped Philippe would seat himself beside her, but he did not; instead he went to a flute-legged armchair, half-sister to the settee. Lily smiled at him and he looked embarrassed.

"I like to dine early with my family, Lily. This is acceptable?" the Vicomte asked.

To Lily the implication of his question appeared twofold: first, it made her feel as though she were someone to be difficult, as though he half-expected her to say "Certainly not"; and, second, that eating was what she was there for and that it had to be got over with as soon as possible.

"Absolutely. Oh, goodness, I don't mind when . . ."

"Bon," he said. The little word volleyed, knocking her exclamations to nothing. "You like your villa?"

"It's beautiful." So they knew. They knew she came from next door; good.

"It belong to my brother. He care to rent it. I can't think why."

"No, it must be very . . ." She stopped, unable to think of

any immediate disadvantage to them; it was, after all, satisfactorily distant.

She looked again at Philippe, smiling more timidly this time. He did not smile, but frowned, and she knew he was hurt. Someone had done something to hurt him.

There was peripheral movement, there, on the terrace: unseen people, fortunate phantoms with a task, while these four remained in uneasy suspension amid the elegance. The maid came to the door, hands shyly folded upon her apron. She glanced quickly about the room, alighting with relief upon the backview of the Vicomtesse. In a childish voice she said, "Madame est servie."

"Merci, Louise."

They seated themselves at the table, Lily with her back to the sea. She felt she should speak, say something sound from which a conversation might spring.

"I'm an only child too, like Philippe. We've talked about it, haven't we? And agreed we prefer it."

At first it appeared there was to be no response to Lily's comment, then without raising her eyes from her white porcelain cup of chilled consommé, the Vicomtesse said, "He may prefer it, but being an only child gives my son many responsibles."

Lily smiled down into her own consommé, but Philippe said, "Responsibilities, Maman." The Vicomtesse raised her face to her son in silent interrogation. He repeated, "The word is not responsibles, but responsibilities."

Her expression became a strange assembly of pride, gratitude and irritation. "My son speaks English extremely well, don't you find?"

"I do, absolutely." This was followed by another silence which, this time, Lily left to them.

Eventually, through the tinkering of cutlery upon china, the Vicomte said, "My son tells me you are an orphan?"

"In a way, yes. But Grace has been my mother, I don't feel like an orphan."

"Your father, he was . . . ?"

"Yes, he was." She was annoyed by the oblique question about which she was expected to decide, then answer. Anyway, you just didn't go around saying "Father unknown." She had no objection to stating it, but not just now to these people, for their sake as much as her own. She observed the Vicomte and Vicomtesse share a glance with downcast heads.

Then the music began. At first Lily thought it came from the drawing-room, that a servant had been subtly instructed to alleviate their discomfiture. But, when she heard the nature of the music (noisy, rude, intrusive), she knew it could never have come from there. With tumbling despair she realized it came from her villa: Grace and company had begun their night.

"Is it always so loud?" Lily asked.

"Mostly," the Vicomte said.

"I'm sorry, I'll say when I go back."

"I think we are accustomed by now, are we not?" He looked at his wife and son, raising his eyebrows, proud of his counterfeit tolerance. "The water about us carries sound very easily, one forgets." His tone was suddenly almost kind, for he saw Lily was nearly crying.

Philippe walked her, without a word, back to her villa. "Why did it go so wrong?" she asked.

He held her hand, squeezing it, releasing it, offering only perfunctory comfort. "It's not your fault. Nothing you can help."

"Will you come in? Meet Grace?"

"No." He was emphatic.

"Please talk to me. Come to the beach later."

Suddenly he looked at her with sincerity and longing, the way he had looked at her years before, that afternoon. "I will." He ran from her gates back to his own.

Lily waited in her room for the others to depart for a nightclub. They would assume she was still next door; too soon to recount the kind of detail they would long for. The villa was quiet again after the cacophony of their departure which Lily heard, not as though it were taking place in the hall beneath her, or on the gravel outside, but as though she were still sitting on the terrace next door, hearing what they would hear, dying a little more.

Past the pool and the drystone wall Lily picked her way down the sandy path through the mimosa grove to the beach. Philippe was there sitting with his back against a tree, head in hands. She knelt next to him without a word. He did not touch her as he would have done in that other world where they loved and talked. Finally she said, "Tell me, Philippe."

He stood up, took some steps away from her, working at a twig, tearing its tendrils of green. He began to speak with his back to her (Lily thought of the maid). "I told them about you, how I loved you. That I wanted to . . . to . . ." She went and stood to see his face. The incline placing her lower, she looked

up at him. He turned away. So this was something to be said
without eyes, without hands, no touch to soften the message.
She did not try to face him, but left him to address the roots of
the grove and the sandy path. ''I told them these things and at
first they said nothing to me. Before you came my father took
me to talk to me, tell me, explain why it could not be; you and
me together. They tell me about your aunt . . . that she is, well,
a lady of the cafés . . .''

''You mean a tart? A prostitute?'' Lily exploded.

''No, no, listen. Not a prostitute, but not *serious.*''

The very word Jaime de Caberro had used and she understood
it, the way Europeans used it; it was not a complaint against
levity, it was describing the quality, the whole fabric of a personality. Lily began to shake. ''It's not Grace in question, it's
me.''

''Yes, but she is your aunt, your background and, Lily, they
say you are not an orphan at all, but that you are a . . .'' He
knew the word perfectly well in English, but for her sake, in
order to distance it, he forged it in French, ''. . . une bâtarde.''

''SO WHAT?'' she yelled, supporting herself against the tree,
wrapping her arms about herself because no one else would.
''SO BLOODY WHAT?''

He continued imperturbably, without turning. ''These things,
they are blood. In families they matter above desire, above
beauty . . . above . . . love; it is blood. I am sorry.''

''How can you change so from the one you were, even this
afternoon?''

''Because I have to, and because then I didn't really know
everything. It is hard for me, too.'' He turned at last and saw
her against the tree cradling herself. He reached out, touched
her shoulder with neither love nor regret, but pity. He walked
away out of the edge of the grove. At first unaware that he had
left her, Lily turned to speak again, then saw him through the
purple and the black and the silver sea; dimmer and dimmer,
not because he moved so fast but because of tears.

She stepped out on to the sand and shouted, ''And screw you
too, you . . . you . . . *Frog.*'' Not great but the best she could
manage just then. A breeze circling in from the sea caught her
words, threw them back at her and on into the trees.

She fell uncomfortably among the roots to cry; it was better
to be uncomfortable, she wanted to be; then she felt exhaustion,
the analgesic for pain. She cried away her birth, her life, and
she cried for Grace. She despised them for despising her and

herself for caring at all. And here was that vessel, a distant doubt no longer, but a ship of misery anchored right in the middle of her mind, no room for anything else. She cried through a shaky, far-off strike of one, then two, slept through three, woke with sore, heavy eyes at four.

She heard voices calling from the villa and wondered what she would do about herself; what she would say. There was a heavy tramping through the grove. One of them was coming, looking, calling. It was Oliver. She stayed still. He wouldn't find her and she would bathe, slip into the house, sleep, appear in the morning (''What? Those boring French, can't stick them, and the boy's a fool'').

''Lily?'' Oliver knelt next to her, shaking her shoulder gently. He thought she was sleeping. She raised her head and right away he knew. He said nothing but settled so her head could rest in his lap. ''Tell me, Lily, tell me.''

She was astounded that she could cry again, anguish freshened from its rest. ''She's not a lady of the cafés, Grace. That's what they say . . . and they said, too, that I'm a bastard. He said it, so I am, but that's not all I am. Is it? . . . Is it? And because of that and Grace and background and blood we can't be, can never be . . .''

''All right, Lily, I've got it, don't go on.'' He paused to think and stroke her hair. ''My God, I guessed as much when Grace came back. Just a little suspicion.''

''Are they right?''

''You know they're not. But there are a lot like them, not only French, all over.''

''You and Melissa are different from Grace, aren't you? Grace isn't an intellectual, I know that, but you two are in a way, and you don't find her just a . . . lady of the cafés?''

''We love her, she'd give anything to anyone, including her heart. She's a child and yet look how she's cared for you and look how you protect her.''

''What'll I tell her about them? What can I say happened?''

''Oh, Lily,'' he turned her head in his lap to see her face, ''I don't have to tell you that. I've seen you shield Grace from the facts since when? Since Spain, remember? The night our baby was born? You can do that better than anyone in the world.''

''I'm tired of France. I'm tired of summer. I'm tired of being seventeen.''

''It'll never hurt so much again, Lily, I promise you that.''

Book
Two

Chapter 7

THE ONLY LIGHT COMING THROUGH THE BEVELED GLASS panels of the front door was from a street lamp variously reflected on the brass of the lift-cage inside. Lily was tired, having driven to North Wales and back in one day. On entering, she turned quickly, leaning hard against the door to shut out the wind before opening the concertina gate of that elaborate lift set in the stairwell.

Six years had passed since the French summer, and Oliver Cary had been right: it never did hurt so much again. Lily never let it. Few came very close to Lily Teape. She was a tall, quiet, speculative girl who would have been surprised at the amount of admiration she stirred in those who knew her. What she did know was that her manner must have advertised some strength or equanimity, for others confided such things as she would rather not have heard. She despised social life; no one had fooled her into thinking that it was anything but a sham, a mummery for passing physical contact. Having studied fashion design and tailoring, she was establishing herself with her unique reconstructions of old garbs, and original designs from antique fabrics. An eccentric dresser, she never wore new herself, preferring the feel of reach-me-downs from unknowns. Things that had been to places she had not.

Her knowledgeable, eclectic taste helped her turn up such things as a Victorian railway porter's uniform, the livery of a royal Edwardian butler, and Paul Poiret gowns. She purchased from junk shops, markets and sales all over the country; would search out more by chatting in pubs. She found peace and pleasure in small talk with strangers. Returning to the home of an

ancient she might acquire this one's grandfather's military uniform ("Seen every battle of the Boer War, that has"); that one's
mother's cap and gown from when she was a "tweeny up at the
big house . . . ."

Lily pulled the heavy lift gate, then stopped, raised her head.
Something decided her to walk the shallow marble stairs. She
did not press the light; it would not last long enough to see her
to the next floor. Unwinding her scarf, removing gloves, she
peered upward between the sway of mahogany banister and lift
before beginning her ascent. The great building breathed quiet
in the darkness.

"Ssst?" While the interrogatory sound she made sailed up,
evaporated, she faced down, eyes closed to concentrate, but
there came no break in the resettled silence. She began to climb.
At each floor she stopped, her form illuminated by the paler
night falling through the long windows, and looked up yet again.
"Sssst?" waiting in the same posture as before. There came no
reply.

She arrived at her own door, the penthouse. Years later she
could still see herself performing that perfectly ordinary act:
key in, turning, opening. Why that particularly? Except perhaps
when reflecting upon the disintegration of a way of life it helps
to pinpoint a specific moment when the status quo decamped;
and it prevents suspicion of all the happy times. There was,
however, one subtle thing that did set this arrival apart: when
she opened the door Lily had an absolute conviction that something came out of the flat, passed her and went away. The current
of it was like the disturbance in the atmosphere on releasing a
trapped bird. But this was no bird; it was something unseeable
unfurling from the confines of the home she still shared with
Grace.

Lily would have called in her customary way, "Grace, it's
me. All right?" had she not known Grace was out on a date.

At fifty-two Grace was still a pretty woman. She had lost some
of her élan but, after all, there had been so many humiliations
in the quest for Happily Ever After. She continued on a decreas-
ing hope-to-hope basis but Grace's unsuitors seemed to go from
bad to worse. After Lily's introduction to any one of them, Grace
would come to her, whipping in her excitement, "Well, Lily,
what did you think? Isn't he the nicest? The kindest? I really
think that *this* time . . . *this* time . . . ." Lily would not mention
Grace's inevitable seniority; or the surreptitious slapping of
Lily's bottom; or the pocketing of the contents of the cigarette

box; or the suspect, mincing hips. No. She would say carefully, "Mmm . . . Seems to be all you say. But, do you know, I can't help wondering about the nose." "The nose?" "Yes. Could you actually wake up, for the rest of your life, to a nose like that?" Thus a cushion would be laid against disappointment and soon after Grace would fall gratefully upon it. "You were so right, darling. What a heartless man, so cruel. And the nose said it all."

However, tonight was different. Grace was seeing someone for the sixth time in less than a fortnight, a man whom even Lily acknowledged was a change from the rest: widower, grown children, similar age to Grace; a successful and genuine and gentle man. It was hard to see what Grace saw in him. There was room for optimism. Lily had been disinclined to single out nose, feet, laugh. He was not the sort of man to be unkind about.

All the lights in the flat were on, not unusual, and Lily would leave them that way for her aunt's return much later. But, as she passed the open door of the drawing-room, there was something poised about the atmosphere coming from that place of fading opulence (still filled with furniture from the country house she had never known, sold almost upon the instant of her uncle's death); it did not seem to be in repose as rooms are when properly vacant.

Lily entered and saw, there on the sofa, feet up, shoes abandoned, though somehow erect and anticipant, Grace. She was clutching a handbag to the lap of her gray, silk-jersey dress, a fur coat cast on a chair nearby. Her hair, still thick, topaz, was carefully arranged and sprayed in place, her lovely eyes made up just a little, but overall there was a mildly exhausted fragility about her; as though she had been beautifully fashioned from used tissue paper.

"Grace. I thought you were going out with David."

Grace shrugged, turned her face away, then brought it back having achieved a smile. She reached for a cigarette box, placed a cigarette in her mouth with a trembling hand and, a little incoherent with the job of lighting it (and something else too), said, "He didn't come."

"Why? Didn't he ring to explain?"

Grace put her head back, shaking it while inhaling deeply. "Uh-uh . . . well, yes, really, he did. Only an hour ago, though. Me waiting here, the booby prize on the sofa."

"I'm sure he had a perfectly good explanation."

"Oh, he did. He'd thought hard, he said, wanted to settle

down. So do I, I said. I know that, he said, and that's why I can't see you anymore; we're not suited to permanence with each other. Those were his words, funny ones, eh? Men always speak oddly when they're oiling out of things. And he said, 'At our stage of life we can't afford to waste time.' " She covered her face, quaking with the repetition, "*Waste time* . . . I ask you."

Lily sat, an arm about Grace. "I'm so sorry." The trick was to make it clear the whole thing was better over with, but for once Lily did not feel that way, was wishing she had forced herself to mention at least his flaccid neck. It would have been useful just now; they might have managed to giggle about it.

Head down, Grace had begun rummaging in her handbag. Not a good sign. Since the incident in Marbella, Grace had policed the extremes of her despair in front of Lily, tried to share only the good times; but Lily knew, and handbag-searching was a regular subterfuge.

Grace finally produced a handkerchief by which time its necessity had subsided. "Do you like my dress? It's Jean Muir," dabbing at her face.

"Yes, I do. You look beautiful. Like always."

"Thank you, dear." Accepting the compliment with weary confidence, shaking her head, returning to the handbag; peering deep into it, she said, "Did you have a chance to pick up my prescription?"

"Yes. Had it made up in Llandudno, of all places." Lily handed over a white packet.

"Llandudno, fancy. How kind you are. Thank you. How did you get on? Found all sorts of lovely things? Anything I can wear?"

"Could be."

"Oh good." She did not ask to see; her attention was dwelling dangerously elsewhere. "If you don't mind, lovey, I think I'll pop along now."

"To bed?"

Grace, over at the drinks cupboard, turned, bottle poised. "Well, you know, sort of."

Lily pointed to the prescription. "Grace, don't take too many of those with the drink, will you? You know what happens."

"I'll be all right, love, don't worry about me. Goodnight," departing, bottle in hand.

A threadwork of concessions, taboos, understandings held their life together in harmony and one major unspoken edict

was: never, never follow Grace into her bedroom once she had
bid goodnight.

"Grace? Wait a minute. Let's talk . . ." Too late. Lily heard
the bedroom door shut. She looked at the front door on the way
to her own room and had a sudden chilling notion that the sense
of departure, so strong, had been the coattails of hope; it had
given up on Grace and gone.

Lily's darkened room was packed with old clothes, the odd
mother-of-pearl button catching briefly some obscure light; souls
shifting uneasily in garments they did not wish to vacate. She
lay fully dressed, fencing with sleep, listening for the sounds
she associated with the restoration of Grace's spirits; the running
of a bath, the television. There was nothing.

It was possible Grace could shut herself into a further room
structured from gin and Valium, looking, looking for the dila-
tory wonderful someone, never to return; leave forever those
who loved her. And there were such, for despite stippling her
life with the miseries of misplaced loving, she poured her own
magic brand of love into others' lives, the way she had for Lily.

When Lily was in her late teens Grace had bought a large house
in Fulham, setting it up—modernized, furnished in her own
intimately elegant, tea-time English style—for children who were
alone in the world. Never more than eight of them at a time:
they were the ones whose parents had suddenly been killed, or
whose only parent had died; the ones who became inexplicably
hated and abused after the birth of a sibling, or after a new
marriage.

In many cases the children there had had every privilege except a place in which to be loved and cared for. Grace called it
The Garden ("because it was in a garden, Lily, that you changed
my life and agreed to live with me"). A carefully selected married couple ran the place; Grace's friend, Angela, handled all
the administration, while Grace funded it herself, with some
large private donations, usually liniment to conscience. It was
Grace who imbued The Garden with wonder. When she arrived
the fun began, any excuse for a celebration; Christmas, Hanuk-
kah, birthdays. If a birthdate was unknown she would decide it.
"What's your lucky number?" "Three." "Favorite season?"
"Spring." "Then it'll be the third of May." A tailor-made
birthday. She took them to cinemas, theaters, on any number of
outings, singly or together depending on who wanted what. She
attended every event at their schools. In all, she treated them as

her own. Even the most reticent, hardened, brutalized child came
to adore her.

The tributaries to the lake of Grace's love were infinite, and
few had any idea of the sinister flows beneath it, dragging her,
pulling her into low, colder currents. Lily had seen her, on at
least two occasions, bruised about the face and who-knows-
where else ("a silly little accident in the car, lovey, nothing to
worry about"), retreating, as always, at such times to her room.
Lily was aware of the truth of it by now, though perhaps not the
extent.

Lily spread herself flat on the floor outside Grace's closed bedroom door; the pile of the carpet being so thick, it was the only
way she could see whether or not a light was burning. If there
was none, then Grace slept, to rise tomorrow, perhaps lunch
with a friend, visit The Garden, attend a private view. It could
be all right after all.

But diffused through the pile pressed flat by Lily's fingers a
light did shine. She listened, considered, entered.

Grace's bedroom, like the rest of the flat, had not altered for as
long as Lily could remember: the light came from two bedside
lamps, fussy situations with pink, silk bows. The big bed, cluttered with pillows, had not been slept in, although the peach
silk quilt had a fatigued look about it. A floral chintz draped
from the tester, looped to left and right, the same chintz used
in festoon blinds at the long windows. On the far side of the
room the door to the bathroom was open. Dozens of framed
photographs were hung or stood on occasional tables, where
they settled with champagne corks grouped together with pink
ribbon, single roses (long since dried), theater programs. The
photographs were of Grace having fun: Grace laughing with the
Carys at a table in a nightclub (there was a rough edge where
someone's image had been torn away); Grace water-skiing;
Grace holding hands with a dark young man outside the Coli-
seum; some dull formal studies of her wedding (a grand, white
affair, an arcade of swords held by smiling young officers).

Lily did not see the live Grace immediately, so diminished
was she by the high proportions and still life commotion of the
room; when her eyes did rest upon her, standing before a cheval
mirror, shoeless in sequined mini-dress, caught in a private
speculative act: half-on to the mirror, head over shoulder, hand
on hip, left foot pivoting pigeon-wise trying to view what others

could from behind, Lily was arrested by how little she looked, terribly little. So this was the blighted, late-night Grace, destitute in the litter of her dreams; a boozy, worn-out frail searching in the mirror for evidence of the compliment she had been paid that morning, or was it yesterday, or was it ever said at all? Had she made it up like all those other carefully scripted scenes ("and be with me, Grace dear, always, always . . . always"), scenes that never came about. Real life fell so very short. She must have known the sight of herself like this would be indelible; had been so careful in hiding it.

Grace gasped and swung round to face Lily, hands clutched over breast as if to cover nakedness. Her stance was unsteady, she tripped slightly, sustaining herself with a hand upon the mirror, then assumed a staccato hauteur. "Lil . . . Lily dear, you shouldn't . . . why have you . . ." She gave up and, with chin lifted in defiance at Lily's expression of distressed solicitude, let herself be viewed until that became too much. She lowered her face. "I wish you hadn't come."

"You worried me."

"I don't want you to do that on my account. I've tried hard for you not to see me like this again. There was once when you were very little; you came in, saw things you shouldn't. Then in Spain: Jaime de Bloody Caberro. I thought then, no more of this around Lily. She absolutely mustn't know."

Despite Grace policing her despair, Lily knew this other woman had been with them, living unseen like a night-shift lodger. To find her all she had to do was open the door to Grace's sanctum, intrude upon unsatisfactory alliance or disappointment. Now she had done that it was hard to find words that might heal, assuage, and when she uttered an inquiry it was meager, not at all what she intended. "So you're all right?"

Grace snatched a look at herself in the mirror, suspicious that her niece had seen a flaw she should have spotted, yet she turned again patting her hair, half-aware of Lily's real inquiry, still half-lost in her own contemplation.

"All right? I think so, don't you? Do you like my dress? It's Ossie Clark." She looked sad, with her chicken's legs displayed, her thin thighs, but Lily nodded sufficiently. "I wore this dress to the first party I went to after Michael was killed. I've not gained a pound. Oh, I was it. They made such a fuss of me. You see, then I was a beautiful young widow, all the more attractive for not being impoverished. One had the air of affluent tragedy about one."

For a moment Grace's gaze rested with vacant delight upon memories until, enamel-eyed, she drew hand to chin. "But look at me now."

"Now doesn't count. You're tired, upset. If you slept a little . . ."

"Hide in sleep? Won't do that . . . Used to, you know, but I found it's all the same by midday. With a good lunch you can push it through to three, four, then, when the chilled Frascati wears off and you remember there's no man who's just for you, it's all the same."

Grace set herself with care on a small dressing chair, hands resting in her lap, shoulders slightly collapsed, head to one side, frowning. Her bare feet pointed to each other. "I thought I'd marry quickly after Michael; clutch at some of that companionship that evaded us as a couple; I was still a young woman, after all. Each morning I'd wake up and think, any day now he'll come along, the very one. I was glad of every night because it made that day closer, just as though we had a real date. Then I began to be tired of waiting, the way one tires of a lover who makes no effort. What's he doing? I thought, and started to suspect that our date had come and gone, he'd stood me up; gone off and married someone else; might even be starting a family. Others were marrying and remarrying all around me. He was probably one of them. And there was I.

"The irony was that everyone said, 'Lucky Grace, you must have lots of men.' And it's not as though they didn't think I was pretty. Lots of painters have wanted to paint me. And, as for people being in love with me, well, I must have at least six copies of that . . . that Prophet thing, that Gibel Khan man."

"Kahlil Gibran," Lily quietly, pale smile lapwards.

"What?" Grace quickly, hopefully; a magic single-word solution might just have been uttered.

"Nothing"

"No, well, that's right: nothing" (what might have been solution turned out to be summing-up) ". . . and I'm sick with shame when I think of how I am." Grace lifted her drink with both hands, swilling it in the glass, then down her throat in one; refilled it, nursed it.

"Tonight, after this David thing, I feel empty as never before; like all possibility is used up. It's not that I'm brokenhearted. I wasn't in love with him. I was opting, like so many people do in marriage, young and old; it's often just opting. Serves me right because really I thought of him as one of my second-eleven. I've always had a team of old buffers whom I thought I could land at a pinch, if all else failed. Well, I felt the pinch and that all else had failed. Now look, the old buffer chucks me. It's no more than I deserve. But I'm sick of my single status, of 'Can anyone give Grace a lift?' after dinner parties.'' She raised her head, pondered, addressed the wall as though it were an audience wherein a guilty party sat. ''I expect someone told him.''

''Told him what?''

''About how I am, where I go, what I do. I say to myself, 'Who that I know would come to this stinking alley, this dock-yard, this bar?' In places like that I deal with my need. Someone slumming might have seen me and told. I think a doctor might call it nymphomania. Some nymph, eh?

''It started off with such a simple wish for arms around me, a man's arms; and not someone who stays just once and doesn't ring, but a man who would stay a while, like for ever. Now it's expectation turned ugly. I've become like one of those women who go around stealing other people's babies because they've lost, or can't have, their own. Their need makes them crazy. My need makes me crazy. I go around stealing love or any damn thing that passes for it. But it's not all the time. Just sometimes I'm cast in this frantic spell of lust; and then the normal chan-nels—How do you do? Dinner, coffee? Will he, won't he? My place or yours?—are just too blasted slow. And, oh God, I love young men, someone the age *he* would have been if I'd first married right. My tastes haven't matured with my body'' (cup-ping her hand and massaging the air suggestively), ''I love the smell of them, the feel of them, their strength and stamina. The way they tremble when they're excited. Sick, sad, shameful and true. Don't judge me, Lily, I beg you not to do that.'' Her voice was calm, considering, yet tears flowed from her eyes while she drew her head from left to right in ceaseless dissent at the situ-ation.

It was no terrible shock; Lily's understanding had developed by degrees over the years. She was reminded of pictures she had played with as a child which started as glossy blank pages but when brushed with water a previously printed image bleared forth, growing sharper as it dried. She had always guessed the scene before the last stroke.

Grace's admission now seemed to prove that she was indeed at the end of something. Her greatest capacity had been that of Let's Pretend. Let's Pretend had brought Grace round and round life's mill of crises, her head rising to the top, bright again, so sure that this time, *this time*, there would be no down-side, no plunge.

Having allowed the confession to dull for them both, Lily said, very carefully, "It's dangerous, what you're doing, living like that, even if it's not all the time."

"I know, dear. It must end before it ends me. I'll stop, I really will . . ." a pause followed by a cynical laugh, "but listen to me promising. It's worth no more than that of a druggy or a drunk. But where the devil do I go to get dried out of this? I'll have to do cold turkey, which is life, time, day by day by day." She swiveled her head to Lily. "Do you know about desire? Longing? Lust? I don't think so. The young, the fresh don't have that brand of desire; those things grow with age, experience, disappointment; and they only fade again when there's no hope left.

"You dropped your heart on a beach in France and never bothered to pick it up again. Dear Lily, so young, so mature. No elation for you? No highs? No lows?"

Lily shouldered-off the approach, the reminder. "Come on now, Grace. I'll help you to bed. We'll talk again in the daylight when the world always seems better," doubting, this time, doubting that the world would seem different for Grace. Never mind the drink, disappointment; even beyond these things the fissure was deep and an awful lot that was of value had fallen in, like optimism, will, belief in Happily Ever After.

Grace allowed herself to be unzipped, maneuvered, laid down. Lily had reached the point of drawing up the covers, hoping any minute to see Grace's eyes shut in the heavy, prompt manner of the drunk, when Grace suddenly thrashed free, grasped Lily's wrists to hoist her slight weight upward, her face close to Lily's, breathing with frantic entreaty. "Find someone, Lily, find someone, before it's too late, like it is for me."

Lowering her to the pillows, "I'll be all right . . . Shh now, shh . . ." reaching to switch off the light.

"No, not that. Not yet. I'll do it myself if I feel it coming, sleep, you know. Thank you, lovey, thank you."

Instead of returning to her room Lily went out of the front door, closing it soundlessly behind her. In the shadows of the landing she leant against the banister, hands on hips. "Sssst?"

"Sssst." The answer came and she descended.

In the dark on the last step of the flight a boy with black hair sat with his back to her, head upturned, mouth slightly parted, facing her with his ear. He was wearing a dressing-gown, striped pajamas and slippers.

"Hello, Lily, sit down." He touched the step beside him, half-closed eyes still to the wall.

Seating herself next to him, Lily tousled his cloud of hair while he reached for her wrist. When she was settled, hands clasped and slung between her knees, the boy turned his head somewhat mechanically, just a little too far so that his eyes were directed to the back of her head. He was quite blind. After a spell of companionable silence, he said, "Good day?"

"Haif and half. You?"

"Bunked out of school. Told them I had another headache. Went fishing in the canal."

"Sebastian, *really* . . . Not again." She allowed her ritual admonishment to float off before, "Catch anything?"

"The usual sort of thing: plastic bag tied tight with something slushy inside. I think it was a rotting rubber Johnny and a plimsoll. You know my real ambition, don't you?"

Lily yanked him closer with his neck in the crook of her arm. "Tell me, tell me."

"Trout-fishing in Scotland. If it's the last thing I do."

"I know." A smile was audible in her words. She had heard his ambition often over the last four years (always said with a fresh "wait-till-you-hear-this" enthusiasm), since giving him a fishing rod for his seventh birthday. They had gone straight to the white stone bridge in Hyde Park and caught an old tartan shirt. Everyone who knew Sebastian heard about it; it was definitely the most exciting experience of his life. For days after he described to anyone who would listen the moment of contact, the tug, the pull, the winding in, adding, to indulge the kindly contained amusement he could feel all round him in his darkness, ". . . and it was a shirt, at least that big," with the exaggeration of the true fisherman: arms spread, head back, beaming to the ceiling.

"How about me making you a promise? I'll take you trout-fishing in Scotland this summer as a birthday present."

"ACE, Lily. Do you really mean it?" He held her upper arm in both hands, turning his knees toward her.

" 'Course I mean it."

"What's the matter?" he asked, releasing her arm to settle in the same manner as she: hands clasped and slung between knees.

"What do you mean?"

"The back of your voice sounds sad."

"Pint-sized Sherlock."

"I'm right, though."

"I suppose. It's Grace. She's very low tonight. I don't think you met her new man, David, but anyway it's over. Which is a pity and she's taken it worse than ever this time."

"Poor Grace. If I was an old man I'd marry her. I think she's really brill and fun."

"The trouble is, Sebastian, if you were an old man she wouldn't want to marry you."

Seeming to balance this obscure reasoning on the tip of his nose and squint at it there, he concluded, "Weird. Anyway, I don't know why she bothers. Mummy says you can waste more valuable working hours organizing husbands than on anything else. Been to The Garden lately?"

"Not since the Christmas party."

"Promise you'll never tell Grace, but I hate it there. It's depressing." Lily began to protest, but, "No, no, listen," he went on. "I know she's done it beautifully and the people are really nice, that it's like a proper family and all; but, when it comes down to it, it's not, and those children know there's no one of their own for them. If there is someone it's almost worse 'cause it means that person doesn't care about them. I mean, the few times I've been there I don't feel I can be normal, and rude, and win the games or whatever 'cause they're so underprivileged in the first place. The least you can let them do is win Gin Rummy. It's just not like real life."

"We're the lucky ones, I guess."

"Yeah," he breathed, reaching again for her wrist as though for a talisman.

"Sebastian?"

"What?"

"I'm starting looking tomorrow. It really is high time. I must have somewhere to work. There's not enough room in the flat anymore."

"Yes, but don't *go*. You won't *go*, will you?"

Lily took his hand, bending the stubby, rough-skinned fingers around her palm. She understood "don't go"; it was what she had always feared herself: those she loved departing.

"No, I won't go. It'll just be a workroom. I'll still live here."

"That's all right, then. Listen, there's Dad."

Lily shut her eyes to concentrate. "Where is he? Outside?"

"Mmm. There's his key in the door."

After a moment there was the sound of the front door closing eight flights and four floors below. An anemic light washed the lower stairs, iron gates opening, closing, a shudder and grind as the lift ascended to stop at the floor beneath where the two sat; it was not constructed to reach the top two floors.

"I'd better go. Bet you're supposed to be in bed," Lily whispered.

Sebastian did not answer; he was focusing his ear below, his fingers splayed tense on his knees.

Oliver Cary's gangly silhouette appeared at the bottom of the stairs; although his head was dropped, his manner exhausted, distracted. After a few steps he paused, looked up when he sensed the larger and smaller forms ahead of him.

"Jesus," he gasped, then, "you scared me. What the devil are you two doing at this hour? It must be eleven." He never carried a watch.

"I'm sorry," Lily said. "You're right, I didn't realize it was so late. I'll go."

"Not cross?" Sebastian asked.

"Not cross, old man," Oliver cupped Sebastian's cheek, "but you'll be tired for school. C'mon."

"Let Lily tuck me in, Dad, please."

"OK, OK, but quick." Oliver stepped past them before they had time to rise, entering the flat calling, "Melissa? Melissa?"

Holding hands, Sebastian and Lily followed. A typewriter chattered somewhere. As they went to Sebastian's room, Lily saw Oliver standing sideways, hands in pockets in a lighted doorway, as though trying to draw together the room and the world outside while remaining apart from both.

"Where's Sebastian?" she heard him say. The typewriter stopped. "No, he's not. He's been sitting on the stairs . . . No, not alone. With Lily. Who else?"

Who else indeed? Who had ventured shyly to the hospital in Marbella to see the baby whose birth caused his parents so much distress, to look at the eyes which were all wrong; to learn from the Monthly Nurse (who stayed for six) how to change and feed him? And, when the nurse left and Melissa Cary remained sunk in a severe post-natal depression, it was Lily who raced home from school to relieve her of these tasks and place rattles in his tiny, grappling hands, bathe him and put him to bed. Overwhelmed with pride, Lily pushed his pram about the park and babysat for countless evenings while her quiet charge slept with his eyes open, and Lily longed for him to wake so they could play. On the days when it did not coincide with her own schooling, she took him to the playgroup, one for ordinary sighted children, and stayed there with him. Later on she escorted him to and from his school, until it was decided he could manage on his own. So he could and he wanted to very much; he was confoundedly independent. When he did fall and break his leg, it was Lily who carried him in his plaster to the sunshine outside, read to him, fished with him and told him stories.

"Ready," Sebastian said quietly. Lily went to his bed. "Make the sheets like you do, Lily. You know, very smooth and really tight."

"Stay in school tomorrow, won't you? This bunking out won't do. You'll get caught."

"You wouldn't tell," he said with certainty.

"Go to sleep, Ghastly. Dream of fishing. I'll see you."

The Carys were at the bedroom door. Oliver came no further but Melissa hustled in. "Lily, honestly, you are irresponsible. He has school, you know. Why do you do this sort of thing? Go on now and just think a little next time."

As Lily passed Oliver his look asked understanding for his wife; they all knew she was testy if her work was interrupted. Lily winked her pardon.

"Oh, Lily," Melissa called, on a friendlier note already, just before the door closed, "don't forget tomorrow evening; baby-sitting?"

"Not BABYSITTING, thank you very much; BOYSITTING, if you must," Sebastian's furious voice.

"I won't forget BOYSITTING tomorrow. Goodnight."

Upstairs she spread herself once more before Grace's bedroom door; no light shone. Grace slept.

Chapter 8

IN THE MORNING, LILY PREPARED COFFEE AND CARRIED IT through to Grace's bedroom. It was their custom to share the start of the day. Lily intended to offer more than the soft breath of encouragement that had been required in the past ("It's aerobics class this morning, Grace. Think of your thighs.") This time Lily would change her plans, not hunt for a workroom, but stay with Grace until her spirits were lifted, invent and guide and stroke her through, as Grace had done for Lily whenever she had had need. However, on entering it was, "Good morning, my love. Isn't it gray and grim outside and isn't it warm and cozy here? Come and sit down, we'll talk about today." Grace patted a place close to her on the wide bed with a sheaf of letters and stiff invitation cards. "I'm having lunch with Angela. Would you like to come? I'm afraid we'll talk 'Garden' non-stop, but you're welcome."

"Well, it depends on how . . ." Lily dried of precise inquiry. Was it a put-on, this resilience? If it was, then would it be fair to lift the lid on pretense?

Proving the sham of preoccupation with the morning's mail, Grace said, "About last night . . ." pausing. "I'm so very sorry. Appalled to think you saw me in that state. But, darling, please don't come in again when I've said goodnight. One has to have some get-out, some privacy to be whatever, without excuse."

"I haven't before, have I? But you were different last night. I was frightened for you."

Grace covered Lily's hand with her own and, after all, Lily had edged off that lid, for a mist of distress filtered across her aunt's features. "Forget it, Lily, please," she whispered, then, trying to toss away those hours as though they were a joke that had fallen flat, went on, "That was another me, a silly me. Mustn't take any notice of that self-pitying old lady, must we?" Inclining her head, she smiled her entreaty to put to one side any recollection of her other than how she wished to be seen: vital and optimistic.

Grace could still pass for forty to the unsuspecting, and it touched Lily that she would wash and make up just a little for their ritual of morning coffee. Just for Lily, it seemed, whom she knew loved her regardless.

With the tips of her long, red nails Grace spread the invitations about the silk cover, her spectacles charmingly precarious on the end of her nose; her manner was that of a fortune-teller seeking out her own future from among the cards.

"What are you looking for?"

"Fun, lovey, fun." She frowned at one and pushed it away. "Every day must have its little treat, mustn't it? And I'm looking for today's. Look here, what about this?" She held up an expensively printed card with a large color plate of a staggered, tortured-looking pyramid of rusting metal. "Now this looks sufficiently ridiculous: 'Johnny Cochrane's *Lyrical Lumber*.' I ask you." She held the card facetiously at several angles, then posed a faint, fanning herself with it. "How *can* they call it art? It's from Dennis's gallery, so I daresay Cochrane is another little bum-chum of his. How that man makes any money is beyond me."

Lily took the card, an invitation to a private view, six until nine that evening, then put it aside, not before she had noticed the window of a washing machine fused into the rest of the rusting metal.

Grace surveyed the other cards but the fingers of her left hand blindly crept back to that particular invitation. She took it up once more, scrutinized it, biting on her amused smile. "Let's go, Lily, eh? Just for a laugh. Look, look it's too silly, *Lyrical Lumber*, I love it." She threw herself back into her huddle of pillows, arms spread, card in fingers, laughing. "Please come too. Everything's so much more fun with you."

"OK. Just for the laugh. *Lyrical Lumber*. Honestly."

Lily was free to search for her workroom, somewhere quiet, cheap, not too far from home. Paddington proved hopeless and by the afternoon she had worked her way through to Ladbroke Grove.

The houses in this area had been grand in another era: many emerging once more into a new grandeur; but there remained the dilapidated ones, even apparently derelict except, perhaps, for a pot-plant on one windowsill, a half-finished bottle of milk on another; curtains drawn here, open there: ubiquitous give-aways of disconnected lives.

It was at a house such as this Lily saw hanging on the inside of its garden gate a handwritten sign, framed behind grubby glass, the single word: VACANCY. It was a street in which some of the other houses had been modernized and sold, possibly for hundreds of thousands, yet this one remained with a singular air of destitution. It was vast, deep, freestanding, rapt in its own sinister secrecy, settled about by an overgrown garden. She opened the gate, walked the path, up the steps which were roofed by a dirty glass arcade and pressed the bell which gave no sound. She thought to ring again when the door opened some inches, secured by a chain. The central track of the woman's face appeared. "Yes?"

"About the sign. Is the room still free?"

The door closed, to open once more, free of its chain. It was run-down inside, although ghosted by its long gone splendor: the fractured plasterwork on the ceiling, a broken chandelier, dead, ignored; dusky imprints where pictures had long hung and gone. The great rooms had obviously been divided into flats cheaply and uneconomically so that their hugeness remained. There was no carpet on the stairs but beauty in the wrought-iron balusters and the mahogany banister.

The woman had large, seriously supported bosoms, voluptuous hips and belly all sheathed in a tight-fitting dress. She was perhaps in her fifties, with brutally blonded hair piled with combs above a bold, frank, heavily made-up face. "It's on the first floor. No lift but you won't mind that being only young. Luggage?"

"Not with me."

"So you won't want it right away?"

"Well I would if it's what I want."

"You can't move in without luggage. House rule."

"I don't really want the room to live in, only to work in during the day."

The woman dropped her head, keeping her eyes upon Lily. With half of her generous mouth lifted in a smile, she said, "Not a tart, are you?"

"God no. I'm a designer, a dress designer, and I want a workroom, that's all. There's no more space in our flat."

"I see." Her tone implied she saw much beyond the words. There was a vulgar worldliness about her and Lily stood embarrassed, impressed, feeling herself becoming known. "Come on up then. I'll show you." She grabbed two keys on a ring from a board, jingling them as she ascended. "The man who was here did a moonlight last week. Three months' rent owing. The sinner. It happens, you know. You're careful, careful, they seem so nice. Talk. Lots of talk. Then wallop. The sinner's gone, leaving the room emptier than it was before . . . and me," reflective resignation in her voice. "I'm Mrs. Gregor. Gill to my tenants."

They came to the Sinner's Flat on the first floor, its door wide open on a high, wide shabby room with three French windows and worn cord carpet, its color given up in wear.

Lily went to stand in the center of the room, lackluster sun slow-stealing from the windows to her feet. There was a poor white-painted wardrobe and chest of drawers; more plasterwork on the ceiling; a center rose from which no light hung. There were dark brown curtains, heavy fabric which swept the floor, running the width of the window wall; possibly they had been there when the house had its Edwardian prime and because of them the room would always look fine, despite its shoddiness and tip-tilting light brackets facing away from each other on the wall.

Lily lifted one of the curtains and held it toward Mrs. Gregor. "This is woollen velvet, you know. Really rare now. They don't make it anymore."

"Yes, dear." Mrs. Gregor stood arms crossed, implacable, proprietorial by the door, watching Lily at ease in the anonymity of the emptiness. "Like it?"

"It's a wonderful room."

"Glad you think so, it's one of my favorites."

"Is there a bathroom, kitchen?"

With indifference Mrs. Gregor opened a door revealing a closet converted into a dreadful excuse for a kitchen. Another door was opened into a small room with a short stained claw-footed bath and unhappy siblings of lavatory and basin.

"How much?"

Mrs. Gregor recrossed her arms, dipping her head sideways to explore another aspect of Lily. After looking down a moment, working on her evaluation, she raised her eyes and brows. "Seventy-five."

"A week?" Lily exclaimed.

" 'Scheap," she said kindly, with a smile upon her ten-minute intelligence of Lily. "Not used to it, are you, love?"

"What?"

"This," she said, without a single gesture, not meaning the room or the squalor but simply a universal THIS.

And Lily knew it. She shook her head. "I will be, though."

"Tell you what: seventy for cash each week, in advance."

The Sinner's Flat became hers and Mrs. Gregor became Gill to Lily.

When Lily was driving home through a narrow road off Baker Street, a woman, shielding herself with a red umbrella against the slanting rain, stepped in front of Lily's car. Lily braked violently and the woman dropped the umbrella to waist height, realizing in sudden terror how near she had come to being run over. The face Lily saw, mouth agape, eyes squeezed with fear, was Grace's face. She raised the umbrella, ran on over and Lily shouted after her, "Grace, stop. Don't go."

On arriving home, finding Grace, Lily asked, although she knew the answer, "Were you in Chiltern Street a while ago, with a red umbrella?"

"Certainly not; and you know I hate umbrellas. Lethal things."

"So you're sure?"

Grace's casual response changed to curiosity. "Why keep on, darling? What are you really asking?"

"I don't know. It must have been the shock; I mean, to nearly run anybody over but then to have them turn round, and the face you see is that of the person you love most in the world . . . silly."

"It's last night, isn't it, that's done this? Lily, listen to me: you must think of yourself, your life; because, me, I'll be all right . . . in the end, you know." And there it was, that look of plea and insistence. See me. I'm smiling, smiling.

Dennis Little's gallery was already full when they arrived that evening; quite impossible to see any of the savage rusting exhibits at suitable distance, yet even without proper viewing Lily felt right away they were not the subjects for humor they had seemed to be on the card. Close to they had their own tactile hostility, for when she reached out, putting her hand to a coarse surface—an invitation they seemed to challenge one with—a rust stain was left on her skin.

Despite the throng there was still a sense of a greater crowd, a confined animation in the tighter knot of people at the far end of the room; an energy came from down there which was absent by the door. Lily knew from other such gatherings that it meant the artist was there: people, pushing near, hubbed around him to soak in vicariously what they could of success, stardust.

Grace was quickly lost to Lily, taken over by acquaintances, and she was glad because Grace was shining again. The chatter amused her, she would toss her head about, laughing, winking, attractively grimacing, confident that the light was right for her. She had a way of putting her fingers into the thick of her hair and lifting it from her head. It gave a charming and totally counterfeit impression of nonchalance about her appearance.

It was typical that Grace was borne directly into the current of people that moved with feigned effortlessness toward the artist, except that she really had made no effort. Dennis Little had called to her across the heads of others, "Grace, darling, over here." She motioned that it was beyond her to push through such a crowd. Clever Grace, he came to her and his presence cleared a path.

Dennis Little was actually a tall man, deep in well-disguised fifties. The nature of his gray hair was such that it could pass for blond. He had the clean, thin-skinned look of the dedicated vegetarian, bore the controlled tan of a sunray lamp and set off his physical coloring with pearl-grays and pinks. He was not the kind of homosexual who could be described as "camp."

He embraced her, planting a full kiss upon her cheek. "Come with me and meet Johnny. You simply must. You'll love him. What do you think? Sheer genius, what?"

"Genius, Dennis, genius. How clever of you to find him," and the last Lily saw of her was as she winked over her shoulder, instinctively knowing, as always, just where Lily was. Grace was on course now; Lily would not have to stay long.

She made fatuous talk with some people she knew, while their eyes flicked beyond her seeking some luminary, until suddenly she remembered boysitting and made to leave. By the door she saw the piece printed on the card, the one that had seemed so funny, with the washing-machine window as though it were an eye lapped in by melting metal flesh. The party was reflected and distorted upon the convex glass, appearing ever littler and sillier than it was. The color and shimmer of it suggested she could snatch it off and play with it in her fingers, while behind that was a profound, watchful blackness, like the vastly enlarged pupil of a creature that dwells in endless dark. It was loathsome.

When Lily arrived at the Carys' flat she thought at first she was too late and that Sebastian had gone elsewhere in order not to be alone for the evening; then she heard his measured step and his voice, "OK, Lily, coming."

He was always confident in things coming to pass as they had been planned: she was late but he knew that when the bell rang it would be her, so much so that he flung the door wide, presenting her with his smile, head as always forced a little back.

"You really must stop doing that," she said.

"What?"

"You must answer the door with the chain on. I could have been anyone. It's dangerous."

"You could never be *anyone*, Lily, not you."

"Let me in, flatterer. I'll get you some food."

As she prepared supper he stood near, eager but silent. He kept feeling his watch. Lily believed he had some fishing exploit to regale her with, only it would be hard because he knew how she felt about his bunking out of school.

At last he touched her arm. "Can we have it in front of the telly?" He loved the television and would sit with his lips practically upon the screen (because, he said, he liked the feel of the static) and there was no point in asking him to sit back. Lily did not have to say, "You'll hurt your eyes"; there was no damage that could be done to them.

"If you like."

He paced around the small kitchen and she guessed that any minute the confession would come. "Aren't you at all excited?" he said at last.

"What about?"

"You've forgotten." He was hurt.

"Oh, my God." Lily hated it that he should be hurt because of some oversight of hers. She always remembered his birthdays, Christmas, school Open Days, plays, and she had no idea now how she had let him down. "What? What? Tell me."

"Mummy's on telly. On *Question Time* tonight."

Lily slammed down the pan in exasperation at herself. How could she have forgotten? Yet she did not mind so much because it was Melissa's moment not Sebastian's. They took their plates through and without turning on the light settled the way they always did before the television. Lily stretched on the floor like a human chaise-lounge, one leg arched so that Sebastian could lean against her thigh and that way she could gain a little distance from the screen.

Since babyhood physical contact had been essential to Sebastian; the common now-and-again touches, trying to assure that something does go on beyond talk, were not enough for him, he needed much more. Even as he sat as he did then (against Lily's thigh, his arm stretched along her body as though along the back of a sofa), his hand would feel unconsciously for hers. Entirely absorbed in the television, head back, mouth agape, rocking to some dim instinct about the movement of the light, he would play with her fingers: sort them, bend them, press upon her nails. He knew her hands better than the tenderest, most assiduous lover.

Melissa had become a national figure: "Melissa Cary Cares" one famous slogan had read. She was highly successful in raising public consciousness and funds; effective, articulate and pretty, everyone wanted her for their cause. This was far from the first time she had been on television but, whether it was this or radio, Sebastian displayed the same proud, attentive excitement.

Sebastian kept leaning forward to feel whether it was the right channel, then feel his watch, and Lily was wondering why Oliver was not there to see the program with them.

At last it began: the panel of four plus chairman behind a semicircular table, ready to deal with questions from the audience. When Melissa was introduced Sebastian smiled, touched the screen with his fingers. "There she is, there she is." Actually it was not. In error the camera had focused upon the woman Member of Parliament. "It's her blue with flowers, isn't it?"

"Yes, she looks fabulous."

"I know," he said.

He knew her whole wardrobe by this kind of description. ("What's it like, Mummy?" pressing his face into the fabric, crushing it, spreading it, stroking it: Melissa withdrawing it firmly, kindly, saying, "Oh, yellow with stripes," or, "Blue with flowers," or, "Black and green.") Lily had wondered what he made of these color-based descriptions, but they seemed to satisfy, and knowing the clothes by feel he would use his mother's description, "You've got on your black and green. I love that."

When the program was nearly over they heard the front door close. Moments after, without turning his head, Sebastian pointed to the screen. "Look, Daddy. It's Mummy. She's terribly good."

Oliver smiled down at Lily. "I know, Seb, I saw the beginning at the studio. She's beautiful and clever."

"Beautiful and clever," Sebastian repeated quietly to himself, adding them to his abstract Identikit.

Even by the spectral light of the television it was possible to see that Oliver was exhausted. He stood about as if unsure where to sit in his home; looked at the screen whenever Melissa was talking and frowned in a way one does about a familiar, unplaceable face in a crowd of strangers. He looked large and shaggy, not suited to conventional rooms, although when he moved and spoke there was a quietness contending with his physical appearance. There was a new quality too: it was weariness; but one beyond that which comes from work. It was as though there was a great unexpelled sigh about him. Lily did not attend to the program herself but observed husband and son watching wife and mother on television.

When the program was over she offered to prepare some food.

"No, Lily, you mustn't do that for me. I'll get it. I know what I want."

They went on sitting, Sebastian and Lily, in the same position with the television off. As Oliver walked down the passage Sebastian followed him with his seeing ear. The giveaway of concentration in a sighted person is usually a frown, but Sebastian had a habitual frown. His giveaway was when he drew his lips inwards over his teeth. He did this now, then turned to Lily and whispered, "What's Daddy got on his foot?"

She laughed and whispered back, "What? You mean like dog's mess?"

"Seriously. One's dragging. Go and look."

She did, because it was not fair to prevaricate with Sebastian. She felt foolish standing in the doorway of the kitchen while Oliver sliced bread on the far side of the table, feet hidden. She could hardly bend and look under it.

"You sure I can't help?"

"No, really, thanks. You needn't stay if you don't want. Seb and I'll chat till Melissa gets back. He'll never sleep till he's seen her, anyway, and it's nice to be alone with him. You know, man to man. He's a great talker. Find I learn from him all the time."

"Yes, he is. Gets it from his mother. She really was good,

wasn't she? And looked terrific." Of course she was only saying what the three of them had already agreed about Melissa, but she concentrated this time on something about his face. He smiled down at the loaf, shaking his head to one side. "Oh, yes, Lily, she's one fine woman." It was there again; the perplexed look mixed in with his smile as if he were talking about someone loved and gone. He raised his eyes, briefly alert. "So we agree, don't we?" The way he said it made Lily want to apologize. He had sensed the other aim in her comment, that she was digging for more, and he was not going to give it. Then she was vindicated by his smile. "Hey, thanks for coming around, Lily, like you do."

" 'Snothing. I like it. Family and all that."

"Yes, well, quite." Somewhere in those three words was that for which she had been previously digging.

She went to the sink, took a glass of water, looking down at his feet as she sipped, then reported back to Sebastian, still in a whisper, "Quite normal. Same old shoes."

"He's walking funny, Lily, he really is."

Chapter 9

WHEN LILY WENT IN THE NEXT MORNING, GRACE WAS already busy on the telephone, a nonsense of feathers on her bed-jacket framing her face, a little more make-up than usual. She beamed, made a face of exaggerated delight at the coffee Lily was carrying, fluttering an inviting hand upon her bed, all without missing a word of the conversation she was conducting, planning a dinner party.

Lily sat down and leafed through Grace's usual mail: dress shows, charity lunches, a hat show, another wedding, more private views. With a curious sort of shock Lily came across the Johnny Cochrane card again; that awful piece of work appearing with the sense of a threat reuttered.

Grace had finished her call and, bracing back a little, as she always did when really interested in her reaction, watched Lily, who put the card aside. It should not have been there anyway. He was yesterday's view.

Grace reached across to where Lily had pushed the card, nail-tapping upon it. "Impres*sive.*"

"Rubbish."

"Really, Lily," she said unusually firmly.

"I didn't like it."

"No, you're not supposed to like it. It's aggressive. It's violent. It speaks about the times in which we live."

"Grace, *please.*" Lily laughed: Grace was never more endearing to her than when she used other people's words, passing them off as her own, as if Lily would not guess. She had obviously come to some such conclusion but that was not her way of expressing it and it more than smacked of last night's phoneys.

The real Grace bubbled through. She blew on her feathers and feature by feature collided into her brilliant smile. "Oh, well. You know, but . . ." She took Lily's hand, serious again. Her changes of mood and expression were lambent as leaves shadowed on an August lawn. "I have to tell you, Lily, he is *wonderful*." Lily turned her face away. "Lily? Don't do that. Don't look away. Be happy."

Mustering the enthusiasm required, Lily turned to meet Grace's face, a gathering of lines between her eyebrows entreating Lily to be as excited as she was.

"Is he really?" Lily said. It was enough.

"Oh yes, darling. Let me tell you . . ." And she did. Things Lily had heard so many times before, Grace was repeating with all the inspiration of youth.

At a point where it did not seem too insensitive to discuss her own life, Lily said, "I found a workroom yesterday."

Grace drew back, startled. "But only to work in? Not 'live'? Lily? Surely not 'live'?"

"Don't worry, not 'live,' but I'll start moving my stuff today. It means I can take on more commissions, broaden my collection. It's exciting, Grace."

"Is it?" doubtfully, then, "Yes, yes I suppose it is," on the floodtide of eagerness. "But you will be here tomorrow for the dinner party and to do the flowers. Please? *He's* coming."

"Is he? So soon? 'Course I will."

"After that I'll come and see your lovely workroom. Really, I can't wait."

Several times Lily drove to the Sinner's Flat ferrying her possessions, with each journey feeling the base of her life spread, her pleasure in the place too. There were no more phantoms of Grace to contend with and the real Grace was absorbed in her preparations for the following day. When that day came their home was chaos from early morning: to have everything moved, cleaned, rearranged was part of the crescendo on which Grace worked prior to entertaining. Lily spent some time arranging flowers and would have left, feeling in the way of the cleaners, except that when she went to take her coat Grace appeared. "Don't go, dear. Don't go . . ." She looked frightened.

"Why?"

"In case anyone rings when I'm out . . . you know, to say . . . to say they can't come. If that happens I want *you* to tell me, not anyone else."

" 'Course I'll stay, with pleasure. But have faith, Grace, *faith*."

"Have I ever said that to you? Have faith?" Grace puzzled.

"No. Not that I remember."

"I should have. It's a good one," she finished, and was off.

Fortunately Grace had her day regimented, observing precisely the pattern she always set herself before her own parties: massage in the morning, followed by hairdresser, manicure, pedicure, no lunch, long rest in the afternoon, then gin and panic at six. That was the moment she decided the hair was not right, the nail varnish wrong and that she had no suitable dress to wear.

The cook, butler and maid had become friends, so many years had they been coming in to help her on these occasions, and now they would help Lily too. "Why, Mrs. Teape, you look wonderful." "Like your hair, Mrs. T, 'snice." "Really, Grace, you're lovely."

"Do I? Is it? Am I? Really? Tell me honestly, darling. The dress: not too young, is it?"

They brought her through to eight o'clock; she was even sitting poised in the drawing-room, patting at her neck, soothing some small, unsettled creature in there, when suddenly she stood up, taking Lily by the wrist with renewed desperation. "Come, come, Lily, do. There's something I've forgotten."

They went into her bedroom. Grace shut the door, leaning against it as though she feared Lily would leave too soon.

"Lily?" (Not fierce but imploring.)

"What is it, Grace?"

Her frightened eyes ranged the room, fixed on the floor, then again on Lily. She moistened her lips. "I'm forty, Lily. *Please*. Forty?"

With a ribbon of smile Lily hid the constriction in her throat, easing the words past it. "No, you're not," Grace drew her breath, brought her clenched hand to her mouth, "you're thirty-nine."

"Oh, I love you so and . . . Lily . . . I'm . . . so happy." Grace was in Lily's arms and she was the one who was crying.

To whom do you turn when your protector becomes the babe in your arms?

They returned to sit in the drawing-room, self-consciously prepared, just as they had been so many times before, not simply for a pleasant evening among friends, but aware that this could be the prelude to For Ever. No words seemed appropriate to the enormity of Grace's expectations except, "Drink?"

"Mmm, darling, thanks. I did say Larry was coming, didn't I?"

"Twice."

"You don't mind? Only Angela practically forced him on me. She kept saying, 'But who will there be for Lily?' I know she hopes you two will get together. But I don't think *him*, dear, do you?"

"He's not into girls, actually, but I don't mind him and I am altering a silk frock-coat for him."

The doorbell rang at last. While the maid was answering, Grace crossed to Lily, grasping her wrist, searching her eyes. "All right? All right, Lily?" seeking to offset her own unbearable suspense by reassuring an imagined one of Lily's.

"Terrific," Lily said with confidence, while sealing herself into the role of observer.

Angela stepped ahead of her son, Larry, and Dennis Little. She had sharp-cut black hair, an angular face with a slightly jutting jaw and ill-shaped lips, but magically, against all odds, there was a lop-sided beauty there that increased as she aged. She had been recently divorced and this invigorated her friendship with Grace who, after all, was an old hand at the single life. Grace would be her coach.

Drawing Angela aside, Grace entered into an intense, whispered conversation with her, although Lily caught the words, "Tell me honestly . . ."

Dennis said to Lily, "A beautiful Paul Poiret. Am I right?"

"Yes. Well done." Lily was pleased. He was referring to the dress she wore, an original, seventy-eight years old, a long tunic affair in green silk.

"So what did you think of the show the other night? Have you been back to see without the crowds?"

"No, I saw enough to know I didn't like it."

"Pity. He's very talented, you know."

"It looked sinister to me."

"There's room for that in art."

"Maybe, but not to live with. His art, I mean."

"You won't find him sinister."

"Oh no?"

"Don't prejudge. Just see." He was smug.

Larry hung about in attitudes, waiting to be spoken to yet

content to be an image: the worn-down one of a lean Oscar Wilde complete with center parting in slack, black hair.

"Nice to see you, Larry. I'm afraid your coat's not ready yet."

"Not to worry, Lily" (floppy, white, dismissive hand), "other things in life, and all that."

Oliver Cary arrived alone, the big man stooping, shuffling in his charmingly hesitant way (it had been understood beforehand that Melissa would be late due to a meeting). He had always been conspicuously shy of entering a crowded room, and to strangers it could make him seem surly, but Dennis Little knew him.

"My dear Oliver, do you know what I've done? I've brought your superb book on the Sahel tribesmen, and I've brought it (a) because you never signed it for me and (b) because I know Johnny will be fascinated."

Oliver smiled his indolent smile at his friend's enthusiasm, and greeted Lily by way of distraction, but Dennis pushed on with the subject of the book and the two became engaged in conversation.

Lily's eyes happened to be upon Grace when there was the sound of the doorbell, almost drowned by their voices, audible only to those listening for it, and they were, Grace and Lily. Lily had been waiting for that pleasant insouciance that would come over Grace once the party was under way, a sort of what-the-hell-let's-have-fun, and it had not come yet. On hearing the bell Grace surprised Oliver, who was beside her but still talking to Dennis, by suddenly engaging him in some senseless and frenzied small talk.

When Johnny Cochrane came to the door there was a second during which the currents that pass between people change, re-arrange, fuse into new complexities. He stood, hands raised slightly at his waist, in a momentary, silent presentation of him-self in black T-shirt, black trousers fashionably loose and gripped at the ankle, emerald-green and pink baseball boots. He was neither tall nor short, with a compact, seething muscu-larity; almost a caricature of the steam-engine brand of male sexuality. He had untidy, black hair falling, curling on to his forehead; brows that swooped into lineless condescension; mouth fleshy and spoilt; and, yes, Lily thought, just so.

The group had subtly, instinctively parted to reveal Grace who remained deep in the room, having a lot of trouble now with that small creature in her throat. She said nothing, seemed even to tremble.

Raising his hands further, gripping his fingers into the air, turning his torso, jutting his shoulder for greater emphasis, slowly surveying Grace from head to foot, he said, "Light of the other night. Light of tonight. Radiant." His voice was deep, resonant with an educated accent chipped down to something coarser and T-less, presumably to meet some necessity of his image (Lily noted, too, the "Radiant" and, mentally rolling despairing eyes heavenwards remembered Grace tapping the card on her bed with her finger and saying "Impressive"; how quickly she picked up the singularities of those she admired).

Letting his oratorical tone drop, Johnny Cochrane all but ran to Grace, saying in a natural voice, "Gracie, fantastic to be here," and Lily heard her murmur, exquisitely frail, breathless in his embrace, "Johno, oh, Johno."

Grace could establish petnames with a stranger in half an hour. She did not do it with everyone but when she did it was the first sign of trouble.

Backs were considerably turned, leaving them to their greeting, for already there was an exclusiveness about them. But no sooner had they picked up, somewhat self-consciously, trails of talk than Johnny Cochrane shouted, "My friend, where's my friend?"

"Oh Johno, you've not *brought* anyone?" Grace was dismayed.

"Certainly have. Oi?" He called toward the door.

They looked. For a moment no one, then Sebastian appeared, head back, shyly grinning.

"Seb," Oliver exclaimed.

"Daddy?" Sebastian reached his hand in the direction of his father's voice and, tottering a little from nerves and the proximity of the small crowd, went toward him.

"What are you doing here? Why did you come down?"

"I asked him," Johnny Cochrane supplied to Oliver. "Look, Gracie, you said top flat, right? So I went and this little fella answered the door wide as you like, a real welcome."

"I thought it was Mummy coming back."

"I told you about the chain the other night," Lily said.

Grace added, "I meant the penthouse at the top."

"Gracie," Johnny Cochrane said on a shaming note, as though that explanation was just not good enough.

"This is my son." Oliver began to try to sort things out. "I don't quite see why you've brought him here. Why did you come, Seb?''

Sebastian looked wicked. It was obvious that he thought the whole thing was a good joke and Johnny Cochrane helped out. "Look, it's quite simple. I go there in error, right? This little tyke opens the door, tells me I'm to go upstairs, tells me his dad's up there too. So I say, 'Why don't you join the party?' He seemed to think it was a good idea.''

"But he was quite happy waiting for his mother, watching television." Oliver was beginning to be angry.

"WATCHING TELEVISION? The little fucker's *blind*.''

There was the predictable moment of unadulterated horror at the possibilities: Oliver's fury, Sebastian's hurt feelings, the extent of Cochrane's insensitivity, Grace's party on a downhill slope; when salvation came in the form of Sebastian's irrepressible, shoulder-shaking laughter. So complete was his amusement that tears spilled from his eyes and Cochrane walked over to him, put his arm around him. "My little friend, he is. Instant rapport, wasn't it, old boy?" Sebastian was still laughing; nodding too.

Johnny Cochrane offered his hand to Oliver in Oliver's own deceptively guileless manner. "Cochrane's the name, Johnny Cochrane." Oliver took it up. He was won over.

The party really did get going then, everyone drawn closer by the varied emotions of the last few minutes. Then Melissa arrived shouting, "Oliver? Oliver?" calling around and through the gathering until her eyes rested upon him, Sebastian hidden on his far side. "I've been downstairs, door wide open, no Sebastian. He's not *there*, Oliver," brinked on hysteria. Then Sebastian moved to make himself conspicuous.

In quite a new voice, tender and modest, Johnny Cochrane went to her, took her hands in his (in the inertia of amazement she let him) and said, "I'm so very sorry. It's all my fault. If I'd thought for a moment I'd cause you or anyone this distress I'd never have done it. I'll explain . . .'' and he did and they all helped.

Melissa was embarrassed, apologetic, won over. She went away to change, taking Sebastian with her, and returned alone, looking, somehow, starlit.

When Johnny Cochrane saw the dining table strewn with flowers in a way that Lily had perfected, he leant back at the vision of it as though it had physically struck him and said, "Who . . . Who did that?''

"Lily did. Lily did," Grace said, absolutely thrilled.

"It's . . ." he struggled to find his word, "masterful."

And Lily thought to herself, Silly, isn't it, how affection is won.

At dinner everyone was inclined to focus the talk about Johnny Cochrane.

"I dropped by the gallery," Larry said, "to see your stuff, knowing I was going to meet you. I was impressed. Outraged and impressed."

"Good. Terrific. See, that's what I want, like, *emotion*. But *you*, Larry, what do you do? I mean you've got a like, spiritual face. Painter, I'll bet. Artist of some kind, anyway."

Fingering a kink in his hair, "Novelist, actually," Larry said.

The food suddenly received more attention than it had hitherto. For six years they had all heard of Larry's novel; worse still, read sections. And here was Cochrane saying, "I'll bet it's good. You can feel these things. See it in a face. One day we'll all be saying, 'Remember that night at Gracie's when Larry was there.' See, like, talent shines. Take old Den here . . ."

"Dennis," he murmured correction into his wine glass.

". . . in he walks to me old garage, sees me stuff; whoops, bang, signed up. If he was a publisher, he'd do the same with you. Eh, Den?"

Since he was not one, Little said with impunity, "Certainly."

"Which art school were you at?" Lily asked.

"Ah . . . St. Martin's, Charing Cross Road."

"That's where I was. Which year?"

"Tell you this, little lady, if you'd been there with me, I'd've known it."

"Are your family artists, painters, sculptors?" Melissa leant forward, conversationally operative.

Johnny Cochrane applied, wordlessly, to Dennis Little, who seemed to nod, and because of it Cochrane asked, "You mean, say, Den? Tell 'em like it was?"

"I don't see why not, if you feel you can."

"Feel I can? Jesus wept, never stopped feeling I can. Well, Melissa, since you ask: family? Got none. Illegit. See? 'Spect me mum took one look and said, 'Don't want this little shithead,' and handed me into the baby shop. They tried to foster me out. Didn't work. But I don't want to spoil this beautiful dinner by telling you why; only to say that life's cruel to kids alone. I know all about the work that Gracie here does, and Angela, Melissa too . . . and, like," feeling clumsily for his glass, self-consciously lifting it, "you know . . . thanks. If not for me, then for them that's like me, who started the way I did."

"But, Johnny . . ."

The praise having settled, Melissa started in again.

"No more, my love, no more just now. Do you mind very much?"

"Oh no. I'm so sorry . . . Do forgive me."

To conclude the interest in his work Cochrane issued a general invitation to his studio. "But," he added, reaching for her hand, "not before Gracie, here, has seen it. Private showing for Gracie, eh doll?"

They returned to the drawing-room and Oliver's book was produced. Cochrane did not touch it but stood, hands in pockets, regarding it with apparent reverence where it lay in Dennis's hands. "But I know it, man. Yeah, got my own copy. Been a fan of Cary's work for years."

"So you've seen all the fabulous shots of the Sahel tribes? You know he lived with them?" Dennis opened the book at a place his finger had held and still Cochrane was disinclined to take the book.

He passed a hand over it without looking.

"I tell you, I know it. Great. Really great. Listen, I've had the book since it came out." So the book was put aside, although Angela approached it quietly and turned the pages while the others talked once more.

Cochrane said, "Fancy dancing, Gracie? Like the other night?"

"Let's all go." Grace rose, lifting her arms, conducting the anticipated enthusiasm.

"It's an idea," Melissa said.

"You hate dancing," Oliver stated blandly.

"Well, once in a while. Come on, Oliver."

"No way. Not for me."

"Then I suppose I shan't."

"Pity. But that's marriage for you, Gracie," Cochrane said.

"I won't join you either," Dennis Little said, "it's quite late enough."

Angela looked disappointed but declined also.

"Lily?" Grace asked with that expression she knew so well.

"No. Not tonight, thanks. I'm dying to finish my book."

"So that counts me out," Larry announced with obvious relief.

"Just us then, Gracie, to bop the night away."

They all left together, praise, farewells and thanks reboant in the stairwell. Lily closed the door. The staff having left, she was alone. In the drawing-room was Oliver's book, forgotten by Dennis Little and still unsigned. She took it in her lap to study again: the faces there known to her as old friends. So Johnny Cochrane knew it too; it should not have been surprising. Was he like the rest? The others who had broken Grace's heart? Yes. He was young. He was handsome, vivacious, common attractions for Grace. And yet the thought of him invoked a smile from Lily.

They would be dancing by now in the hot, dark noise of a club, intimate among strangers; Grace close to him and not so strangely matched now the fuse of her youthfulness was yet again ignited. Are you lonely, Lily? Yes, but not for that, not for that pain she would surely, sooner or later, assuage for Grace.

There was a ring at the bell, Dennis's voice on the intercom. Lily buzzed for him to enter.

"Forgot the book, didn't I?" he said, shy.

Lily was glad he was there; she wanted to postpone sleeping, postpone waking, postpone tomorrow or the future at all just now.

"Is it love?" he said across the room as she poured drinks for them both, meaning Grace and Johnny.

"I suppose so, Dennis, if that's what it's called."

"That's what it's called all right, only I'm surprised. I thought Grace went for the aggressively male type and he's not like that at all, you know. He's a dear boy, vulnerable, loving. He's had a hard time. The way he talked tonight was restrained. You should hear him when he gets going. He was thrashed, abused, violated. He got a bit drunk one night, told me all about it. It was all I could do not to weep. Oh, Lily, what happens to children? Do you know he's not mentioned it once since then? I'd like to ask him more, like how it wasn't found out, you know, details. But you can't. You just can't. In any case, he swerves off the topic every time, like he did tonight. The poor devil. Who wouldn't?"

"Are you *very* fond of him, Dennis?" trying to convey what she couldn't quite ask.

"Become so, yes," tipping his drink to his mouth to hide his expression.

"I'm sorry. It must hurt very much."

He went over, seated himself beside her, took her hand, said nothing.

* * *

In the morning Lily decided not to take coffee through to Grace; she had developed an instinct about these things. Sure enough, as she stood at the kitchen window, her hand upon the kettle waiting for it to boil, there was a movement in the passage, the door to the flat opened and closed. A minute or two later she saw through the window, way down below, Johnny Cochrane punching his arms into a leather jacket as he diagonally crossed the peaceful street to a massive motorbike. He stood there, turned away from the building, arms spread, head thrown back; when his head turned Lily could see his mouth was open; he appeared to be drinking in the rain, revitalizing himself from the sharp air. Then he shook as though he were divesting himself of something. This done, he turned his attention to the motor-bike, his jacket beginning to shine in the drizzle.

He took a cloth from some compartment in the machine to dry the seat. He touched it here and there, kneeling closer at one point to study something about the engine, like a rider re-assuring a horse before mounting, then he swung his leg over and, without looking up, ravaged the morning quiet with 1000 cc's.

Lily felt there were other eyes upon him, one window along; eyes anxious and uncertain.

So, she thought, then it's begun.

The following period in the life of Grace Teape would be af-flicted with tension. Lily would use the telephone as little as possible, and for her to receive a call would cause Grace awful distress so she steered clear of the flat altogether. This would go on until some pattern or understanding had been forged be-tween Grace and her new lover. It would be a time when Lily was of no use to her. Nothing she could say would encourage Grace if he did not ring; Lily could only pick her up if she fell completely.

At the end of the following week Lily went to Cornwall where the contents of a large house near Truro were to be auctioned. There had been publicity about it: the rich widow of some peer had died at the age of ninety-two; she had been a dancer in Paris before her marriage and with her husband had led a fabled life. The possibilities her clothing might offer were too interesting to be missed although every dealer would be there.

She crossed paths only once with Grace during that time and

then Grace appeared to be so relaxed and happy that Lily dared, "How's it all going?"

"What in particular, darling?" She only wanted Lily to say his name.

"With Johnny. Johnny Cochrane. *The* Johnny Cochrane."

"Oh, Johno." She gave a half-hearted attempt at indifference, then flung her arms in the air before wrapping them about herself, swaying in her own embrace. "Wonderful, wonderful, wonderful. I've never been so happy."

"Good. That's . . . well, like you say, 'wonderful.' "

She touched Lily's face, at the unspoken cynicism there, sadness for her in her expression. "Dear Lily. So young, so mature. No elation for you? No highs? No lows?"

Lily did not think to tell her she would be staying away one night in Cornwall, and when it did occur to her she was already at the hotel and it was late in the evening. She did not want to ring and have it only be her just in case Grace had been waiting for another call.

When she returned to the flat the next day Grace greeted her with, "Lily, my dear Lily, we've been so worried" (keener to convey the "we" than anything else). The other component of the "we" was couched and grinning on the silk-covered sofa which barely ten days previously had supported Grace's lonely and dejected form. Johnny Cochrane had moved in.

It had never happened before because it was understood that Grace's someone wonderful would have somewhere wonderful to go with him, that she would be transported to a new and better life.

"It is all right, darling, isn't it? You are pleased, because we felt so sure you would be."

"Well . . . I don't know what to say . . . it's surprising and . . . and . . ."

". . . wonderful?" Grace helped, eyes bright.

"Wonderful." When she decently could she went to her room to think, only there was no time before someone knocked softly. Before she could answer, Cochrane entered. "Can I come in?" he said.

" 'Course. Sorry it's such a mess. It's all this new stuff. I'll move it to my workroom tomorrow."

He looked for a space to sit, decided against next to Lily on the bed and chose the floor. He pulled out the doings for rolling a cigarette, placing matches, papers, tin of tobacco before him, then hesitated. "Do you mind if I do? I mean with all this stuff about?"

"No. Can I have one?"

"Sure." He seemed pleased to be able to give her something and that pleased Lily. "What's this?" He grasped the royal Edwardian butler's livery, scrutinizing the buttons. "Look at these. Lions, aren't they?"

"Yes. And look here," drawing his attention to the rich braid.

"I do see why this stuff grabs you like it does. I mean *really.*" Their heads were close together as they examined the garments. Without moving away from her, without looking at her, he said, "I love her, Lily."

"Good."

"No, really."

"Do you mind me asking . . . how old are you?"

"Thirty-three." He began a studied smile; he knew what she was thinking and now Lily could think of no comment. She dared not show surprise but she had hoped for thirty-eight at least; there was a worn look, a hardness about his face that would match that. "Think I'm too young for her, do you?"

"No. Good heavens," (damning her inability to lie) "she's only . . ." (Now how old was Grace supposed to be?)

"My little Gracie's fifty, if she's a day. I know women, Lily, I know their faces and what's more my Gracie's not too hot at her numberwork. So far she's been thirty-eight, forty-three, then when she tried to give me the year she was born she was fifty-seven, till she'd thought it out. Little lady. Love her."

"Well that's all right then."

"Do you mind?"

She did not like talking in this manner to Grace's lovers. Ever since Jaime de Caberro she had been frightened of what she would hear. She never wanted to be close to someone who would hurt Grace. But here he was, living in their home. "I don't mind. I'm happy about it. I want happiness for her. She's very . . ." Lily stopped, frightened of betraying some quality Grace might be seeking to hide. You never knew with Grace how she was trying to seem.

"She's very what, Lily?"

"Sensitive."

"I knew that the moment I set eyes on her. Don't worry."

Grace tapped with her fingernail on the door. "Hello, you two. Interrupting?"

Johnny Cochrane stood up and went to her, taking her hands. "Gracie, I don't think Lily here minds me too much."

She came to Lily and held her.

"Darling Lily."

Grace touched the punctual tears in her eyes and said, "Hanky, Johno?"

After some tugging he produced a vast, filthy, entirely repellent handkerchief, handing it to her without a work of apology. Her eyes fluttered at its appearance but, with a reticence so slight that only Lily, in her arms, could perceive it, she placed the grotesque item to her immaculate cheeks and returned it with reverence.

"Thank you, Johno."

Chapter 10

L ILY STOOD AT THE BOTTOM OF THE STEPS TO SEBASTIAN'S
school among the mothers, nannies, au pairs. It was a
small school of high academic standard for normally
sighted children, housed in a haughty, dark red–brick Victorian
building. Some of those about her were familiar faces, for she
had waited thus many times to collect Sebastian and spend what
was left of the afternoon together. Each one felt a brand of pride
in their particular child who would rush down the steps when
the bell rang.

At three-thirty the boys began to bubble forth like the tapping
of a spring: first the youngest in desultory fashion, cock-eyed in
their over-large uniforms; then the older ones; finally the eldest
(Sebastian's class) stumbled out, grazed at the knees, askew,
shirts and ties adrift.

As usual there were tuts of pity and amazement when Sebastian coursed down the steps without due care, shouting, "Lily?
Lily?" His head moved like a radar, certain of picking up her
presence.

"So what do you want to do?" she asked once they were
away from the building.

"I know exactly" (he always did).

"Well?"

"I want to go to Daddy's studio"—and before Lily could
protest—"seriously, Lily, we've not been for ages. He'd really
like it. I want to find out what he's doing. Please."

In the past they had been frequently, and Oliver would take
them to tea afterwards if he was able to free himself, but there
had always been a plan beforehand.

91

"I'll ring from the next call-box."

"Oh, for goodness' sake, Lily, be some fun. Let's surprise them all. Come *on*. They'd like to see us at the studio."

She could think of no reason why not other than a general reserve; but she thought it was not really her business: she was only bringing son to father after all. ("Dear Lily, so young, so mature. No elation for you? No highs? No lows?") She was suddenly tired of heeding her instincts, tired of undertones.

"Great. We'll even take a taxi," she said.

In the taxi Sebastian felt for her hand. "Is it true?"

"What?"

"Is it true Johnny's moved in?"

"Yes. Who told you?"

"I heard Grace telling Mummy. She's very happy, isn't she? I'm glad 'cause I think he's really nice. You know he said that we're friends? He called me his 'new friend.' Are you glad too? Don't you think he's nice?"

"I suppose I do, only I'm still surprised that I do. I was so sure from his work that I'd loathe him, it's awful stuff, sort of vicious."

"Oh great. I'd love to get a feel of it. Bet it's exciting. He is, isn't he? I mean, he makes things happen."

"He does that all right and, like you say, he's making Grace happy . . . at the moment."

Lily wanted to talk some more about it, to sort out her feelings aloud, for there was something in her dislodged, a misgiving, but Sebastian was not the right person and anyway his attention had already gone from the subject.

"We must be nearly there," he was saying. "Can I pay the driver, *please*? Give me your purse?"

Oliver Cary's studio was formed on the second two floors of a warehouse in Ridinghouse Street. There were two parts: the commercial section which contained the reception area too; down there worked a secretary, stylist, assistants; the number of people would depend on his workload, it could be as many as twelve. Upstairs he had a smaller studio where he did what he referred to as his "own work." This would be his abstract or still life designs: domesticity made strange; peculiar surrealistic nudes, occasional portraits of famous people. Up on that second floor, alone or with some favored assistant, he produced works of art with no selling function, simply beautiful in their own right.

When they entered the studio Esther was sitting at the desk

which formed the reception area, separating it from the rest of the studio. She was an obese woman with Cleopatra-styled, hennaed hair, given to wearing massive Hawaiian print shirts and skirts and who traveled to and from work on a great tricycle. Oliver had told Lily once that she was married to a homosexual and that the studio was her life. Modesty made him say studio because all knew that Oliver was her life; her protection of him was prodigious and everyone associated with the studio was in awe of her. She was the person to ingratiate oneself with to gain access to Oliver Cary. One of the duties Esther performed best was keeping away from him the many visiting models with their portfolios, ''go-seeing'' photographers without appointments, desperate for work and mainly unusable. But Esther could be relied upon to spot a rare face, raw beauty, and would send that happy girl through to see the famous man.

''Hi Lily, Sebastian. Where've you been all this time? Haven't seen the two of you for ages.''

''Told you they'd be glad to see us,'' Sebastian nudged Lily. He wandered further into the studio with complete confidence, answering the greetings that met him all around. A pair of blue jeans high on a scaffold erecting a camera for a bird's-eye view called down, ''Hey, Sebastian, it's a room set we're doing for a boring old catalog, but if you go and sit on that chair, right in front of you,'' Sebastian pointed inquiringly, ''there to the right . . . to the right . . . that's it, then I can focus on you till the model comes out of the dressing-room, IF SHE EVER COMES OUT . . .'' he yelled over his shoulder toward the dressing-room.

Sebastian looked pleased and felt his way forward on to the set. *''Take your shoes off,''* the blue jeans shouted. ''Sorry,'' Sebastian said, quite unperturbed by the shout and settled on the floor to remove his heavy, leather-soled, lace-up shoes.

It was a curious anomaly in Sebastian's taste that generally he was particular in the clothes he wore, the way they felt, the cut, shirts with collars just right; always fashionable; he had to have the latest-style jeans but he always wore clumsy, heavy, lace-up schoolboy shoes with hard soles. Every season he and Lily would go to the shop and every season he would choose the same. Lily would hand him more fashionable things, which he would bend about in his hands, then return to her without a word, would not even try them on.

While Sebastian sat there, confused by the echoing, conflicting sounds but happy, self-important in his role, head ranging to assimilate all he could, the model emerged from the dressing-room.

Lily had never become inured to the inner-lit, ethereal quality possessed by models made-up and ready to work; they were not always beautiful, feature for feature, but there was a shine, a breathlessness, the air of fantasy made flesh. For all that, the crew in the studio seemed barely to notice her as she stood on the edge of the set, placid and somewhat bored, having her shoes taped to keep the backdrop clean.

When she approached the chair she was supposed to sit in, her placidity was galvanized by converging emotions: first it was clear she was irritated that someone was where she was supposed to be but almost simultaneously she saw he was only a boy, blind too; also in that instant a vast bank of lights was switched on, isolating the two of them within the set, making the rest of the studio no more than animated depths of shadow.

She stood a moment staring at Sebastian, who stared back somewhat in her direction. There must have been eight of them in that crepuscular outer area and the vibrancy of the silence alone proved that most of those eyes were on that singular confrontation, yet no one spoke.

The model, blinded by the light to any world beyond the set, raised her hand to shield and strain her eyes, seeking some assistance from the invisibles who surrounded her. "I say . . ." she faltered, "there's someone . . . someone . . ." She motioned toward Sebastian in the chair, then gave it up, doubting any continued existence, the existence of anything beyond her brilliant embarrassment.

It was cruel, although unintentional. The incident had come about by accident but now Beauty had to prove itself, as it always does, by breaking through the ribaldry, the hostility that by its nature Beauty provokes. She stood a moment wringing one hand in the other, then decisively turned to crouch beside Sebastian, touching him with one of her lovely made-up hands. He jerked his head round to her.

"I'm the model." She spoke very gently. "They've said I must sit there to do the shot but you can do it if you like. *I* don't mind if *they* don't."

"No. No, I'm for focus only. Here, sit down." He levered himself up but she took his arm to guide him slowly, slowly to the edge of the set, looking down for him at where each step should be placed while he assumed, in order not to abuse her consideration, a faltering hesitancy.

The studio came to life again and Lily began to feel in the way.

"Where's Oliver?"

"Working upstairs. Always is these days." Esther sounded disgruntled. "You can go on up, seeing it's you two."

They tramped up the wide concrete steps, opening the door to his private studio with more deference than they had shown below; this was, after all, Oliver's private world where he made his imagination tangible, then, having photographed it, rendered it once more intangible, merely visible. There had always been an immaculacy about this place that was not below; everything was put just so and to touch or move anything would be a mistake; it had always been kept scrupulously clean and dustfree. None of these aspects one would especially associate with the appearance of Oliver but, again, this place was the reflection of his mind.

When they entered that day, however, there was no immaculacy; things were disarrayed and dusty. Right away Sebastian sniffed and whispered, "Hasn't been cleaned lately." The fustiness was palpable in the air. This was another vast high-ceilinged room divided by screens and equipment. It was gray in there, light seeping through the one-third of the window not covered by a black blind.

Lily was about to leave when she saw Oliver's coat on a chair. They held hands as they moved without speaking further into the studio; Sebastian began to squeeze Lily's hand, and she looked down at him wondering why he should be nervous; why she should be.

Pouring from the dressing-room at the end was that seductive glow caused by lights set in around a mirror. From there voices came, soft with concentration. They moved over, stood in the doorway. There was no one sitting at the make-up bar before the mirror but on the floor was Oliver Cary's great body, head at Lily's feet, naked from the waist down. All she could see of the girl beneath him was a tousled white blonde head and two skinny arms, two skinny legs wrapping him.

"Daddy?" Sebastian called, pulling his lips hard in over his teeth and releasing them, "Daddy, are you all right?" He was twisting his head and shoulders in an effort to ascertain why the sounds his father made were coming from the floor. Lily pulled at Sebastian but he clung to the door frame.

"Lily . . . Oh Christ, Seb . . ."

"No," the girl explained quite conversationally and unoffended, oblivious to Lily and Sebastian, "Kaye's the name, K-A-Y-E, Kaye," then she rolled her eyes upward and saw them. "Gawd."

Lily forced Sebastian's hand from the frame, dragging him behind her. "No, Lily, I want to see Daddy."

"He's too busy now," she shouted.

Sebastian lessened his resistance. He had always had great respect for his parents' work and never demanded their time, never imposed his presence; it had saddened Lily sometimes that he should have relinquished that childish right.

"But is he all right, Lily? What were the funny noises?"

"Of course he's all right, never better." Lily was moving as fast as possible through the filthy studio; even in her horrified haste she was stunned by the change in the place. It looked as though no work had been done there for months. "I'd hardly leave him if he wasn't all right. He's just terribly, terribly busy."

"Was he fixing up a model?"

"That's it exactly; he was fixing up a model. Really well. Mustn't interrupt."

Out on the pavement he said with some reticence, as though he feared Lily's anger at his continued concern, "Was . . . Lily, was his foot all right?"

And she laughed, "His foot's just fine. Come on, we'll get a hamburger."

Chapter 11

L ILY AVOIDED THE CARYS' FLAT FOR A FEW DAYS, FEARING she would meet Oliver, that he might try to explain. She did not want to hear those crippled excuses people lay at the feet of infidelity from Oliver, whose marriage she had held in such high regard. On the Friday she suggested to Sebastian they go fishing the following day.

She spent the Saturday morning shut in her room hearing the sounds of Grace and Johnny rising: their talk, their soft laughter. She no longer took coffee through in the mornings.

Grace knocked upon her door at one point. "Lovey? All right? Awake, are you?"

"Yes, fine thanks."

"Sure?" Lily knew she would have to open the door to prove it. "Oh, not dressed yet? Happy, darling?"

"Fine."

Grace looked quite beautiful, more tranquil than Lily had ever remembered her, flutter and anxiety all gone. To see her so fine made Lily warmer still toward Johnny Cochrane.

"What'll you do today? Only we're going to the country, Johno and I, to meet some friends of his."

Johnny swung in around the door frame and Lily clutched her voluminous Edwardian nightdress to herself. "Don't you look pretty? Doesn't she?"

"She always does, Johno."

"Come too," he said. "Nice, eh Gracie, the three of us?"

"I'd love it. Do, Lily." She meant it.

"No, really. I'm fishing with Sebastian this afternoon."

Just before she closed the front door behind them, Grace called

back, "By the way, dear, painters in later, all right?" but did
not wait for an answer.

The only home Lily had ever known was changing about her;
familiar furniture was disappearing, new items in leather and
steel arriving. The pale mauve silk curtains, their innerfolds
weakened, threaded by sun and years, they went; the round
tables with their long cloths and deep fringing; the porcelain
Grace had collected, it had all gone. Painters came with tall
ladders and white sheets and in a matter of days altered their
gentle home with its memories coiled in corners, spread about
in unexpected places: Lily would draw a curtain, lift a book,
turn a cushion, sit upon a chair and some recollection from the
past would reveal itself to lend a still moment some happy den-
sity. Her life as it had been with Grace was being painted over;
the flat was becoming a sleek, pale gray throughout with black
gloss woodwork. No more photographs, no more mementoes,
no vestige of past.

She was lonely there now. She wanted to go.

Later that day she sat beside Sebastian on the earthy towpath
of the Regent's Canal somewhere near the Zoo; the two of them
wrapped against the freezing fog, sharing a Thermos of soup.

Lily would feel close to Sebastian at such a time, almost more
than any other, sitting doing little except watching the water for
some movement, as though she had entered the timelessness of
his world. He was an unhurried person, not pushed on by changing hours and light; he would let the world hasten him just so
much but left to himself he lapsed into a reflective peace, un-
cluttered by sight and talk.

The fog isolated and deadened the few sounds about them,
disembodying footsteps behind their backs, lifting occasional
voices from the Zoo on the far bank. A growl magnified by the
halted air came from some indistinguishable beast, its lofty
proximity making it seem to be free, upon them any second.
Mostly Lily heard just the treacly lap-lap of the water about the
float on the end of Sebastian's rod and against the stone banks
of the canal. They could have found a more propitious spot for
his fishing but were accustomed to the canal; it was nearby and
a roach or perch had been caught sufficiently often along that
stretch to give them hope. The catching of a real fish had ceased
to be the point; sitting there had come to do with peace and
thought with only the remote possibility of distraction.

Lily felt for Sebastian's pocket.

"What's that?" he asked.

"It's a tape of that Irish record of mine, the one you wanted, remember?"

"Great. Thanks."

"Listen, Sebastian, at the beginning of the tape I've said the address and telephone number of my workroom. I'm moving in there, see? It's better, now things are like they are for Grace."

"But what about boysitting and evenings and prep? Oh Lily, please . . ."

"I won't do it all at once. It'll all feel just the same. Don't worry, I'll be around whenever you want. And think: you can come and spend the weekends with me when you like."

"Mmm . . ." He was becoming interested in the possibilities. "Do you feel a bit out of it at home?"

"I just don't want to be in the way, that's all."

"I know that feeling," he said, and she wondered why he should; placed an arm about him and he bent his head a little to acknowledge her.

As they sat thus, a cameo of companionship framed by the quiescent, roaming fog, Oliver found them. "Hey, you two. Thought you'd be here. Mind if I join you?"

They separated, letting him settle between them.

"Soup?"

"No thanks, Lily." He spread his square hand to decline. "Any luck, Seb?"

"I don't know . . ." Sebastian said contemplatively. He would never say "no" outright.

Oliver looked at Lily over the collar of his worn leather coat, then away, uncomfortably, at the white air and the plank-like span of black water. He said, "I can't just sit. Makes me stiff. I'll walk along a bit and back."

"OK, Daddy."

"Join me, Lily?" He paused. "Or not?"

"Or not" was the point. Are we friends, or not? Do you despise me, or not? May I explain, or not?

Lily rose to walk with him, touching Sebastian's back as she did so. "Careful, eh? Won't be long."

"I'm fine." Lily saw him cock his ear to their footsteps, no doubt listening for the troubled foot.

They gained a little distance from Sebastian without speaking, then Oliver said, "Are you very disappointed?" He checked Lily's face to see that she understood to what he referred and was satisfied.

"I suppose. But it's not . . ."

"It *is* your business, Lily. You're family. You've as much right to expect my loyalty as Sebastian; after all, it's you who's helped me to . . . helped *us* bring him up. It wasn't the first time, what you saw. Can't pretend it was."

Lily glanced back but Sebastian was shut away from them by the fog; it was as though they moved alone through a limitless, unfurnished room, only the gray shoulders of shapes about them. It reminded Lily of how the flat was beginning to look. Their voices sounded secret, urgent.

"I didn't think it was, actually."

"It's not been my way in the past, don't think that, but I've not been talking, you know, and it makes a person lonely not talking to the ones he loves. I mean really talking, revealing yourself, confusions, fears and all. It makes you reach for the wrong kind of intimacy."

"Do you have fears then? Confusions?"

"Uh huh."

"Can't you tell Melissa? I'd have thought she'd be the easiest person. After all, that's her thing isn't it, other people's problems?"

"Yes. That's her thing. But the fact is I'm sick, Lily, and I don't really want to tell her that. Not yet. Not unless I have to and perhaps it won't come to that."

Lily stopped and he urged her on, huge and hunched in his coat, face taut with cold. Lily thought of his foot, and Sebastian, and realized they had walked a long way from him. "We had better turn back. Is it your leg or foot?"

Oliver stopped. "Why?"

"Only because Sebastian's been on about your walking oddly. I haven't noticed anything but he's been really worried."

He moved to the edge of the towpath, head down, hand to his face. Lily left him for some moments, then went to stand beside him. Pretending to look at a swan (whiter against the white) over his way, she confirmed that there were tears on his face. He snatched them off, rubbed them away in his palm, nodded. "Jesus, I love that boy."

"So he's right."

"Yeah, yeah. Stiff. Tendons. Dizzy. Something, something, don't know what."

"Have you seen a doctor?"

"Yup. Appointment with a specialist soon."

"Is that anything to do with your studio being such a mess? I've never seen it like that before."

"I hide up there, you see. They leave me alone. There's enough work to keep going downstairs for a while. Think I can cover up till I get myself sorted out; there's a lot of shots they can do without me so long as I design them."

"Please tell Melissa."

"No, Lily. She's on the crest of a wave right now. She's worked hard for it. I wouldn't spoil that for her."

"Will you let me know when you've seen the man, the specialist?"

He slung his heavy arm around Lily's neck, pulled her neck on to his shoulder, released it. His mood was altered already. "If it's something really gory and interesting, I might tell you. If it's just that my balls are falling off, I'll keep it to myself."

"Well . . . doesn't look like that's the problem."

They laughed together, establishing his apology, her forgiveness, their continued unimpaired affection. As they laughed they heard a shout and another, louder one.

"Help, help, Dad. Quick Lily, help."

Fear, like a heap of sickness in her throat, stopped Lily breathing as she ran. Nearly choking, she reached the spot where Sebastian was, Oliver some paces behind.

Sebastian was straining to pull his line from the water; every time his hands reached shoulder height something dark and living was to be seen twisting on the end of the line. Living, for the first time something living.

"I've got something. There's something on it."

"Well, pull it in," Lily shouted, longing to grab the rod herself. "Don't let it go . . . look it's going."

" 'Course I won't let it go, but . . . but . . ." He was not strong enough to raise the rod higher. "He's gonna get away. I know it."

"It's all right, Seb, you've got him. Here." Oliver stood behind Sebastian with his knees about the boy's shoulders, his large hands covering Sebastian's small ones. Together they raised the rod from the water; on the end of it a fish that must have weighed six or seven pounds, the color and nature of a vast dull goldfish. "It's a carp, Seb. You've got a carp. A bloody great carp."

They landed it thudding at Lily's feet. She leapt away and looked down at its anguished struggling.

"Where? Where?" Sebastian was feeling around the towpath. "I want to touch it." He reached the fish and it slipped from his hands.

They were quite unprepared. "Where's your net?" Oliver was shouting.

"We never bring it anymore."

An odd constricted voice came from offstage, as it were, into their scene still circumscribed by the fog. "You want a keep-net for that."

"What?" they said to each other, then looking round for the bodiless voice, "Who said that?"

"I did. You want a keep-net for that." As the fish still thrashed and gasped, a slightly bibulous dwarf in denim overalls and jacket swayed into their vision; he had frizzy gray hair and pebble spectacles. "Ain't you got no keep-net? No business fishing without a keep-net."

"Have you got one?" Oliver asked.

"Naa. Don't fish myself. That there's a carp. Holds the secret of eternal life, that does."

Over Sebastian's head Oliver and Lily smiled away their laughter at the purposelessness of this dialogue. Sebastian had had his head far back, mouth open, ear toward the voice, but now he too dismissed it.

"What do you want to do, Seb? Shall we eat it?" Oliver bent down, holding the fish firmly in Sebastian's lap. "I could do with some eternal life."

Sebastian ran his fingers about it. "It's got dusty, gritty, poor thing. It's dying. I want to put it back. Take the hook out, Dad. Let it go free."

They bought fish and chips to celebrate and took them back to the Carys' flat.

Melissa was there when they had supposed her to be elsewhere.

Oliver said, "I thought you were on Radio 4 any minute?"

"I am."

"Then why are you here?"

"It's a recording, Oliver, and my afternoon meeting was cut short, so here I am. All right?"

"Sure, just surprised to see you, that's all. It's good. I'm glad. We can all be together." He did not say "for once," but the look she gave him was as if he had.

They all sat at the kitchen table. It was rare Lily saw Melissa at home lately; her working hours seemed to be erratic.

Lily found the corporal Melissa to be less real than that severely witty achiever wearing bright colors and a smile on the television. I don't really know you at all, she thought, as she watched the small, paler article lounging at the table in jeans, sweater, pretty black hair piled up and falling a little. Lily decided that was the price of television fame: it rendered the actual so very second-hand.

Although Lily had had eleven years of Sebastian in common with Melissa (not to mention Oliver, Grace and the general intertwining of family life), she found it harder than ever to talk to her. Lily felt her topics should all be about what Melissa was known for, like charities, pressure groups, the common good.

Nevertheless, Lily was happy to be here with the three of them; they had done this often in the past, just sitting round "being together" like Oliver said.

". . . and there was a funny lady, Mummy, who said we should have a keep-net."

"It wasn't a lady, Seb, it was a man, a dwarf."

"Just a miniature person, you mean?"

"No, that's a midget," Melissa began in her typically factual way. "They really are quite different. You see, a midget is perfectly proportioned, nothing medically wrong, but a dwarf looks odd because his bones have stayed the same size as when he was, say, seven or eight, although the muscle and tissue have gone on growing around them to maturity. You don't see so many now and you'll see fewer still because there are drugs to make the bones grow." Just like Melissa, no stone unturned.

"And what about Johnny Cochrane then, Lily?" Melissa sucked her fingers and lowered her head to study Lily's face.

"Honestly, I'm really pleased" (answering the unasked). "Have you seen Grace in the past few days? She looks beautiful. So calm. You can't argue with happiness."

"Well said." Melissa reached for Oliver's hand, who looked surprised and pleased, reinforcing the gesture with his hand over hers.

Lily felt inexplicably alone; it only lasted a second, that feeling, and vanished when she said to Sebastian, "Scrabble? Best of three? Bet I win." Yes, it did vanish, and she wouldn't think about it again, or try to understand the way seeing those hands made her feel.

Scrabble had been Lily's latest present to Sebastian and they had become addicted. Lily would blindfold herself just as she had when she learnt braille from the teacher who came to Sebastian, back in the days when she pretended he was her own son, fantasized about being mother to one so dear as he. Several hours a week Lily would enter into the acute world of the blind wherein ordinary sounds became specific in profound isolation. She had joined Sebastian and his teacher, a gray, gentle woman, blind herself, with a voice soft and precise like a distant bell across a still evening. There had been no time for Oliver and Melissa to learn, or any necessity, but Lily had enjoyed being bound by common learning, stumbling through books together in shared exasperation. He had always been better at braille than Lily and Scrabble was practice for her.

They returned to the sitting-room, the room Lily had always considered rather bare with the polished boards, rugs, white walls, strange objects (Melissa had never altered it); but now it had the familiarity that nowhere else held for her. It was cluttered in comparison with what her own home had become.

"Just you two, then," Melissa said when she saw Sebastian setting out the board for four.

"Oh Mummy, *please*. There's print too. You can see the letters. Look . . ."

He pulled her toward the board.

"Well, only for a bit. You know I'm no good at games. Oliver, you too?"

"Of course."

Very shortly Melissa became restless. She began to look at her watch; Oliver regarded her furtively, waiting for the moment she would rise. And she did. "I think I'd better be . . ."

"Don't tell me you're going somewhere." Oliver had almost shouted, and she was startled by the rare pitch of his voice.

"In a minute, then. I have a meeting, you see."

"What possible meeting can you have on a Saturday night? When the devil can we be a family?"

"It's a women's group. I promised I'd go."

"And what about their families? Don't they want to be with their husbands and children either?"

"Well, they're lesbians, actually. Not everyone lives in a family. We're lucky, and since all this media hype that I've had, everyone wants me. It's what I work for, Oliver, to have an effective voice. People need that on their side; they need me."

"*We* need you," Oliver said.

Sebastian and Lily did not say a word because they knew Oliver and Melissa were arguing about more than her presence.

Melissa delayed her departure and they played, somewhat discomfited by her reluctance. When they were halfway through the second game there began a loud, insistent banging on the front door. "Well, really . . ." Melissa pretended annoyance, although glad to have a distraction. She rose and stumped to it, swinging the door open with an aggressive "Yes?" Almost at once her voice slid on to a note of affable embarrassment. "Oh, it's you, sorry. Come in."

Johnny Cochrane entered the sitting-room ahead of Melissa, arms raised. "Hi, hi, hi," he rapped out, one for each of them, "listen you lot: Gracie and I wondered if you'd like to come on over to the studio and look around. Like now." He hooked his fingers into the air, "Like this very minute," as though there had never before been a present moment in the history of man and it had to be exploited.

"Oh, yes please." Sebastian stood up.

"That's my little mate. Atta*boy*. You? You? You?" he applied to the rest of them.

Melissa stood with her hand pushed into her hair, her other arm limply resting on her hip with uncustomary indecision. "I don't know because, well . . . I don't think . . ."

"Melissa's got to see some lesbians, but I'd like to," Oliver said.

"Oh well, if Melissa's seeing lesbians." Johnny then turned to Melissa with indeterminate facetiousness. "I mean, I know your work is very important. I've seen you, you know, on the box and I hope you don't mind me saying I think you're terrific, only: how's a man to keep his mind on those, like, serious issues, with you being so pretty?" Having paid the compliment he lessened the intimacy of it by seeking Oliver's agreement. "Eh, Oliver? Eh?"

"Absolutely."

"But why don't you bugger lesbians tonight and come to my studio instead. It'll be fun. Show you me arc lamp, darling. AND, if you're very good, me oxyo-cetalin welder too. Now there's an offer no girl can refuse."

No one ever spoke lightly of Melissa's work and Lily expected her to be at least piqued, but she remained irresolute, even amused. "Well, I'll have to ring. See what they say."

Oliver watched her at the telephone with wordless interest and when she lightly proclaimed her availability his expression was remote, distantly exhausted once more.

"And you, Lily. You want to come?" Johnny Cochrane tossed casually in her direction.

* * *

The fog had given way to rainless, damp-skyed night. There was no one about the tawdry street of two-story houses in Westbourne Grove, most of which were turned into shops: seedy second-hand electrics, a take-away, a betting shop. Standing detached was a large, battered, wooden garage with a cockeyed, paint-peeling sign hanging above it: "A. E. GANGE. CRASH REPAIRS." This was Johnny Cochrane's studio.

They stood on the rackety pavement stamping their feet, turning on the spot, while Johnny Cochrane swore ritualistically at the massive padlock clamping the doors together. Grace had remained in the car: she must have known from experience that opening-up took time. The doors ground hoarsely open and Cochrane disappeared inside; soon a washed-out light probed a little at the inner darkness. "C'min, c'min then. Don't hang about," he shouted from inside.

Melissa stepped in first, then Oliver leading Sebastian. Lily hung back to call Grace. She was still in the car, sitting swathed in fur in a smudge of warm, marmalade light, peering into the mirror on the inside of the sun flap, patting at her face, an icon of glamour in the desolate street.

"Come on, Grace," Lily called loud enough to be heard through the closed window; Grace looked round, startled for a minute, then beamed at Lily, her smile disintegrating behind her breath as it materialized upon the window.

Lily stepped straight into a rainbow-hearted pool of oil just inside the door. The low-ceilinged building was piled high with scrap metal stacked in unreliable heaps; the edges of gear-wheels bearing their unhappy teeth; the blade of an old bacon-slicer; the door of a railway carriage; an electric fire with broken bars, the wires spiraling out. There were buckets and grill plates, car engines, radiators, ancient stoves and refrigerators in unexpected positions. Sand had been scattered over parts of the floor to counteract the oil which was everywhere. There was a space cleared in the center, the working area, and something was in progress: four groups of three scaffolding poles, each bound together with bicycle chain, stood upright at the four corners of six feet of cross-barred metal.

Oliver approached it, walked around it, crouched, fingers linked to study it better. He was giving it real artistic consideration, while Sebastian ran his fingers over the twisting bicycle chain. There was a crunching of sand as Grace entered and came into the pool of dull light, erect, careful, masking her distaste for the general filth with laughter and admiration. She was like an unsteady moth accidentally landed and doomed. "Isn't it exciting, though, the atmosphere here? What do you think, Oliver. Lily? Isn't he clever. Do you know what this is, Melissa? Have you guessed?" She was holding one of the groups of scaffolding poles. "Have you told them yet, Johno?"

Johnny Cochrane was standing back, arms crossed, watching. Grace gestured for him to speak and noticed grease on her hand as she did so. "Oh dear." She looked at it, then raised it across the gloom toward him. "Hanky, Johno?"

He pulled out a filthy rag (just like the one Lily had watched being passed before), reached across to her with it and she took it without the slightest apprehension. She lifted her eyes, very slightly, in the direction of the others to see that they watched her as she thoroughly rubbed her hand into it. "Thank you, Johno. Do tell them, darling, what it is."

He cleared his throat. "Well, it's a bed, isn't it? See?"

"So it is," Oliver said, "a four-poster."

"And tell them too, Johno, you know . . ." Grace pressed.

He moved to Grace, picked her up and sat her on the iron crossbars of the bed, with the scrape, winge and grind of rusty metal. "This is my present to Gracie. I make the bed, she's gotta lie in it. Joke. Right?" No one laughed: they waited because Grace was waiting, her face strained upon him. He took a breath. "All right then, this is my wedding present to Gracie. We're gonna get married. Soon. Aren't we, doll?"

During the following silence Grace continued to look up at him, then round to the others, drawing her hand to her neck, her eyes glistening. Cochrane was standing aggressively, hands on hips, as though preparing to deal with outrage.

"Aren't we all supposed to say 'Congratulations'?" Sebastian said. "Will you stay living in the flat? Can I come and visit you here? I think it's great. Lovely smell too."

"Tell you what, Sebastian, old boy: you're a grand little kid and you're welcome in my life anytime you like. Right?"

"Right," Sebastian answered, moving nearer to Johnny Cochrane, taking his hand.

That had given them time, so then everyone spoke at once, words of surprised approval, and through the noise Grace put out her hand toward Lily. "Lily dear, all right?"

Lily went to her. "Yes, Grace, all right. You'll be very happy, I know it." She didn't, she didn't at all.

"I will be, darling. I will be, really. We'll all be."

Lily moved from the light so they could no longer see her

face. She rested against a table where, in grubby disarray among tools, lay more rags like the one Cochrane kept in his pocket. She looked hard without seeing them, picked up a metal pipe just for something to absorb her grip. Johnny Cochrane came to her while the others gathered around Grace. "Hey, that's my arc lamp, I'll show you." He took it from her hand, giving her in exchange a large, heavy, three-sided mask with glass let into it at eye-level. "Hold that in front of your face," he said with the tool poised, finger on an electric switch. Lily supported the mask in front of her with both hands, he flicked the switch and a searing violet-white stream of light gushed out with a roaring hiss. He held it out, its brilliance and sound isolating them from the rest of the room. He put his head next to Lily's behind the mask. "Weld with it, see?"

"This mask is heavy. Do you wear it?"

"Yeah. Wear it, don't I? I mean, got to have my hands free. What d'you think then, Lil?"

"Lily."

"Sorry: Lily. What do you think?"

"About the studio?"

"Nope."

"Getting married?"

"Yep."

"Don't know. You're very quick."

"That's me: fast worker. Don't hang about. Know what I want and it's Gracie. She's my girl now. I'll take her part. She's not going to have to wake up alone anymore 'cause I'll be there with her. And when she gets a bit tired, like she does and pretends not to, I'll be there, still telling her she's pretty, a looker, the way she likes. What she needs. I'll say all those things that change her face from that scared look. Know the one? 'Course you do. I'll be there, see? All the time. Giving her what she needs."

Was he clever to know her so well so soon? These things that, it seemed, had taken Lily years to learn he understood with ease. That was the nature of love, then, the love of a man. Lily had been the locum, done the best she could, now he would do it right.

"All right then, Lily?"

"You're like her. She keeps asking me, 'All right?' "

"Yes. Well. You don't say much, see? I don't feel I know you." He turned the candescent light until its outer edge touched the mask, searing across the glass covering her eyes. "What then, Lily? Are we going to be, like, friends?"

"We will be, especially if Grace is happy we will be. A bit of time, that's all, I'm not good at quick friendship."

"Not like Gracie, eh?"

"No. Not like Grace."

"OK, girl. Fair enough."

He switched off the arc lamp, returning the two of them from the light and noise into the wretched garage, reuniting them with the littleness of the others' voices, who were carrying on unaware that the two had spoken alone.

"So let's all celebrate." Melissa, perched on top of a huge, smashed fish tank, slapped her thighs, her breath huddling from her mouth into the cold.

Here it was then: Grace Teape's Happily Ever After. Not at all what she or Lily had imagined; nor even those who speculated upon that woman's future.

This twenty-year street of Lily's life with Grace had ended; a street lined with holidays where the smart set holidayed; dinners where they dined. Champagne for little Lily while she watched, watched, watched lest Grace be hurt again. They had been there, where one ought to be, because that was where for Grace someone wonderful would be found, was found. And see what threshold he brought her to (after the laughter, the plans, that evanescent, ever nascent hope of hers): a dank, damp garage with an odious iron structure as her wedding bed.

Chapter 12

GRACE AND JOHNNY BECAME SO INVOLVED, SO BOUND, SO thoroughly "we" that Lily found herself inhibited in their presence. She did not want to announce the decision to live in her workroom to the two of them, but to Grace alone, so they might be mutually assured of no offense being taken, and that for Lily to bow out at this point, live alone, was the natural course. There had been scarce moments when Cochrane was absent; Lily had tried, "Grace . . . ?" in an introductory way, carrying a low-key plea, and Grace had turned, beamed, "Yes, dear?" but bright, immediate, pressed. Lily found she could not say it; a dilute fear restrained her. Was it selfish to depart? Should she stay around a little longer to be sure that all was as it seemed? "Nothing. It'll do later," and Grace would pass on through in a rush of palpitating happiness.

Yet Lily came to understand that her departure was tacit in the absence of talk; in the new decorations; the daily changes in the flat; items she had known all her life gone, and all happening so fast.

Late one afternoon, when she thought she was alone in the flat, in her room, performing a final clearing, Grace came to her. Souvenirs of the forgotten were cast about, pulled from drawers, cupboards, and she had come across the dress she had worn that night in Marbella. The one she had never worn since—the one she had hidden from Grace's sight and her own—was lying now in year-yellowed tissue paper.

There was an unobtrusive tap upon the door followed by Grace's head, shy, reticent, around it. "May I?"

It was evident what Lily was doing and Grace made no protest. It seemed she had come to her to help, not unkindly, not hurriedly, but just when Lily was ready because the time was right.

"Are you going to your workroom then?" Grace asked as though the question were an impertinence.

"Yes. It's huge and really lovely or it will be when I've finished with it."

"I'm longing to see it but, Lily, you will keep your room here, won't you? I mean we won't touch it, we don't need it and we'll close the door so that whenever you come back it'll be just as you left it, always home."

"Thank you. I'd like that. And you know you can come any time to my workroom but I'd quite like to make it fabulous first. On the other hand, I want you to see where I am. But admit: you have been a bit taken up lately."

So they were talking alone like they used to.

"Yes, yes. Isn't it . . . well . . ." she grimaced an apology at her own silly repetition, "wonderful?"

"You've got the right word."

Grace settled on the bed, examined the things there with a kind of wistful recognition, folded them and placed them in the gaping suitcases with a final touch, as if selecting fragments of what had been to settle them finally with a benediction.

Lily reached too late to cover the Marbella dress. Grace raised it to her face, stroked her cheek against it. "Oh, Lily, Lily, that awful night . . ."

And Grace had even remembered what Lily had been wearing, as Lily knew she would.

"Come on then," Lily said, "let's pack it, shall we? Or throw it out. It's all over now, that sort of thing. You've found Johnny, happiness, so let's throw this away as a sort of gesture."

Grace did not move, remained with the dress pressed to her face. "No, we couldn't do that because, you see, the memory of you in this dress is the only sweetness from that dreadful night. Give it to me to keep, would you? So that when my happiness with Johno becomes something that had no beginning, when it seems he's always been there loving me, I'll take it out, you see, I'll take it out and remember and make him wonder why I should kiss him out of the blue." She rested the dress on her lap, sunk her head. "I'm doing it right, I hope?"

"What?"

"Letting you go like this."

"There you are, that's what's worried me: that you'd think I was going for the wrong reasons or that you'd made me in some way. It's not true, Grace. I want to go, it's right to go. It's high time, really, and I'm looking forward to it. It'll all be the same but a little different . . ."

"I so want to get everything right from now on. One's made so many mistakes. If you were still little I wouldn't let you go; you know that, don't you? But, honestly, sometimes I even feel you're older than I am. Silly, isn't it, but you're so . . . so adult, like a very old soul who's seen it all before many times. Oh, but sweet, Lily, so sweet . . ." a breath of laughter to reassure and defuse. "And I worry about you being alone, for too long, that is. It's so good to have someone. Start to live, lovey, eh? Have some fun? Bring your heart back from the beach?"

"I'll be fine."

"Lily?"

"What, Grace?"

"Tell me honestly . . ." Lily averted her head but Grace pierced with her gaze until Lily faced her again. "He does love me, doesn't he?"

If only it had been her face, her figure ("You, Grace, fat? Oh come on"). She had never been asked to confirm love before. " 'Course," she managed, ashamed of her effort, then with improved energy, "Listen, Grace, he tells you, doesn't he?"

"Yes, but they do, don't they? Men."

"You must trust him more than that if you're going to marry him."

"He doesn't know my age."

Now some relief; Lily could smile. "He might have guessed and love you just the same."

"And I think he thinks I'm a little richer than I am."

Relief passed away. "Why should he do that?" Grace only shrugged with a dead-eyed smile. "You haven't misled him, have you?"

"Well, I am quite rich by a lot of people's standards and I've sold some things he didn't like, the French commode, remember? And the Hepplewhite bookcase?"

Yes, she remembered. "I did wonder where they'd gone." Her home, her past, yet not hers at all.

"You do like him, don't you, dear?"

"Yes, but you know how I am: slow to respond. I can't just fall into friendship with him like you've fallen into love with him. The thing that matters between Johnny and me is you. And if he makes you happy, then I like him for that and I daresay in time I'll get to like him for all sorts of other things as well."

They were both aware that Johnny Cochrane had been presented as a *fait accompli*. Lily had been deprived of her usual opportunity for voiced circumspection. It was too late to say she found his art spurious and his pump-house sexuality embarrassing, distasteful. Lily could barely even admit these things to herself, so intent was she upon shining benign light over Grace's chosen course.

Then he was there: Johnny Cochrane pushed open the door and leant in the frame for some moments with the air of knowing what had passed between them. He said nothing, merely imposed his presence, pleasant but definite. He went and placed his arm around Grace. She held the tips of his fingers where they touched her shoulder while still looking up at Lily.

"Johno, Lily's going to live in her workroom but I've told her that this room will always be here for her, waiting, just the way she leaves it."

He looked hard at Lily. "You're going then?" (Did she hear an unspoken, "At last?")

"Yup."

"Well that's really . . . like . . ." as was his habit, he paused to select his word, and Lily waited for *terrific, great, good,* ". . . really sad."

They left her, Grace taking the Marbella dress, and Lily stood amidst her unfinished packing with less resolve, hearing only those unexpected words: really sad. An emptiness entered her, accompanied by fading confidence; she wanted just a little more of Grace and Johnny's company before closing this part of her life.

She went to Grace's bedroom door which was partly open, heard their voices, pushed the door further. Grace was in Johnny Cochrane's arms, clutching in her hand, with the Marbella dress, that filthy handkerchief.

Johnny looked up and said, "What do you want?" in a voice so far from "really sad."

"Sorry . . . I . . ."

"Oh Lily dear . . ." Grace turned her head into Cochrane's shoulder; she had been crying.

"What's the matter, Grace?" Lily asked.

" 'Sall right, Lil. You can go. I'm in control; not your business now."

"Oh Johno, don't. What is it, dear? Why did you come?"

"I just suddenly wondered if it would be nice to do something together . . . I don't know what, just something."

Grace raised her nestling head to Johnny. "Sorry but we're going out." He answered for them both and Grace asked, "All right, Lily?"

"Fine . . . fine . . . Anyway I'm dying to finish my . . ." Grace broke from Johnny's embrace to stare at Lily, "my packing."

In the Sinner's Flat, with proper solitude rather than that created by absence, the emptiness abated to re-form as misgiving. Had she left too soon? Should she watch some more, anticipating a fall that might never come? Was it right to stay here being quietly amazed by the extent of her possessions (mostly her collection of clothing and accessories) as she unpacked trunk after trunk? It seemed remarkable that she should have contained her life for so long in one room.

There was a picture rail running around the wall of the workroom and from this she hung flat at different heights the uniforms, the tail-coats, the frock-coats, a jacket from Schiaparelli's Circus Collection, a rare Chanel dress in black chiffon and lace, an exquisitely pleated Fortuny in pale green silk. Punctuating her work with unanswered calls to Grace, Lily spent hours hanging garments such as these to overlap here, reveal there, finally creating a peopled atmosphere, as though a party of soundless gaiety were taking place; this was reinforced by three old dressmaker's dummies standing about with their odd pigeon-breasted shapes clothed. She set up her pressing table and her sewing machines, one old black model, elaborately etched in gold, the other electronic. She bought furniture to supplement the room's own sad items. For several days she worked like this while her mind trod involuntarily, incessantly from past to recent events and back again, kneading at half-gained impressions. (So what if Grace had been crying? Hadn't tears always been in the process of her happiness? Of course they had. " 'Sall right, Lil, you can go. I'm in control.")

Late one afternoon she sat down, looked around. It was as finished as a room ever is: low, wide bed in the corner covered with a dark Paisley print; two shell-backed armchairs conversationally placed, their tattered blue brocade too lovely to hide; a small round table between them; the dummies; her worktables; a bureau. Crowded, idiosyncratic and fine, just fine.

She went to the telephone beside her bed and dialed. "Hello

. . . it's me. Yes . . . I've finished my workroom and wondered if you'd like to see it, both of you, of course . . . Well I'm not doing anything tonight . . . Oh, I see. Tomorrow? . . . No, Grace, really that's fine . . . no, don't worry. Have you got my number? . . . Good. So everything's all right, then? Marvelous. Bye for now.''

She looked down at her hands in her lap, raised her head and in a mirror hanging behind the clothes against the wall saw her reflection curtailed by a cuff, a hem. Hadn't she sat, just so, years before in a whitewashed room on a hot night? Hadn't she raised her head to look past herself at another? And what was it she had said then: ''She's awfully proud . . . worst of all . . . don't think she'll marry you now . . .'' And the silence and the voice, ''Say it again, Leely?'' And after that, the shame. All over now, that and the rest of it. All over.

Lily went to the Victoria and Albert Museum with one of her acquisitions from that day in Llandudno. It was a full, long dress of woven silk. She pressed the bell beside a varnished wood door at the end of a gallery on the first floor. After a short wait she was let into the textile department where anyone could take items for identification and valuation. They knew Lily well, for she frequently brought something of interest. Lily's friend there, Lea, a mature, round, untidy woman with an infinite love and knowledge of old and historic garments, greeted her. ''Well, Lily, something nice? Where did you find it?''

''Llandudno.'' With care Lily unwrapped the antique dress, laying it on an elongated mahogany table that stretched the length of the tunnel-like room in which they stood. The ceiling was arced, the walls lined with long narrow drawers wherein any garment could lie flat; it was windowless, airless.

''Good heavens . . .'' Lea whispered. ''Do you know what you've found?''

''No, not really.''

''Come here. Come and see.''

They moved down the long room, stopping at a particular drawer which Lea pulled open. Carefully she withdrew from it a dress of identical fabric to the one Lily had brought but badly decayed. Setting the two together on the table, Lea said, ''The silk is an Anna Maria Garthwaite design, and see the flowers?'' Her fingers ran over the woven flowers which were lightly, gracefully disposed on the open background. ''So real, exact. It's a very important piece and in such fine condition, so much better than ours. I'd date it at seventeen-forty to forty-five; not before because this style marks the change in her work from the baroque, heavy stuff to this beautiful natural line, perfectly observed. Do you know she was unmarried? Lived in Spitalfields among the Huguenot master weavers? Remarkable for those days, and nothing now, is it? A woman alone pursuing her career, her life . . . Lily? Are you all right?''

Lily was holding her head trying to stifle a faintness. ''I think I'll go into the passage, get some air.''

''Of course. You know it's the excitement. This is terribly exciting . . . Can you manage?''

''Yes. Stay here, I'll be fine in a minute.'' She left Lea happy with the dress, went into the cool of the corridor, pressed her head against a cold windowpane, eyes shut. When the spinning stilled she opened her eyes, gazing down into the central courtyard of that massive building.

There was a woman down there among the people moving this way and that, all hunching against the rain beginning to fall from the black pearl sky. The rain fell harder, the people moved faster, except for that woman dead center. She stood with no covering against the rain, her hands clutched to her mouth, searching frantically about her. It was Grace. If Lily ran now, through the various galleries, down the flight of steps, here and there, to the courtyard at last, she would surely be gone, lost to her somewhere in the museum. So Lily stayed motionless, mesmerized, seeing Grace's red hair become streaked wet against her face as she turned and turned on the spot where she stood in apparently silent hysteria; until out of one of the doors leading from the museum a little girl came running, dressed in a blue raincoat with a hood, quite protected from the rain. The child approached from behind and touched the woman who was Grace. She swirled round and crouched to embrace her and stayed holding her, oblivious to the rain.

''I don't suppose you would like to donate it, would you?''

Slowly Lily leveled her eyes upon Lea who bore that wry smile she used when trying the unreasonable.

''No,'' Lily was vague and frowning, ''no, I don't think so . . .''

''We might buy it, you know. You look very pale, Lily. Shouldn't you sit down? What's the matter? What can you see out of that window?'' Lea aligned her eyes with Lily's. ''Rain, is that it? It's raining?''

"Can you see a woman down there with a child, or a woman alone? No coat, no covering from the rain?"

Lea conscientiously scanned the scene below: gray, distant and uninteresting when there was an Anna Maria Garthwaite to be enjoyed. "If she was there, she's gone."

"Yes, she's gone, hasn't she? And the child too . . . Keep the dress, Lea. I'll come back for it."

On returning to her flat Lily telephoned Grace and when the Ansaphone picked up she prepared herself for Grace's recorded voice, stilted and stagy, delivering the message that amused Lily so: "It's Grace here but I'm not in. However *do* say something, won't you?" The voice this time was not that of Grace. "Johnny Cochrane speaking. If you have a message for Grace or me, speak after the tone. Thanks." Lily said nothing. She dialed another number.

"Larry? It's me. Your coat will be ready for fitting tomorrow. My new place, remember. About five? . . . See you then." She dialed again. "Elizabeth? Lily . . . I'm finishing your wedding dress tomorrow. Would you like to come round Thursday morning to collect it? No need to fit it again. You've got my address? Great. Bye."

She stalked her room a while appraising it, readjusting a fold, a feather; played a record of Bach's cello suites; made herself a sandwich. Then she remembered: Wednesday tomorrow. Wednesday: her day for collecting Sebastian. They would come back to her flat, have tea, do any prep, then . . . no television. Hadn't thought of that. Never mind for one day. She would have one by the weekend.

The next morning she worked swiftly and pleasurably, hulla-baloo in her head all gone. She went out to buy the things Sebastian liked best for tea, chocolate éclairs mostly, and returned to prepare the table before going to collect him.

Because it was far too early she walked the distance to the school anticipating his response to her new home. He was the best person to see the flat first because he was always so interested, so positive.

She stood outside the school enjoying the familiarity, watching the various greetings as the boys came down the steps; as always the little ones first. At last Sebastian's class appeared. She knew all their faces and some of their names. Today Sebastian was not among the leaders as he usually was.

The last mother went with her boy. "Bye," she called to Lily, "Sebastian hanging about today, is he?"

"Suppose so, bye."

The headmaster's wife came to the front door having overseen the departure of the boys; she released the brass bolt that held it open, was about to close it when she saw Lily. "Why, Miss Teape?"

"Hello. Sebastian's not come out yet."

"Oh, my dear, he went home much earlier with one of his headaches. Didn't anyone tell you? What a pity, I am sorry."

"Don't worry, there must be a misunderstanding," masking her initial anger. "I'll find him at home."

Then came the fear so closely allied in dealing with Sebastian. When he had broken his leg that fear subsided awhile, the worst had happened, but as time went by it sidled back: there could be another accident any time. This, surely, was one of his phony headaches? But he had never done it before, not on her day, not on a Wednesday. She hailed a cab.

Lily was unready for the sensation of unbelonging as she let herself in through the great street door and mounted those stairs she knew so well, for the first time as an outsider. It had only been a week.

Her ring on the bell was unanswered. Even after it was apparent there was to be no answer, she continued to ring the way one does when there seems little else to do; until she remembered she had a key and let herself in.

"Sebastian?"

There was movement in the kitchen. Lily went to the door and saw the cleaner there rubbing at the stove in her skin-tight ski-pants and low-cut T-shirt, her frothy brass-blonde hair tied back with red chiffon. "Hello. It's you," barely looking up from her task.

"Yes. Why didn't you answer when I rang?"

"I've told Oliver and Melissa time and time again: I won't answer no bells. You get all mixed up with messages and signatures and all sorts. I'm here to clean and that's what I do."

"I don't suppose Sebastian's here, is he?"

"He was but he went out a while back."

"Where?"

"He went with that Mr. Cochrane of Mrs. Teape's. Said something about going to his studio."

"No message? Nothing?"

"Didn't say anything to me."

"So he was quite all right, didn't seem as though he had a headache or anything?"

"Fit as a flea like always. Larking about with that Johnny Cochrane he was, nice to see him like that. Lovely little boy, isn't he?"

"Sweet." And the way she said it caused the cleaner to stop and look at her.

All elation and expectation decanted, she went upstairs to Grace's flat. "Grace?" she called, once inside, but knew there was no one.

The last thing in that place to clutch at life the way it had been was the smell: wool carpets and fresh flowers. Now that too had let go, annihilated by black rubber flooring laid throughout the passage with its own industrial fume.

Opening the door of her room with apprehension, Lily found it was the same, as they had promised. She sat on the bed, looked about. It was forlorn there and she saw that she had taken from it all that represented her as the woman she had become, leaving it simply as the little girl she had been: the toys there, the storybooks and, in the wardrobe among the school dresses and pleated skirts, the Marbella dress placed back where it belonged with all else that was done with.

Without looking at the other rooms she went away, took the Underground and down there, despite its brouhaha, clangor, 'Scuse me's and thrash, that emptiness drifted back.

Chapter 13

L ARRY WAS LAZING IN A SHELL-BACKED ARMCHAIR WHEN
Lily arrived home. Smoking a cheroot, legs stretched, ankles crossed, he studied her nonplussed expression while
eating a chocolate éclair.

"Your landlady let me in. I take it these were for me?" waving the éclair.

"Why not? Actually, I'd forgotten you were coming. I'm glad
you waited."

"So am I now. It's always a pleasure to look at you, Lily.
Although this time you seem a trifle despondent."

"It's nothing."

"Don't tell me someone's got your heart at last?"

"Nothing like that. Just depressed, that's all. Come on, let's
do the fitting."

"So independence at last." He was sauntering in front of a
cheval mirror with his ivory-handled cane as Lily approached
from behind with pins. "Are you going out? Entertaining? Ex-
ercising your freedom?"

"There's nothing new in my freedom. I feel I've had that a
long time."

"Yes, but no Grace now to watch over you, wondering what
time you'll return and all that."

There was no point in enlightening him, so she said, "I'll
lead my life in much the same way. It suits me." She knelt to
attend to the hem.

"You're absurd, Lily, the way you go on. You're asked out
and you don't go. Do you have any close friends besides Sebastian?"

"Plenty. You for a start," she said simply to disconcert.

"Oh, Lily, if only that were true; you're *my* friend, you know that, but am I *yours*? You don't give. Think of all the delicious confidences I've shared with you and what do I know of yours? . . ." ("Yes, well Lil, you don't say much, see? I don't feel I know you.") ". . . I mean, *can* you love, Lily? Is it blood in your veins or a steely river of dressmaker's pins? You'll end up all alone, you know, while the rest of the world is holding hands in twos . . ."("And I worry about you being alone.") ". . . You're young, you're beautiful, enjoy it. Stop wasting time." ("Start to live, lovey, eh? Have some fun. Bring your heart back from the beach.")

"You can take it off now."

"What?" He looked down as she rested back on her heels by his feet.

"The coat, of course. I've got the hemline. If you wait I'll sew it."

"Have you listened to me at all?"

"Yes. What do you think of Johnny Cochrane, by the way?"

"I liked him, he made me laugh. He's genuine."

"He flattered you."

"Oh, so that's it."

"What?"

"You're jealous, aren't you?" He watched her for a while with her head turned firmly away, then stooped, brought her face toward him. "Why, Lily, tears? I'm sorry. I didn't mean to hurt you. Whatever's the matter? You're not yourself at all."

"I'm not jealous. I do have fun and I can love. I'm not good at social life, that's all. I don't really enjoy it."

"Well, you're going to learn. Come out with me tonight. Come out, be beautiful and have fun."

("If you were still little I wouldn't let you go . . .")

"Very well, I'll come." Yet there remained something intangibly repellent about him that had made her refuse when he had asked her in the past.

He stalked the room while she sewed the hem. "I think I'll wear the coat now. Perfect, don't you think, with these?" Gesturing to his soft-collared shirt, pink satin waistcoat, stovepipe trousers, patent leather pumps.

"Perfect," without thought, without raising her eyes.

"And you can wear this." He lifted the green silk Fortuny dress from the wall.

"That's a bit much for a quick dinner or a movie or whatever."

"I'm not the quick dinner or movie type, Lily, you should know that. I'm taking you to meet some interesting people and people who will appreciate you wearing something rare. So, come along, finish the hem quickly and dress." ("So, dress, dress, darling, I'll see you downstairs . . .")

Having changed into the clinging, trailing Fortuny, Lily made herself up to achieve a suitably theatrical mask, haunted, black-eyed, red-mouthed, and took pleasure in her appearance: that of a specter wandered in from some Venetian palazzo. Larry touched up his own make-up too: eyes, mouth, a little white powder.

Covered by a midnight-blue silk-velvet cloak, Lily descended the stairs behind Larry and was accosted by Gill in the hall. "Grief. What have you two come as?"

Larry said, "I'm taking Miss Lily Teape out, my good woman, to enjoy herself. To be herself. By that I mean to be young and beautiful. Like the song says," he sang the words in an odd falsetto, "keep young and beautiful if you want to be loved."

Gill had at first crossed her arms, head to one side, in sceptical assessment of Larry, but when he sang that line she shifted her position, looked away and said, "Yes . . . well, there's truth in that." She glanced at Lily, prepared to see her face alive with prospective enjoyment, but what she saw beyond the mask of makeup was a closed nervousness: and Gill was sorry, it seemed wrong. "Hey," she said to Lily, "don't you listen to me. You look lovely, really, and he's right: you should have some fun, being only young like you are. What if you do look like a couple of ghouls, very attractive ghouls. Go and meet some other ghouls and have a laugh. God knows, we could all do with that."

The ambivalent blessing warmed Lily and she felt that being young and having fun, if that is what they were to do, might be the right thing after all.

They arrived at a stone-fronted house at the end of a badly lit cul-de-sac. Its studded, wooden front door and steep stone step imposed right upon the narrow pavement with no introductory path or garden, giving the place an air of sudden dominance. The blackness behind the mullioned windows was so complete that rather than suggesting emptiness beyond them, it suggested the opposite: hidden, secret life, something hung there to block out daylight, moonlight, eyes.

Larry raised the massive metal knocker, letting it fall just

once, then turned his back on the door, looking at Lily in silence
with an air of certainty. After a period, just long enough to imply
the occupants were absent, the door was opened and they entered. Lily did not turn round to see who had actually opened
the door, for right away she was embraced in a world without
date. It was no longer night outside or even England; it was as
though this house were poised in some perpetual, invented space
and hour; confined, warm, complete as a womb.

Inside was unexpected depth and proportion so that vast room
followed room, up a stair, down two, with no apparent archi-
tectural rhythm. Larry led the way down a corridor, the walls
of which were massed with dark, gilt-framed paintings, to a
door which he opened, then closed behind them. There followed
a moment during which they tussled in darkness with a copious
woolen curtain that had been hung all about the other side of the
door, presumably to stop drafts. As they pushed and prodded
at its softness the sound of subdued festivity filtered through and
because no one came to assist them in their protracted entry the
effect was that of being in a social decompression chamber, for
when Larry did at last draw aside the curtain, with a clack of
the wooden rings on which it hung, Lily found herself tuned to
the gloaming room. It was partially lit by gothic wooden lamp
standards with parchment shades and by a wide, leaping coal
fire. There was massive furniture, and huge brittle arrangements
of dried flowers, shriven of name or season, struck rigid from
great brass urns. If there were any windows they were covered
by tapestries. Commanding the whole of the wall directly opposite, above the fire, was a lifesize painting of Shire horses
pulling a plough, followed by a young man, all on an umber
field. The varnish on this train of tossing manes, reins, shafts of
steel was so browned that it beset the whole scene in an unnatural, almost post-nuclear sunset.

There were people there; hard to tell how many because of
the dimensions of the room and their disparate socializing, but
the apparent quiet, low key of their voices was striking. Dressed
in varying modes, yet all so as to make Larry and Lily seem
quite unpeculiar, they stood about in groups or alone: some
eating, some drinking, some talking; one singing to an audience
of two; a girl in a black tutu practising a *pas de chat* unwatched.

There was an everflowing quality about the gathering, as
though there had been no beginning, or if there had been it was
long ago; there would be no question of an end, but perennial
spontaneity. Yet, for all that, the coal fire was maintained,

plates of delicate things to eat were about, trays of clean glasses, bottles of wine, spirits; in all an oblique choreography to the whole affair.

No one acknowledged their entry. Larry handed Lily a glass of wine and took one himself. They began moving among the people who seemed to know Larry, treating him as though he had been everpresent; with Lily they were neither cordial nor cold. This stylized crowd were simply acquiescent to her presence.

For perhaps half an hour she stood making light conversational remarks, listening to others, taking in the eccentric surroundings, becoming gradually assimilated. She idly spun an antique floor-standing globe until, on finding Africa, she remembered the note she had never seen: "Gone to Africa." Oliver had never mentioned his illness again, so it could not have been serious. Then came the first sign that reality was disintegrating: when she withdrew her hand from that old world, Africa came with it and melted through her fingers. She looked about quickly to see if anyone else could see that great continent dribbling off her palm. Slow motion commenced and soon after she felt she had quite literally stepped outside of herself.

Lily saw her pale green form talking to two strangers, a man with a Mozartian look and a girl with pink hair: she saw herself taking a sip from her glass and gesturing to demonstrate some detail of her dress. Her consciousness stood apart from her body and to reunite them now would require a maneuver she could not quite complete. It was frightening yet the procedure of fear was beyond her and all the while, most amazing of all (for all she really wanted to do now was depart), her body moved among these people with her own voice uttering things she had not expected to say. If a consciousness can frown, hers did then for she saw what others saw in her. How cool she was, confident, remote, secure. There followed a period during which she found the trick of reentering her body but not to remain in it. In a moment when she was at one with herself, she grasped Larry's arm. "Help me, Larry, I'm not right. I don't feel right. I want to go." His face loomed close and that intangible repellence was intangible no longer: he was a sharp-toothed rat, twitching, rapacious.

"You'll be fine," he said, "just relax, don't fight it, take another sip." On the same breath he said to another, "Here's Lily Teape, I told you I'd bring her."

A supremely tall, black-haired woman with fierce glyptic

beauty slid into view. She wore tight purple satin trousers and was naked beneath a black chiffon blouse. She smiled, reached out a long arm and touched Lily's face. "So you're drinking the wine, that's good. You see, you'll feel quite marvelous."

With her separated mind Lily saw herself do the one thing she instinctively did not want to do: take another sip from the glass. The woman reached for Lily's hand and placed it to her breast beneath the black chiffon. With what remained of reason Lily snatched back her hand and fought to reunite mind and body. She found in the moment of success that she had no recollection of arriving at this place or of any time that she had not known these faces which had taken on a grotesque familiarity. A frenzy overtook her and she pulled at the tapestries on the walls in search of an exit. Voices came coolly observant from somewhere: "I think she wants out." "Has she had it before, Larry?" "I don't like the look of it." "Someone take her away."

Alone then she was punished by cold wind and rain, on an unkind street in a bombazine night; there had been no leaving that place; now the hot interior of a car surrounded by a haywire cinerama of light. Again, no arrival, just another image: she was on her bed, knew that Paisley cover, clutched it with relief. For a while she lay watching an eerie and delightful scene; her collection of clothes came from the wall and to life. They were pirouetting, bowing, curtseying and appeared to lean over her from time to time in affectionate concern. The Schiaparelli jacket somersaulted and danced with a dummy. Lily laughed. She laughed and laughed until, without warning, she passed from consciousness.

Chapter 14

AWAKE, LILY REMAINED BEHIND SHUT EYES JUST BEYOND a tangle of dreams still roaming her head with an ache. She breathed air stiff with the odor of defunct revelry. The fractions of incident that came to her were not all dreams: the ones most clear and horrible she knew to be fact. If she opened her eyes any one of those night strangers might still be there, spent upon the floor. So she stayed wondering about a faint, discordant tinnitus until curiosity made her open her eyes slightly.

Through lash-feathered vision she ascertained she lay in vacant chaos. Eyes fully open, without moving her head or a limb, Lily looked at the room on which she had spent all those hours of care. The furniture was tumbled about, one shell-backed chair on its side, the other with a now unclothed dummy stretched across it, her work-tables strewn with glasses and bottles, spilt and smashed. One curtain had been pulled to the floor and the light streaming through gave the room an uncommon brilliance. But, besides the disarray, the stench, something more was different: her room had a solitary deserted air. And there was the reason: the walls were bare, no clothes hung against them; no butler's livery, railway porter's uniform, no Schiaparelli jacket; only the skeletal wire hangers each tapping with a different note at the wall, animated by a yawn of morning air through the open window.

She sat up. A streak of pain passed from neck to stomach as she retched. When she rose unsteadily she found she was still wearing the green silk Fortuny, stained and crushed. Her possessions had been pulled from place and thrown around like

126

debris. She searched on her knees for the clothes it had taken her six years to collect. They were not there. With her head resting on the stained, cigarette-singed pressing table, she cried. She cried exhaustion, she cried desolation; until there was a touch on her shoulder.

"Lily? Lily dear?" A voice doubting that she was Lily at all. It was Grace looking fresh, alert, concerned, all part of this morning hour. Lily remained with her head on her arms, broken down. Carefully pulling back Lily's hair to study what she could of her profile, Grace said, "What's happened, my darling? The mess in here. And you."

"Look what they've done to my home, Grace."

"Who?"

"I don't know."

From near the door Gill's voice came, "I chased a dozen out last night. I came up 'cause of the racket. Thought she was having a party but saw her passed out on the bed so put a stop to it all. Expensive-looking crew, they were. But nasty, you know, nasty. All dressed up, and laughing fit to bust. Had a look to see Lily here was all right. Didn't want her choking or anything. She looked OK so I left her."

Lily turned her head on the table to speak. "Were they wearing my things?" But Gill had not seen her collection. "Was anyone in a jacket with a circus design on the buttons?"

A short silence followed, heavy with exchanged looks, until Gill said with kind tolerance, "Didn't see the buttons, love."

"Was there a bright pink jacket, then?"

"Yes, there was, and a girl in a man's uniform, old style. All sorts."

Lily began to shake and was helped back to bed by Grace and Gill who then left them. Johnny Cochrane was standing by the door hands in pockets, looking at his feet, discreet.

"So what made you come?" Lily asked, as though regretting their presence.

"We were sorry, you see dear, that we couldn't come over last night or tonight. You sounded a bit low and we were worried. Mrs. Gregor let us in. Who were they? They must be people you know?"

Lily explained about Larry, about arriving somewhere and feeling strange.

"Drunk? Were you drunk?" Grace helped.

"No, I hardly had anything. One glass of wine, if that . . ."

When she described her disembodiment (leaving out about

Africa melting), Johnny stirred. "Where'd that ponce take you then, Lil?"

"You know that wide cul-de-sac off King's Road . . ."

"You went to Mona's. Thought so," he interrupted. "They gave you acid, that's what they did."

"Acid?" Grace put her arms around Lily, protecting her from the very word. "You mean drugs? Not Lily. Lily doesn't do drugs, Johno."

"No, doll. In the wine. She wouldn't even know it."

"But why?"

"They do, see, at Mona's. Sort of joke. Sick crowd."

"How do you know them?"

"Well, toss around the London art scene a bit and you soon get to Mona's. Sort of pseudy lot they are, know what I mean?"

"And they've stolen Lily's collection?"

"Na, not stolen. Just sort of borrowed, a prank, I'll bet." He sat on the edge of the bed, reached for Lily's hand. "Tell you what, I'll get 'em back. Might take a day or two but I'll track 'em down through that old dyke Mona. Give me a list of what's missing I'll be off."

"Everything. Just everything," Lily said, beyond being impressed by his offer. She didn't believe he'd do it. It was all show for Grace.

"What, that butler's whatnot with the little lions? Fancied that myself."

Grace wrote a list with Lily's disjointed help and handed it to Johnny Cochrane who studied it and clarified a few details. Without lifting his head he squeezed Lily's hand. "OK, Lil, I'll be off."

"Lily," she said firmly, with her face to the wall.

He did not let go of her hand but when she turned to face him he was staring back at her, hurt and inquiring. Then the tone of her voice was absolved by a fine change in her expression. She had had some vague intention of wordlessly challenging him for going off with Sebastian yesterday, but seeing his face she could not sustain it. "I'm Lily, not Lil," she said with her eyes dropped, returning a faint pressure in his hand, almost ashamed now of her insistence.

He grinned, winked. " 'Course you are: Lily. That's right, girl. Tell you what, Lily, you pop round my studio this afternoon 'bout four and see if I haven't turned something up." He crossed over to where Grace sat watching them, hands linked in her lap, leaning forward, smiling, urging their friendship with silent eloquence. "And you, lovely lady," pausing to touch her hair as though tinkering with perfection, "I'll see you tonight."

After he had left Lily asked, "Will he manage it?"

"Oh, he will. He really will."

"It's sweet of him to bother."

"Oh, but he would, you see, Lily, he would. It's just like him."

"I'm sure it is. Well done."

"What for?"

"For finding him." She wanted to come home from the isolation her mind had placed her in this past week and be in on their happiness. Down with Lily the sceptic.

"Bless you, Lily." Grace leant forward confidentially. "You'll never guess . . ." She was biting her pleasure on to her lower lip and Lily laughed wearily but a laugh just the same.

"Go on then, Grace, what?"

"He knows my age."

"Never."

"Yes. I can't think how. But he let me know that he knew and that it's all right."

Lily gave herself up to laughter and Grace braced back, watching her with satisfaction. "There, dear, I knew I could make you laugh. Now then," quite changing her face and manner, "why all this? Why Larry? You've always quite rightly avoided going out with him. Poor Angela, even she admits he's not much good. I don't understand, Lily?"

"I was trying to be young. Go out. Have fun the way one's supposed to." If she admitted confusion Grace would take the blame.

"And the drugs? Is it going to be all that again? Is it Lily? I watched your mother go down, mind gone, skin and hair wretched. Ice-cream was all she ate from morning till night.

"Such friends we were once. I met Michael through her; the fun we all had. I loved her despite her making it nearly impossible. We tried to help her kick the habit. I found her once in an outside lavatory. She'd taken an overdose. God knows how long she'd been there. Got her out, to hospital. She pulled through, obviously. We sent her on an incredibly expensive cure. A week after she was discharged she was back on the drugs. They changed her personality, she became devious, dishonest, stole from Michael . . . and me."

Grace had been addressing the window, the sky, the street outside; now she snapped her head back, speaking bitterly.

"Is it going to be all that with you? Will I be dragging you out of fetid lavatories, pulling you round only to have you turn on me. And they'll say, 'What could you expect after being brought up by Grace Teape?' And they might well be right."

Having raised herself on the bed, Lily was staring at Grace. She had never had to excuse herself before. She had never hurt Grace before. There was so much to address but no words would come; except finally, "I was low, depressed. Forgive me, Grace . . ." (Grace was muttering, "No . . . no, not 'forgive,' darling, that's not it . . .") "But it was just one mistake and you're condemning me already. Just once, Grace, is it fair?"

Grace nearly screamed her response. "Don't you see, *yet? Once is all it takes.*"

"I'm not druggy and won't be. I made a mistake. I won't make it again, I promise."

"Haven't I made enough mistakes for both of us? Couldn't you learn from mine? And your mother's? No. That's not how life is, is it? Should we get a doctor, dear, to make sure you're all right?"

"No, I'm just tired . . . and kind of . . . shattered." She lay back down, closed her eyes.

While Lily rested Grace made coffee and began to restore the room. She was stepping about righting furniture, collecting glasses, when Elizabeth arrived. Little Elizabeth, graceful and snowdrop-fresh, only eighteen and embarking on the burlesque of marriage: for her Lily had found a Victorian country wedding dress.

"What's happened here?" she asked in that lisping, lilting voice of hers, so nearly still a child.

With her nerves unstrung, the thought of the dress being certainly gone with the rest made Lily turn away on her bed and sob. But Grace said brightly, "It's nothing really. Lily had a housewarming, that's all, and she's a little tired."

"I've come for my dress."

"Oh the pretty muslin one, of course. Now let's see . . ." Grace made no demur, just as though they were in a boutique and all was to hand.

"It's gone, Elizabeth, with all the rest of my things. Stolen," Lily moaned through her hands.

"What?" Elizabeth was startled.

"Don't listen to her," said Grace. "It's a wedding dress so it has to be here somewhere. We'll look around."

Elizabeth seated herself with downcast eyes, dimly understanding what had happened. "What'll I do? There's no time to get another one." She studied the room and Lily on the bed with her back to her. That was Lily Teape? Unwashed, hungover, matted hair, vile rag of a dress? She had wanted to confide something, draw reassurance about a small issue, it was not essential but it was nice to do that with Lily because she possessed such maturity, wisdom. You could ask her things you could not ask your mother. Who would have thought she would be like this the moment she lived alone.

In her search Grace restored the room and it was not so hard. Nothing except glasses and bottles had been broken. With the curtain rehung, furniture set straight and with fresh air, all was much as it had been before, except of course the collection was gone, the lovely clothes, Lily's silent companions.

"So," Elizabeth said at last, "no wedding dress."

"Wait, wait, It *will* be somewhere, I know it," Grace said, betraying some desperation. "You'd want to keep the dust off. You'd put it away. If it was hidden, there's a chance it's here . . ." On an inkling she crossed to the white painted wardrobe, standing shabby in a corner. She opened the door and, as though quickened by life once removed, like a ghost caught at hide and seek, the opaque muslin of the wedding dress sprang forth with its frills and flowers.

"Look, Elizabeth," Grace sang out to the little girl engaged in controlling her dejection.

She raised her pale face and saw. "There it is . . . there it was all the time. I knew Lily wouldn't let anything happen to it. I knew she wouldn't let me down."

"Of course she wouldn't. Not Lily. Never," Grace said.

Nevertheless, Elizabeth made a grateful and speedy departure.

Grace continued to fold silk shawls, pair off gloves, restore the furniture, until there was no more to do, then she took a newspaper from her bag and settled to read it casually, glancing (less casually) at Lily from time to time. A while passed and she said, "How do you feel?"

"Better, thanks."

"Like to get up?"

"Yes."

"Tell you why. I've just seen here there's a sale of film and theatrical clothes at Christie's, South Kensington. Viewing this morning, sale at three this afternoon. We could view, then have lunch somewhere nice."

"That'd be good but, before anything, I'm going round to Mona's to see if I can track my stuff . . ."

"But Johno's doing that."

"I know, but I want to as well. I can't just rely on him. He can't possibly know all the items, and anyway he doesn't really understand what it means to me. I'd like to see that Mona by daylight, give her hell . . ."

"Don't, Lily. Just let Johno have a go. You saw how pleased he was to be doing something for you. It's his chance to . . . to gain your, what, respect? I don't know exactly but let him try, won't you? Then if it doesn't work we'll see that dreadful woman together. How about that?"

"All right, but I swear to God if I don't get my stuff back this afternoon, I'm calling the police. Then Larry'll be sorry."

"You *are* feeling better, aren't you? Well done. That's what you have to do, see? Life knocks you down and you get up again. It's as simple as that."

Lily was washing in the bathroom when she heard Grace scream. Kicking open the door, towel in hand, she saw her aunt holding the newspaper wide, gazing at it with delight. "Look, look, it's us. It's Johno and me at last night's party . . ." She backed to Lily so the paper could be viewed over her shoulder. On the gossip page was a photograph of Johnny Cochrane in the center of a crowd, eyes stared by the flash, hand stretched out as though to fend off publicity, yet done with a smile as though in cahoots with the photographer.

"I see, but where are *you*?" Lily asked.

"There. Look. There's my arm. You see, he's holding my hand and there's my arm on the end of it." Quite satisfied with her degree of exposure Grace read aloud, " 'Johnny Cochrane, the young British sculptor, whose exhibition *Lyrical Lumber* is at the Dennis Little Gallery, with his fiancée Miss Grace Teape.' Miss. Don't you love it? Just as well they can't see my face. But, oh Lily, isn't that lovely? Now everyone knows. Just everyone."

Lily found an elaborate 1907 corset in the saleroom and marked it in her catalog to bid for later but what restored her most was finding a wide-shouldered, striped lady's suit. Walking to the restaurant, Lily's vitality began to return. "That suit's a Gilbert Adrian, Grace. Just think what it could mean."

"Yes. I am thinking. Goodness," Grace answered with quick

enthusiasm, pausing then to let some meaning dawn, which it did not, so added tentatively, "What *could* it mean?"

"He designed for MGM for twenty years and particularly for Joan Crawford. This could even have been worn by her."

Throughout the crystalline clatter and chatter of lunch in an Italian restaurant, Grace spoke *we*. No longer did *she* think this or that, or *she* do the other: *we* thought and *we* did. Lily was careful to fall in with the unspoken implication that any mention of Grace Teape singular might destabilize happiness.

At a strategic point, when the main course had been served, looking at and lightly twisting her plate as though its correct positioning was integral to what she had to say, Grace said, "Lily?" in the tone of voice Lily knew so well.

"Listening," Lily confirmed and was surprised to find she did not fear "Tell me honestly:" instinctively she knew that in this short time a door had closed on all of that too.

"Lily, we're thinking of moving abroad. To Italy, actually."

Lily sat dumbstruck waiting for a corollary while Grace remained quiet with eyes averted, so Lily said, "You mean selling up? Completely? Just like that?"

"No. We'll keep the flat but as a bolt hole." Still not looking at Lily, she toyed with the base of her wine glass. "We thought we'd go straight after our wedding as our honeymoon. But, you see, if we find the house we like, our honeymoon will be the rest of our lives."

Grace smiled privately upon some recent recollection; no doubt the phrase was not hers at all.

"You do really want this, Grace? I mean *you*?" Lily spoke firmly, trying to drag the woman she knew from the roller-coaster of change. If she could extract, "*I* know what *I'm* doing and *I* want it," it might be enough but Grace only said, "Yes, we've talked it through . . ." and her eyes flitted to Lily just long enough to establish that she was not to be deflected from *we* ". . . and it's what we want."

"What about The Garden?"

"Yes, I know." There was regret in her voice, then a flash of uncertainty when she realized she had been caught out in the singular. "But we'll come back regularly and The Garden was set up financially by me a long time ago. Angela does all the admin and loves it. We'll visit, Johno and I, and keep a strict eye, and take the children out and, why . . . even have them to stay in Italy, why not? It'll all be lovely. You'll love it too, Lily, won't you? You've always loved Italy."

"Yes, I have. Well . . ." Lily raised her glass against her detractions and doubt, "Good luck." What else could she say?

Having navigated that conversational headland, Grace felt safe to level her eyes upon Lily's. Raising her glass too, she said, "Thank you, dear, and . . . and good luck to you."

It shouldn't have been, it couldn't have been, but it felt just like farewell.

They finished lunch talking about plans for the wedding in a couple of weeks and, Grace having demanded confirmation from Lily that nothing like last night would happen again, they parted with two-way promises to ring very soon.

Lily bid successfully for the corset, the Gilbert Adrian and a bolt of fifty-year-old Jacquard silk. She paid a little too much but that befitted her mood; the acquisitions would assuage her spirit and on the way to Cochrane's studio she collected her Anna Maria Garthwaite from the Victoria and Albert to rethrong her life further with the kind of company that put her at ease.

Chapter 15

T HE SOUND OF DRUMMING POUNDED THROUGH THE GA-
rage doors of Johnny Cochrane's studio and into the street;
a fast elaborate rhythm from one drum was conflicting
with another played by a heavy and artless hand.

Lily pushed at the door, slowly focusing through the gray light
upon Johnny Cochrane at the far end of the garage, seated on a
stool, clutching between his knees a set of bongos. He was
leaning over, elbows flailing, head to one side, letting his ear
receive the full volume of the sound made by his rapid hands.
Opposite him sat Sebastian, also with bongos, only he was upright with head cast back. The arhythmic knocking against
Cochrane's gifted playing was coming from him. Both were lost
in concentration, with Cochrane shouting from time to time,
"There you go, man, great. Faster, faster," and Sebastian obey-
ing with a wide, open-mouthed smile.

Lily watched from just inside the door. When at last they
finished and were wiping their foreheads in a self-congratulatory
way, Lily's clapping came thin through the air still bruised by
the previous noise.

"Who is it?" Cochrane shouted to the shadow.

"It's me."

"Lily," Sebastian exclaimed, standing up, letting the bongos
fall.

"Hey, careful." Cochrane snatched them up, brushing them
off tenderly.

Lily went toward them. "Hi, Lily," Sebastian said, insecure,
interrogative, when she was close.

"Hi yourself," was all she said but it was enough. Sebastian began to move from foot to foot, hands in pockets, hands out, his head minutely oscillating: all his signs of acute distress and Lily did not want to do it to him; not here, not with Cochrane. She would tick him off another time for yesterday. "Terrific playing. I was listening quite a while."

"Yeah, the kid's got the motion." Cochrane winked, smiling with indulgent conspiracy, for he and Lily had both heard that a sense of rhythm was not among Sebastian's assets.

"And where did you learn to play like that? Sounds really professional," Lily said.

"Here and there. Round about."

"I hope you haven't bunked out of school again, Sebastian."

"No. It's all right." He was relaxed now. "Johnny collected me and Mummy knows. Really. Johnny's teaching me to weld."

"You're crazy," Lily shot at Cochrane.

"Naa, naa," placating with spread hands, "watch him, don't I? Quite safe, aren't you, Seb?" nodding at Lily to imply there really was no harm.

"Just because I'm blind doesn't mean I can't do things like weld, you know. So there."

Irritated by this uncharacteristic remark from him, but containing what she would have said if they'd been alone, Lily gazed at Sebastian, whose face was rigid with sullen defiance directed to where she stood, a little apart.

Johnny Cochrane, thumbs hitched in jeans, let his eyes pass from Lily to Sebastian and back with a voyeuristic interest in the friction between them until, as if bored, he said, "I've got something for you." He raked in the corner among pipes, stoves, buckled wheels and produced more than a dozen plastic bags. Stuffed inside them, grubby but unharmed, were the Schiaparelli jacket, butler's livery and nearly every other item of her collection.

Infused with gratitude and shame, Lily stood gesticulating her thanks, but actually said, "I'm really sorry."

"What for, for Pete's sake?"

"Oh, just because I really didn't believe that you'd find them. Actually, I didn't think you'd even try."

"Didn't trust old Johnny, eh?"

"Well," was all she said, letting her shoulders say the rest, then, "Look, would you like this?" holding out the butler's livery, "I mean, you said you'd fancied it yourself and I'd like to give you something."

"Don't be silly, girl, that's yours. Now what about a cuppa tea?"

Lily meddled with broken-handled mugs and tea bags in the foul corner of a kitchen, considering her confusion of feelings toward Johnny Cochrane now. She liked him for having made that effort, all the more for succeeding, but . . . but what? She despised herself for liking him on such grounds. Through these thoughts sifted an awareness of Sebastian quietly, furtively nagging Cochrane, who was testing rusty embellishments for the four-poster which still held centerstage in the garage.

He was standing on the cross-bars forming the base of the bed, holding above his head the wheel of a racing bicycle, from which hung fine metal chains.

"If I can fix this dead center, see, then spread out the chains like a metallic sunburst . . . great . . ." He was talking more to himself than anyone.

". . . but you *said*. And I told him we'd go . . ." Sebastian was reaching across the bed, pulling at Cochrane's ankles to gain his attention.

"How you do go on, you little bugger . . . What is it?"

"Bugger yourself. You *said* we'd go to Daddy's studio. I want you to see it."

Lily had turned to study the exchange, registering the intimate banter as the mark of some time having been spent together.

Cochrane threw down the wheel. "OK, OK, come on then. Lil, forget the tea, we're off to his dad's studio. Wanna tag along?"

Suffocating her resentment at "tag along," she went with them.

Sebastian sat on the jump seat in the taxi, feeling, sorting the money Cochrane had given him to pay the driver. Lily sat opposite with Cochrane next to her, slouching with his legs spread apart, studying Sebastian.

"So. What'd you say your dad does in this studio of his then? Painter, is he?"

"No. A photographer." Sebastian was distracted, head down, concentrating on the money.

But Lily sat round and forward on her seat, eyes galvanized with disbelief on Cochrane. "You *know* he's a photographer."

Cochrane looked at her briefly as though she were a stranger, said, "That's right. Just testing," then looked away, singularly engrossed with the traffic outside.

Lily insisted on reporting to Esther at the reception before going upstairs, "Yes," she said, "he told me Sebastian would be coming. He's up there."

The dusty, disused appearance of his studio had gone and opera stormed through the stereo system, obliterating any sound of their entry. In the brilliantly lit center of a dark periphery Oliver Cary stood, bent at the waist, his left hand stiffly held behind his back as though paying homage. His right hand, with the meticulous precision of a surgeon, was placing a tiny white ceramic brick, no more than a centimeter square, at the top of a model skyscraper made of dozens of the same bricks. Standing on the table in front of him with this building were others, taller, shorter, wider; the whole was a model Manhattan, a miraculous, miniature, clean-dream of the place, its glazed bricks shimmering in the brilliance of the light. Oliver stepped back to where his camera stood to study it through the lens.

"What's he doing?" Sebastian whispered to Johnny Cochrane, although whispering was unnecessary because of the loud music. This music was what told Sebastian work was in progress; Oliver always played Verdi when he worked.

Johnny Cochrane returned also in a whisper, "He's got, like, a fantastic little New York on a table."

When Oliver removed the back from his camera and went with it to the refrigerator where he kept his film he saw the three of them standing in mute respect and shouted, "Hey. How long have you been there?" He turned down the music, flicked off the umbrella spots, leaving them in a more even light. "Hi, Seb, I've been waiting for you." Oliver crouched to hug him, which Sebastian allowed for a moment, then released himself. "Dad, Johnny's here."

"I know. Well good. I'm glad you all came, only I don't know that there's anything interesting for you to see. Hi, Lily, want a beer?"

"I'll have one," Johnny Cochrane said.

"Oh, yes . . . 'course," hesitant and surprised that their ritual greeting actually held any meaning. He went back to the refrigerator and took out a can, threw it to Cochrane who, catching it, pointed to the brick Manhattan. "That's amazing. What's it for?"

"Err . . . cigarettes," waving his hand unconvincingly, as though he had forgotten the purpose of his shot. "But it's not like being a sculptor, is it? I mean, what you see there isn't the image I'm after exactly . . . I don't know. I'm going for something beyond that which hopefully will be captured only in the shot. It's hard to explain.''

Sebastian went to feel the fragile buildings, so precarious that any sighted person might fear even to stand close by; but Oliver watched him knowing that under his fingers not a brick would fall or be dislodged.

''It's beautiful and smooth, Daddy. It must have taken days to build. Did you do it all alone?''

''Yes. Three days, I think.''

''Listen, I hope we're not interrupting or anything?'' Johnny Cochrane said, but Sebastian answered for him.

''No, it's all right, isn't it, Daddy? He's been expecting us. He said so. Last time we came he wasn't expecting us and he was fixing up a model girl so we had to go.''

''*Was he?* Lucky devil.''

Oliver looked crisply at Lily who was shaking her head adamantly at him. Well, of course she had not told Sebastian. This exchange did not escape Johnny Cochrane who once more watched as he had watched Sebastian and Lily in the garage, with leisurely impudence.

Oliver dismissed the moment by saying, ''This is the stuff I've been working on lately for a book,'' adding with diffidence, ''I think you said you've got my last one.''

''Absolu*tely*.'' Cochrane took the pile of monochrome photographs that showed gulleys and folds of indefinable flesh going on to the edges of each print like landscape; no telltale lips, toes or nipples, but close, close and abstract as only a lover's eye can see.

Leafing through them, twisting them this way and that to guess, Cochrane stopped at one: held it far, then near. Moving over to Oliver, nudging him, he said, ''Here, I know what that is . . .'' first lowering his voice, then raising it with the mock shock of a music-hall bawdy, ''that's a, it's a . . .''

''No, it's not,'' Oliver said quickly, laughing and dropping his arm around Cochrane who stood some inches shorter than he. ''Really, it's nothing like that. That's the point. To make people think it's something it's not. Corny and crude and it's been done before really but there's money in doing the book.''

''Fanta*stic* . . .'' Cochrane mused on the print.

''Well, Seb. Happy now Johnny's seen the studio? I mean, there's nothing else to see here really. We could go home now if you like?''

''All right, let's go home. Will you come too, Johnny?''

"Sure thing. Back to my Gracie. Gotta go out tonight."

"Well, in that case I'll be making my own way then . . ." Lily said, and Oliver became suddenly agitated, stepping back away from Sebastian and Johnny.

"You mean you won't come with us? Why?"

"Well not unless . . ." She did not want to say "not unless Sebastian wants me." She did not want it to be like that.

"Look here," Oliver said to Sebastian and Johnny, "would you two mind going on ahead. There's something I want to say to Lily."

"But Daddy you just *said*," in an outraged whine.

"I know but . . . only a minute, Seb, please. Not long, you can wait downstairs if you don't want to go on without me. *Please.*"

The chilling intensity in his appeal was lost on Sebastian but not on the other two.

"Blimey O'Reilly, Seb. '*You* said this and *you* said that.' Got us like a bunch of bloody puppets, incha? What? Listen, you come with me, old son, there's something I want to buy you on the way home."

With a "Promise you won't be long?" Sebastian went away with Johnny Cochrane. While Oliver watched them down the stairs, Lily returned to the little Manhattan, switched on the lights again to set it shining and stood in wonder.

She heard the grind of Oliver's shoes on the concrete floor but could not see him standing beyond the light. She said to where she thought he was, "It couldn't have only taken three days."

"No," with disembodied voice, "more like two weeks."

"Which cigarettes?"

"It's not for cigarettes."

"I thought you'd said that oddly. What for then?" There was no answer. She looked to where his voice had come from. "Secret?" she said lightly but puzzled.

He stepped into the light, his eyes fixed on her with a frozen, contemplated anger. She had been resting her hand on the table and she dropped it to her side. He came closer with his eyes steady, and she saw in them that he expected her to know something.

His left arm was still fixed behind his back as it had been all the time since they first entered. When he raised his right arm high Lily did not stand back from the blow that seemed certain, not because she was unafraid but because she could not move; all she could do was look back into the stir of rage and frustration in his eyes. He brought his arm down past her and around to the table, sweeping the buildings to the floor. Leaning against the table then, head sunk, he swished some remaining bricks from it and walked away.

Shaken, disconcerted, Lily brought her hands to her face for the second time that day. She was remembering another incident, entirely different and enacted by strangers, but it had left her feeling exactly as she did now: she had been on the Underground, it was the merest incident of racial tension, a white man obliging a black to pass purposelessly this way, not that, down the aisle of the train; the following confrontation of eyes, of expression, the physical was leashed, but the air was rank with hostility. She had got off at the next stop, not where she wanted to be, but only to get away and had become hopelessly lost down there. This irrelevant memory put the present into perspective, calmed her. Oliver's action was neither violence nor hatred, it was desperate entreaty.

She lowered her hands and walked off the set. Behind a tall screen he was stretched on an old mahogany and cane deckchair beneath a window that was, all but three inches at the bottom, covered by a blackout blind. Mauve evening swelled through those three inches, falling on to the profile of his face and body. His right leg still rested on the floor as if it were too heavy to lift beside the other and his right hand was now held rigid across his breast.

Lily knelt beside the chair. His eyes were closed.

"Sorry," he said, speaking low, facing ahead. "You've seen a couple of pretty bad sides to me recently, haven't you?"

Since this was true, it was a little hard to respond. Disinclined to muster the necessary brutality for the affirmative, she said, "Well . . . but why? I mean, why did you ask me to stay, then just do what you did? It's hurtful, actually, and it makes me feel as though you're trying to pay me back for some hurt I've done you."

He reached for her hand; within the warm strength of his grip was a trembling. "You've not hurt me, Lily, but in a funny way you're right: I suppose I was trying to hurt you and only because I confided in you."

"You and the model in the dressing-room? About that?"

"No, not that nonsense; about being unwell."

"Why mind about that? You're better, aren't you? You're working again and you said you'd tell me if it was anything serious."

Only now did he turn his head to face her. Increasing his grip, he moved his eyes to their clasped hands, inviting her attention upon them. She looked, frowned, felt a distinct and steady tremor. "Why are you shaking? Has something upset you so much?"

"No. I can't help the shaking, Lily. Remember I said I was seeing a specialist? Well, I did. There's something going on with my body; like it's in revolt. They tell me I'm very sick."

She pulled his arm toward her, placed her forehead hard on his hand and felt the tremor stop beneath her pressure. Smiling up at him briefly, hopefully, about what she had achieved, she found he had not even noticed; she had only momentarily stopped a tail-end symptom. It began again even before her smile had faded. She attempted to voice the rush of questions all knotted up with emotion but he said, "Shh . . . shhh. Please listen, that's all I want. I want to talk about it so much. I've said nothing to anyone since I saw the specialist two weeks ago and I'm really confused. Frightened too, if I'm honest. And as soon as you came in today I decided I was going to talk. I think I'd been waiting to see you without knowing it. Can you understand that? I mean you were in and out of our flat most days at some point, weren't you, mucking about with Seb? Now things are different with you having moved away and him spending so much time with Johnny. So when you said just now that you were going back to your own place I had this mad sense of being betrayed. The only person who knew I was ill wasn't going to let me talk. Silly, unfair, cruel. I'm sorry. I'm doing quite a few things that aren't like me. The funny thing is that since I've seen the chap, had the tests, I've felt worse, not better. I didn't shake a fortnight ago. It's like my body's acting up, falling in with what the doctors say I might expect. I wish now I'd never asked in the first place."

"Tell me," Lily began carefully, carefully, "about the Manhattan. Why build it if it wasn't for a job; what has that to do with being ill?"

"To prove I could. I'd had the bricks specially made for something and they arrived as I returned from the first time the doctors implied something serious was up. They told me it was my right side affected so I built it with just my right hand. Kept my left behind me all the time and didn't even sit down to do it. A sort of test. Defiance. Also I had to create some sort of impression of work going on up here, particularly since Seb's been going on about bringing Johnny. Says Johnny's been begging him to come here.''

Mentally smiling at Sebastian's methods of getting his own way, Lily put her head on Oliver's lap. They might have sat thus many times, it did not feel new or different; really it had only been once before and neither remembered that just then.

"Has it got a name?'' she asked.

"Some fancy Latin thing. They've done loads of tests . . . amazing, really, what they can find out. Seems it goes back to something I got in Africa over fifteen years ago.''

"There must be drugs, Oliver?''

"Yes, I've started. They make me feel sick.''

"You'll get used to them. You'll get the dose right.''

"Yes,'' as though he did not care.

"When you say you haven't told anyone, do you mean not even Melissa?''

"Not even her.''

"Why? Now you know it's so serious, you *have* to tell her. It's no longer a question of 'not bothering' her. Think what she will feel when she knows you've kept it from her all this time. She'll want to be helping you, supporting you. You're not really being fair to her.''

"Oh, Lily . . .'' and he was almost laughing in a dry, sad way.

Surprised, she said, "Is that so silly? It *is* how she'll feel. It's natural. I know I would.''

"Yes, Yes, you would. Tell you something: that poor little model you caught me out with, that didn't feel like infidelity, not really. But *this*, telling you and not telling Melissa, is the real thing. The greatest infidelity.''

At those words coldness dawned through her and slowly she began to withdraw from him, but he did not want her to move and placed his hand on her head, pressing it into his lap with gentle insistence. She stayed. He was talking on with no idea of what he had just done, that he had isolated her in a state of unfounded guilt. Something else was also happening to Lily; the coldness was turning to a flowing of desire for this man who had been a family figure since she was eight. Here she lay with her head low on his stomach, one arm along his thigh, one hand within his hand. When she had settled thus, only minutes before, there had been no harm, no meaning, in where her head, her hand, lay: it had been right and to do with caring when words aren't enough. Now there was shame in feeling the geography of his body under her face, through his clothing, disgrace in holding the thick of his thigh.

And all the time he was talking, and he was saying, "But, Lily, it's not all that that I wanted to tell you, to talk about. There's something else I'm feeling which is stranger even than my symptoms. You must listen because I feel as though something is impending and yet at the same time . . . This is so hard . . . It's like I have something to do, or somewhere to go, something really important that I've forgotten about. All the time my mind is working at it. It won't stop. What could that be, Lily? Is that what being unwell, badly unwell, is like, do you think? Can you help me understand it? Will I have to go on with this suspense?"

She heard his words, knew his need, and if only she had not had this wild, irrational change in feeling, then she could have responded. But to speak now, when he was lost in the ocean of his illness, would be impossibly dangerous.

It was certain he did not know what had happened to her, what his words had done, that even now she was thinking that if she raised herself she could lay her body against his, or if she stood she could bend to put her mouth to his mouth, his eyes, touch his hair.

"Oliver?"

"Yes?" he said with expectancy, as though he believed she might already have the answers to his questions.

"This talk must be for Melissa, not for me. Please understand."

His hands released their grasp on her; he seemed to subside and whispered, "Yes . . . yes, of course you're right. I have to talk to Melissa."

"Will she be home now?"

"She said she would be but you know how she gets caught up."

"If I came and stayed with Sebastian, would it make it easier for you to tell her this evening? You could take her out or something, do whatever you do when you talk to each other properly?"

"Perhaps it would. Home's her office, the telephone never stops ringing. It's hard to get her whole attention. I'll take her somewhere quiet if I can."

"Let's go then, shall we? You told Seb you wouldn't be long."

Having moved away, she watched him get to his feet and was shocked to see he was stiff, slow. Could it be that, as he said, his body seemed to act up to the knowledge of his sickness, so she might now observe all kinds of details in him, labeling as symptoms habits he'd always had? "Oliver?" she said.

"Yes?"

"It'll be all right. It *will* be."

"Yes."

As soon as Oliver turned the key in his front door there was a shout of, "Waahoo, they're here . . . Quick . . . They're here . . ." It was Johnny Cochrane who had opened the door, too fast for Oliver to remove his key.

From further down the passage Sebastian called back into the sitting-room, "They're here, Mummy, ready?"

While Johnny Cochrane propelled Lily and Oliver down the passage before him they heard two shots in quick succession and saw on entering the sitting-room Melissa standing arms lifted in a declamatory way over two frothing bottles of champagne.

Although she was clad in a tailored city suit, her black hair fell with unmanaged charm and her face was alight with excitement and pleasure. Grace was standing near her smiling, hand raised to acknowledge Oliver and Lily but waiting for Melissa to make her announcement.

"Guess, guess. Go on, guess," Melissa sang out.

Oliver was instantly transformed from the unsteady, frightened man of the last two hours. He entered into the required mood and, all stiff slowness vanished, he walked up and down wringing his hands with delighted perplexity. "You've . . . let's think . . . You've . . . been adopted as an SDP candidate?" he threw out with vigor.

"Nope." Melissa grinned, drawing her head decisively to the left and waiting for another try.

The change in him was inexplicable and Lily felt mildly outraged. Had it all been an act then? Real symptoms can't go just like that. Oliver guessed again. "You've been voted Woman of the Year?"

"Nope," drawing her head back to the right, exuberance brimming.

"Oh I must get it. I must. Let's think harder. Help me, Lily. Give me a clue, Seb."

"Clue, right, clue . . ." Sebastian pondered.

"Box?" Johnny Cochrane said to Sebastian.

"Brilliant. Box, Daddy, box." Sebastian moved over to the television with an extraordinary gait, lifting his feet high and placing them with emphatic care, like a duck on a wall, and Lily thought it was part of the clue.

"I can't stand it anymore," Oliver said. "Tell me?"

"A talk show." Melissa nodded away any disbelief as she spoke, "A talk show of my very own once a week. Yorkshire Television. It's true."

"Oh my darling, you've done it. Brilliant woman." Oliver threw his great long arms around her and she looked pretty, neat, small and safe in his embrace.

While the champagne was being poured Grace and Johnny Cochrane closed together and Sebastian approached Lily, still stepping peculiarly.

"What do you think?"

"It's marvelous, Sebastian. I'm really thrilled for her."

"No. Not that. The boots." He hopped on one foot while lifting the other for her to see. He was wearing purple baseball boots like Johnny Cochrane's. The kind, the very style, she had suggested often in shoe shops and he had rejected.

"Smart. Just like Johnny's."

"I know. He bought them for me on our way home."

"Spoilt brat," she said and ruffled his hair.

"I know," he said again, infinitely pleased, and duck-walked back to where his parents stood.

Melissa was describing the kind of show she wanted it to be. "So you see I'll have on people who are really doing things, not just vacuous personalities, passing film stars. I'll have artists of all kinds to talk about and explain their work. I'll have charity workers with clever ideas, the kind of people who don't usually get much air space. The whole premise will be to stimulate rather than just entertain. But entertain too, I hope."

"So I'd do?" They all looked with mild surprise toward Johnny Cochrane who was standing arms akimbo to display the offer of himself.

"Well . . . well yes," Melissa stammered at first but warmed to the idea. "I mean, why not? You're exactly the type because your work is actually recycling scrap metal. Turning rubbish into art, there's a lot to say about it. And you too, Grace, with Angela talking about The Garden."

"Oh, I don't know about that. We like a low profile on it, you know, but now then . . ." she held her glass aloft, "let's all drink to Melissa, to her success and to all the good work she has done for so many." That done, she said, "And now, Johno, darling, we must go, we'll be so late."

Johnny Cochrane went to Melissa and with his inimitable candor, more effective because it rose out of his effusive boy-ishness, he put his hand on her shoulder, looked hard into her eyes until she adopted his seriousness and returned his look. With quiet emphasis, he said, "Well done, Melissa. Well done *you*." She gave a demurring, embarrassed laugh and lowered her eyes from his.

The moment he heard the front door close on Grace and Johnny Cochrane, Sebastian bent down and unlaced his baseball boots, seating himself to remove them, picking them up and cradling them.

"Wear them, darling, why not? They're fabulous," Melissa said.

"I . . . I don't want to get them dirty."

"What, in here?" Oliver said. "Anyway, Johnny's are filthy. It's all part of the look."

"Well not yet. I want to save them."

He felt for the bag in which he had brought home his old leather-soled lace-ups, produced them, put them on.

"Will you help me with my prep, Lily?"

Oliver and Melissa had settled to a discussion of her television contract and Lily left them, wondering how he would bring the subject around to himself or if he would.

Later, when Sebastian was getting into bed, Lily went back to the sitting-room. She would know right away if anything had been said. Intuition caused her to knock upon the part-open door and it was not misplaced for when she went in they were sitting with a freshly separated, warm-tousled closeness. But when Lily said, "Excuse me," and Melissa said jauntily, "No really, Lily, it's fine, come in," Lily knew he had said nothing yet.

"Oh, Lily, you're blushing. You've caught us kissing before. Come in. Sit down."

But she couldn't, she couldn't. It was all different now. "No thanks, really. I only wanted to say that Sebastian's in bed but if you wanted to go out and celebrate properly, or something, then I'd be happy to stay."

"We don't want to go out, do we, Oliver? Anyway, I am expecting a call."

"I thought it might be nice to go somewhere . . ."

"No. Let's not. There's the champagne to finish and plenty in the kitchen. Really, Lily, you go. And thanks, eh?"

Lily feared to look at Oliver: in the second of a glance Melissa might read collusion. From her solitary place in the heartland of confidences, she said to Melissa, "No need to thank me, you know I love it, but I'll go now, if you're sure, and say goodnight to Sebastian on the way out."

"We can't persuade you to stay to supper?"

"No thank you," Lily said firmly, risking her eyes upon Oliver to let him know what she expected of him. It would be harder for him to tell Melissa about his illness now, but he might still try right there in their own sitting-room with the possibility of the telephone ringing at any minute, exactly as it was ringing now, and Melissa was up and at it with her usual alacrity.

Oliver crossed the room to Lily. In the privacy the moment offered, he said quietly, "You look so tired, Lily. I've never seen you look that way before."

"I am tired."

"Lily . . . ?" Apology and confusion in his eyes. "Lily, what have I done?"

"Just tell her, that's all. Please tell her tonight."

Lily went to Sebastian's room. He was lying in bed with his hands behind his head, the only light being that which came from the passage. Beside him on his pillow were the baseball boots. He moved over to let Lily sit beside him.

"What are you thinking about?" she asked.

"I'll bet he thinks I'm wet."

"Who?"

"Johnny."

"Why on earth should he think that?"

" 'Cause I'm blind."

"Grief, Sebastian, I'm going to get angry with you," and the tone of her voice suggested she already was. "What's come over you with all this ' 'cause I'm blind' business? You did it in the studio this afternoon as well. *That's* wet, talking like that. And while we're at it: what did happen yesterday when I was supposed to collect you? I mean you just went off, no message, no note, nothing."

Sebastian felt for her hand, began to play with her fingers. "I am sorry, honestly. Actually, Johnny did say he was going to write a note but I think he just forgot. And you know how sort of fast and exciting he is. He doesn't wait, does he? And I thought that if I'd hung around he'd go without me."

"And that's being wet too, if you ask me."

"Well, I'm not asking you. You just don't understand."

She changed the subject because she could see in the diminished light that sullen expression returning to his face. "Great boots."

He touched them, confirming their proximity. "I know."

"Tell me why you won't wear them? And it's not about dirtying them, you can't kid me."

"No, it's not. If I tell you, you promise you won't tell Johnny?"

"Promise."

"It's because I can't hear where I'm walking with them, and they sort of dull the feeling of what I'm on. It's the rubber soles. You won't say, will you? He'd be so hurt."

"That's why you've never let me buy them for you?"

"Yes. I thought you knew."

"No I didn't. How would you like to go fishing this weekend?"

"No thanks. I'm helping Johnny finish the bed for Grace. He wants it done before their wedding and it's holidays next week and he said I can spend every day at his studio if he's there. You can come too, if you like."

"I don't think so, thank you. Well, I'll say goodnight, then, Ghastly." She kissed him.

"Goodnight, Hideous." He wrapped his arms around her, then turned over, reaching one hand out from the bedclothes, checking on the boots.

It was a long way from Regent's Park to Notting Hill and Lily walked it, evenly weighted by her purchases and the clothes returned by Johnny Cochrane. She paced away from the world of her people: her Grace, her Sebastian and, although she had thought of neither Oliver nor Melissa as hers in the same sense, their union had formed one of the bastions of permanence. That was different now. She had become a guilty interloper in their marriage, a watching shade.

There was something disproportionate, misplaced, even sick in this wayward emotion of hers when all Oliver had been seeking was solace, support. What she was feeling could not have been born from pity because that was not a quality of hers, although practical compassion was.

She felt every step of the distance she was putting between herself and sleeping Sebastian; stepping away from Grace occupied with Happily Ever After and speaking *we*; and stepping away from them, from Oliver and Melissa, from her success and his groping toward candor.

They would never guess what had come over her and it would die. Wouldn't it, just die? Ignored and unencouraged, these things do.

He would have told Melissa by the next day and it would all be the same again. Or had she, Lily, lost her place among them? And if so who sat on her seat in the Musical Chairs of family relations? Was it Johnny Cochrane with his " 'Sall right, Lil, I'm in control . . ." and his "Wanna tag along . . . ?" Maybe no one was there, perhaps it had simply been removed; removed by Oliver and his "greatest infidelity." Or, more truthfully, had she not relinquished it by her shameless change in feeling for Oliver? Perhaps there was no one but herself to blame for placing her on this eastern reach, this Nod.

Night-time London likes the lonely, the way the streets of cities do; they console with distorted pavements, with office buildings waiting steady for tomorrow, with smaller places dishing out vitality, laughter, doubletalk and violence. Any kind of sentiment can be laundered, lost in those streets, rinsed in the greater senselessness of it all. It is rooms that send one mad, immuring anxieties and insecurities. But she could not walk for ever, she had to arrive and she did; and when she let herself in it was not so bad. Things were arranged with Grace's touch as they had been left that morning.

It was cold inside, for the window was still open wide admitting a howl, this time, of night air. She hung her Gilbert Adrian, Schiaparelli jacket and butler's livery on some of the wire hangers, while the othes still chimed unloaded against the wall. She shut the window to settle them; shut the curtains too; shut it all out. Getting into bed with the bolt of old black Jacquard silk beside her, she ran her fingers over its varied surface for inspiration. Tomorrow she would make it into something beautiful. She would work. She would not think. Oliver was there, though, Oliver in a new light, through another lens, with his huge ailing body storming her senses, but it didn't matter now. There was no one to see or to know what went on in her head alone in the Sinner's Flat.

Chapter 16

SOME TIME DURING THAT NIGHT LILY MADE THE DECISION not to cut into the Jacquard yet but to go away for a few days, drive north in search of markets and sales. Before leaving she drafted a letter to Larry convincingly threatening legal action unless he made some effort toward returning the few items still missing from her collection. He might rightly assume she would never do such a thing to him, friend of years and Angela's son, but she banked on his fear of having much to hide in the druggier aspect of his life. Having done that, she rang Grace whose answering machine picked up the call. Lily left the name of the village in Yorkshire for which she was somewhat arbitrarily heading but no word of how long she intended to stay.

As she drove she tried to force her mind on to her work, expansion perhaps, employing more seamstresses, opening a shop: she had always had that as a goal. Although she tried, it was all less real and important than the figure standing offstage in her mind. There were questions she wished she had asked, like how long would this state of his last? Could they cure it or merely allay it? Might it just fade as it had come? He must have told Melissa by now and she would have asked these questions, taken things in hand; her efficient approach would eclipse his fear and rub out any memory he had of that moment which forever finished the way he and Lily had been together over fifteen years.

When she reached North Yorkshire she stopped to buy the local and regional newspapers before driving on toward her chosen village; however just before she reached it she came to a pub standing in gaunt solitude at the highest point of Swale Dale and went in for lunch. Very soon she was indulging in the intimate anonymity of bar-talk with the locals; starting with the whereabouts of antique and junk shops, working on to themselves, she found out who had been down the pits, in the mills, on the barges, who shepherded in the hills. On discovering there were rooms to let upstairs she decided to go no further.

The rest of that day and all of the next she walked the spongy, giving ground of the moors, rested against drystone walls, moved through flocks of sheep that frothed about her like dingy spume, their bleating racking the silence.

Springtime demurred in that part of England; its warming fragrance was there in the moments when the wind stilled, only to be whipped away leaving just its honey, honey light.

The physical exertion restored Lily and that first night she slept beyond dreams. By the end of the second day her waking mind was freed too. When she entered the pub that evening, hair awry, smiling without knowing, an acquaintance of yesterday hailed her. He was a stick of a man, crooked by years, prickly with tweed, his sharp, shining eyes and beak nose clamped between grubby flat cap and jutting jaw: an apparently irremovable pipe was pushed into the line of his mouth indicated only by a radiant of whiskered wrinkles.

"Ee, lass," he said, "ye look champion now. Cum over 'ere. Want a beer?" Her unconscious smile broke, and he must have seen for he added with concern, "Ye don't afto 'ave one, lass."

"No, I will. Thank you." She leant with him at the bar. "Now tell me more about your grandad, coalheaver on the barges, right?"

"Eee, right . . ." And he settled in to tell, for he had reached the age where his history had the clarity of morning.

Later two contemporaries of his joined them to slip in their own memories of escapades as boys, each in his own style giving way to wild fabrications which, with time and repetition, were hallowed as truth. One would slap another and only have to say, "Do ee remember the time when . . . Do ee? . . . Do ee? . . ." with no further prompt, and they did; their minds colliding and colluding in a long-gone space of time and the three would double up and wheeze like worn-out squeeze boxes until laughter could find its vent.

Younger people in the crowding pub jeered with kindly scepticism: the old boys were obviously giving Lily the works. Head back against the dark oak, high-backed settle where they had ensconced themselves, Lily was laughing too. This was contentment.

As the place filled people stood about holding their drinks; having been pushed accidentally against the table where Lily sat with her companions, a rubicund, middle-aged man turned to nod an apology simultaneously taking in the stranger, the three locals and the accumulation of beer glasses before them. He winked at Lily and, understanding it to be the drink, the talk and her gabbing friends, she winked back. He was indicated as being the local doctor.

The door clattered open, admitting yet another, a woman this time, in a black raincoat. She could hardly be seen through the throng but Lily judged her to be unknown because of the lull in the chat as she worked her way to the bar. Lily went to the bar herself to order a second plate of chips while the three veterans seemed to require no sustenance but beer. Reaching through those seated on high stools at the counter, Lily called to the landlord, "George, more chips please," leaving her hand resting there with a fiver in it to secure attention. "Coming up," George said, but she remained in her awkward position waiting to feel the plate in her hand and pull it back. Instead of that, however, she felt another hand on hers, a woman's hand, small, soft, urgent. Lily saw through the bulks of bodies in front of her that the hand protruded from a cuff of the black raincoat. Initially Lily thought it was an effort to snatch the note from her fingers, until she heard lifted above the general turmoil of voices, "Lily? Lily? Here, over here."

Lily edged forward until she touched the bar, then craned to the left where the hand came from. Down past elbows, shoulders, the battery of glasses, she saw, so familiar as to be almost abstract in these strange surroundings, Melissa's face.

It took a minute or two to push behind the people and find her, pale, weary, still unserved and hot in her raincoat. She snatched Lily's arm. "Thank God I've found you, Lily. I wasn't expecting you to be here and just came in for directions. I was going to look for you in Reeth. Grace said you would be staying there."

"Tell me what's happened? Is it Sebastian? Is it Grace? Is it . . ." She could not say Oliver's name.

"No, everybody's all right. It's not that sort of thing. Really."

"But how would you have found me in Reeth? I didn't know myself where I'd be."

"Michelin . . ." she held up the red book, almost bashful at

her unfailing logic. "There's not much there. I'd have asked at
every one."

Lily's fear having subsided, oblique anger was taking its place.
"Why didn't you just ring round. No need to come all this way,
surely?"

"I couldn't ring. I had to talk to you urgently, I have to. But
please not here, somewhere quiet. Where are you staying then?"

"Upstairs. Go into the lobby and I'll join you in a second."

The disquiet and anguish she had slept and walked away over
the past two days now fell back on her, hating to relinquish
this cheery fellowship for the grave intensity promised in Melissa's face, she eased over to the squeeze-boxes who were tilted
and cackling once more, no doubt over another boyhood mis-
demeanor. "Hey chaps, I've got to go. See you tomorrow,
maybe."

They raised three hands in surprised farewell, looked askance
at one another, shrugged, continued where they had left off.

"Come on," Lily said to Melissa in the narrow, stale, tobacco-
brown passage, "up here." She ascended the hugger-mugger
stairs and Melissa followed uncharacteristically humble and acquiescent: so much so that Lily stopped halfway to look down
at her just one step behind and below. Melissa lifted her head
to meet Lily's and let herself be seen defenses down. Her tan
eyes, usually so alive with inquiry and interest, were slowed
with doubt and something else harder to ascertain; her neat,
busy red mouth screwed to hardly more than a dot; her hair in
dank waves.

Lily turned away and continued to the upper passage identical
to the lower and opened one of the four doors there. Inside were
two unusually tall, wood-framed single beds, each loaded with
a full bosom of floral quilted eiderdown. Although the carpet
was swirled with gold and orange, and the curtains (with no
more substance than a handkerchief) were dark green, the room
still contrived to be a continuation of the brown outside the door.
Apart from the beds, a chest of drawers, a basin in the corner,
there was no other furniture. One picture hung impartially between the beds, its scene depicting the surrounding hill with
half-hearted redolence.

Melissa entered, sat herself on the side of a bed with not even
a cursory glance for the absent chair. She pulled off her raincoat
to let it fall about her, revealing the jeans and sweater she always
favored at home. Reaching into her large saggy, leather bag, she
produced a bottle of brandy. The effort seemed to finish her for

she sat looking at it in her lap. Lily took two mugs from beside the basin, opened the bottle and poured. Handing a mug to Melissa, she said, "So . . . ?" and was a little shocked at an unintended impatience in her voice. Melissa was clearly abject. The natural thing to do would, surely, be to place an arm about her but, without knowing why, Lily could not do that; she could only amend her invitation to speak. "What's the matter, Melissa? Do tell me," adding, "now you've come all this way," and regretting it.

"You're annoyed, aren't you? It's an invasion, I suppose, me coming like this without ringing or anything." That was not a question, merely an acknowledgment, but when she went on quickly, "Oh, my goodness, are you with a boyfriend, I hadn't thought of that, it never occurred to me?" it was a question.

Lily's anger accumulated. "I came here to be alone."

"Not hunting around like you usually do?"

"That too."

Melissa peered and reached into her bag again, produced a packet of cigarettes, shook one out and bag-scrabbled once more for a lighter. It all took time and Lily stood near wondering.

"It's about Oliver," Melissa said, finally anchored with the cigarette, eyes down on her drink, her feet not quite touching the floor beneath the bed.

Fear exploded in Lily and she lunged at Melissa, gripping her upper arm. "You said everyone was all right. He's not dead? He couldn't have died?"

Melissa stared at Lily, some of that fiercely intelligent vitality returning to her eyes. Calmly she said, "Why do you ask that? Why should he have died?"

The response proved he was alive: you don't fence when announcing a death, not if the other has relieved you of your task by a guess. Lily retreated to the window. People were departing below, bending from the rain: the single forlorn yard-light setting the backs of trooping heads and shoulders in relief upon the night. The sound of the feet on the gravel, the convivial good-byes, the slamming of car doors, starting of engines all chiseled into the echoing air.

"Lily?" Melissa called to bring back her attention, obviously quite lost, and to Lily the voice came surprisingly close, almost as though it were inside her head. Lily turned to see Melissa put her hand over her eyes. The necessity to speak, the import of what she was about to say had apparently driven away any suspicion, and inclining her head, artless, unpracticed in the act, she began to cry. "He's sick, Lily, very sick."

Lily prepared to perform a contemptible show of ignorance, ask some questions to which she knew the answers, before she could ask the essential, the obvious question. So she went to Melissa, placed about her that belated arm and Melissa, cool, bright, brilliant Melissa, independent, self-assured, turned her head and wept on Lily's shoulder.

The emotion shortly ebbed and Melissa dammed it finally with, "There, there, that's enough of that. All over now, not like me at all, as you know." Back to the bag for a handkerchief this time, which having wiped her face, she proceeded to shred. "Listen and I'll explain," she said. Lily would be relieved of questions after all.

"On Friday after you left we talked for ages about my show and we read through my contract and by then I was flaked so I went to bed. He said he'd come in a minute. When I woke later he'd obviously been in bed, I could see by the blankets, but he wasn't there anymore. I waited a bit then went to look for him.

"I could hear him walking up and down in the sitting-room even before I opened the door. I suppose I looked in quietly, although I didn't intend that, and I saw him. He had stopped the pacing and was standing naked in the middle of the room with his back to me. I could see his hands were sort of gyrating. I mean it was only a small movement but it was the only movement in the room just then, and it was odd somehow. Do you know what I thought he was doing?" She turned to look at Lily close beside her on the bed, as though to check that she was ready for it and decided she was not, for she went on, "I can't tell you." She looked away but changed her mind. "No, I will tell you. I thought he was masturbating. Standing up doing that. That's what it looked like. I must have sounded outraged when I shouted at him and it gave him a terrible shock and in turning round he fell over. That was odd, too, really, and made me think he was drunk. So there he was naked on the floor and me standing above him. I don't know what came over me but that's what I thought he was doing, there was no doubt in my mind. And right in the middle of our sitting-room. I mean his hands were down there and kind of jerking; it seemed obvious. 'Please leave me alone,' he said from where he was at my feet and I said something like, 'What the fuck do you think you're doing?' And, God forgive me, he began to cry; I don't mean properly. I can't even explain how, but he was and I knew it and didn't

stop to think.'' The dam on emotion began to crack but she
stopped it up by throwing her head back, blinking at the ceiling,
heaving her breath. ''So . . . well, there we were: him naked
on the floor and me over him for all the world like some bloody
matron catching out a boy. 'I'm sick, Melissa,' he said, 'I'm
sick and I'm frightened.' 'Yes,' I said, 'you certainly are sick,
doing that in the middle of our sitting-room.' Dear God, one
could almost laugh.''

Lily had removed her arm from Melissa's shoulder to her hand
which she clutched while facing away and down, her features
contorted. Melissa's other hand reached over Lily's, the con-
soled now consoling, but she continued with the savage force of
recollection.

'' 'Doing what?' he said from down there like a great baby
at my feet. 'Wanking,' I said, 'I saw you.' Well, he altered then.
The strange kind of crying, which was not crying at all, stopped
and he was . . . oh . . . oh furious, but terribly contained and
quietly so. If I didn't know him better, I'd have thought he was
going to hit me. But you know what, Lily? I've seen that look
in his face before, these past weeks. And other things too, physical things, but simply didn't register them on any upper level.
We get so busy with our work we're often too tired to talk, really
talk.

''He got up then, very, very slowly. I was still thinking he
must be drunk, it was all such an effort for him. And he stood
in front of me and to my horror he was still doing it, that movement. But I could see then he wasn't touching himself at all. His
hand was just sort of jerking. I thought he was making fun of
me. 'Stop it,' I said. 'I can't,' he said, very very calmly, 'I can't
stop it, Melissa.'

''Lily?'' Lily was still hunched and facing away. ''Lily?'' she
said again; Lily nodded stiffly. ''Lily, he's terribly ill.''

The reiteration of the hideous scene appeared to restore Melissa in some part, as the repeated confrontation of any horror
can. It was diluted for her in the sharing; perhaps if she told
twenty people she might reduce the whole memory to trivia.

Lily had to retrieve her imagination from that room she knew
so well with its green plants, polished boarded floor and Oliver's
African treasures. She had to leave him standing naked and
shaking before Melissa. A question was due, Melissa was waiting for one before she could go on.

''So what did you do?'' Her voice fractured. Not the ideal
question. What she wanted to ask was: Did you hold him? Did

you take his shaking hands and pull them to you? Did you reach up to his shoulders then because you would have to, wouldn't you, you who are so little in comparison with him? Did you reach up and lay your head against his naked breast and feel his warmth on your face? And hear the deep-going thud of his heart? Were you unclothed from bed as he was? Did you press your body hard on his? Did your shame make you slide to your knees with your arms around his long, large legs placing yourself below him as he'd just been below you? And on your knees with your mouth in the heat of his groin did you make it all right, did you redress the balance of pride? Did you? Did you make love with him? "What did you do?"

"I got him his dressing-gown."

"And?" Because there was something unsaid, with them there, like an ache in the room.

"We talked for what remained of the night. He gave me all the details he knows at the moment. It's not much. It's one of those things with no given course. He's on drugs already. You see you'd be too young to remember but when he was in Africa he got very ill with a brain fever; something called *Encephalitis lethargica*. He was unconscious for ages. The specialist says it's that, it can come back, it seems, but different. Apparently, if he has a surge of adrenaline the symptoms go for a bit, just while he's excited, and they say, too, that . . ." All the facts, all the facts. She went on at length, fervent, hectic until Lily could bear it no more and cut through the details and terminology.

"Melissa?"

". . . but if he leaves off coffee and tea, alcohol, cigarettes, red meat, all dairy products and certain other foods, I checked this at the library on Saturday, there would definitely be . . ."

"Melissa?"

"What?"

"Where is he now?"

"At home," glancing at her watch, "in bed, I expect."

At last the essential obvious question. "What are you doing here? Why have you come?"

There was a long pause before Melissa uttered an involuntary "Ah . . ." as though something had stabbed at her and she went back to work on that dam: took deep breaths, another cigarette, lit it, cupped her hands over her face. Another "Ah . . ." was for a while all she could manage and still keep control.

She got up from the bed, walked the room staring at the floor. Arms outstretched she squared her hands in front of her as though

centering a block of print and began, "After he'd told me . . ."
but rejected that prologue. Waiting a moment she tried again.
"The thing is . . ." leveling with one hand this time. Letting
out a shuddering groan, she gave it up and fell against the wall,
hiding her face in her elbow stretched above her head and stayed
there sobbing.

Lily went over to her, turned her, embraced her, which Melissa allowed with unaffected simplicity, then she held Lily's
arms so as to distance herself a little, facing Lily directly, head
tilted up to Lily's height, fingers pressing hard into Lily's flesh
as she spoke.

"After he'd told me and I'd got his dressing-gown and we sat
down and we talked, after all that he put his hand on me, rather
shyly . . . Oh, I don't know what I felt through the second of
that touch, but, yes, it was shy and timid and ashamed. I mean
I knew he wanted something of the sort from the start. I could
see he was longing for physical comfort. But I can't do it,
Lily . . ." Her eyes were wide with the shock of admission. "I
can't bear to touch him or have him touch me, because along
with those other things I felt through his hand I felt the shaking,
his infirmity. I wanted to be sick, to throw up. I jumped away
from him. 'Stop it,' I shouted. 'Don't touch me.' I'd said it
before I could stop myself. I can't help it, Lily. It's a deep, deep
thing in me. And he said, 'Please, Melissa.' He just said that.
Not pleading. It was dignified. But he knows how I am. You see
he's understood for years how close contact, physical contact,
with disability affects me. It's something I can't control.

"After that we pretended he had no physical need of me and
that I had no inadequacy. This last day and a half we've been
circling each other pretending and being polite. I'd see him taking a pill: 'All right?' I'd say; 'Fine,' he'd say. And then I'd
catch him looking at me and he'd catch me looking at him and
all the unspoken was said without a word."

Her speech came with speed and passion and Lily's quiet
strong voice was in curious contrast. "Melissa, it's happened
now. He's got it. You know about it. You're together. You have
to face it, don't you? The greater ordeal, surely, is his, not
yours?"

"You just don't see, do you?" She had moved away and was
pointing, accusing, menacing, brinking on hysteria. "You, of
all people. I was certain you'd understand. It's the only reason
I came. You understood before. You helped before."

"What do you mean?"

"With Sebastian, blast it. You helped me then during those Godforsaken months, years even. All I ever wanted was a healthy, normal baby. It didn't have to be clever or good-looking. And what did God send me? A little groping baby . . ."

"Don't."

". . . and I said to Oliver long before Sebastian was born, 'If it's not right,' I said, 'it'll have to go. I'll have an abortion.' But the amniocentesis test showed all was fine. Oh yes, fine. But even then, just in case, I made him swear that if by any chance the baby was not normal we wouldn't keep it. Have it adopted. And what happened, eh? What happened . . . ?" Still pointing, head shaking, with the power of her voice undiminished, "Born bleeding eyeless. Dear God. 'Well, that's it. He's wrong,' I said, 'I won't keep him.' But Oliver said he wasn't wrong, he was normal but just blind. Blind didn't count. He forced me to keep him."

"But you love him. You *do* love him."

The pointing finger was dropped, she closed her eyes. "Oh, I love him. I worship him, but, Lily, I can't bear him. The shuffling, the bumping into things . . ."

"Hardly ever."

"No, but sometimes. And that abnormal expression on his face; that gaping mouth . . ."

"I can't listen to this."

"No, because what I'm admitting about myself is grotesque. If they knew, those who associate my name with caring for the vulnerable in this world, just think what a sham I'd look. I know that really I'm trying to absolve myself by dealing in general with what I can't handle in the specific. Don't think I'm proud of it. If I worked as I do from now until the end of time it would never make up for not holding Sebastian a whole year after he was born, or taking Oliver in my arms last Thursday night. You were the only person in this world I could talk to about it. I thought you sensed how I was, understood and that's why you took over so much."

"I 'took over,' as you put it, because at first I was curious about Sebastian, as any twelve-year-old girl would be about a baby, and I quickly grew to love him. Everything I've ever done for him has been because of that, nothing to do with helping you."

"Well do it again, Lily," now an impassioned whisper, "*please*. Do it for Oliver this time."

Lily gripped the bar at the foot of the bed where she stood as though to restrain herself, for she was leaning on past her arms toward Melissa. Her voice was superficially cold, steady, but the alarm signal was pitching and lurching in her words. "Now just listen to me. If I'd thought way back then in my little girl's head that I was helping you away from confronting your feelings about Sebastian, or really looking after him, I don't think I'd have been around as I was. And what is it you're asking now, actually? I mean, what is this? Pass the Parcel with your husband as the prize in the middle of the wrappings . . . ?"

"Please . . ."

"What precisely am I supposed to do? Nappies, if he becomes incontinent, like I did for Sebastian when he was a baby? Feeding with bottles . . . ?"

"You don't want to understand . . ."

". . . potties and wiping bottoms? Doesn't he remain an adult, a sensitive, proud man? Could you possibly be asking me to hold him for you? Feeling the shaking you can't bear? Take him to bed, even?"

"You're disgusting."

"Disgusting? Oh, sorry. My duties would stop at sex, yes? He will just have to learn to do without that. Serves him right for having this . . . this whatever-you-call-it. Have you really thought it through, Melissa? Does he know you're here?"

"Of course not. I had to come to Leeds for my show anyway."

"The show, naturally. Well I decline your request, so what will you do now? Tout him about until you find someone to say yes to whatever it is you're asking? Will he have any say in this? Is he to be left any dignity?"

"Why are you like this, Lily? I don't understand what I've done to you to deserve it. I thought we were friends. I've confided in you things only Oliver knows, things I admit I'm ashamed of, and you attack me. Is your gentleness for Sebastian and Grace only? Nothing for Oliver, nothing for me?"

"You ask too much, and yet you're asking nothing at all, because what you want can't be done by anybody. You want me to hide his sickness, hide the ugliness, the embarrassment and leave you the man he was. Well, I can't, and if I could it wouldn't be for me to do. Go away and face it, Melissa."

Throughout Melissa had been standing, swaying back, fending off the words with spread hands at waist level; now she collapsed on the side of the bed, head sunk, hands clasped between her knees.

Lily would not sit but remained still and fortified against any renewed, rearranged approach.

"I didn't mean it to be like this," Melissa said, "or to come to ask what it seems I've asked. What a mess. I just wanted to talk to someone. I'm not big on close friends."

"There's Oliver. There's Sebastian. Grace."

"Oliver doesn't want Grace to know yet, he doesn't want to spoil her happiness and I don't want Sebastian to know. I mean it's a visual disease. He won't see the symptoms. He's no way of knowing."

"I wouldn't be so sure."

"I don't remember ever making such a fool of myself."

A spring of tenderness rose weak but steady in Lily. "And you haven't now. I'm sorry if I sounded hard. It's ghastly and I guess we'll all react in different ways."

"You don't ever, do you?"

"Ever what?"

"Make a fool of yourself."

Of all they might be discussing this seemed the least necessary but it had some unfathomable importance to Melissa and made Lily think of Larry, Mona's, her collection and of her unforeseen, baseless desire for this woman's husband, which had driven her to this remote spot. She said with feeling, "Often, often."

"You're right: I didn't think out what I was asking. You will be the same, won't you? Come round and be with Sebastian and us when we're at home. If you don't anymore it'll all be my fault."

"Where's Sebastian been since Oliver told you? How did you hide the tension from him?"

"He's been with Johnny at the studio almost all the time. I think Grace was there too. Sebastian and Johnny are mad about each other at the moment. They'll be together all this week during Sebastian's holiday, working on the bed. Thank God for Johnny." Lily intended to agree but was somehow too late and Melissa continued, "Can I stay, Lily? I'm too tired to go on tonight."

"Yes, of course you can stay."

"And in the morning we'll pretend I haven't been so ridiculous and everything will be just how it was."

Lily laughed. "Know what? You sound exactly like Grace. That's just what she would say."

With a blue smile, Melissa said, "Grace is a wise woman in

her way, isn't she? But, you see, the difference is that Grace would say it and believe it and, in believing it, make it true. Whereas when I say it, we both know, you and I, that it's only words. I don't have the kind of imagination that makes things come true, I've only intellect and it's not worth a twopenny damn.''

Melissa curled on to the bed and, even before Lily had covered her with the other eiderdown, she slept.

Chapter 17

IT WAS DAWN OF THE FOLLOWING DAY BEFORE THE ROUND-about of remorse, indecision, conviction, doubt began to slow. Lily heard the cows trudging parlorward with a sound like locomotive bellows, the draymen arriving to rattle metal-barreled ale to the cellar, then finally she slept. When she awoke Melissa had left.

It would have been comforting to pretend for a while the visit had never taken place but that was made impossible by the stale cigarette smoke, the tooth mugs, the brandy bottle and the crush of eiderdown and pillow on the next bed. There was a scrap of paper on the chest of drawers reading, "Thank you, Lily. Melissa." Quite what for was beyond her because the only thing standing in the rubble of her night's thought was her cruelty, for which any just cause had misted away.

Her visit was ruined. She took one last walk, and found her composure lay forever ahead on the next hill. She gave up and returned to London.

A few days later, with designs for the Jacquard advanced and cutting begun, Lily paused in her work. She considered that although calm appeared to be restored she was nonetheless in a state of apprehension. Whenever the telephone rang she lurched to answer it and none of the various voices dispelled her sense of disquiet. Even opening her mail she felt stifled agitation. She received an envelope from Larry containing a generous check and told herself then that this nonsense would depart but it didn't. She remained on subliminal alert. Self-deception, however, is possible for just so long: she knew. She knew all right and was glad when Grace telephoned to request Lily's company while collecting her wedding dress. Only after several Sure-it's-not-a-bore's and Promise-you're-not-too-busy's did Lily convince Grace of the pleasure it would give her.

When they met at a coffee shop Grace was still bathed in that tranquil glow of happiness but it was overlayed by a fervor, a haste in all she said and did, as though she felt herself to be a sieve for the passage of time and she was using jim-jam industry to stop up the holes.

"Why the hurry, Grace? Relax."

"But, darling, don't you see? There's so much to do, to buy and be seen to. And it's only ten days. Think of it: ten days and Johno and I will be man and wife. So drink up your coffee and come and see my dress. It's wonderful. Oh I hope you love it."

However, at the shop, when she put on something stiff, satin and turquoise, Grace was distraught. "It's not right at all, Lily. It's not . . . well . . . it's not *Johno*. Whatever made me say yes to satin and turquoise?"

At first Lily and the tall, soft-voiced Flemish designer, with his fine suit, slender hands and beautiful young male assistant, tried to laugh Grace through until they saw she was serious. Naturally "But it's not Johnny who is wearing it" was no good.

"He has an image of me, you see. When a man loves a woman, he does, doesn't he? And I don't want to step out of that image, not even for a moment, but especially on our wedding day. Actually I'm still not quite sure what his image is but it's not this. This is . . . oh, forgive me, Wim, but this is aging."

They left Wim gallantly reserving his dejection and his bill—"No, Mrs. Teape, not at all, there will be other occasions, other dresses"—and they proceeded down Knightsbridge, up Bond Street and made dashes to out-of-the-way shops as the day drew on.

Nothing was going to be right, be "Johno." Hopelessly Lily suggested that Johnny Cochrane come with Grace instead of herself. "But it must be a surprise, Lily, you do see that, don't you?"

When it appeared all inspiration and energy had gone, they happened upon an inauspicious-looking leather shop, on the way to somewhere quite different. Inside they found a skirt and jacket made from the flimsiest stroke of suede in a murmur of lilac. To Lily's relief it was judged not only to be "Johno" but was also very Grace.

"Darling, are you busy tonight? Why not come back with me? We're having supper with Oliver and Melissa. It would be so nice to be all together."

So she could see him, as easy as that. Say "yes" and go, just as she'd often dined there. But it would be settled between them, Oliver and Melissa, while nothing was settled in herself. "Not this time, thank you. How is he?"

"Who?"

"Oliver."

"Oliver? Well, fine. Why? Actually, I've hardly seen him but you know Oliver's always the same."

"Yes."

They agreed the wedding lunch would be at their usual Italian restaurant, that Lily would arrange it, and that, other than Oliver, Melissa and Sebastian, the only guests would be Angela and Dennis Little. Then it quickly became apparent that Grace, for all her activity, had made very few practical arrangements.

"Why don't you leave it all to me?" Lily said. "I don't just mean the restaurant but the other things too?"

"But what other things, darling? I mean Johno's booked our flights to Italy for after lunch, and a hotel in Florence. Is there anything else, do you think?"

"Yes, a few things. Leave it to me."

"All right, but remember, we do want it small, Johno and I. Nothing showy. No silly announcements or anything."

"Rely on me."

How changed Grace was, how mature in her approach. Where was all the "And the world will know I'm loved again, they'll know because I'll tell them . . . show them"? Perhaps she understood that it required no statement, that her appearance alone was that of a loved woman.

They parted, but before two yards were between them Grace called, "Oh Lily . . . Lily wait." Lily walked back to her. "Johno says we must spend the last day and night apart, that it's bad luck not to. Meet at the Register Office, he says. I'm to stay somewhere wonderful and he'll stay at the flat. So I've booked a room at the Berkeley. Will you come with me, Lily? I won't want to be alone and there's no one I'd want more than you."

" 'Course I will. I'd love to."

"Meet you there Friday week then, about six?"

"Can't wait. Hen party for two."

Lily immersed herself in preparations for the wedding lunch: booked a part of the restaurant that was a little separate, but not so much as to diminish the pleasure of lunching out; she planned the menu; organized flowers at both Register Office and restaurant, and two chauffeur-driven cars from the former to the latter, with yet another to take Grace and Johnny Cochrane to the airport. She also arranged for a small wedding cake.

During those ten days she tried to confront the restlessness in herself: she wanted to see or speak to Oliver, ascertain his state of mind, but she did not trust her motives. For whose sake did she want that? For his? Seriously. For hers, then? For them both? She thought of any number of reasons to go round to his studio or just to ring. In the end she could bring herself to do neither. She would wait to see them at the Register Office, at the lunch afterwards, and would judge what kind of understanding he had forged with Melissa. She would see Melissa coping, the panic in his eyes allayed and there would be no possible excuse to see him alone.

Lily half-expected Grace to be ringing from time to time with small crises and concerns but that did not happen; and when she arrived at the hotel the night before the wedding it was a composed, but pleasantly exhilarated Grace that greeted her.

"Lily dear, you've arrived." Grace stood with her back to the window framing the evening, a sheer curtain softening the view, double-glazing doing the same for the unending shunt of London traffic. Her scent took the edge off the anonymous snuff of carpet and new paint. Her wedding suit hung on the wardrobe door, her nightdress lay on the bed.

"And you've arrived too," Lily said. "This is it at last, isn't it? I'm so happy for you, Grace. I know it'll all be just as you want it to be. Here." She handed Grace a package bound by silver and gold strings with a star sewn on the end of each one.

"It's too beautiful to open. You make an art out of all the little things of life, don't you? You always have . . ." This last she said wistfully.

Having unwrapped it with reverence she held up a small brass box. Her eyes rested inquiringly on Lily, a trace of a smile. She opened it. The hoarse, miniature sound of a musical box began. Head to one side, concentrating, Grace then joined words to the tune of "The Way You Look Tonight," her voice a trifle unsteady.

"Thank you, thank you, darling. I shan't ask you how you found it. It must have been by magic. Come here." She placed her hands on Lily's shoulders, then removed one to touch her cheek. "You've been everything to me for so long. Thank you for that too. And for letting me bring you up. I hope I've done it right.'' Just in time, before her own tears became inevitable, Grace threw her hands in the air, spun round on one foot and said, ''And now, lovey, we're going to have some fun. Tell you what I thought: room service, eh? A delicious dinner up here?''

Lily kicked off her shoes, threw herself on one of the beds. ''Fabulous. That's what I hoped you'd say.'' One of their mutual delights had always been room service in hotels like this one.

''And guess what else? I've brought our photograph albums. All the way back to when you were six. We'll have an evening reminiscing, that's what one does do on a wedding night, doesn't one?''

''One does.''

They giggled away some hours with: ''And look, remember being there?'' ''Remember him, Lily? The old man who took a fancy to you and followed you all round Nice until I warned him off. Polish Count, wasn't he?'' Grace even looked with equanimity upon a photograph of Jaime de Caberro which had miraculously survived the holocaust of his image eleven years earlier. ''Look at him. Handsome, but what a vain and silly man he was. Whatever did I see in him . . . ?'' Eclipsing him with a flip of the heavy cardboard page, she scrutinized another set of forgotten faces, showing such transient, half-completed expressions as are caught by snapshots.

When they had finished dinner, pushed aside the white-clothed trolley, Grace watched Lily. Hesitant about the possible reaction, she began, ''Lily . . . there's something I forgot to tell you. I've known a couple of weeks and it went right out of my head. I'm rather ashamed. You see the solicitors wrote to me to say that old Prudence Teape died. But, darling, I *couldn't* mind, you know. For one thing she was fearfully old but I had written to her every year with photos of you and saying how you were getting on. Not once did they respond in all these years. Old Henry Teape's sold up and gone to life in a supervised flat, one for the elderly. You're not upset, are you?''

''Honestly, I don't even remember their faces. But I do remember the feel of being there. No details but the gray, the cold, the quiet. Especially the quiet, and I remember you, on a sofa, holding me.''

''Lily?''

''Yes?''

''What is it?''

''What do you mean?''

"Each time we stop talking I watch your face alter. I see a distress there I've never seen before. Why?"

"It's really nothing," she said, looking away to hide that altering face.

Grace reached to cover Lily's hand. "Yes, dear, I understand. The nothings are always the worst, aren't they?"

It's a glum place, a Register Office, and efforts to relieve it die with the kiss of bureaucracy. The flowers Lily had arranged and delivered the day before had been lined indifferently against the wall beneath a sign reading "No Confetti to be Thrown Inside or Outside of this Building."

Oliver, Melissa and Sebastian were already there. Oliver went, hands out, to greet Grace. "Hello Grace. Happy day, eh?" Over her shoulder to Lily he said, "Hi there, want a . . ." He did not finish and Lily tried to acknowledge the half-greeting without facing him.

I won't look. I won't see his face or let him see mine in case it tells tales on me, the way it did to Grace last night. Lily went to stand beside Sebastian, awkward in his baseball boots.

"You do look lovely, Grace," Melissa said, "and what a pretty outfit. Did you help to choose that, Lily?" Her eyes arrested Lily's with cloudless candor. There had been no pub in Yorkshire.

Dennis Little and Angela arrived to participate in the ritual fussing over Grace who accepted it all with something akin to amusement; for once she seemed to require no reassurance, but everyone else felt self-conscious, each wondering whether the others shared the particular fear. After all, though, where was he? Johnny Cochrane?

It was Grace who admired the flowers, smiled, exchanged greetings with the other wedding group due after her ceremony and gathered early for their fifteen-minute slot of civil espousal.

The brass handle on the inner door of the waiting-room moved downward, pressed from the inside; all looked instinctively toward it opening. A very young couple came in. He had an insignificant neck rising, skinny, out of a ring of overlarge important-looking collar. He was spotty and looked seventeen; she the same and looking younger still. They moved timidly through the quiet and the eyes while he held her hand, gently drawing her on behind him, as, no doubt, he intended to do through life. Before they passed out of the door on the other side

of the waiting-room, Grace called, "Good luck," which un-
corked general goodwill and others did the same.

The young man's pallor turned to the color of his spots.
"Thank you very much. Most kind . . . Really very kind . . .
the same to you as well." It was clearly more of a Te Deum
than he had ever expected.

"Mr. Cochrane? Mrs. Teape?" At the inside door stood a
male figure with the unsettling quality of seeming to be an entirely empty suit.

Dennis Little, Angela and Melissa were all looking watch-
wards; Oliver went to stand near Grace. "We're not quite all
here yet."

"It *is* eleven-fifteen," the suit said.

Grace leant forward from where she was sitting, lifting her
hand as though indicating an unspotted vacant seat on a crowded
bus. "Would you care to . . . ?" addressing the other group.

"What? Do us first then?" The aging Teddy boy with a sau-
sage of greased hair over his forehead, draped jacket, crêpe-
soled shoes like submarines, said to Grace, "Ta very much,
duck. Come along Daisy. In for a penny, in for a pound." He
maneuvered her before him, as though she were a porcelain
figurine, dressed all in white, his massive bride, made more so
by advanced pregnancy. The party of six disappeared through
the door.

Angela went to the window. Melissa tidied Sebastian's shirt,
Dennis Little raised his eyebrows to Oliver, Lily sat near Grace,
thought she might take her hand, decided not to. Three eternal
minutes passed thus until Grace said serenely, "Will you all
please stop it?"

"What?" they murmured, quietly confused.

"Stop thinking he won't come, because he will, you see. I
know you think he won't, but he will." There was nothing in
her voice to suggest she was insisting on the unlikely. She really
believed.

No more was said, the vestige of her words straggling in the
deadly wait.

At last there was a rush and slam of the outside doors; stamping, banging, a shout. Johnny Cochrane was with them. For a
carefully judged moment he stood with his arms raised to display himself, to be admired, for admiration was due: he wore a
supremely tailored suit, white silk shirt, rich but discreetly pat-
terned silk tie; and baseball boots.

"Hey, hey, hey," he said when their exclamations had subsided. "There she is, my Gracie. My lady. My wife. Give us a kiss, girl."

When Mr. and Mrs. Johnny Cochrane entered the restaurant there was a cheer from some of those friends who knew today was The Day, had heard the plan and booked themselves tables just to see . . . well, just to see. The waiters led the party through the restaurant with light-hearted flourish and even strangers watched as they passed exuding their happiness. Such a very handsome young man; and the lady with him, beautiful, interesting. Not his wife, surely? Really? Fancy.

Johnny Cochrane insisted Grace sit on his right and Sebastian on his left. Lily sat between Sebastian and Dennis Little. It fell that Oliver was opposite Lily between Grace and Angela. As the momentum of the festivity gathered and others came up to congratulate the couple, Lily allowed herself to regard Oliver. For all that she had not properly seen him at the Register Office, she had been aware of his energy and of no apparent ailing. Now she saw he was tired. If no one was requiring his attention he fell into introspection, not vacant, but cocking his head as though a voice outside their environment was nagging him. When he was called into the conversation he came to quickly and convincingly.

"Lily? I say, Lily?" It was she who was caught out, inattentive. Dennis Little was talking to her. "You were miles away. Did your friend find you?"

"What friend?"

"Well I say 'friend.' I don't even know if you know her, but a girl came to my gallery asking for you."

"Why to your gallery?"

"Search me. She was a poor little thing, wretched-looking. She asked for you. I was a bit surprised myself but I gave her your address. I hope that was all right?"

"Yes. I wonder who it was . . . ?" She was about to ask for more details when Grace jumped to her feet with a screech, jerking the table, brushing at her suede skirt over which red wine was spilt. Oliver was half-raised apparently trying to re-stand the fallen bottle with a violent erratic thrust of his arm. Every time he succeeded he knocked it over again with an opposite, involuntary lurch.

"Oliver? Oliver, what are you trying to do?" Grace was saying.

"Daddy? Daddy? Are you all right?"

Dennis Little reached over, took the bottle from Oliver and gestured to a waiter to clear the mess. All the time his eyes were fixed on Oliver as though with sudden enlightenment, watching him caught in the action of pouring and straightening a bottle he no longer held.

"You stupid clot," Melissa burst out, "look what you've done to Grace's skirt. It's ruined . . . it's . . ."

"Stop it, Melissa," Angela said softly. "It's only an accident. Poor Oliver."

When she saw everyone at the table was staring at her, Melissa hid her face, said, "Oh, God . . . I'm sorry . . . but I just can't bear it . . . I can't." She left the table in a hurry.

Grace turned her stare to Oliver, in her eyes the same dawning as had been in Dennis Little's. "Oliver, dear?" placing her hand on his arm.

Released now from his trap of motion, he shook his head. "I'm really very sorry, Grace. I've ruined your lovely skirt. Melissa's right. I'm a clot."

"It's nothing, nothing at all," Grace said slowly, "but you . . . ?" She knew she could not go on, however. This was not the time, not the place.

Throughout Lily had been perfectly still watching Oliver, watching Melissa. She made a decision and having done so felt a greater peace and strength than she had felt in days. While she remained thus, letting the others resettle on to the train of celebration, a small, rough hand felt for hers in her lap. She took it, held it, looked to her right. Sebastian's head was forced back, oscillating almost imperceptibly, lips drawn hard in over his teeth.

"It's all right, darling. Don't worry," she said, but he did not release her hand.

There was something of the thespian in both Oliver and Grace, for it was entirely due to Oliver's following performance that gaiety was completely restored. Having joked away the problem with his arm, blaming it on a pulled muscle, he became his easy self. When Melissa returned she too joined in with the "pulled muscle" number saying, "Poor Oliver, it's been beastly for him."

It helped, of course, that everyone wanted their pleasure re-established and contributed their own effort. They ate, they drank, they laughed. That little hand left Lily's. The lunch was a success and all were charmed by the tiny wedding cake when that was produced.

Rocking back, arms stretched expansively around Grace's chair to the right, Sebastian's to the left, Johnny Cochrane said in a low voice to Lily, ''Well, Lil. Here I am then, eh? Member of the family, step-uncle, what? Didn't I think I'd come through, did yer?'' There was an edge to his voice.

'' 'Course I did. Don't be silly,'' but not convincing, ''and anyway, like you say: you have and I'm really happy for you both.''

''Can't kid me, girl. I know what's in your head, see? It's this knack I have, like I know people, feel 'em, don't I? Take old Olly . . .''

''Olly? . . . You can't call him Olly.''

''Sorry. Keep your hair on, Oliver . . . he's sick as a parrot.''

''Not now, please . . .'' Her eyes indicated Sebastian leaning forward between them.

''No, well . . .'' Still rocking back on his chair, he surveyed the party around the table and his expression was the one of casual impudence she had seen before. It was, indeed, as though he could see into their heads and was looking coldly at the weaknesses, vulnerabilities they struggled to conceal. With his eyes upon them in that manner, each became unwittingly futile. Lily was absorbed in consideration of his face with no thought formulated, just a feeling, the same one she had had about him before. Yet hardly had it touched her than he turned, smiled, winked delightfully, ingenuously, blotting out all doubt. Once again she was left feeling private guilt for being the one to read chicanery into happiness.

When it was time to go to the airport Johnny Cochrane said, ''Come too, the lot of you, why don't you?''

They declined except Sebastian. ''Oh please, please let me. I so want to see you off, Johnny.''

So Lily and Sebastian went in the car with Grace and Johnny Cochrane. There was little time before they had to go through to the departure lounge. Grace took Lily's hand. ''Well, my love, we've done our goodbye's, haven't we? And either we'll be back if we don't find somewhere, or else you'll come out and see us. And you will, won't you?''

''Like a shot.''

''Check the flat, darling, see Johno's left nothing on. Take the albums back if you don't want to keep them.''

''I'll go round there now with Sebastian. Don't worry. Come on, Sebastian, I think we'll go now.''

Sebastian was standing close to Johnny Cochrane holding his hand. Johnny slapped his back lightly.

"Bye, you little bugger. Watch how you go on, eh?" He came over to Lily while Grace and Sebastian made their farewells. "So long then, Lil. Thanks for the nice wedding, the lunch, the cars and all . . ." He kissed her cheek. It was the first time.

Without turning again Johnny Cochrane led Grace by the hand through the door in the partition; while she, not allowed to slacken her pace, twisted awkwardly to blow kisses with her free hand. Sebastian waved. When they were out of sight, Lily said, "Come on." Sebastian still waved.

"Is he waving, Lily? Is he waving?"

"No, darling. They've gone now. They're on their way."

Chapter 18

WHILE LILY COLLECTED THE ALBUMS, PAID THE BILL AT the hotel, Sebastian investigated the lobby amidst its hushed activity. She returned to find him crouching before the coal fire, relishing the warmth on his face.

"I really love the smell of fire, Lily. There are all different kinds when you think of it. I mean, none of them smell the same. Imagine having one here in a hotel. Just like a real house, isn't it? Gosh, it's grand here."

"Would you like to stop for tea then? Chocolate éclairs?"

"Oh cool."

Watching Sebastian tucking into his favorite food, Lily saw a large plaster on his wrist nearly hidden by his sleeve.

"What's that?" She reached out, touching it.

He blushed.

"I slipped."

"You don't cut there if you slip. Come on, why not say?"

"You'll be cross."

"Try me."

"I was welding with Johnny. Burnt myself," chocolate éclair halfway between plate and mouth, head turned fractionally to hear her expression.

He's gone now, thank God he's gone now. The thought was formed before she knew it and Lily was appalled at herself.

"I know what you're thinking," Sebastian said.

"No you don't," as lightly as possible.

"Lily?"

"Look, it's none of my business."

"No, not that. What's the matter with Daddy?"

175

"Well it's . . . I don't really know. Why?"

"So you're going to lie to me as well. Mummy does. God, I get sick of people hiding things from me. Things I know about already. Johnny wouldn't, he treats me like a man."

"Ask him yourself. Have you tried that?"

"No, 'cause I didn't know if he knew. I mean, sometimes people are ill and everyone knows but the person, don't they? But at lunch today I knew that Daddy knew because he lied too. About saying he'd pulled a muscle."

"So you ask him, eh? That's the best."

"I'll do it tonight."

It was nearly dark by the time Lily dropped Sebastian at his front door. When she heard Melissa's voice inside, she said to him, "I must be off. Bye for now. Come and see my place soon, yes?"

He nodded eagerly but an intent had come over his physique; even before the door had shut he called, "Is Daddy home?"

Lily climbed the last two flights to the penthouse flat. Funny about the front door, it looked different; it wasn't, hadn't even been painted, but it had an element of antipathy.

Balancing the albums on her knee, she put the key in the lock and almost fell through when it opened. Blasted place: all rubber, gray and black. How could Grace put up with it? She smiled, thinking that she knew very well Grace would put up with almost anything in pursuit of happiness.

She switched on a light, smile waning. There was still something strange, so much so that she lodged the albums in the front door to keep it open and with a degree of personal embarrassment called, "Hello?" Heat rising in her neck. "Who's there?"

Her footfalls deadened by the rubber flooring, she moved tentatively down the passage to Grace's bedroom. The door was ajar, she pushed it wide with her foot. There was the bed with its scaffolding poles, bicycle wheel now in place with hundreds of fine metal chains draped to form a silver canopy that clinked in the draft. Some of Johnny Cochrane's clothing lay about, nothing that belonged to Grace. Only in one corner of the bathroom were signs of her existence: jars, scent bottles, tubes of cream, a pair of stockings limp on the towel rail and all of it somehow reticent, apologetic.

More briskly Lily checked the rest of the flat, finding several of Johnny Cochrane's ghastly structures. These were unsold items from the now closed exhibition, and no wonder, not that the few that had sold were any more acceptable. She checked taps, cooker, plugs, everything safe for a long absence, if that is what it was to be.

She had had some vague intention of staying in her own room awhile and left it to the end of her rounds. When she reached for the handle there was once more an overwhelming sense of another present, inside there. So strong was her feeling she even looked to see that the front door was still propped open. With absolute conviction now that she was not alone, that a person in that room had been listening to her moving through the flat, waiting for her to come here, she flung open the door. The force of her action caused the door to bounce on its hinges and close to, so revealing the interior for just an instant. It was long enough, however, to see an unnaturally tall figure standing in the center of the room, a long arm thrust out pointing directly at her.

Fazed by fear Lily remained unable to run. When at last she could speak she whispered through the crack in the almost closed door, "Who are you?" No sound, no movement. "What do you want?" The motionless presence was so powerful she could have sliced it. "For Christ's sake, say something."

No answer. Look then, look inside. She pushed her bedroom door slowly, slowly. There, dead center, was a huge figure, metallic, shining about with smidgeons of borrowed light from windows over the street.

She snapped the switch by the door and there illuminated was another of Johnny Cochrane's grotesqueries; but this one was far more horrible than the rest because it was undoubtedly intended to be she, Lily. Standing, surely, eight feet high, the legs were wrenches hideously welded, resembling anatomical intimacies of a cripple. The body was a kicked-in galvanized dustbin, the head another racing-bicycle wheel, bright, silver, with deep-socket eyes made from decaying paint cans. Its long hair was more of the fine metal chain used on the bed, a fringe cut across it just like her own. The drainpipe arms were bolted through at the elbows; the pointing fingers, old spanners; the feet, shovels.

It wasn't funny and it wasn't supposed to be. He had set it here purposely, knowing she would come. It was his statement.

Damn you, Johnny Cochrane, why are you afraid of me?

She walked around the construction touching it, getting to know it, minimizing her fear, shock. Clever how he had made it her; the long silver hair and fringe were obvious but there was something cunning in the stance, something she had recognized about herself that disastrous night at Mona's when her mind stood aside and watched her body. Everything else in the room was left the same, as Grace had promised it would be. It was certain she did not know about this.

Lily left the flat, double-locking the front door. She took satisfaction in doing so, as though caging that thing inside, giving it no chance to follow. She did not descend directly but went to sit on the stairs the way she used to with Sebastian in the old days, eight weeks ago, before Happily Ever After.

There was movement in the Carys' flat, voices were discernible. They were all three there, together, being a family, and all she had to do to be one of them was knock on the door, say, "Hi, it's me. May I come in? Be with you all?" She could tell them about the figure; take them up, show it to them and they would laugh, relegate it to its proper place of ridicule. Yes, laugh and all would be the same again. Could it be that Sebastian had helped him build it? Is that what they'd been doing in the studio, how he'd burnt himself? Did he know what it was intended to be?

She stood by the front door, hand covering the bell beside it. Sounds: typewriter, telephone, television; Melissa's voice just the other side of the door. "Sebastian . . . Oh sorry, darling, I didn't know you were talking to Daddy . . . carry on . . ."

That decision which at lunch had given strength and peace was undone. Lily went down, out, away.

It was always a tricky business opening the garden gate to Mrs. Gregor's house due to its rusty latch, noisy too, because the hinges were in the same condition; but Mrs. Gregor kept it that way so she might hear when it was opened. She had any number of methods by which to know who was around.

The deep, wide garden leaved and tendriled its way in darkness on to the path. If someone did not cut it back soon there would be no path at all. Enough light came through the glass panels either side of the front door at the top of the steps to give direction and shuffling, murmuring foliage made Lily disinclined to linger. She tripped on a lifted slab of the path, uttered an oath while bending to rub her foot, and on straightening was surprised to see a young woman standing off the path, obscured in part by a rhododendron bush, but clearly intending to be seen. She emanated nothing menacing, indeed a reticence about her stamped Lily's mind momentarily with the image of Grace's stockings and few possessions in the bathroom.

"Hello," Lily said.

"Hello," the young woman answered dully. Her youth was apparent only in her demeanor, her features were hardly visible, her height marked by the lightness of her short, ragged hair.

"Are you looking for a room here?" There was a large suitcase beside her.

"No . . . Looking for someone. Waiting."

"Oh I see. I'm sure Mrs. Gregor would let you wait inside."

"Are you her?"

"Who?"

"Miss Teape?"

"Yes I am. I'm sorry, what's your name?"

It was then Lily began to be aware that the young woman was not alone, there was something hidden deeper in the bushes behind, movement, sound: the nature of it made Lily assume it to be a dog perhaps; anyway, nothing unfriendly.

"Carol."

"Were you, by any chance, the person who was looking for me at Dennis Little's gallery?"

"Yeah."

Lily felt the young woman's eyes upon her.

"Well . . . ermm . . ." Lily started but that life within the bushes became more vital, there was a snuffle. "Are you alone?" Carol looked over her shoulder as though to decide. "No . . . no, not really." It still seemed open to doubt.

"Have you got a dog there?"

"No." There was unutterable lethargy in her every response.

"Can I see what you have got then? Lily had unintentionally adopted the cajoling tone one uses on a truculent child.

Without a word Carol pulled from out of the bushes a double baby buggy containing two sleeping children: one a girl of perhaps three years, the other a dark-haired boy of about eighteen months. She carelessly rattled the buggy on to the path, yet still the lightly clad grubbies slept, heads lolling.

"My goodness. Are they yours?"

"Yeah."

"Aren't they cold like that?"

Carol looked at them sideways without moving her head; the question seemed to bore her, if boredom is distinguishable in a state of such torpor. She said, "Are you the Miss Teape that's marrying John Cook?"

"No. I don't even know any John Cook."

"Well, Johnny Cochrane then?" Carol amended with a giggle, embarrassed at saying the name.

Dennis Little had been right: she was wretched, her children too. "No. No, that's my aunt, Mrs. Teape, Mrs. Grace Teape. She married Johnny Cochrane today. They've gone to Italy. Why?"

"They be gone long? Is it, like, a honeymoon?"

"They plan on living there, looking for a house."

"Italy, eh?"

"Is he a friend of yours?"

There was a silence. The girl still registered no actual emotion, yet there was something there beyond the apathy. Defeat? "No, not really," she said, "only I'm his wife and these here're his kids."

Book
Three

Chapter 19

PASS ON, SUFFERING, DOWN THE LINE PLEASE; YOU'RE A risk to others' peace of mind. Grace would never have said that, even when it was her own happiness at stake. "OK . . . up one more . . ." Bump. Bump. This is what she would have done; you don't turn children away into the night. "Carefully now . . . nearly there . . ."

Carol's destitution was real, no act: she might be able to play out the lethargy of the hopeless, but not the sick face, impassive eyes, the indifference to physical state. "Life it up a little . . . no, up . . . up . . ." Besides, Lily had crouched, there in the garden, to see the children better and in the sleeping boy's sensual features was the apparition of Johnny Cochrane.

"Turn it sideways, Carol . . . that's it . . . that's it, now we're getting somewhere. Watch you don't get their feet caught in the door frame . . ."

They were maneuvering the buggy with its somnolent occupants into Lily's flat. The hall and stairs had been easy but her own front door was, for some reason, harder. Mrs. Gregor had come out, arms crossed, with her usual air of patient contemplation on the procession of life through her house. "Well I never, whatever next?" was all she said, which was a relief.

Outside Lily had asked, "Why are you looking for my aunt and not this . . . John Cook?" The girl had swayed, looked away, deciding whether the answer justified the energy. Speaking not to Lily but the night she had said, "Thought she might be kind, see the kiddies and understand, like, make him do something . . . don't know really . . ." The last words had been said over her shoulder as she made for the gate.

To tell who she was, whose children they were, had been her last card and then she had shown it to the wrong person, the wrong Teape, so she had turned to go.

Lily had watched her heft the broken, busting suitcase along with the buggy to the end of the path and knew the truth of it: that Carol would sleep rough. ''Where are you staying?'' It had been said, there could be no retreat because it was not a genuine question; Lily knew what the answer would be and the consequences to which her own nature would drive her.

''Oh . . . here, there, round about.'' Spoken without intent, no stopping of the slow struggle with the gate; she had not expected to be asked in.

''You mean nowhere.''

''Didn't say that, did I?''

It was then Lily should have said, ''No you didn't,'' taken advantage of the pride of the poor and broken, but, ''You'd better come in for a bit,'' was what she did say.

Carol did not accept or decline, she merely acquiesced in a way beyond relief, surprise or gratitude. Once inside the flat she stood looking at the floor, hands in pockets of her drab raincoat beneath which the hem of her skirt drooped; stockings orange, laddered, mud-spattered; feet in worn-out trainers several sizes too large; hair cut in lumps, angles and bleached to death for half its length, the inner part dark brown.

''Do you think we should put them on the bed?'' Lily gestured to the little ones.

''Don't mind.'' Carol dragged from her pocket a packet of cigarettes, a box of matches, hands shaking as she lit up.

The boy began a luxurious stretch and in doing so swiped his sister in the face. She set up an instant wail, alert even in sleep for fresh distress. For some moments the boy watched his sister with drowsy interest, then collected his features into a gradual studied imitation of her expression and turned it upon his mother, adding his own wail on a different note.

Carol did not go to them but watched unaffected. After a couple of minutes, she said flatly, ''Shurrup,'' then faced away as though the word might make them vanish and she did not want to watch it actually happen. They continued to cry.

Lily closed the curtains, turned on heaters, lights, thinking that ignoring the babies might make their mother attend to them; but when she had finished Carol was standing as she had been and still they cried.

''When did you all last eat?''

Carol shrugged.

"Chips this morning, s'pose."

"Look. Do something with them. Pick them up or put them on the bed, only we've got to stop the racket or there'll be complaints and you'll have to go. I'll fix something to eat."

. That worked. Carol first went to the boy, lifted him saying, "Come on. Come on. What's all this then, eh?" Kneeling beside the girl with the boy in her arms, she cuddled her as best she could. "It's all right, love, don't cry. The lady's going to get you something to eat. That'll be nice, won't it, eh?"

The change in Carol's voice and manner stopped Lily in her egg-breaking at the cooker to watch and realize Carol's carelessness had been her last defense: to blind herself to their cold when she could not warm them, their hunger when she could not feed them, was the only way left to go on. When there was something to offer that would really be of use, then she could afford to give them love with it. She settled them on the bed and they began to crawl around.

"What are their names?"

"He's Damian, she's Chloë."

"Nice names."

"Yeah," adding in a scathing undertone, "Johnny Cochrane . . . blimey . . ." and giggled as she had done on the path. It was an odd noise—dry, solitary, no mirth before or after it—as though she had dipped into her giggle ration and now there was one less for the rest of her life.

Lily handed her a mug of coffee. Carol looked at it in wonderment which she then hid with a brief "Ta."

"Here's some bread for the children to be going on with. I won't be long with the rest."

As she turned bacon in the pan Lily heard behind her, "There you are, love, lovely, isn't it? Bread and butter. Nice."

They would have to spend the night. Then what? Oh God, then what? Give her some money; let her wander off to here, there, round about? Ring Grace: "Hello, having a nice time? I say, guess what . . ."

Carol's voice filtered into her thoughts.

"Did you hear me? She's got an umlaut on her e."

Lily turned, spatula in hand. Carol was sitting on the edge of the bed squeezing her daughter's thigh. Vaguely guarded, Lily said, "Oh . . . I'm sorry. Poor little girl . . . on her knee?"

"No . . . no." Carol's irritation made her more vital than she had been hitherto. "An *umlaut* on her *e*. You know those two little dots on top."

"Oh, I *see*. In her name. Oh yes, very good." Lily turned away with her spatula and amusement.

"I thought, when she was born, I thought: Chloë's all right. It's a nice name: Chloë. But then I thought if she had an umlaut, like I'd seen it done on a book in a shop window, children's book it was, well, I thought, that'd make them sit up and think. You know, at school and such. They'd see her name writ there with all the others and they'd see her umlaut, and they'd say, 'Look,' they'd say, 'that's Chloë with an umlaut.' Then they'd remember her. 'Cause it's not everyone that's got something like that, is it?"

"Certainly not."

"And you've got to have something, God knows . . ." Carol stopped speaking. Lily turned again to see her wiping her nose with her sleeve.

Lily took a plate of bacon, egg and fried bread to her. "Here, you eat this and I'll help the children if they'll let me."

"Oh they'll let you. They'll let you, all right."

Carol bore her plate with reverence between both hands to the table. She sat down looking at it a while before raising the knife and fork, turning them in her fingers, then began to eat with no rush but steady deliberation. Not once did she lift her head but paused occasionally to push the fried bread across the plate, saving the treat for last.

Lily, having cut the food into small pieces, was spooning it into the children's mouths in turn. No sooner had she filled one than the other was open again, like birds in a nest. She managed during this rhythmic task to observe Carol furtively.

Her drawn, once-pretty features reflected hunching in corners with the filth of dustbins, sleeping on benches in railway stations and the hangouts of the down and out. No need to ask if she had stolen to eat, if she had fought to protect herself and her children while moving on, resigned to despair. It was all there in her face and yet beyond that smashed mirror of hardship Lily saw a familiarity so striking she was driven to say, "I can't help feeling I know you, that I've seen you somewhere."

"Yeah," Carol answered, uninterested, but in a manner that suggested familiarity was to be expected.

As she ate her face came closer and closer to the plate, and when Lily saw she was about to lick it she said, "There's plenty more, if you'd like it?"

"Yeah . . ." Carol breathed with real enthusiasm this time.

"How old are you?"

"Twenty-three."

"How long since you've seen Johnny . . . John?"

"Couple of years."

"Why wait until now to find him?"

"Tried, didn't I? Never could, then I seen his picture in the papers. Going round and round on the Circle Line, we were. Picked it up for something to look at, the paper. Wearing a tux, he was, with all the smart set. Happy. Said about 'Young British Sculptor' and I thought, Sculptor, my foot, I thought, but that's him."

"What will you do when you find him?"

For the first time Carol lifted her face from her second plate of food, directing upon Lily a gaze of scorn and pity as one might upon a brutal idiot. "You rich?" she asked and looked round the room gathering evidence to back her assumption already made.

"Well . . . what's rich?"

"You're rich then. That's a rich man's answer," Carol scoffed but added, "Nice of you to take us in, though, give us food and that. Kind, you are. Your aunt kind like you?"

Lily ignored the question. "Was Damian born before your marriage broke up?"

"No. Didn't even know I was pregnant then, did I? But we never, like, broke up, see? He didn't say nothing, John, he just went out one day and didn't come back. But I knew he was pissed off with being poor. He always had big ideas. But he loved Chloë ever so. I always thought he could leave me, but never little Chloë."

"There's no need to go hungry, sleep out. There are people to help you, all sorts of Social Benefits, organizations, charities that will feed you and the children, give you somewhere to sleep. Help you get set up, even."

Carol nodded at Lily with ponderous sarcasm. "Oh yeah . . . love*ly*, love*ly* . . ." (Cochrane's mannerism coming from her mouth was chilling.) " 'Authorities,' you mean. What do you think I'm bloody running for, eh? Do you think I want that lot to get their hands on my babies. Never give them back. Bring them up in a home like I was . . . ?"

"And Johnny too, right?"

"What? John? In a home? Don't be funny."

"It could be you're after the wrong man."

With a resigned sigh Carol went to the suitcase, unfastened it, felt without looking beneath the contents and pulled out a framed photograph, handed it to Lily: a bride and groom standing on the steps of a church; long white dress, veil, bouquet, that was Carol; top hat, morning coat, grin . . . "Yes . . . yes, it's him."

" 'Course it's bloody him . . ." Carol poked about the inside of her cigarette packet with no success which seemed to finish her in some oblique way for she threw it on the table, brought her sleeve to her nose again, but this time to mask her voice and face. "And it's not that I don't love them, little bleeders, but I can't do it anymore . . . push them round the streets all day, sleeping where we can, cold, hungry, bored, tired. And him in his tux having a good time. He'd love them if he saw them, I thought. Who wouldn't? Never mind me, I'll be all right on my own, but there's nothing more I can give them."

Carol crossed to the children, slumped herself by the bed. "Have a little sleep, loves, eh?" She pulled back the Paisley cover, encouraging Damian to the inside, Chloë to the outside. "There, nice bed, warm. That's right: you suck your thumb . . ." They were disturbingly obedient and when their heads were on the pillows she lullabied them:

> You can't get to heaven in a biscuit tin,
> A biscuit tin,
> 'Cause God won't let no crummy ones in.
> You can't get to heaven in a bottle of scent,
> A bottle of scent,
> 'Cause God won't let no smelly ones in.
> You can't get to heaven in a bottle of gin,
> A bottle of gin . . .

She stopped, kissed one, then the other. "You'll be all right, loves, your mum loves you. She does."

She got up, stood looking at them, their eyes closing, opening to flutter closed again, more firmly each time. "You got any fags?" she asked with her back to Lily, eyes still upon her children.

"No, I'm sorry."

"I'll pop out then, get some."

"I'll go. You can't leave them in case they wake. They'll be frightened if they don't see you."

"It's all right, they won't wake up, not with their little bellies full up like that. Nice to 'ave a little walk on my own, like, not for long. Fag machine nearby, is there?''

"I don't want you to leave me alone with the children."

"You're all right. You done it before. I can see that."

"That's not the point. You can't go away. I'll get the cigarettes."

"Leaving my things here, aren't I? Case and all. Got to come back. Just a little walk, that's all, get some fags."

Lily began to feel her fear that Carol would not return was unjustified; after all, she had seen her face when she had finished her lullaby. She could never leave her children.

Carol had watched Lily, divined her thoughts, for she wheedled, "Let me. Just a little walk for some fags, please?"

"End of the road on the left. It takes fifties. You got the right change?"

"Shouldn't think so." She did not even bother to search her pockets and apparently had no handbag.

"Here . . ." From her own purse Lily took some fifty-pence coins. "Don't be long, I'd hate them to wake."

"Yeah . . ." At the door she turned, "Ta-ta then," half-lifted her hand, part-wave, part-salute.

The gesture made Lily rush to the banister, call down, "Be quick, won't you?"

"Yeah . . ." The pallid face with haunting familiarity looked up through the gloom of the stairs. "I'll be quick."

Lily returned to her room, went straight to the window. She saw Carol emerge on to the path, walk to the gate, through, turn left, nothing more. Lily picked up the plates, stopped by Chloë and Damian deep-slumbering, breaths burbling. Ten-fifteen, her watch read. She cleared up, washed up, all the time surprised at not being surprised, shocked not to be shocked. In the shell-backed chair she leant forward, face in hands, stunned that even with two children asleep in her room, in her bed, she could feel so entirely alone. Ten forty-five, back any minute now. At eleven o'clock she suddenly dashed to the door, down the stairs to the street, impelled by no conscious thought or decision.

There was no one about. "Carol," she shouted, standing central in the broad road; her eyes searched the next-door gardens as she thought, I know you're here somewhere, I know your dashed eyes are seeing me. "Carol."

She did not shout a third time.

Chapter 20

L ILY SAT IN THE SHELL-BACKED CHAIR; NIGHT UNFOLDED. Just once she returned to the street and stood as she had before to sense whether Carol's eyes still watched, but she felt nothing: Carol was away now, no doubt miserable with her lonely freedom, her "little walk" might take a lifetime.

Lily crossed the room to rearrange the children's limbs when Damian, the darkly innocent Cochrane clone, came too close to his sister in his tumbling sleep. In Chloë's fair hair and skin was a mystical luminosity and Lily saw herself lying there as she might have been years ago when her life was of no account to anyone but her drug-crazed mother, and even that was uncertain. She had probably slept dream-free and deep, as Chloë did now, through the tortured nights of others' lives and had, for sure, woken one day to find herself abandoned as Chloë would tomorrow.

In the early hours Lily made herself a bed on the floor and although some kind of sleep came there was no turning over into the arms of unconscious. Worm-blind her mind earthed back through the casts of experience to settle at a rainbow, a sofa, a voice, a touch, something but nothing at all. When she did awake thought had been up before her, was already searching for some clause that might prolong Grace's short lease on happiness. Opening her eyes, she found the reality of the situation all the more ghastly for daylight. Clothed and uncomfortable she slowly became self-conscious and, when she turned her head to the bed, saw why: Chloë was sitting up on the side of it with her arm around Damian, both staring at Lily, unmoving, bemused. Lily shut her eyes at the sight of them, only to feel that double stare. When she could bear it no longer she got up, said in a voice intended to guard against involvement, "Morning, you two."

Lily washed, put the kettle on, their eyes following her incessantly. Their instinct told them they were alone now, that Lily controlled them until such time as they were passed to another. She gave them the last of the bread, some milk, and returned to her chair to think. But that was hard, because looking at Chloë was still like seeing into a cuddy of time past and there she was herself at the bottom of it, abandoned, humiliated, vulnerable, struggling to be brave. Until this moment Lily had had no specific recollection of what it had been like when her mother had died and strangers collected her, and assumed it could not have been so bad because there was no noxious residue in memory. But too terrible to cling to and carry around was what it had been and the worst of it was this, their predicament now: sensing they had been foisted on some unwilling adult and confused, frightened by the coldly contained outrage. Lily was, to them, a Prudence Teape, administering without tenderness. All she would have to do is lift the telephone receiver and the police would take them away. She need say nothing about Johnny Cochrane, postpone the showdown which would inevitably come. By lunchtime they could be grouped with other children such as they, lost, abused or unwanted. Easy.

Damian could not manage his bread well and Chloë tried to aid him. After a minute of watching their efforts Lily helped them both to eat and when done Damian slid off the bed to finger the hem of the Anna Maria Garthwaite now displayed on one of the dressmaker's dummies. As he did so, filth began to stream from his nappy.

Chloë looked up at Lily. "Where's Mum?" ("Gone to live with Jesus . . . d'you see-ah . . . d'you hear-ah . . ." You dreary little burden, you inconvenience, you stone on the path to tranquility . . . Unsaid, all that, yes, but felt and remembered until Grace came with her dreams to blot it all out. The rainbow, the sofa, the voice. Where had her mind been during last night's shallow sleep?)

"She's not far, Chloë, She's . . . she's having a rest." Left you, left you; she might just as well have said it because that was what Chloë knew, it was there on her smudged face. Lily knelt with her arms about Chloë's legs to reassure with gesture where words would not do. Chloë put her hand to Lily's cheek, touching the wet of tears, and lifting her mouth in an uncorroborated smile, Lily said, "Yes . . . yes I know. Silly me, eh?" thinking Grace might have said just that. She knew it was alarming, although interesting, to see a grown-up cry but could not help herself, so turned away from Chloë. Whatever course she took betrayal was involved, either of Grace or of Chloë as a distant image of herself; maybe it would not be too long before Carol returned, perhaps a day or two. Come back, blast you. Come back to your babies . . .

It was then the front doorbell rang. There was no such luxury as a direct bell to any of the flats so Mrs. Gregor usually answered. And so she was: stump, stumping through the hall below. Lily looked at her watch, seven-thirty . . . It could only be Carol at this hour. Who else, for goodness' sake? Footsteps up the stairs. She had come back.

Chloë was oblivious to what was happening; the sounds of this strange place meant nothing to her. She joined Damian by the dummy, not to play, just to be near, her eye upon Lily when she thought she was unseen.

Don't open the door, wait for the knock. Weary, shuffling footsteps, nearer, nearer, pausing outside. There. There it was: the knock on the door.

"Thank God," Lily said and as she passed the children she touched a promise upon either head that all was to be well.

In that instant before greeting the expected one, when even the most genuine feeling is distilled into a kind of ceremonial pretense, Lily prepared a welcoming admonishment to deliver to Carol for what she had put her through these nine hours, then opened the door.

Oliver stood, head to the floor; he half-raised it, not to see her but only to enlist her attention for the speech he had prepared. Harassed face, done in, he too must have been sleepless.

"I know it's early and I'm sorry if I woke you but there's something I have to say . . . it's important. Can we talk, Lily? Will you have me in?" He lifted his face to her fully, and freed of his introduction viewed her better. "Lily? What's the matter? You look terrible. Have you been crying? But why?"

He went forward to take her hands, which she pulled away and high, hopeless of explanation. Eyes closed, head shaking, trying to deny her words before they were spoken, "I need you, Oliver. I'm absolutely lost and I need you."

He brought her hands down, enclosing them in his against his chest. "How wonderful. You've just said the very thing I've needed to hear. Come on."

Lily did not move so he led her through the door which had closed to. Inside she stood blank-faced while he looked around admiringly. Chloë and Damian had returned to the bed, side by side, owl-like with their alert immobility.

"It's marvelous in here, Lily, so much to look at it's hard to take it all in. It's . . ." Then he saw them. His intense gray eyes snapped back to her for a questioning instant before approaching them, squatting on his heels, hands linked between knees. "*Hello*. Look at you . . ." Having gently cupped their cheeks, stroked their heads, he stood up, thumbed over his shoulder toward them, said quietly, "Who the devil *are* they?"

Lily's voice was dazed. Still focusing on nothing, she said, "That's exactly what she said. Those were her very first words to me: 'Hello. Look at you . . .' Kindly, kindly. I've not been kind to them. Do as you would be done by . . . I didn't. Grace did and she was the rainbow I dreamt about last night. It was the sweater she was wearing. I can suddenly see the whole room as it was; and her . . . and them. Those two, the Teapes, they did the best they could, you know. You can't blame them. But then she came along and gave to me everything she wanted for herself. So much love . . ."

"I know, Lily, I know . . . but listen to me. Hey . . ." He moved her hair from where it fell across her eyes, trying to bring her into the present. "Whose children are they? What are they doing here?"

"False pretenses, see? Nothing's what it seems. And in here, the Sinner's Flat, you'll find all the answers and the lies because I am the vacant space where other people drive their shames, disappointments, half-cock dreams; they leave them with Lily the Parking Lot. But you must understand that I can't leave because I trail a clatter of secrets behind me and the wrong person might hear what I know. I can't go to Grace because I know the truth now. I am the trustee of her happiness and I can count it out day by day. I can't see Melissa because . . ." She stopped, was silent a while, frowned. "I'm sorry, Oliver. I've no idea what I've been saying. I didn't sleep too well. What did you ask me?"

He ignored her apology, was dwelling on her previous words; only with an effort did he stop his contemplation to say, but now almost as though it were unimportant, "I was wondering whose children they were."

"They are Johnny Cochrane's children." Deadpan, even bored.

"So he *has* been married before. It doesn't surprise me but why are they here?"

"He still is married. His wife's twenty-three, destitute and gone. She's left them here and I don't know where she is."

Pushing his hands into his pockets, throwing his head back, Oliver inhaled deeply, not releasing his breath until he was at the other side of the room facing out of the window.

"I knew it," he said without turning, "you did too, didn't you?" He could not have seen her nodding but continued, "Yes, 'course you did. We all did, didn't we? We just didn't want to poke about in Grace's dream for fear of finding the maggot."

As they remained without speaking Damian slid again from the bed, returning to the dressmaker's dummy; Chloë went with him and they began a game of hiding behind it and spinning it. Damian guggled his laughter but Chloë, with even-handed attention, watched Oliver and Lily as well as amusing her brother.

"I've got to bathe him," Lily said.

"What?" Oliver swung round out of thought as if brought to by a mad suggestion.

"I said I've got to bathe him. Her too, really."

"Lily, you're not to get involved."

"A bath hardly means involvement and it's only practical. I mean, can't you smell . . ."

"Yes I can, but with you a bath means involvement."

She couldn't deny it but took the two to the bathroom just the same.

"Have you any clues about her?" Oliver called as she undressed them.

"Her name's Carol Cook. That's his real name: Cook. Otherwise nothing. She left that suitcase, though. Can you look inside to see if there are any fresh clothes?"

Lily set the little ones in the bath together and with the foam and warm water even Chloë shed her pitiful maturity, splashed and chortled. Kneeling with her chin on the side of the bath, the steam moistening her face, Lily forgot who they were, remembered Sebastian at the same age and how she had sat in this manner with the same pleasure.

"Lily . . ." Oliver warned.

To where he stood in the doorway she said, "It's all right, I was thinking of Sebastian really. What's that?"

He held a large leather portfolio under his left arm, his right index finger separating two pages. "I found this at the bottom of the case. Is it her, by any chance?"

He held the portfolio in front of his face so Lily saw a larger-than-life photograph of a girl, full-smiling, one eye with an incipient wink. "Yes, that's her. My goodness," Lily wiped her hands on a towel, took the portfolio, "but it's not her anymore. God, you should see the change."

"Don't you recognize her?"

"Well, she's a model. I knew she was familiar, even said so."

"But Lily, she was the Milk Girl. Don't you remember? Her face was everywhere; posters, commercials, magazines. She was the embodiment of healthy, youthful, innocent sexuality. It must be five years ago but they've never had one that was a patch on her. I can't understand why she should be penniless now; she must have made a small fortune."

In the portfolio there were magazine covers featuring Carol Cook, as well as dozens of fashion and beauty shots of her. "Did you ever employ her?"

"No. I don't often use models and when I do they tend to be artist's models. But I know who's around. They come and see me, show me their work."

"Yes . . . so they do." Eye to eye they remembered and he flicked his hand at the vision, dismissing it.

"Here." He threw a tangled bundle of clothes on the floor. "That's all I could find for them to wear. Better get them ready now."

Lily sorted through the expensive children's clothes, all too small and mostly ruined, but found enough to dress them for warmth if nothing else. Taking Chloë onto her lap to dry her, Lily had a sudden replay of Oliver's last words and, still with the little girl in her arms, she went to the door of the bathroom. "Oliver, what did you mean, 'Get them ready.' Ready for what?" Oliver was cradling his large body by the telephone, the receiver to his ear. "Not the police, Oliver. Not yet *please*. We must give Carol more time. I know she'll come back. You didn't see her: she loves them." He looked at her without attempting to speak, and she went on, "Don't make me hand them over. I can't. It didn't happen to me . . . I wasn't put in a home. I could've been and wasn't . . ." She was halfway across the room smothering Chloë against herself in swathes of towel, bending toward him. "And *you* didn't let it happen to Sebastian when Melissa . . ." She straightened with the realization of what she had begun to say.

At this Oliver brought the receiver from his ear, toyed with it. Lily observed the tremor in his right hand for the first time

that day, then some sound from the receiver made him return it
to his ear.

"Please, Oliver . . ." Lily said and he turned his face away
from her.

"Angela?" he said into the receiver. "Good morning, it's
Oliver . . . Yes. Lily and I need your help. Yes it is urgent. Do
you know where her flat is? Can you come over now. Thank
you . . ."

With a mask of vitality on his face, all his features doing the
right thing but unlit, ineffectual, and holding hard on to his right
hand to still it, he said, "Would you mind if I lie down a while?"

Without waiting for an answer he did so. Lily watched him
stretch on to the bed, check his watch and, apparently relieved
by the hour he saw there, pull from his pocket some pills which
he swallowed. Chloë on her hip, Lily brought him a glass of
water which he hauled himself up to take.

Holding on to her hand with his trembling one, eyes unrest-
ing, ranging over their shared and part-shared lives, he said, "I
think I just heard the clatter of one of your secrets." Then he
lay back, releasing her hand. Lily returned to the bathroom,
concluded the dressing of the babies.

Upon Angela's arrival Oliver effected one of those complete
changes from stiffness and apathy to vigor that still confounded
Lily. There was no way that Angela could have guessed, by his
manner, that seconds before her entry he had been prostrate and
apparently comatose.

Chic, angular, gangle-legged, smelling good, Angela seated
herself, taking in her surroundings with wordless admiration;
Chloë and Damian along with the rest, but also without question. She wore an original 1930s Chanel suit which Lily had
once found for her and, indeed, Angela had the look of Coco
Chanel herself with her black sharp-cut hair framing her strong
features.

Angela knew how to wait, how to let people reveal a circum-
stance in their own time; in fact after saying "Good morning"
her only words, up to the announcement that they were Cochrane's children, were, "Thank you dear, that would be nice,"
in response to an offer of black coffee. As they explained her
eyes traveled swiftly about as though examining the verbal mural
Oliver and Lily were creating.

Even when they had finished she sat on, erect, one hand placed
palm-up in the other on her lap. Then she reached down to the
maroon leather bag she nearly always carried. Placing it on her

knees, she clicked open the gold fasteners with the air of a doctor seeking his stethoscope. One by one she produced a dozen small clockwork toys, knelt down to put them on the floor and proceeded to wind them up: little boots walking, a bear somersaulting, a top hat swiveling, a clown dancing. Still with no word or smile she crooked her finger to Chloë and Damian who had resumed, on her entry, their watchful immobility.

After three long minutes the fascination proved too much for them and they crossed the low-level vastness of the room, past the unfamiliar feet of Oliver, Lily and three dressmaker's dummies to Angela and the toys. With their attention now lost in the tick-tick-ticking animation of that tiny world, Angela reseated herself and began to speak at last, bending now and again to rewind, in a detached fashion, a slowing toy which she seemed to notice without looking.

"I take it your idea is that we should place them in The Garden?"

"Exactly," Oliver said. "But, Angela, have you nothing to say about it? Aren't you surprised, appalled? I don't know, but something?"

"What day is it?" she asked. Oliver and Lily had to consider.

"Sunday," Lily said.

Angela let out a great sigh. "Sunday. It was just yesterday they were married . . . even about this time. I expected the axe to fall then with him not showing. But he did. Admit, we were all surprised. Then I knew it was just a matter of time. I hated myself for not trusting him, but I never did." Oliver and Lily did not need to state their mutual feeling, for Angela added for them, "Of course we didn't," and fell reflective.

"What do you think about taking them to The Garden? Just until . . . until . . ." Oliver prompted.

"You do realize that it's Grace's money, and hers only, that runs that place? In a roundabout way we'd be compounding Cochrane's injustice to her."

"So we take them to the police station," Oliver said.

"No." Lily was quietly vehement. The other two raised their eyebrows at her. "Grace wouldn't do that."

After some time Angela said, "I agree, she never would. But, you know, there's no saying she doesn't already know about these children. He might have told her and she might have accepted it."

"And you think he told her about still being married, too?" Oliver said. "Angela, haven't we all fooled ourselves enough?"

"You're quite right. So it had better be The Garden for a while. See what happens. Give their mother a chance to return. You think she might, Lily?"

"I know she will."

"So be it. Just for now. If Grace weren't abroad this couldn't happen, and as it is we're rigorously checked by the authorities. It can't be for long." She suddenly dropped her professional manner, relaxed into her chair. "Poor, dear, Grace. We'll let her have her honeymoon . . ."

"Their mother's name was Carol Longman," Oliver said when Angela was already reaching down to gather the clockwork toys. "I know the woman who used to be her agent. Tomorrow I'll talk to her, see if we can track her family."

"She was brought up in a home," Lily said coldly, implying there was a fault in that, not hers or theirs, but attributable to the world at large.

Angela prepared the children to go with her, still without addressing them but with a universal kindliness of manner requiring no unearned endearments and they responded quite happily, even eagerly. Lily picked up her own coat.

"No, Lily," Angela said firmly, "you mustn't come." And when she saw Lily about to embrace the children Angela put out a restraining hand. "Time to go now. I imagine you'll be telling Melissa about all of this, Oliver? But other than her I think we should keep quiet until we can break it to Grace ourselves, in our own time."

"I won't even tell Melissa. She's got quite enough to think about, so it's just the three of us for now. OK?"

"OK."

They helped her to the car, Chloë and Damian in the back seat, suitcase in the boot. Just before she drove away, Angela leant across the passenger seat craning her face to Lily. "I forgot to tell you yesterday; Larry sent his love. He left Friday."

"Left for where?"

"You didn't know? Colombia. That's all I know and I didn't know that until Thursday but assumed you would have; I thought he confided in you. I sometimes wish I'd had a daughter; envy Grace a bit. Bye, bye, love. Don't worry about the little ones."

On their way up the stairs Oliver said, "There you are, things are looking up already."

"What do you mean?"

"I mean, there's a secret you didn't have to keep, about Larry going off."

"Yeah. Can't say I'm sorry."

Back upstairs Lily felt bereft rather than relieved. "What made you come here today in the first place, Oliver? And so early?"

"Ah . . . well now." On arriving he had said he wanted "to talk," but this was not a "talking" voice; this was an "I've-got-a-surprise-for-you" voice.

"Last night Seb formed up to me about my illness. He's hurt, and quite right, that I've kept it from him. I've told him as much as I know and that the prospects aren't too hot. He's observed so much for so long I'm ashamed I didn't confide in him sooner. I underestimated him. He has wisdom, you know. Funny how some have, regardless of age . . ." Oliver thought about that for a minute, then went on, "Anyway, we decided we'd go on a fishing holiday. I can't work until I get some sort of a grip on myself, let the medicine settle down. At the moment I wake up every day worse, when I'm lucky enough to wake up that is, most of the time I can't sleep at all. So I've rented out my studio to an old friend and he's let me borrow a little place he has in Scotland. I'd always planned to take Seb there one day. Well 'one day' has come and it's going to be tomorrow."

"I'm glad. I've promised I'd do something like that with him."

"I know you have and we'd like you to come. Say you will."

"But I can't. Not yet. Not tomorrow."

"Why?"

"Because of Carol. Of waiting for her to come back. I'll have to take her to The Garden. And, anyway, you said tomorrow you'd speak to her ex-agent."

"I'll do that in the morning. We're planning on catching the sleeper at eleven P.M. Leave a message with Mrs. Gregor for if Carol comes. You've got to leave this behind you, Lily. It's not your responsibility or mine. An answer will present itself in its own good time. The children are safe; we've done our best for now. Let Grace have her honeymoon like Angela says; let's see if he makes her happy. In the meantime let it be."

"You really want me with you in Scotland?"

"We both do."

"What about Melissa?"

"She can't come."

"No, but . . ."

He frowned at Lily, stood up, walked about stiffly while re-arranging some mental burden. "She's . . ." shoulders dropped, rummaging in his pockets for reasons, "Well, as you know, she's got a hell of a lot on, like I told Angela. She's spearheading this Children Suffering thing, and now there's her show and still her column, endless articles. They even want her to do a book on something or other, and I do believe she's said she will. She's a wonderwoman. In a way it would be a relief for her to know we were away enjoying ourselves. It makes her feel badly thinking we're at home alone and . . .''

He was warming up, getting faster and prepared to go on explaining, qualifying, justifying with his back to Lily, talking to the Anna Maria Garthwaite on the dummy as though it were more inclined to understanding.

''I'd love to come,'' Lily said.

He sat in front of her again, leaning forward, hands on knees. ''You would? You really would?'' So open, so bright she averted her face. Did he know how things were with her? That she felt guilty and ashamed to hold him in the manner she always had? Did he guess that to be with him for ten days would be a defective pleasure? Sliding her eyes to him, she saw he continued to lean forward awaiting her affirmation. Not so open now, not so bright, but resolute. His head was very slightly nodding. His affliction? Or answer to her thoughts?

''Yes,'' she said, ''yes, I really would love to come.''

Chapter 21

"YOU'RE IN THIS ONE, LILY. COME AND SEE, IT'S EPIC."
As soon as Lily arrived at the train Sebastian was pulling her along the corridor to her compartment. "We're right next door. I'm in the top bunk. You won't be frightened, will you, being alone in yours?"

" 'Course not. You be careful you don't fall out."

This he ignored. "Look, look . . . a pot to pull out and pee in. And when you push it back in, it empties. Somewhere here . . ." feeling in the corner, "I'm dying to try ours. The stink's frightful when you open it but it's good fun. Are you excited? I am."

"You bet," Lily said, slinging her bag on the berth. "Now show me where you are."

Sebastian entered in front of Lily, who put her head into the narrow wagon-lit cluttered with fishing rods and open cases. Oliver was stretched on the lower bunk.

"Hi Lily, want a beer?"

He actually had one to offer and she sat beside him drinking while Sebastian hung upside down from the upper berth.

"Dad, Lily. Listen. Listen, they're slamming the doors. It means we're going soon, we're really going."

Once the train was moving Sebastian was eager as never before to be in bed and, having opened and shut the chamber pot a dozen times, taken the footmat from its plastic container and stood purposefully upon it, wiped his shoes (his old heavy-soled ones) with the complimentary cloth, he was happy to lie in his bunk flicking the switches a while before sleep.

When Lily climbed the ladder to kiss him goodnight, he whispered, "You see, Lily, dreams do come true, don't they? This is my dream coming true. Have you got one?"

"Well, this. Going on the fishing holiday we've always talked about."

"No but that's your share in my dream. It's better to have one of your own, although I'd like a share in yours too."

"Well I might have, I'll work on it."

"Then it'll come true. I promise. Night, Hideousness."

"Night, Ghastly."

Oliver lumbered up the ladder to kiss him—"Night, old man"—knocking into this and that. "I'm not made for this sort of space."

They sat on the bottom bunk finishing their beer in alternating light, dark, light, dark, caused, unwittingly, by Sebastian above still playing with the switches. They said nothing. They did not mind. When they were left in a prolonged darkness and their eyes sought the window with its intermittent streaks of flash and glare, Lily felt her way back up the ladder. She could tell by the looseness of his limbs that Sebastian slept and, in a rectangular swoop of neon from a sped-through station, she saw that he did so with his eyes open in that alarming way he had. She returned to Oliver's side and watched the window's peep-show.

"Did you get anything? About Carol, I mean?" Lily asked after some hesitation. There was no chance of Sebastian hearing even if he had been awake.

Oliver brought his attention from the window but unsteadily, double-taking as if there were something there requiring his observance that he was reluctant to offend. At last, by fixing his gaze to the floor and holding his right hand with his left to still its insistent nag, he said, "It's all so pathetic and wasteful and sad. Look, if I tell you now, can we not talk about it again this holiday? Because we're going to have to face it when we get home, sooner or later."

"All right, I promise. Go on." But Oliver had become once more absorbed in something about or beyond the window. She touched his arm. "A rough idea?" Lily urged, yet looking herself to see if there was something particular there.

"Yes, of course," to the floor again. "Carol turned up at the agency one day, this is going back a few years, and said she wanted to be a model. They would have rejected her because she was far too short, only five three or something and most of the girls are giantesses now, I mean six foot is normal. But her skin and hair and features were so undeniably marvelous they thought they'd take her on to see if she had any luck with beauty shots. Apparently she had nothing: no home, no money. She'd been brought up in homes, as you know, and they had tried fostering but she'd had bad luck, was beaten, I think, so she wouldn't ever go to another family.''

"But that's what Johnny Cochrane says happened to him.''

"Yes, well. It seems he took more from her than just money. He took her past and her confidence too. When she started she was very sure of herself, cocky, outgoing, likable. The agency even loved her in a way, treated her like their child, but the little thing wasn't brainy.

"Almost right away she landed the milk contract out of three hundred other girls and became a minor celebrity in that world. Made a lot of money, got a flat, met Johnny. The agency knew about Johnny. Apparently he had leeched off other models and they warned her but she married him. They said that right away she started to go downhill. Hard to understand, really. I mean, there she was: she had her career, her money, her man, but apparently her confidence began to ebb and it got so she could hardly face a lens anymore. In modeling, without confidence, some almost disproportionate sense of self-worth, you simply can't do it. No matter how great you look, if the lights go off inside that's it: finish. That's what happened to her. Then she got pregnant, while all the time he lived in high style off her money. Soon after they were together he made her leave the agency, said he would be her manager. She tried to get work after the first baby, but no go. After their not hearing anything of her for ages, she wandered into the agency one day, another baby due any minute. He'd left her. She begged them for work, maternity wear, anything, offered her little girl as a child model. They gave her money out of pity and affection, but there was no way she could do a job. Her skin was terrible and her whole being was the antithesis of the vibrant, healthy, sexy thing she'd been. They tried to keep tabs on her, help her out, but she just drifted away from them as things got worse for her; she had pride. And, do you know, it seems that old Johnny comes from a perfectly respectable, middle-class background; minor public school, all that. And elderly parents who gave up everything for him . . . so, there we are.''

"But . . . Oliver?''

Too late. Once again his eyes were toward the window and as the minutes passed Lily had an increasing sense that he was, inexplicably, profoundly absent.

She was considering leaving him to rest when his hand sought hers wrapped about her beer can. Gently prising her fingers from it, he linked them into his own. Still with his eyes to the window, he brought her hand against his lips, turned it and lowered his forehead into her palm. There was wordless consent to the undertow of feeling between them.

He faced her as if to speak, but simply put his left arm, the firm one, about Lily's neck, bent his head, kissed her mouth as though concluding a long dialogue in the only way possible. He pulled his head back then, while hers remained in the crook of his arm, and studied her face in such wandering light as there was. He drew his thumb across her lips, removing a trace of moisture that remained, then suddenly looked away to the window. Lily disengaged her fingers and, although he responded with faint pressure, he let her go, kissing her departing hand without dropping his attention from that something other, out there beyond the night.

The door rattled sharply when Lily pulled it open, which brought Oliver's attention back. "Lily?" he said in a way that made her feel some statement was required, or an absolution.

"I'm . . ." she began.

"Yes? Yes?"

"I'm very, very happy."

"So am I, Lily." No mask-like face straining for vitality. Just then he was free of all contortion, pain, distress and Lily shut the door before she would have to see those things return.

During the night the train stopped and Lily woke to the clangor of a station, probably Crewe. When it started again she was nearly thrown from her berth and lay worrying that Sebastian may have actually fallen from his. With the train rhythmically under way she decided to see. The next-door compartment was not locked and she pulled the door as quietly as possible. Sebastian was sleeping, safe, but Oliver was not there and it appeared that his berth had not been slept in.

Stumbling from side to side down the corridor she found the lavatory, vacant. Past the concertina joint to the next carriage Lily saw Oliver sitting on a pull-down seat by the blast and freeze of an open window. His arms were braced to the wall and door, head forced back unnaturally far in the posture adopted by Sebastian when he was concentrating. For the first time Lily registered the certain likeness between father and son. When she was close she saw his eyes were wide-staring and fixed, yet on nothing, only out, away.

Putting both hands to his cold face, she shouted above the roar from the window, "Oliver . . . it's me. Come on." No response. She pulled his hand from the top of the window to shut it and they were slammed instantly into the intimate interior rattle of the train. "Oliver," rubbing the circulation back to his hand which began to relax. "What is it you see there?"

"Sorry, sorry. What? What is it?" The daydreamer exposed to the teacher in class. He was released now; himself again.

"Why do you keep staring out of the window?"

"I don't know . . . The movement? The speed?" He began to turn his head toward it but with her hand on his cheek Lily averted him. "But there's something, Lily, like I told you, something very important . . . I do wish I could remember, or see."

"Don't try now. Could you sleep a little?"

"I think so." He seemed to totter down the corridor before her, but perhaps it was only the movement of the train that made him do that.

When he was on his bunk and Lily drew up the blanket, he grasped her wrist. "You see how it is with me now? I, in a way, get stuck. Don't really want Sebastian to know about it. I think it must be frightening. Is it, Lily? Is it frightening?"

"Yes."

"Don't be. Please don't. I'm not, you see."

So she wouldn't be; couldn't be; not now he'd asked her.

"All right. I'm here for you and I'm not afraid."

She went to the window, scanned the unending night for that other thing out there, then pulled the blind down against it.

On leaving the train in the morning they hired a car; Lily drove, Oliver navigated. After two hours he asked her to stop. They were away from any collection of human life, under a whitened sky, on a high narrow road ribboning rough folds of murrey and ochre hills, with a loch down to the left like a massive opal dropped in cloth.

"OK, here. See the track?" Oliver pointed.

Lily pulled on to it to find it was no track at all, just a large cleared space over which heather was trying to creep if no one watched. "Are you sure?" she said as they got out, walked about. All the while Sebastian was saying, "God, it's quiet, God, it's nice, I like it," nuzzling his face into the lazy breeze.

Oliver's eyes searched with patient conviction. "There," putting his arm about Lily to direct her, "Seb, over here." Sebastian moved to his father whose arm encircled him as well. "We're on a hill, Seb, one among many that go on and on repeating their slopes and colors. At the bottom of our hill, at our feet, is a loch."

"How big? This? This?" Spreading, spreading his arms as though to embrace its circumference.

"It would take us a day, or a day and a night, to walk round it." Sebastian nodded his satisfaction. "And on the far side is a beach with one lone bothy."

"You mean someone's nude there? Gosh. Which way? Point me." Sebastian grinned up to his father to be affectionately cuffed.

"Bothy, twit, not botty. A stone house, hardly more than a room, slate roof, and that's where we're staying. We have to go over there by rowing-boat which I've just spotted. Look, Lily, see?"

Sebastian looked too, with his ear. "Do you, Lily, do you see?"

"Yes, and thank goodness it's got an outboard."

They loaded the boat shouting convivial abuse at one another, mostly instigated by Sebastian, flat echoes of their voices and laughter clinging near them, unwilling to depart through the softly, softly Scottish air. Once they were settled in the boat, Oliver rose to pull at the starting cord of the motor, jerked it once, feebly, entirely without effect. He slumped down on the cross-seat while they swayed with the violence of his movement. Putting his head on his arms, he snapped, "Fuck it."

"Daddy? Daddy?" Sebastian, who had always hated discord, quickly beamed in on his father's distress.

"It's all right, Seb, I'm not cross, just pissed off. Lily? Have a go?"

They lurched about until they had rearranged themselves, then Lily made an attempt and turned to grimace to Oliver about its failure. On the fifth pull it started and the little boat with its load broke into the shield of water.

The bothy had a picket fence before it that staggered this way and that like bad teeth in an old face, and a surprisingly generous, doleful-looking window either side of the dim blue, paint-peeling front door. This door sported an ostentatious knocker, peculiar in the spacious solitude, like an embossed dinner invitation offered to a starving man.

They let Sebastian discover the gate in the fence, go through, find the front door. He banged the knocker resoundingly, enjoying its weight.

"There's no one there, Seb. I told you we'd be alone here."

"I know, but it's still fun to do." So they all had a go.

The walls of the room inside were lined with match boarding stained the color of molasses and pungent with resin seeping from it in golden globules. There was old brown lino covering the floor along with woollen rugs strategically placed; a black iron fireplace with two dear slovens of armchairs disposed toward it; peat for burning stacked neatly aside; a table; rush-seated chairs; a cooker with a blue calor gas tank beneath; a porcelain sink with a brass tap dripping above. Instead of exploring further, calling, enthusing, the three came together in a spontaneous hug and Sebastian said into their bodies where his head was pressed, "We're here at last. We're all here together." Rocking in one another's arms they chanted, "We're here, we're here, we're here at last . . ." and in that moment's perpetuity, no one, absolutely no one else existed.

Doors at the back of the main room led into two bedrooms, modest additions to the body of the building. These offered between them four beds, only one of which was sufficiently solid to bear Oliver with any comfort.

As soon as he saw it Oliver lay down and Lily watched Sebastian from the door unrolling the sleeping bags and placing one over his father. "All right, Daddy?" Feeling his face, stroking his hair.

"All right, Seb. Just a little rest, eh? Not a proper sleep."

" 'Course." Sebastian unpacked, arranging his own belongings near the bed beside Oliver's. "I'll be right next to you, Daddy, so you don't have to worry."

"That's good, darling, that's good."

Lifting his hand above his face Oliver checked his watch, reached for his pills. Lily brought a glass of water to the doorway, whispered, "Sebastian . . . here." He went to her, she put the glass in his hand. "That's for Daddy, he's taking his pills."

Deep-nodding his understanding, he carried the glass with an air of diligent importance, leaning a little backward, sensing with his left hand fingertips his way through the unfamiliar surroundings. "Daddy? Daddy?" As he drew near, Oliver's eyes were shut. He looked gray, drained, increasingly stiff. Sebastian seated himself by his shoulder. "I've got some water for you."

Oliver levered himself to his elbow, drank, replaced the glass in Sebastian's hand and pulled the boy's head on to his breast.

"Love you, Seb." His eyes drifted toward Lily in the doorway. He regarded her a while, still pulling Sebastian's head almost savagely against him, then said, "Love you too, Lily. You too."

Lily swung out of the door frame back into the main room, pressed herself against the wall unable to bear what she had heard. Sebastian would feel this madness if he didn't already. Nothing for Oliver to say he loved her. No. Not before (although he never had). But now? Now he'd kissed her? Now things were as they seemed to be between them? Was he crazy?

When she heard Sebastian moving away from Oliver toward her, Lily made herself busy with the boxes of food they had brought. He shut the bedroom door carefully behind him, advanced through the room and out, without a word.

She watched him approach the gate, walk the shore to the water's edge, and stand just as though enjoying the view. She let him be a while before following.

Side by side they stood, neither looking into the other's face nor speaking. Lily pushed her hands in her pockets, dug her toe in the shingle, watched the water swirl away the impression it made, let her eyes slip to Sebastian's face. He was crying. She wanted to put her arm about him, but where was the worth in that when it was she who caused the pain? She was considering offering to leave, perhaps the next day, when something in his expression caused her to wait.

His mouth was pulled in over his teeth, head way back, and Lily was struck by the reverse image: last night she had seen son in father, now she saw father in son. For all that his eyelids nearly covered his eyes and tears came from the only parting, a fearful sense of vision emanated from them. Lily turned to what his line of sight would have been, frowned out across the water and the hills with the shadows of clouds cast on them, and felt that, just like last night when she'd looked through the window of the train, something looked back at her.

"What are you seeing, Sebastian? I see water, hills, sky. What is it you see?"

He closed his eyes on whatever it was, said, "He's dying, Lily, isn't he?"

"Don't be rid . . ." She stopped, ashamed of her voice of shallow pretense. Yet not once had she really thought that, not even back in Yorkshire when Melissa arrived and she had said then, "Is he dead?" "I don't know. I hardly understand what his sickness is. Why do you say it? And how can you?"

"I can feel it in his body when I hold him, like he's going.

Not just weak but going. Can't you? And if we can't say it, then how can we help him? If we make out like he's doing something rude or disgusting? He can't help it." His eyes were open, his face in a knot as though resisting glare. Once more Lily looked to where he did.

"Equally, Sebastian, it's not just to be accepted or invited. We have to fight it with him, you know."

"It must be worse for you," he said, "because you can see him. Does he look very different?"

"Sometimes, yes. A lot of the time now really."

"Mummy sees it too. She hates it."

"How do you know?"

"I sense her being embarrassed. You know. Like she was at the wedding lunch. I think she's ashamed for him like he was for himself today in the boat. She doesn't really like 'looking after,' 'doing for.' Can you understand? She likes her own people to be strong. It's the same if I crash into anything or hurt myself. I think she thinks I'm too good to be blind and Daddy's too good to be ill. I know he wants her to hold him. He sort of puts himself in her way, and she'll move. I hear her say, 'Don't, Oliver . . . Not now,' in a special low voice, trying not to be cross. It's worse when we're in a little room together, like the kitchen. It's so busy, with him wanting to be near her and her moving, that it's like there are six of us in there. He doesn't do it anymore, though. He sits and she'll go to him and talk about all kinds of interesting things and he talks back, like people do at a party, making an effort. It's very hard for her. You can see that, can't you? Because it means there's no way for her to show how much she minds. And she really does. We can, though, can't we? So it's better for us. Poor Mummy. She cries too, you know. I hear her."

Lily let a silence come down between them. She knew why he was talking about his mother now. It was his way of warning her off, and quite right too. How had she let it come to this: to be cautioned by her beloved friend, an eleven-year-old ancient, wrapped in eyeless wisdom, fingertipping his way through the interior of others' lies.

"Lily?"

"Mmm." Only just managing the assenting noise, she owed it to him, after all, to let him speak; she was the transgressor.

"I'm glad he said 'I love you' to you as well."

She looked at him. His attention on afar had dropped, he had come back to himself, he was a boy again, was even blushing.

"I know about all *that sort of thing* and I'm trying to say, I'm glad there's you because I can't really help him on my own. See?"

"Sebastian, it really isn't 'that sort of thing.' Well not . . ."

"I say?"

"What?"

"Have you got any éclairs in that food box?"

That evening and successive evenings the three went fishing from the boat. Sebastian and Oliver sat back to back in the stern with their rods, Lily stretched out in the prow reading while the light held, then stared skyward at the ever-deepening violet closing down. Calm water, calm air, stroked once by the collective, melancholy call from geese in flight; frequently by the swish and burr of the fishing lines.

Sebastian was the first to catch. It was a large trout. Oliver showed him how to remove the hook, kill it with one sharp knock on the bottom of the boat. Sebastian picked the fish up when it was dead, put it to his nose, his cheek, lowered his face to it as though forcing sight and Lily watched, wondering if he would catch and kill another. He did, and after that first time made no business of it except to be quite certain the fish was dead.

When they pulled the boat up on shore it would be dark. By the light of paraffin lamps they cooked the fish and, after five nights of eating what they had caught themselves, the thrill and taste of it palled just a little. They played Scrabble and Oliver read aloud from *The Lord of the Rings*, but when Lily thought back to that time she could remember little talk between them. It was as if, with the passing of the hours, peace, such as Sebastian always had, affected Lily and Oliver. There was no need or desire for many words. Closeness counted, however, for where with the sighted a "Hi" delivered with a smile could cover much, with Sebastian there had to be contact too. For him, touch was that smile; and it began to be so for Oliver and Lily. More and more Oliver came to her just to be near, sometimes drawing her against him as though recharging his dissipating energy. Sebastian often knew when they were holding each other and would join them, muscling in on their embrace, diffusing any embarrassment by his obvious pleasure. One time when Oliver had gone to Lily and bound his hands about hers, pulling them low against him, Sebastian had found the camera Oliver always kept nearby like an adjunct to his body. "Hey?"

Sebastian called on several notes which meant he wanted to establish their exact whereabouts. Oliver and Lily turned their heads saying at once, ''Here,'' and Sebastian, laughing, took their picture, supporting the camera askew somewhere near his mouth.

Lily began to note a cycle to Oliver's disease: until midday he displayed almost manic activity. He would walk, beachcomb with Sebastian, skid stones across the sepulchral loch, make plans too: ''When I'm better, Sebastian, I'm going to take you to Africa,'' and he would tell him about that continent, or, ''I'm going to do a series of shots on these hills, Lily, can't you see how like a human body they are? They have all the mystery of folds of firm flesh,'' or, ''They're like the heads of giant ginger and tow-haired children huddled together with a secret.'' But, in the space of a minute, his vigor would go, along with the hopes, plans. His distraction would begin and Lily would ease him to his bed where he lay stiffening. The initial fury and panic in his eyes gave way to a detached wonderment so powerful that again Lily was driven to ask, ''What is it you see?'' But usually by then he was beyond speech.

It was apparent to Lily that he was worsening almost by the day and so it was inexplicable that their happiness should have seemed to be so complete: but it was (''Do you remember, Sebastian, when I dropped my book in the loch and nearly fell in too?'' ''Yes, yes, and the time we made Daddy gut his own fish or pay a penalty, and he wouldn't so we made him sing a song?'' ''Wasn't it the best?'' ''The very best,'' repeated down the years).

Oliver never appeared to sleep at night. Lily would lie in her bed listening to him pacing, sometimes going outdoors, even if it was raining. She feared to go to him at such times, despite Sebastian's sanctioning ''all that sort of thing''; and anyway she doubted he really knew what he had said then. It was in those low, solitary hours during their last night that Oliver came to her.

He had been moving, moving, and it sounded as though he were talking to himself. Lily was sitting on the side of her bed, feet to the floor, willing herself to remain where she was, when he opened the door, just a crack at first as though to confirm she slept. Finding she did not, he entered, closing the door behind him. He was fully dressed and damp from the night air. The lamp in his hand flushed the space about him amber, her white pajamas too, as he drew near. He placed the lamp on the floor,

his hands on her shoulders and knelt. Closing her arms about
him, Lily leant forward, her hair curtaining them both. His limbs
shook from the involuntary tension in the tendons which made
his hands clutch her to the point of pain, which she did not mind
at all. With her returning touch she tried to take away that awful
quiver but knew by now it was not possible. He undid the buttons of her jacket and she felt traveling against her breast his
dry lips and the moist heat of his breath. As she put her fingers
to his scalp, drawing him closer still, Sebastian's words returned, "I can feel him going, not just weak but going," and
she knew what he meant. She held him against her trying to feed
him life through her own flesh and she heard herself say into the
muddled complexity of their bodies, "Don't go. Please don't
go."

Any other man at such a moment might have feared the chilling dawn of possession; any other woman might have feared to
utter such words. But Oliver knew she addressed what was happening to his body, which cried out to any sensitive hand upon
it, "Give me more life. I'm trying not to go, Lily. I'm fighting
very hard. Help me."

"I'll help but . . ." With her hands about his face she forced
him to break from her breast, to look at her, and almost angrily
said, "But you've got to promise to win the fight. Promise me
you won't go. You won't leave . . . *say it*," gripping his head
now as he gripped her.

"I promise. I promise." They fell against each other, limp,
drained, pretending they could not hear the futility in their words.

They remained without moving or speaking until Oliver
said, "Home tomorrow . . ." She may have nodded; could not
speak. "Will you let me come to you then? Back home? And
we can be . . . be together?"

"Yes."

He got to his feet, took up the lamp, held open his arms,
while his huge and partial shadow did the same across the floor
and up the wall behind him. "Look," he said, bright, strong,
proud. "No shakes. You made me firm again. Means my adrenaline's pumping. Better go in case it pumps too hard. Seb'll
wake soon."

Chapter 22

THE TRAIN CRANKLED INTO LONDON AT A GROTESQUE hour of the morning, an hour that doubtless was being beautiful elsewhere, but not here with the shove, hustle and, above all, the goodbye. Lily managed to grasp Sebastian's arm before they entered separate taxis.

"It was all right then? The coming true? The dream? Not disappointing or anything?"

"Oh better than the dream 'cause in the dream Daddy wasn't there. Will you come round soon and look at the photos?"

"Sure. Or you bring them to me."

She lifted cases into their cab for them, and to Oliver on the back seat where he had folded his frame, outsized for such a space, she said, "Well . . . goodbye then."

Goodbye *then*, as though they had discussed the alternatives and it was to be goodbye. She wished she had not added "then," just said, "Bye for now," or better still, "Come to me soon."

"Goodbye then," Oliver copied and looked away. Was he taking his tone from her? Did he mean: "Goodbye, because we know it can't possibly be: us together"? Hadn't she known that all along? Hadn't she?

Lily was without sleep, hungry and depressed. As far as she was concerned this day was done with. Yet there remained a coil of anticipation. "Will you let me come to you . . . back home? . . . Be together?" Would he? Could he? And, after all, was it right? She decided to sleep herself away from all this, and awake hoping to find life resettled, go back to work on the Jacquard designs.

The first and last part of that plan she executed well. As for the middle part: Mrs. Gregor came up during the course of the evening. She ledged her bottom, sheathed in shiny black, on the edge of Lily's work-table: arms crossed, head on one side, considering something about her feet or shoes as she spoke. "She was here, then. Your friend. I told her where her kiddies were."

"So she *did* come back for them. I knew she would."

"Well, as it turned out, I went to her. See, she'd been hanging around on the corner watching the place for a day or so. I remembered her face from that night I saw you both on the stairs with the pram. Being as I had the address to give her, I just went up to her and gave it. Had to shout it after her 'cause soon as I approached she made off. Slowed down and looked at me when she understood what I was saying. I suppose she heard me but said nothing, not so much as a nod or a thank you."

"When was this?"

"Three, four days ago." Mrs. Gregor was sulky, clearly put out to have played a key role in a drama about which she knew little.

"Mrs. Gregor, she was just a bit down on her luck. That's all. Nothing sinister."

"What? And had to get her kiddies' address from me? All seems very fishy. Not that I'm judging, mind you," lifting her hand against the explanations she felt were bound to be coming, "never was one to judge. 'Spect you know that by now. But being as I am you can't help seeing, and what I see in this place is nobody's business." Having delivered herself of that she was prepared to leave, and did.

Lily rang Angela.

"Hello, Lily. How was it . . . ? I'm so glad. And poor Oliver? I met Melissa the other day, she told me about his illness. It sounds very strange, but he's a strong man, he'll pull through."

"Of course he will. Mrs. Gregor gave Carol the address. Has she been to you?"

"No, but she's about."

"What do you mean?"

"I've seen her watching the house. Unfortunately she must have seen me first, knows I'm to do with it so won't let me approach. Obviously she wants to catch sight of the children, but she won't for a bit. We let them play in the garden a little while each day, but that's all for now. You see, they've both got chest infections, lice, eczema, you name it."

"Maybe if I came . . ."

"For the last time, Lily, don't get involved. I've taken this one off you. I'm doing the best I can and Carol's here watching, that's a start. Any word from Grace?''

"A postcard, but you know her writing. I made out Wonderful, Fabulous and Johno.''

"I got the same. So it sounds all right. Well, bye for now, Lily, and keep in touch, won't you. I long to hear any news of Grace. I think I still have some notion that he might make her happy. God, how one clings to hope.''

"Quite.'' The weight of agreement in that word was lost on Angela. "Goodbye.''

Lily turned the postcard over in her fingers; not the predictable Florentine or Sienese rooftops, but a dustily beweeded road cutting an interminable way through two fields of sunflowers in full bloom. The print on the back said simply: Girasoli, luglio. The words Grace had written were even more slapdash than usual and Lily twisted the card in every direction in an oblique expectation that Grace's state of mind might surface there.

Days passed and Lily worked on the death of her own hope that Oliver would come to her; yet every ring of the door or the telephone, every step on the stairs outside her flat, brought back the birth-pangs of conviction: this time, surely . . . this time. There was no hour that she could be free of the suspense of his imminent arrival, because she knew that even night no longer held anything for him but wakeful misery and contemplation. Did he think of her during those hours? Or was it possible that Melissa had changed?

Wednesdays with Sebastian were temporarily canceled due to it being summer term, late swimming practice. There was no doubt Sebastian required her less altogether these days due to commitments with friends and other pursuits. He was growing up, that was all. She had known that would happen, too.

What Lily tried to teach herself to live with, that there was to be nothing more between herself and Oliver, became quite suddenly insupportable; it happened completely, all at once, after two weeks of industry and decided concentration on her work. She slammed down her tailor's shears one morning and with no plan made her way to Oliver's studio.

The large lower floor he had let out to his friend, but upstairs remained his; she could bypass Esther at reception (saw her full, painted face bobbing behind the porthole of glass in the swing doors) and go on up the concrete steps to the top.

It was darkened inside, dusty again. She knew right away he was not there, moved noisily to the window, released the blind to let in some inches of daylight, enough to see better this place where he was most himself. She lay down in the mahogany and cane deckchair behind the screen where he had been that evening when, head in his lap, her feelings had turned, emerged. On the floor were still the ceramic bricks he had crashed there. He had altered even since then, was sicker, weaker, more withdrawn. At that time he had wanted to communicate his outrage at what was happening to him, but when she last saw him he had either lost or stowed those feelings and was struggling against inexplicable distraction.

Sounds came from the studio below: the roar of a fresh backdrop being pulled from the huge roll of paper hung high; telephone ringing; a shriek, a laugh. And it had been like that when he had commanded the place: all vitality, creativity.

Lily heard the muffled thud and huff of this studio door opening and closing on its pressured hinge; someone coming toward her. She did not recognize the step. Was it Esther, having heard movement, as Lily had heard movement below? She remained concealed by the screen. Whoever it was, they came closer but slow, as though looking around as they went.

Oliver appeared at the far end of the screen, head sunk to the floor. She sat forward, he looked up, "Lily," his voice curiously unemphatic, "how wonderful."

She stayed unmoving, unspeaking, watching him as though wading through water. When he reached her he smiled and she said angrily into that smile, "Why didn't you come to me? You asked. I said yes and I've waited and longed and been so lonely. Why did you do that to me? Is it because it's all right at home now?" He shook his head. "I didn't think it could be, then why?"

"For your sake. I've nothing to offer you. It would be shameful to take advantage of your pity. It felt different when we were away from the world, in Scotland. I felt so close to you then, but as soon as reality hit, that very morning reaching London . . . I knew I couldn't."

"So who's pitying, and what about some pity for me? Can't you understand that I . . ."

"And there's another thing too. Although I put it as my second reason, it certainly matters as much."

"What's that?" Lily felt fear; she could have argued her way through the former.

"Vanity. I want to make love to you, you know that. To be honest, I've wanted it since . . . Oh Christ knows, but the first time I was really aware of it was here, when I sat where you are now. But for all my desire . . . and these drugs make me ridiculously horny, more than I've ever been. Seems I'm to be left no dignity in any area. Despite that, I don't know that I can do it anymore, or certainly not to give any satisfaction . . ." She made to speak; he butted in. "Yeah, yeah. I know you're going to say you wouldn't mind. I know that line, but a fellow does, see? I do. I mind like hell. I don't want to make an idiot of myself, not with you."

"You make it all sound very base. There's more to it than that."

"Of course there is; to erase something it's easier to begin by debasing it."

"So you're debasing me. If you hadn't been ill I believe nothing would have begun between us, but it has and now you turn from it *because* you're ill. There seems no room for me either way."

"Too much room, Lily. Hours and hours to think of you, the way you talk, the way you feel, the quality of your companionship. And here you are sitting exactly where I've prayed to find you every time I come into this place."

"If I hadn't come, would you have come to me?"

"I think maybe not."

"Well I have." She began to rise. He put out his hand to halt her.

"There's another thing too, a thought that nags me. Does ghastly illness exempt one from the rules, excuse infidelity? Does it allow me to take advantage of your, if you don't like the word pity, then compassion? Too easy to be without honor at such times."

Lily could have advanced arguments defusing his doubts, mitigating his honor; but you do not do that for another without paying for it in the end. And anyway she knew now his questions were voiced, not asked, and that, in the same way she had come to the studio, he would do the unavoidable, the imperative.

After a while she said, "Oliver, please come to me at the times when you would be alone. I can't think of clever things to say to persuade you, only that I'm desperately unhappy in a way I've never known. Not unhappy for you but for me without you. I'm jealous too, of whatever it is that distracts you, takes your interest when your mind goes away. Give me some time as well, don't give it all to your sickness and let it take you over."

She got up, stood against him. He closed his large square

hands hard around her head, bending slightly to draw his mouth
over her features, murmuring at the same time, "So you're prepared to enter this horror with me? Be there while I go down?
You have no idea what you're saying, offering, with your absurd, insane courage . . . If I were a better man than I've ever
been, then I'd turn you away now."

Oliver was never specific about when he would come to Lily,
but right away it began to be part of every day or night. She gave
him a key so that she might, and did, have the pleasure of arriving home to find him there. She never went out for long because
of that: her life and mind fast becoming fused with his. He might
roll up at three in the morning or the afternoon: the difference
had ceased to have much significance for him, he was increasingly living on his own time-plane.

Lily discovered gradually, without questions, how things were
at home: that it was Oliver who was there for Sebastian when
he was not at school; that those two were closer than they had
ever been; that Melissa had hired a live-in housekeeper-cum-
nurse to cook, drive, generally organize during her own frequent
absences. It was no longer safe for Oliver to be alone with only
Sebastian to help. Lily learned, too, that Oliver and Melissa now
slept in separate rooms. "Better, really," he excused, "I'm a
bore at night." And Lily felt private shame at the lenitive effect
of the knowledge.

They agreed they would fight his sickness in the open, with
discussion of every new symptom: the nodding head, tottering
step, loss of control over his voice. If these tics and gyrations
made him absurd, which they did at times, cruelly so, then they
would ridicule them as visiting devils to his body. Treat them
like an enemy. No holds barred. You can't frighten us. Go back
to where you came from. Go to hell.

If Lily saw his distraction coming upon him she would say,
"Hey, hey . . . no you don't. Where do you think you're going?
You don't walk out on me, see?" Sometimes it worked and he
would stay, with a look of shame, mingled with regret toward
what it was she had drawn him from.

They found he had to beware of repetitive motions and sounds.
On one occasion his attention became trapped by the foot of her
sewing machine humming along a seam. He had been sitting
beside her and she was enjoying his propinquity and study of
her work; it was only by chance she looked up to see that pleasant attention had become contorted abstraction.

He grew confused about taking his drugs, overdosed, under-
osed, and Lily devised a chart with hour, day, date, on which
  cross off the six daily requirements which were soon to be-
ome twelve. On two occasions she had left him, one to go
nopping and the other merely to turn over at his side in bed and
eep a while. Both times she returned to find him struck in a
intastic posture and he would stay thus indefinitely, gazing,
azing away. When he relaxed out of those vacations from re-
ity he would answer with awe to her "Where do you go? What
o you see?", "I go somewhere, Lily, I do see things." And
nce, terrifyingly, "It's a secret." That time she thought, I'm
osing.

All of this was countered with lucid periods, times when his
ymptoms vanished so utterly that Lily remembered why, once,
ne had doubted his sickness, and she could believe that, cer-
inly, one day all of this would pass from him. Occasionally,
ith crazy optimism, she thought that that time had actually
ome. For instance, when he arrived at her door looking for all
ne world like the man she had met years before. Grace's "little
rother" back from Africa, who had turned out to be that big-
uilt, lazy-easy, gray-haired, gray-eyed man, with a kind of
ined strength, shyly, gently observant and amused. And how
ne had feared it, that note she never saw: "Gone to Africa."

When he arrived looking like that she would ask him, "Where
ave you been? What have you been doing?" and he might say,
Swimming . . . in the warm pool at the hospital. Therapy, you
now." And she would remember that the well-being was prob-
ly an illusion, or, at best, transient.

The real Oliver reaching frantically past the sick impostor to
omeone who, it seemed, could save him, and that someone
aching back and saving, saving for all she was worth, that was
nly part of their alliance. Equally intense was their desire for
ach other and joy from time spent talking, loving long and
ourishingly. He was a man who possessed the rare art of inten-
ty, who was able to make the present moment more real, valu-
le than that one past or waiting ahead. Never, never had the
ste of life been so keen.

They had been sharing their lives in this manner for nearly a
onth when Oliver entered early one evening. It was an unusual
our for him because Sebastian would be home. When Lily
eard the key and saw him there she beamed, for it was the well
an who came toward her, arms lifted. "Hey, darling," wrap-

ping, rocking her in those arms, then waving a packet aloft, "want to see what I've got?"

"Isn't Sebastian at home now? He's not alone, is he?"

" 'Course not. Out with a friend till nine, so I'll have to be back before that because Melissa's leaving for Yorkshire any minute. Now do you want to see or not? It's the photos of our holiday. I dropped them in the studio to be developed and forgot about them. Esther brought them round today while I was at the neurologist; nice of her really 'cause she's been a bit hostile since I won't let her interfere as much as she used to. My shots are good but the best are Sebastian's."

There it was all over again, their place, their Scotland, their time together, in rectangles of delight, along with Sebastian's personal views of chair legs, shoes, the bottom of the boat with a fish in it, aslant, out of focus. They lay on the bed passing the photographs to and fro.

"And look . . ." "And there . . ." "And that . . ." And yes, yes, yes.

"We will go again, won't we, Oliver? Soon?"

He did not answer so she turned her head on his shoulder and looked into his face. He was staring at the ceiling. "Oliver? Don't, Oliver . . . stop it . . ."

"It's all right. I'm all right."

"Then why don't you answer me? We will go again, won't we? With Sebastian?"

"Lily, at the hospital they're talking about me going in, living in. This day-care business is starting not to be enough. We know I'm getting worse, old thing, let's face it."

She brought her leg over his, leant her shoulders across him so her face was above his. "But we *do* face it and you're not getting worse. Think of all the times . . . think of now. You're prefect now . . ." vision blurring, voice shaking.

"Don't cry, darling." With his hand in her hair he drew her face even closer to his. "We have to prepare because it's coming to it."

Before Lily could begin a fresh attack on his reasoning the telephone rang. She reached for it, holding him with her eyes, warning that she would not let the subject drop.

"Yes?" she said into the receiver with impatience, then she fell away from Oliver on to her back, grasping the air in her astonishment. "*Grace*. I can't believe it. At last. I could murder you, it's been so long. Three measly postcards. Did you get my letters? How are you? Where are you?"

Oliver settled on to his elbow to watch Lily and when she glanced at him, eyebrows raised, he shook his head, indicating with his finger that he was not there; Lily nodded without breaking the conversation. ". . . So you've found one already . . ." repeating what she reasonably could so as not to frustrate Oliver's avid interest. "Is it an old villa? . . . Called La Pietà . . . Beautiful? Well it would have to be, wouldn't it . . . Oh, so you can only rent it. But two years is about right, isn't it? How nice, so you won't have to buy furniture . . . No, well, I suppose Johnny doesn't like it if it's antique, but still . . ."

Oliver mouthed, "How is she?"

"And what about you, Grace? How are you? Happy . . . ? Grace . . . ? What is it? Grace . . . ?" Lily shrugged incomprehension to Oliver, then back to the telephone. "Oh, Johnny. I was talking to Grace. What happened?"

Both Lily and Oliver altered their posture, becoming more erect and guarded. Sharp-voiced, Lily said, "Well if you don't mind I want to ask her myself . . ." Oliver touched her arm, she saw his hand held out flat, and tilting, indicating: steady. "Sorry . . . I only meant I was a bit worried by her voice. How are you? Are you having a lovely time? Good. Great news about the villa . . ." Lily covered the mouthpiece, whispering to Oliver. "He's just spoken to Melissa, got her as she was leaving . . ." She uncovered, said, "You mean for Sebastian's halfterm? That's in less than a week. Did she say yes? I see, the three of them? Really?" She whispered, "You're all going to stay with them for halfterm, going out Friday, coming back Monday. Melissa said you'd love it, the change would do you good." Oliver rolled his eyes, hid his face.

Lily was speaking again to Johnny Cochrane. "Well of course I'd like to come, but if it's all the same with you, can I talk to Grace about it? Please . . . Thanks. Bye." Lily rested back on the bed intent upon what she could hear happening at the other end, finally, "Grace? Hi. What's going on there? You're not crying, are you? Oh I see laughing. Must be the line . . . Yes, I'd really love to. I'm longing to see you again. So you want us all to come together. And Dennis and Angela? Blimey! Is there really room? . . . Goodness. Oh, must you really go now? There's a lot I want to ask you . . . OK, then. Miss you too. Bye."

Oliver watched her nursing the dead receiver as though it might still give up a little more news of Grace. "Well?" he said.

Lily sighed, placed the telephone back by the bed. "She sounded . . . oh well . . . very excitable."

"Oh dear."

"Quite."

Still lying on the bed they held hands, Lily's eyes wandering over the aqueous stains on the ceiling, Oliver's eyes closed. At last she said, "Could you manage it? The journey? Being there?"

"I have to, somehow, for Grace. See for myself what's going on and let her see what's going on with me. It's only fair to let her know."

"It means we'll all be there together; you, me, Melissa, Sebastian. I could say no. Go later."

"Would you find it very hard? Pretending?"

"I can't imagine. But I'm sure they'll guess about us; that it'll show in the way I look at you, touch you. I mean, I used to, didn't I, touch and all that? But how did I do it before when I didn't know and love your body like I do now?"

He squeezed her hand. "Be there, if you can bear to. Please. Who else would help me when I, if I, well, get like I do? Who will be there to understand, not to be frightened?"

"Sebastian."

"Lily, you know he can't alone. It's not fair."

"Of course it's not fair. Don't worry. I'll come. But what about those children? They're still at The Garden. Carol's never shown, not really. What'll we do about knowing the truth?"

"*You* ask me? You, the Keeper of Secrets? Well what does one ever do about knowing the truth, except dish it out measure by measure, kindly, gently, and then only if you have to. We'll play it by ear, Lily." Lily felt a sudden coldness through his hand, the tensing. "Must get back now, darling, help me home."

Only after she had driven Oliver to his front door and was returning alone did she recall his talk about living in hospital. The memory came with such force she stopped the car, wanted to go back, argue it out with him, rant against the inevitable. But no, she could spare him that. She drove on.

There was nothing for it but to go to Italy, look in on Grace's happiness with knowing eyes. She would dissemble too, for the sake of them all; she would be the old Lily, the Lily who would never be again: the girl in their midst whom they had loved, trusted, treasured.

Chapter 23

IT MUST HAVE APPEARED A BIZARRE GROUP OF SIX WHICH
descended from the morning flight from London into the
June dazzle of Pisa. Lily, in a forty-year-old, cream tussore
or suit, flanked Oliver, who staggered between two sticks.
Sebastian was on his other side, carrying a white cane musket-
yle at his shoulder, only tap-tapping when he had to. His head
ack, mouth open, he stroked his face against this new warm
r as he duck-walked in his baseball boots ("I know they said
ey wouldn't come to the airport, but in case they do, in case
does, he must see I'm wearing them"). Melissa pranced in
ont of these three in tight, bright trousers, pursuing an earnest
onversation with Angela who, with typical British mistrust of
e weather, was still swathed against the slate-skies she had
ft. Walking behind the rest, sad-faced, came Dennis Little.
e was creased and Maughamesque in flapping, off-white linen,
anama hat, carrying a rattan suitcase; in all looking indefinably
bsolete, like a balloon a week after the party: reflation was
ossible but unlikely it would hold. His dejection was so appar-
t that Lily inquired more than once, "OK Dennis?"

"Wonderful."

They hired two taxis at the airport, then came the first test,
e first false front.

"I'll go with Dennis and Angela in this one."

"*Lily,*" Sebastian and Melissa in outraged unison, then Me-
ssa alone, "What's the matter with you? Come on, there's
asses of room." She was kind, encouraging. It was hard to
ar.

When they had met at London airport Melissa had grasped

Lily by the shoulders. "*Great* to see you, stranger, after so long.
I *mean* it: great," driving home some conclusion she wished to
have drawn; it was all but an embrace because that was not
Melissa's way.

Of course to travel with them was the natural thing to do, but
Lily did contrive to sit in front beside the driver.

After nearly two hours the driver slowed down, pointed.
"Guarda laggiù, quella è La Pietà."

They saw the villa across the valley poised on a hill, separate
like a dream, in a fumid shimmer, honey and ochre nobly decaying; sentried by cyprus trees; clustered about with lower,
ancient, acolyte buildings.

Melissa peered forward between the front seats, her hand
casually resting on Lily. "My goodness, how lovely. Eh, Lily?"

"It's perfectly Grace, isn't it?"

"Well done, Grace."

They began descriptive exclamations for Sebastian's sake.
Straining round in her seat to endorse her enthusiasm with a
touch to Sebastian's knee, Lily registered Oliver drawn up in the
corner and that all was not well with him.

"Melissa, look."

Melissa did so. "Oh my God. Oliver? Not now, Oliver, we're
nearly there, love. Come on. Oh God. Lily? What shall we do?
Shall we stop?"

"I don't think that'll help now. Has he taken his pills?"

"I don't know. Oliver? Have you taken your pills?" Loud,
staccato, as though to one who did not speak the language. But
he was beyond it, abstracted.

Lily said, "Look at his chart. He'll have crossed it off if he's
taken them."

"Chart? Chart? Oh yes. That paper. Right." Melissa reached
gingerly inside his jacket, whipping out the card in the manner
of one snatching meat from a lion. "Let's see now . . ."

Lily deferentially turned the card the right way about in Melissa's hand.

"Oh God," Melissa said again, "how stupid of me."

"Don't panic, Melissa. Would you like me to look?"

"Would you? Thank you."

"Now then." Lily studied the graph set out in her hand. "No.
Looks like he's forgotten his dose. We can't give it to him here
in the car. We'll have to wait till we can get him on his back."

"What'll Grace say? Poor Grace. She has no idea. I should
have warned. I know now I should have."

Lily did what she had originally turned to do, reassure Sebastian with a touch. "Everything's all right, Sebastian. Don't worry. Jolly nearly there."

Silent, his face searched the interior of the car. Melissa put her arm about him. "Daddy'll be fine in a minute, darling."

The two cars ascended an unmade, winding road, slowing as they passed the dwellings in the lay of the villa, around and out of which ran scraggy dogs, children waving. Not an adult in sight; no doubt sleeping through the thud of the afternoon heat.

A stretch of tall, elegant, tranquilly rusting railings, with center gates, closed off the beweeded courtyard in front of La Pietà. Everyone but Oliver left the cars. One of the drivers who seemed to know the place walked to the left end of the railings and pulled at an iron rod. Deep inside the building a bell choked. Immediately came footsteps with the otherworld echo of ringing tone; they drew closer, and now the shunting of bolts on the far side of the double front doors.

Smiling, ready for Grace to appear in this ideal setting, they watched one of the high doors open. Out came a short, stocky, black-haired woman with floral apron, bare-legged in moccasins. She moved brusquely, head down, saluting with her right hand, shouting harshly, "Ciao, Benedetto."

"Ciao, Anna. Come va?" the bell-ringing driver answered.

With no response she continued her choppy progress across the courtyard, arms held waist-high, wading the air. She unlatched the gates and the drivers helped her pull them backward in their dusty ruts. A rapid conversation then ensued between the three. Lily, Melissa, Angela and Dennis stood about feeling amused and extraneous. Sebastian had returned to the car, opened the door to stand protectively beside his father.

Their attention on the front door had dropped when Grace appeared, so they heard her voice first. "Darlings, loveys, you've made it. You're all here . . . how marvelous." She traversed the courtyard with her hands lifted to support the brim of a very large straw hat, strewn with dim-hued, antique silk flowers, the shade of it obscuring her features. Her white dress flowed, glared in the sunlight, every step faster, tripping slightly in high-heeled sandals. "Lily, Lily, Lily, my darling girl. Come," and Lily was taken in under the hat, thrilled, happy and shocked; shocked at the feel of the fleshless body holding her. Grace dipped backward to see Lily's face and Lily saw hers: strained, haunted but lightly tanned and smiling. She left Lily to adjust her reaction but still retained her hand while greeting the others. "Angela,

dear. Lovely, lovely; and how well you look. Dennis, sweetie.
You're so nice to come out when you're so busy. But aren't you
glad, now, that I insisted?'' with a gesture that encompassed the
villa, the hills, all. ''Melissa, so much to catch up on. But I hear
about you, you know, even over here, and read about you in the
English newspapers.'' She called out, ''Hello, Sebastian, darling. I'm coming right over. You'll never guess what: we've got
a stream, with fish in it, just longing to be fished.''

Before advancing to Sebastian she held Anna close by the
upper arm, confirming her cherished status. ''Listen everybody,
this is Anna and she's wonderful. Aren't you, Anna?'' Anna
pulled her head into her shoulder, grinned, coy. ''Now Anna,
this is Lily, my Lily, whom I've told you so much about.''
Anna apron-wiped her hand before offering it. ''And Melissa
and Angela, and Dennis and over there's Sebastian, and . . .''
Grace broke off. Anna made away at this point to get on with
more pressing matters such as suitcases. Grace's arms fell limp;
putting back her head to gain vision beyond the extent of her
hat's brim, she said, with awful dismay in her voice, ''But Oliver, where's Oliver? Is it him I see there? In the car?'' Her voice
unnatural. Funny how the soul knows before the senses.

''Grace, now look there's something . . .'' Melissa was already walking back toward the car as she started to explain.
''Oliver's not been well. We didn't tell you because he didn't
want that. Not to spoil your honeymoon. I know now I should
have warned you but . . .'' She knelt at the open door of the
car; Sebastian, apart now, detached himself in the way he did
when he knew he could be of no help. ''He has these sort of,
what, fits really. He's having one now and you mustn't be
alarmed. Try not to be . . .''

Grace, one hand spread at her breast, slowly wide-circled the
car, stooping to view inside. As Melissa swung Oliver's legs
round, slotted his arm to lift him, straighten him to the upright
position, then so did Grace become upright, full-facing with
horror the great palsied figure of her brother teetering foot before foot and craning his head back as though being forced from
a fabulous vision.

The drivers displayed the usual embarrassed pity of strangers
uncertain what is required of them, but Dennis and Angela uttered their shock aloud. Yes, they had been warned he was ill;
appalled by his appearance at the airport, but this? This clenched
loony? Melissa had given them no idea at all.

Oliver suddenly convulsed, trapping Melissa's neck. ''Oliver, don't. You're strangling me. It's hurting. Help." Locked together they lurched hopelessly.

Lily had turned her back in a show of admiring the scenery but really so as not to see him first appear. However, when she heard Melissa's cry she went straight to them, fiercely yanking Oliver's arm from Melissa to load his weight against herself.

"He can't help it," she breathed through her struggle. "He has no control just now . . . you have to do it for him . . ."

With her own leg wrapped behind one of his, she dragged it forward.

All were paralyzed by the spectacle until Anna pumped purposefully forward. Her head no higher than Oliver's chest, she hoisted his flailing arm around her, securing it with her hand and together with Lily hauled him forward saying, in a let's-get-on-with-it voice, "Allora. Andiamo."

Dennis Little and Angela went across to console Grace who remained struck, speechless. Lily heard him say as she entered the fathomless shadow of the villa, "Why don't we all go inside, then Melissa can explain. Please, Melissa. The whole thing's . . . incomprehensible."

"Yes . . . I will. If I'd thought for a second . . . I'm so sorry, Grace."

Through the front door was what amounted to an interior courtyard, stone-floored with an identical pair of doors opposite. From the ceiling hung a massive wrought-iron candelabra bearing fat, yellowing candles in glass funnels. To the left and right of the area rose broad, marble-balustered steps to the first floor.

All the time Lily and Anna negotiated Oliver forward, Lily talked to him in as normal a voice as her efforts would allow. "You're going to love it here, Oliver . . . Look up, see the light there, candles too . . . bit like a church, I'll bet, when they're lit . . . Steps now, steady . . . that's right. Can you see the marble? It's almost pink, incredible."

Initially Anna cast dubious looks to Lily across Oliver's lumbersome body, then, accepting light talk as being what was required, joined in. "Yais . . . issa very nice 'ere . . . Eet belong always the church, many, many years . . . Diversi cardinali hanno abitato qui. È la verità."

"Hear that, Oliver? Interesting, eh?"

They had reached the top, turned right along a short gallery overlooking the enclosed courtyard. The others were entering

now. Anna put out a hand to open the stout door before them.
"Arrivato," she puffed.

At the end of a dark passage they at last reached a bedroom
where a wide, canopied bed loomed center in the shuttered light.

Because of their exhaustion Oliver was almost flung upon the
bed and immediately Lily rolled him on to his back and, kneeling on his arm (Anna holding down the other), she took out,
sorted and administered his pills, pushing them to the back of
his throat, following with water tipped from a carafe.

All this done Lily fell across his body. "I know you can hear
me, my love. Please, please be well. Fight on, darling . . . Fight
on for yourself . . . for me."

His arms fell on her back, with terrible weight, pushing her
against his body which, if she could, she would have entered,
to remain in some deep recess of it, cause trouble there, insisting
on life. She might never have moved herself were it not that
another hand came on her back, after who knows how long,
perhaps only minutes. Anna's hand. Lily looked up. Anna
pointed to Oliver's head, saying in a tone of reverence and recognition, " 'E sleepa now." He did seem to be sleeping but
you could never be sure. "We go, yais?" encouraging Lily to
rise.

"Yes." Lily swiped her sleeve across her face to remove what
she could of giveaway emotion, and faltered, uncertain of what
this woman must now be thinking. "He's . . . he's a fine man,"
she said by way of explanation, excuse, and just because she
wanted to talk about him.

"Yais, 'e is," Anna breathed. Although she was looking at
Oliver she seemed to be seeing someone else as well.

"Thank you, for helping me."

Wagging her brown, knobbled hand with impatient appreciation, Anna said, "Come. Signora Grace ava the beautiful tea-
time ready."

Across the passage Lily entered that long, umbrageous room
running the depth of the villa; the log fire burning there made
appropriate by the distance of the elegant windows at either end,
so far as to make their images of languorous summer seem mere
holograms. Arranged beside the fire were two deep sofas with
a massive, gilt, consul table behind each one and a low coffee
table between. Lily knew the furniture did not belong to Grace
but it had her touch. It was here the company and Grace were
seated.

Melissa interrupted herself. "Oh, Lily, how is he?"

"Resting."

"I was just trying to explain . . ."

"Well, so you have, Melissa," Dennis said gratefully, but firm, obviously sated with detail. "Very clearly. Thank you. I'm sure it'll make it easier for all of us to understand and help. Don't you think, Angela?"

"Yes. Yes. Definitely," though doubtful.

Melissa moved up to make room for Lily on the sofa. "I have to say Lily's been incredible, Grace." Lily was startled. "She went with Sebastian and Oliver to Scotland, did you know? On a fishing holiday. I couldn't go and they couldn't have gone alone. I'm very grateful to her."

"What I don't understand is, well, is he, will he, I'm trying to ask: is it terminal?" Angela blushed.

"Well no." Melissa still managed calm lucidity. "That's the thing, you see. There's no reason why he can't go on for years. And that's why," for the first time her eyes cast down, "we've agreed, Oliver, Sebastian and I, that after this," gesturing to the room, still without lifting her gaze, "these couple of days here, he's going to go into residential care." Now she looked at each in turn, quick and reassuring. "He'll be with quite a few others just like him. There are even still post-encephalitics alive from the epidemic back in the twenties." Her phrasing was cold but forgivable: it was information received, correct. She listened a moment to the quiet she had caused, added, "I'm sorry, Lily, you didn't know, did you?"

No, she didn't know. So she was on a par with the rest, being pounded out of her ignorance. Her head turned involuntarily toward the door through which, back across that passage, through another door, he lay. Had he known? Had he decided and not told her? When? Yesterday? Before? Was it already fixed a week ago when he first mentioned it? Whose idea, anyway? His? Melissa's, or theirs, the medics'? Sebastian was playing no part in the explanation but exploring the room with polite constraint while this chapter that, no doubt, he knew too well was being re-read. Even he had not come to her, warned her, and after all they had shared in Scotland.

Unexpectedly Angela asked Lily's question for her and was observing Lily as she did so. "So when was that decided? About him going in?"

"Only last night. We'd talked about it a bit, but only last night, really."

Lily shut her eyes, releasing her grip on a cushion. Please God, don't let them be looking at me. She opened her eyes. Angela was.

"It's all ghastly, just ghastly." Melissa said it half-aloud and in a different voice altogether. "So hard to know how to say it all the right way, and do all the right things. I want to very much. I really do." Constricted, on a breath.

"Mummy?" sudden, concerned, down the room.

"It's all right, darling, I'm all right, really."

Grace sat twisting a lace handkerchief and staring around the slate floor as though all Melissa's words were split there for her to pick over. Without particularly breaking her reflection she dangled the handkerchief ahead. "There's tea over there, if anyone would like it."

All but Lily moved off; she crossed to Grace who lifted a bewildered face. "I can't believe it. It's so hard to understand. Africa. It all stems back to Africa, to when he went to sleep. But, Lily, that was fifteen years ago. I didn't ask questions then, one doesn't somehow. He came back, that was all that mattered, came back and was well. Until now."

"Grace, sometimes, a lot of the time, he's his old self. You'll see, soon he might be up. Come on, Anna says you've got a beautiful teatime ready."

Grace laughed a bit. "Oh yes. Her English is sweet, isn't it?"

Tea had been set in front of a window upon a white-clothed table with every kind of confection—iced, crystallized, creamed—and strips of toasted savouries; a silver kettle on a silver stand, a flame beneath.

"Look, try one of these." Grace handed a plate of sugared chestnuts and, shyly determined on some levity, said, "Capezzoli di Venere. Nipples of Venus. Salieri's favorite. Remember the film?" They dutifully tasted, appreciated, and she went on. "See there," pointing through the half-open window, leading on to stone steps going left and right down to the garden. "See beyond to that hill directly in front. If you look hard you'll see a path right up the center of it. Well that was made by some Cardinal centuries ago. It seems he was fearfully jealous of a rival and arranged to have him murdered. Having done so he was stricken with guilt and had that path cut. As a penance to God, every day for the rest of his life he walked from here to the top of the hill and back on his knees."

"Umm."

"Goodness."

"I say."

"Tough."

Sebastian said nothing.

Grace went on, "If you feel like it, I'll take you up there after tea. Knees if you like, but you don't have to."

Laughter. Agreement. Silence.

Of course they had all been wondering since they arrived; well it did seem, on the surface of it, just a little odd, but no one wanted to be the one to ask. No one except Sebastian.

"Grace?"

"Yes, my love, what is it?"

"Where's Johnny?"

Chapter 24

"SIENA, I EXPECT, DEAR," GRACE SAID, ATTENDING TO A thread at her shoulder, the knot of her sash, something about her hair. "Johno likes to go to Siena."

"Will he be back soon?" Sebastian persisted.

"Oh yes. Any minute, and he'll be thrilled to see his old friend is still wearing the baseball boots."

They climbed the hill, rested, bathed and changed for dinner then congregated once more in that room. Still Johnny Cochrane had not arrived; and Grace's enthusiasm was increasingly brittle.

"We do everything but sleep in this room, you see," Grace responded to Angela's admiration of it. "We relax, take tea and breakfast overlooking the garden there, and dinner down that end overlooking the courtyard. A kind of bedsit in a stately: it makes it cozier, more possible for two."

The dining table was set upon the loggia, its silver, crystal and flowers on damask vivified by candlelight, cut in relief against the night. It had the air of a hallucinatory stage awaiting the moment to make spectres of them all.

Melissa entered with Oliver. Except for Johnny Cochrane they were the last to appear. Oliver was, to a point, his old self, as Lily had said he might be; but his old self having had the being pulled out, shaken and stuffed back, like used linen in a basket.

Grace and he wordlessly embraced and that embrace both explained and accepted all that was necessary, for when they separated the atmosphere was lighter and there was no talk of his condition.

Having had Sebastian open the way for them earlier, it was easier to refer to Johnny Cochrane.

"Is Johnny working at all?" Dennis inquired of Grace.

"Working?" momentarily at a loss. "Oh, *working*. I'm sorry. I'm so vague. Well no, not yet. When he's a bit more settled here; there's a good building for a studio lower down the hill."

"I thought maybe that's what was keeping him in Siena, a studio there."

"No," pondering, "no, not a studio. Don't worry, Dennis, he'll have plenty more pieces for you to show very soon."

"Oh . . . Oh super." But the prospect was not apparently exhilarating him.

Grace crossed the room to the loggia, leant against the rail there, seeing out to the direction of Siena where, across the dark distance, the lights of cars beaded a line of motorway.

The company tried to sparkle for her, but at nine-thirty she said, "I think we'll start. Poor Johno must have been kept. Siena's madly crowded at this time of year."

Grace seated herself and, with a hand on the chair next to her at the head of the table, said, "We'll leave that for Johno. Melissa, you go there on his other side, Dennis next to Melissa, then Lily next to Dennis. You don't mind having your backs to the view? No? Good." She watched them obey her directions, one finger to upper lip, considering. To have the seating exactly right was integral to her pleasure. "Oliver, darling, next to me here, then Angela, then Sebastian. This way, my love . . ." She rose to lead him to his chair. The far end of the table was left vacant.

Anna produced two platters of pasta and wine and they settled, becoming immersed in that other light of the loggia, all part of the room, yet not; chiaroscuro altering their intended, pretended expressions.

They had not been dining long when Sebastian said, "Listen, a car. Do you think that's Johnny, Grace?"

"Certain to be, darling. Oh good." Grace leant against the balustrade waving to headlights which stopped with a screech. A car door closed.

"Hello, girl. Home again." Johnny Cochrane's voice from below.

"Johno, where have you been, darling? I was so worried. We're all here. Here, and dying to see you."

The sound of his footsteps crossing the courtyard was followed by that of another car. "Who's that, Johno? Whoever is it?"

No answer but the slamming of the front door. Grace remained where she was; they all went over in time to see a young man and woman climbing out of a car. He carried an enormous portable stereo that blasted the air with rock music.

" 'Ello, 'ello. Here's me, then, ladies and gentlemen, the man you've all been waiting for."

They turned as one to see Johnny Cochrane standing mid-distance, arms aloft, displaying himself, grinning; nothing new, except the style: Italian-cut, white suit, open soft silk shirt, Gucci loafers, predictable tan; quite a bit of gold about.

Lily could not help a sceptical one-corner lift of mouth and opposite eyebrow to the suppressed amusement of Oliver and Angela.

"Hello, Johnny. Great to see you." Sebastian had saved his greeting until everyone else had done.

"Watcha cock," was all he got with a light slap on the head, but he seemed prepared to make do with that.

Johnny Cochrane sat at the head of the table. "Oi, come on, Gracie, tuck in."

Grace would not sit. "Who are those people, Johno? They've crossed the yard, come inside."

The door opened, the couple from the car were ushered in by Anna. The man was almost black-skinned, with an inane, irregularly-toothed, loppy-lipped face; he was skinny and cheaply, gaudily dressed. The woman was olive-skinned, fulsome, succulent with every hallmark of the fresh young whore. She scuttled across to Johnny Cochrane as best she could in her short, tight skirt, and with her hand about his forehead pulled his head backward into her profound, luscious, well-exposed breasts, saying, "Joany. Carissimo Joany."

"Ah, get me head out yer bosoms, girl," he said, roughly freeing himself, then, "Very forward, these Italian girls, and lusty. Oi, Anna, two more places. Everyone, this is Gina and this is Franco. Brother and sister." He pointed for the girl to sit beside Sebastian and Franco next to Lily, from where they began loud talk in Italian across the table to each other.

"They don't speak a word of English, folks, so feel free."

"But *you* don't speak Italian, Johno, and *who* are they? *How* could you? Tonight of all nights." Grace was standing above him in her anger.

He looked up and in a kind voice, but obscurely threatening, said, "Sit down, Gracie, you know I don't like scenes." She sat. "So then? How do you all like our little place?"

They tried to be natural; to ignore for the sake of things, but Grace would not say a word; left her food untouched.

"Come on, Gracie, eat up. Don't want a scrawny wife, do I?"

"I can't."

"Well you'd better start, old girl. There's no man wants a bag of bones for a wife. Eh, Oliver?" Still his voice was friendly, but contained (or was it only Lily who heard this?) implicit menace.

"Grace has always been slender and a small eater." Oliver was icy. Perhaps he, too, had heard that other in Cochrane's tone.

"Well, never too old to learn." Johnny Cochrane put his arm around Grace, took a forkful of pasta, pushing it toward her mouth, cajoling, "Come on, girl, eat up for Johno, eh?"

Everyone was watching, the two Italians shrieking with laughter at the apparent force-feeding of a middle-aged woman. It was an ugly scene and Lily, stifled by the odor of sweat and garlic from her left, said across Dennis and Melissa, "You shouldn't make her eat if she doesn't want to. Leave her alone."

"Hey, hey, steady on there." He put her fork down, pointed at Lily, smiling. "You don't want to come between man and wife, Lily. See? Mind yer own, that's what I say."

Dennis and Melissa appeared to be mildly amused or perhaps that was the expression they had chosen; but, after all, was it all so very bad? Wasn't he being just a bit wicked, outrageous, the kind of thing one might expect from Johnny Cochrane? Wouldn't they view it differently if they, Lily, Oliver, Angela, had not known what they did? Grace was upset but not extravagantly so; one could believe that his had happened before and she knew how to handle it.

Melissa even said indulgently, "You're a naughty boy, Johnny. I can see you've got a thing or two to learn about marriage."

"Some parts of it, maybe, but I *am* a naughty boy, you're right." He leant close to her, his delivery so loaded as to make Melissa turn her face away, smiling, blushing, protesting, "Really, Johnny."

Lily had been observing Oliver: no twitch or tremor, only that which came from restraining anger. He looked in this light, at this moment, as he had looked to Lily fifteen years before. Now the change in him from that afternoon was so pronounced that

Angela noticed, said, "I can't help saying, Oliver: you're looking wonderful tonight."

That was taken as a cue to turn the subject from their hosts.

"You do, darling, it's true," Melissa exclaimed.

Dennis raised his glass. "So let's drink to a happy visit." No one took him up on it for their interest in Oliver had become more intent. "All right, don't let's." Dennis replaced his glass, chuckling amiably.

Oliver had pushed himself away from the table, was leaning sideways in his chair, one arm resting across its back, the other next to his plate; legs stretched out, he was coldly composed, eyes narrowed and locked with Johnny Cochrane's.

"Lily," Oliver began so oratorically as to galvanize all but the two Italians who yattered on, and Oliver lunged his huge shoulders round, simultaneously slamming his hand, roaring, "Smettetela voi due idioti. Voglio parlare." The two melted to silence.

"I never knew he spoke Italian," Angela breathed almost petulantly into her bosom, as though affronted by the discovery of a secret.

Oliver continued as before. "Since *he* keeps talking about what *husbands* expect, I think it would be interesting if you told *Grace's husband* about the young woman you met on the day of his marriage."

We'll play it by ear, he had said. Terrific. This was his ear, not hers. She was unprepared, had no idea how much he intended her to reveal. Oliver guessed her confusion, helped. "Just some part of it, Lily, not all. It's a good story."

All but Angela were still hoping for a subject to take flight from the original cue about how well he was looking, and were putting Oliver's curious manner down to his infirmity. Lily was still finding it hard to speak.

Melissa looked past Dennis. "What young woman, Lily?"

Dennis said, "Not the one who came looking for you at my gallery, by any chance? That was the day before the wedding."

"The very one."

"Oh, good. She found you, poor soul."

"Yes, she did. Like Oliver says: it was the day Grace and Johnny got married. I arrived back home, it was dark. She met me on the path. She was cold, hungry; worn-out shoes, perished raincoat . . ." Oliver directed Cochrane's attention from himself to Lily with a sagacious nod toward her. Cochrane was bent forward, fingertips on the edge of the table. ". . . I had never

net her before. She was looking for someone with a name very
ike mine, made a mistake, you see.''

"But at the gallery she definitely asked for . . .'' It was
Dennis, this time, who was silenced by the barest motion from
Oliver.

"I might never have asked her into my flat but for the fact
that she had two little children, a boy and a girl; about eighteen
months and three. Nowhere to go. No money. I thought the least
I could do was feed them.''

"Absolutely,'' Melissa murmured.

Johnny Cochrane slowly surfaced from his trance-like attention; felt in his pocket for cigarettes, gold lighter. He lit up,
inhaled, exhaled with his head back. He was not creating a
distraction with all this, nor was he bored, it was just that he
was relaxing into the pleasure of a jolly good yarn. He refocused
on Lily, head to one side, interested in a pleasant, courteous
way; delicately removing a shred of tobacco from tongue-tip.

"While I prepared some food she talked, told me her name
was Carol. Carol Cook.'' Lily paused, turned her face upon
Johnny Cochrane. Not a flicker, not a wince. ''And that her
children were called Chloë and Damian.'' Not even a cooling
of that smiling interest. He did move but it was only to inhale
on his cigarette and reach his arm about Grace, exhaling above
her head, then pressing his lips into her hair (all of which she
enjoyed, quietly responded to), but none of it was done to spoil
Lily's story.

"She told me that Chloë was spelt with an umlaut on the e.
She put great store by that; she felt it would make her little girl
noticed in some small way. 'Chloe with an umlaut,' she kept
saying.''

"How charming,'' Grace said, ''but sad,'' linking Johnny
Cochrane's fingers into hers against such sadness.

"Carol was the Milk Girl. Do any of you remember that really
famous one, a few years back? Her face was everywhere.''

"I do,'' Melissa said.

"So do I. She was that wretched creature at my gallery? It's
tragic. So what happened, Lily?''

"By the morning she was gone; she didn't want to stay. I
don't know where she is.'' Lily wondered if Oliver would agree
that that was how she might leave it. She saw his face; he did
assent, in a way only she would understand.

They began to talk in general terms about the nature of destitution, except Lily, Oliver and Angela who were longing to

speak alone, hoping that one of them might have spotted some
giveaway, some subtle agitation.

Sebastian had not sustained his concentration on Lily's story,
because during those minutes he had been waging a peculiar
war of his own: Gina, at his right side, recovering from the
shock of being told to shut up, had become bored. For a while
she and her brother amused themselves by making faces at each
other, crossed eyes, protruding tongues; that quickly cloyed, but
they did not dare speak again. Franco found distraction in the
business of trying to hang a spoon from his chin by first warming
the bowl of it with his breath. This left Gina entirely at a loose
end; that is until she saw Sebastian properly.

When first she had sat down she had been so involved with
the food and wine, in talk with her brother, she had seen nothing
else. Now she was intrigued by Sebastian. He had been sitting
very straight, facing ahead into the night. He made some movement in Gina's direction, while eating or feeling for his glass,
and suddenly Gina saw his eyes. She flapped her hand at her
brother to look at the oddity but he was too busy with his spoon.
She wriggled her fingers in front of Sebastian's eyes, her own
head rudely close and oscillating like a snake's in her excited
curiosity.

Sebastian sensed the movement and having never encountered
this kind of behavior did not expect it. He responded to the
motion in front of his eyes, put his hand to it. Nothing there. It
came back; still nothing. Something small hit his cheek, fell to
his lap. His fingers found and registered a tiny ball of bread.
Now there was a happening just above his head, like flies walking there. He hit out. Suddenly he knew there was a face right
next to his, peering into his crippled eyes with brutal inquisition.
So he peered back exploring and exposing with his features
what, he was certain, was a dim-brained cretin. He pushed his
face right up to it, following its retreat from him, causing finally
an imbecilic squeak. He turned after that battle and, unknown
to him, settled in exactly the same posture as his father seated
one place down from him.

Gina's squeak caused Johnny Cochrane to remember the presence of the Italians. "You still here. Oi, Gina, Franco . . ."
Franco, who had only just succeeded in suspending the spoon
from his chin, let it clatter to the table. With his arm still about
Grace, Cochrane said, "Do you want them to go, love, would
you like that?"

"Yes please, Johno."

"All right, Gracie, if that's what you want. You two; clear ff," waving his hand to outside. They affected not to under-tand. "Oliver, you speak Wop. Tell 'em to go. They've had heir dinner."

"You brought them. You tell them to leave," Oliver said.

"OK. OK. Keep yer hair on," cordially and, getting to his eet, he raised Gina unceremoniously by her armpits, pointing er to the door. "Bugger offa nowa. Gottit, girl?"

"Joany, carissimo Joany." Slithering her body against his, rms all over him.

He untangled her. "Pusha offa . . . Oh God . . . Gracie, elp, she's gonna rape me. Blimey, get yer 'and out . . ." Franco, thinking the party had begun, switched on his stereo ull volume. "Oi, Pinocchio, you can turn that off for a start nd pissy offy . . . Christ, Oliver, give us a hand here, can't ou?"

All of them, even Oliver, laughed until Anna came to help Cochrane dispose of the two unexpected guests who protested olubly.

Grace presided by the open door. "Goodbye, goodbye. I do ope you enjoyed your dinner. It's been so nice. Goodbye gain." She closed the door on all four.

It reopened almost immediately with Johnny Cochrane lean-ng in backward, still holding Franco in a half-nelson. "Back n a minute, love. Give us a kiss." She did so.

The shouting grew distant before reemerging into the court-ard.

"There you are, you see," Grace, with her palms up to the bvious, "he's hopelessly kind. He can't say no. They're poor, hey're hungry. It makes him ashamed that they have so little vhen we have so much. Like you, Lily, really, taking in that irl and her children. He'd have done the same."

By the time Johnny Cochrane returned Grace, Melissa and Dennis were talking about Melissa's Children Suffering appeal. He joined them and Sebastian approached. "Look, Johnny," ifting one foot.

"What?"

"Baseball boots."

"Yeah. That's right," as though he were merely naming ob-ects.

"No but these are the ones you bought me. I've looked after hem."

"So you have, son. Good lad." Cochrane was more interested in gaining some leverage in the conversation. "What about your show, then, Melissa. When are you having me on?"

"Well, Johnny, here you are living in Italy and I'm afraid my budget won't allow me to bring a team over. Worse luck."

Sebastian had put himself next to Johnny Cochrane, apparently unoffended, waiting for another opportunity to gain his interest.

"Lily? I want to go outside a minute. Give me a hand, would you?" Oliver called from the glass doors.

Carrying over his sticks, Lily saw he was at the tail end of his composure.

"May I join you?" Angela asked, joining.

Light from the windows swelled on to the steps, across the gravel to the grass in paling degrees, and beyond it they found chairs and a wooden table canopied by a complexity of pleached lime. Another stone balustrade fended a drop to the terrace below. Angela went to sit on it with her back to the viewless night; not so much as a star. She watched Lily ease Oliver into a chair, lean his sticks close by. "So what did you think?" Angela asked them, out of their sight but her voice impressively close in the clothy humidity.

Oliver muttered, "Damn it, I was too fast. Too fast. I lost my temper with the bastard; just couldn't stand to see him like that with Grace. The little shit. I could kill him, but now all I've done is prepared him. Hell."

"That doesn't matter now," Lily said, "because you know what? I was looking; I saw every little movement he made. He's not the husband. If he was . . ."

"But we saw his photo." Angela's voice was still coming like something that had no beginning except in their heads. ". . . the wedding snaps. He was the man all right. And Grace: happy, do you think?"

"Are you asking me?" Lily stalled. She was seated in the dark at the far end of the table from Oliver, out of an instinct of propriety.

"Yes you." It was Oliver's voice demanding, disparaging her cowardice. "Tell me what you see in her eyes." There was the tish-tishing of her dress recrossing with her legs while she planned equivocation. "Say the truth, Lily."

"All right, then," blindfolded by the night, the heat, the scent of lime, "I see frantic unhappiness."

"That's right, the hopeless pretense; and her hands are shak-

ng again like they used to. She's drinking or something,'' Oliver
concluded for Lily.

Angela added, "I'm afraid I see Grace as I've seen her so
many times in the past: ankle-deep in a dream in which she's
trying to drown." She made a brisk movement, her shoes grazed
the stone; she whispered, "I say, look there. Johnny's just come
out. He's looking around."

Johnny Cochrane could not have heard their voices from where
he was at the top of the steps, but must have sensed some strum
of animation from where they were for he crossed over with no
hesitation, halting at the table.

They watched his dark shape muscling out a cigarette from a
soft-pack; holding his lighter at arm's length he glowed it upon
the motionless, watchful figures of Lily and Oliver, then drew
it near his mouth and lit up. They saw his features golden, smoke-
hazed, gone. Only his voice now in the blind after-shine of light.

"So . . ." he said, pausing to inhale, tip head back, exhale,
"it's . . . ah . . . Chloë with an umlaut, eh? Good story, that,
Lil."

"It's not a story."

"No? Well life's full of them, see? That sort."

"What sort are they?" Lily asked.

"The walking wounded."

"And who's wounded them? In this case her husband, the
father of her children, used her youth, her confidence, her money,
then left her and never divorced. What's he doing now, do you
think? Hunting new ground? Ruining another life?"

"Could it be, Lil, he's holding someone's life together?
Thought of that, had you? Take our Gracie, how do you find
her?"

"Terrible. Thin, nervous . . ."

"Yeah, yeah, well now, why? She's got her house, she's got
her husband, he gives her what she likes. I'll tell you why:
'cause your auntie's cracking up, see? She was cracking when I
met her and still is. She's into this pill and that pill from the
doctors; little drinks when you're looking, little drinks when
you're not. The lady's on the edge."

"If she's on the edge it's you who put her there."

"Wrong, girl. Gracie thought that when she married me the
clock wouldn't just stand still, she thought it'd turn back and all
those little lines and bags and sags would disappear; and they
haven't and it's not bloody my fault that she's old and getting
older and . . ."

The next moment Cochrane's words were swallowed with gut-retching as his figure doubled up and backward in slow motion.

Oliver having delivered his punch was dragging Cochrane forward to the table, their silhouettes entangled, barely relieved by any light save that coming from the villa. It was hard to see exactly what passed, but in seconds Johnny Cochrane seemed to be kneeling at the table, his head upon it, apparently held there by his hair in Oliver's clutch.

Oliver's voice was flat, unhurried, peculiarly conversational.

"I've been waiting for some word of curiosity from you about Lily's visitor and the children; concern about Carol Cook whose life you smashed . . ."

"Lemme up . . . for fuck's sake . . ." The words chipped off into a groan of pain as his cheek was ground into the table.

"I've been waiting for you to say, 'Chloë, is she grown? Is she talking? And Damian . . .' "

"Damian. Never heard of bloody Damian. Trust Carol to pick a poncy name like that. Bet he's not even mine . . ."

When he dropped his hand from Cochrane's head, Oliver's shape separated to be one man again. Lily and Angela were still on their feet as they had been since the violence began minutes before. There was silence; all four supporting the unexpectedness of admission.

"Johno, Oliver?" Grace's voice sang inquiry from the villa into the cooling night. "Where are you? Angela, Lily?"

Cochrane rose, brushed at his clothing, shouted, "Over here, Gracie . . . my love," adding the last two words for their ears, not hers. "You going to tell her, then, Olly, old boy? Eh? 'Cause you know as well as I do what that'll do to her. What she'll do to herself. She'll top herself, won't she, eh? See, you can give her the truth but what after? Bloody nothing. Think about it."

They watched him go toward Grace, who stood at the top of the steps. As he drew closer, she said, "Johno . . . your clothes . . . your face . . ."

" 'S OK, love, slipped, that's all. Too much of the old vino rosso. Tell you what, doll, let's get into bed, shall we?"

"Yes, yes, but," pathetically torn between desire and sociability, "what about the others?" She called now toward them, "Lily? Oliver? Angela? All right, are you?"

Lily replied, "We're all right, Grace. Goodnight."

Chapter 25

THAT NIGHT THE WALLS TALKED. LOCKED INTO THE STONE and mortar, behind the smooth finish, pig-blood Italian plaster, plangent voices cajoled, protested, insisted, implored and, sleeping, Lily heard them.

She lay in a tall narrow bed, an open window as tall and no wider directly above, its calico curtain ushering in the night. Those walls were close either side in her long room; to the left slept Oliver and Melissa, forced together for the first time in a while (Slept? Slept? Surely not?). To the right were Grace and Johnny Cochrane. The four of them pressed into the thin sleep Lily had wrestled from consciousness. When she did startle into wakefulness, in a game of Grandmother's Footsteps between dream and reality, the intrusive voices stopped instantly but Lily could sense fingers pointing elsewhere, raised, stilled in the act of instruction, eyes slid upon her, all waiting for her to rest back, commencing once more when she did so.

Where's Johnny? . . . Siena, I expect . . . Mind yer own, that's what I say . . . You're looking wonderful tonight . . . Please, Gracie, come on . . . Why now, Johno? . . . Please . . . All right? (Don't say it's not; for *my* sake. Let's hold hands and pretend together.) All right. All right. All right.

Lily awoke late to find the others had begun their day without her; and Anna stopped the clearing of breakfast to bring her fresh coffee, warm bread.

"Where is everyone, Anna?"

"Signor Cochrane, he take the Mrs. Melissa and Sebastiano to Siena. He crazy man. Siena isa terrible, terrible today. Molti, molti turisti oggi. È la verità."

243

"And the others?"

"I thinka maybe garden. Who know?" evidently tired of placing the missing.

After breakfast Lily wandered down the stone steps, along the wide, grassy walk lined with cyprus trees that would eventually lead to the penance hill. Pushing between the gathered branches of the trees to the outside of the walk, Lily looked back and saw the balustrade where Angela had sat last night. There she was now, stretched, swimsuited, on the terrace beneath, littered about with the impedimenta of sun-worship: a bottle of oil, a tube of cream, a nose guard, a towel, a scarf, a book, a pad and pencil, a newspaper, sunglasses, spectacles, wrap . . . at this point Lily stopped listing. Angela, hat covering face, was having trouble with a fly which had apparently landed on her foot, then on her stomach, shoulder, only to settle after brief respite on her knee. It was all too tiring to watch.

Further on there was a break in the trees on the other side. Through it Lily saw a stone-built folly some yards away with a semicircular seat around its inside curve. Oliver and Grace were sitting there; Grace with her whole body inclined toward him, one arm reaching forward to his.

Reassurance? Affirmation? His head, bent low, nodded once, twice with intention.

They did not see her and she passed on in the hot, paley lavender suspension of sunshine wherein life slow-motioned.

Pausing, with a mild interest in the distance she had covered from the villa, she saw Dennis Little not far behind; his figure a light, unsteady blur moving closer.

"Morning, Lily." The stillness lifted his voice nearer than expected.

"Good morning," she answered as he drew up pulling a handkerchief from trouser pocket, wiping his forehead, lifting his face to the prospect in an eloquent substitute for spoken admiration. As they walked on together without a word, Lily remembered how occasionally in the past she had enjoyed the undemanding simplicity of his presence.

But then he said, "What on earth's going on, Lily?" She looked at him, his eyes down to the tawny grass on which they walked. "Come on, the atmosphere's unbearable. I mean, even without Oliver's situation and the fact that we've not found Grace to be all we might have wished, I can still feel . . . I don't know, but like I've walked into one play having learned the lines for another. Well?"

Lily stopped splitting the green stem in her fingers to push back her hair behind her ears, revealing her profile; explanation was imminent, but she let Dennis see that more prompting would help.

"It's to do with that girl who came to my gallery, what was her name . . . ?"

"Carol Cook."

"Yes, now. It *was* you she was looking for, wasn't it?"

"Grace."

"Who is she?"

"Johnny's wife."

Dennis stopped. Lily walked on a few paces, turned in time to see him with one sharp shake of the head, dismissing surprise as inappropriate. "And the children?"

Lily explained, concluding with, "Johnny knows we know and he's almost defied us to tell Grace. He says she'd kill herself."

"What do you think?"

"It's a fear I had once a while back; Oliver too, I suppose. There's enough in it to stop us rushing forth with the truth. She'll have to know. The problem is, when. I think to myself: what's the point in spoiling the little that's left, this moment, that moment, the next. I've tried to blame you, actually, for introducing them, but it won't stick."

"Thank you."

"But you might have guessed he was her type."

"But not she his, Lily; I had good reason for not suspecting that."

His emphasis invited the conclusion. "Then, after all, you were lovers, you and Johnny?"

Dennis nodded and, to annihilate doubt thoroughly, added, "Yes." Lily did not expect him to say any more; it was a private knowledge that would have made little difference to anyone; but Dennis went on. "I fell for him like a fool, suddenly and completely, the way Grace did. He gave me something that's hard to define. Maybe it was only the same old buzz that's harder to come by and dimmer as the years pass. It was like he handed me back a sheaf of years all wrapped up in his vitality and enthusiasm, things which he made me feel were born out of my existence alone. Then I saw it. What was to come. At Grace's dinner party I watched him shifting his beam, saw him operate, and understood."

"What did you understand?"

''That he preys on the weak. I knew he wasn't really gay, although I wasn't the first man in his life, that's for sure. He doesn't mind who he goes with so long as it's to his advantage. I simply didn't see it at first and was fool enough to think . . .'' Dennis lifted his face once more to the penance hill, no longer any appreciation there. ''At Grace's party I began to understand. The obvious one to make a play for was you, surely. But no, he was afraid of you. Remember you asked him when he was at St. Martin's? He never was there. You're too strong, too straight. Grace and Sebastian were the ones he latched on to.''

''Sebastian's not weak.''

''One wouldn't have thought so. I sat at that table and seemed to have vision for the first time. I watched him singling and sorting; he went for Larry, steered clear of Oliver; wouldn't even touch his book, I remember.''

''He wouldn't touch the book because he said he knew it, had owned it ever since it had been published, and yet only days after he asked what Oliver did in his studio, was he a painter.''

''It's typical. Johnny's only a smalltime operator, easily exposed by those who wish to do so, which is why he picks on the ones he does, dealing in the currency of things to hide, petty shames, dubious desires. To the right types, like Grace and me, the very silliness of his lies makes him attractive in a childlike way. Don't think Grace hasn't spotted his inconsistencies; she's weak but she's not stupid. Even by the time he met Grace I'd lent him a great deal of money; tried to make it seem businesslike by buying his sculpture. You were right when you said his stuff was spurious. I knew that, but it was good enough. I could rely on selling sufficient to cover the costs of my infatuation.''

''And have you?''

''The thing is, I can't. The day before the wedding he hired a van, went around to the gallery when he knew I was away and took every single piece of his work; all of which I'd bought and paid for.''

''Someone must have seen him. Tried to stop him.''

''He flattered his way past my daft girl. She said he was so sure of himself that I must have known. That's why I didn't want to come out here, but Grace insisted so, and I suppose I thought he might just explain. As soon as I saw him, of course, I knew he wouldn't. That's not his way. He just shifts ground. I also wanted to see if Grace and he were happy.''

''And you have.''

''Mmmm.''

"It's theft, isn't it? Won't you challenge him?"

"I don't think so. And he knows that. I won't because of Grace and because . . ." He stopped and let her see him shrug at the inevitable, then lowered his eyes from her contempt. They walked on.

"I know where his stuff is. It's all in Grace's flat in London. You could get it back."

He glanced at her and away. "So I could, Lily. So I could." His tone was ambiguous though perhaps amused at her practicality, insensibility to some finer mesh of life. He put his arm around her and they turned for the villa.

Was that how it worked then? People make a fool of you, use you, walk away? No retribution? "Dennis, don't you want to get even? Get back?"

He produced a laugh of sorts. "Oh, Lily, Lily, don't you see? One doesn't. One simply doesn't."

Johnny Cochrane, Melissa and Sebastian were due back for lunch. They did not arrive. So Grace lunched at the table under the pleached limes with the four that were left, all of whom now knew the truth that would sooner or later be broken. They watched her face, tired, perplexed ("Mozzarella, Lily, in oil with black olives? Very nice."), working at pleasure for her friends ("A little more wine, Dennis?"), frowning, twitching when she thought they did not see ("Angela, rice? Salad?"), lifting the dishes, struggling to smile, isolated in her ignorance.

Oliver, Lily, Dennis and Angela talked quietly to each other out of deference to Grace's apparent weariness.

"Grace and I chatted all morning; more than we have for years," Oliver said, "perhaps not even since we were children. It was wonderful. What did you do, Lily?"

Dennis answered for her. "We walked to that hill, very pleasant. Did you have a nice time, Angela? Watch out, you're getting burnt."

"I know. I'm very silly about . . ."

Suddenly Grace interrupted and, as though suspecting the very subject at bay, started in with, "You see, Johno's so terribly restless . . ." then stopped, hands in lap, eyes searching her companions as though for a clue as to why he might be so.

Angela returned with her therapist's tone, the dangerous deceptive one that by its apparent obtuseness causes an outpouring of all that was planned to be withheld. "Is he, dear?"

"Oh, yes, yes. Don't you see it? I thought you must have,"

hands flailing explanation. "Even last night, after we were all in bed, well, we didn't have a row. No. Not that. But quite out of the blue he tells me he wants us to go away, travel, India then China and who knows where else. He begged and pleaded for hours. I didn't understand. Said so. We have this, La Pietà, I said. It's what we came in search of, it's well, Happily Ever After . . ." a rush of panicked laughter and her brief animation was all expelled; she shrank within herself.

Angela leant across the table, stayed Grace's hand in the act of lifting a glass. "Grace, if it's not working with Johnny there's no shame in pulling out. That would be the right thing, the brave thing. There's much more for you in life, just wait . . ."

"Not working? Not working?" Snapping on vitality. "Good heavens, did I give that impression? How silly of me. Oh no, Johno and I are, oh *so*, in love, really." Searching around the faces. "Really we are."

Oliver saw Lily's eyes pass from Grace to himself and he conveyed with an inward, despairing smile that, yes, it was exactly the line she had been feeding him all morning.

"Grace, I was hoping," Angela began, "that this afternoon we could go through some Garden business. There are several questions that need your attention and I have letters from all six children. They've sent you presents, too, little things they've made, paintings and more pencil-holders from loo rolls, you know the kind of thing."

"Oh I love pencil-holders from loo rolls. Just what we need here, too. I haven't any. And letters. I can't wait. I miss the children so. I'm determined to have them all out here this summer . . . that's if we're still . . . still here . . . Oh God, why won't he settle?"

"Shall we tell them, Grace?" Oliver said, shifting, becoming restless. He would be going to his room soon, Lily thought. More hours of separation. Which pain was the greater: to see him, yet not to speak and touch as they had come to do? Or to have him out of sight, suffering, when she could be there enjoined in his physical anguish which was becoming hers?

Grace drifted her attention back and when it settled on his words, she was alight again. "Oh, Oliver, yes." She went behind his chair, leaning over to embrace him. "Oliver said this morning he would like to stay on here a while, isn't that wonderful?"

"Well, I'm only going back to go into care. Don't mind postponing that for as long as I can."

Was he making excuses? Was he even looking at Lily? So there was to be nothing, it seemed, for the two of them but severance.

"I think I must lie down a bit," Lily said, rising, trying to look around the company impartially, all strength gone from her eyes. "Too much sun, probably."

She had reached the steps when Oliver called her. Turning, she saw him lunging about for his sticks. "Give me a hand, Lily." She began to walk back.

Grace had her arms about him. "It's all right, Oliver, I'm here. I'll help you to . . ." She stopped, drawing back a little, still with protective hands about her brother. Her eyes traveled between Lily and Oliver, brow folding slightly as though trying to divine the source of a faint melody. Lily waited. Oliver waited too; his head forced down now by that alien power. Grace dropped her hands from him, saying, "Why, of course. Lily will help you . . . Lily will."

Grace watched the two figures, leaning, supporting, close, stepping back to the villa, then turned to face Dennis and Angela who were looking at her. It was clear they had been waiting for her to see what they had understood for some time.

At the door of his room Oliver said, "I have only two weapons to use against Cochrane. One is the truth, and we all fear that. The other is my presence, such as it is. Ha. I'll hang around a bit just to see exactly what it is he does to her. I'm needed, Lily. There's really something I can do." He went into his room.

Alone a while, then, she would go to bed, safe there from the possibility of more confidences. Nothing here would speak to her: the stout, dark-wood chair; the carved double-fronted wardrobe; the thunder-blue slate floor; the walls, ah yes, the walls, they would keep their peace this afternoon. Lily looked at the small door to the left that must adjoin the next room where Oliver was now alone. She could go through, take his body in her arms, risk herself in the vice of his unnatural strength; and she drowned in her desire to do it. But no. His family, his people —Melissa and Sebastian—could be back any minute. She had no right. No right at all.

Chapter 26

WHEN JOHNNY COCHRANE ARRIVED WITH MELISSA AND Sebastian they came with masks, belts and picture postcards, costume dolls, flags and other tourist truck. They caught Grace kneeling at the low table before the fire, enraptured with her letters from The Garden children. She had been reading aloud to Angela, Dennis and Lily, laughing with delight at the contents.

"We've all been so silly," Melissa burst out pleasurably on entering, the other two crowding behind her with an aura of heat, dust and crowds. "We've wasted our money on rubbish and pizza and wine and had the best of fun."

"Certainly have," Johnny Cochrane confirmed.

"Really ace," Sebastian said, but with an emptiness there that made Lily twist in her seat to see him. His grubby face was strained into a smile left on too long, set there to cover what she recognized to be prolonged fear; though it was gone now, its shadow remained; and Lily thought, I know you too well.

"Would you like me to run you a bath, Sebastian?" she asked and he came to her, put the sweet roughness of his hand to her neck and she felt him drawing relief.

"Yes please, Lily," almost whispering.

"I'm glad you've enjoyed yourselves. We have too, I think, haven't we?" Grace held her arms high, envelope in one hand, letter in the other. "But my highlight is now. Johno, I've had letters from all the children. Sealed up and filled with their little secrets and thoughts and plans. Goodness, they're sweet and funny. I was just reading Imogen's. She's seven. Her mother's a wildly rich alcoholic and gets monstrously violent. Father not around. The poor woman begged us to take Imogen, didn't she, Angela?''

"Yes. She's capable of killing her daughter but loves her like nothing else. A dearer and more loyal child one couldn't hope for.''

"True," Grace said. "Listen, she says here: 'Went with Mummy to the Zoo and *Modom Two Sods* . . .' " Grace spelt out the words and, still kneeling, threw her head back, laughed, pounding the floor with relish. "You know she means Madame Tussaud's, don't you? Glorious. And listen, let's see . . ." tracing her finger along the page. "She goes on to say, 'Life's peppy here at The Garden. I like Chloë but she doesn't talk much . . .' " Grace paused, turned to Angela. "Chloë? Who's Chloë? We don't have a Chloë.''

"No. No." Angela almost snatched the letter. "Let's see. She obviously means someone at school.''

"That's not how it reads," Grace insisted.

Johnny Cochrane was standing with his back to the group by a consul table on which drinks were kept. A large mirror hung above, its silver oxidized over the years, offering phantoms among its reflections. In this Lily saw his image paralyzed, bottle poised, glass raised; he stared across to her. Could it be, at that moment, he was seeing one of the mirror's ghostly extras, perhaps that dreadful figure he had made to look like Lily and left in her room, its accusing arm thrust out pointing now at himself?

His black hair waved down his forehead, tanned skin glistened with well-being, the corners of his full-formed mouth fined into lines of witty ellipse, but he was not smiling now. Lily thought, yes I do see it, you are handsome; and trapped. He turned his head from the mirror to face her in reality, a minute twitch about his jaw, unalloyed hatred in his eyes.

"Grace, she's only seven," Angela was saying. "It's a wonderful letter. Modom Two Sods. Priceless." Her eyes pleaded assistance from Lily.

"Goodness," Lily said, "never wrote letters when I was seven. So you had a great time, Melissa? What's Siena like?"

Dennis Little added, "Yes, what's Siena like?"

"Just fabulous. I wish Oliver had seen it. Is he resting?"

"Oh, Melissa." Grace stood up. Interest repositioned, she folded away her letters in a marbled-paper file. "Oliver's made such a lovely suggestion. I do hope you'll agree.''

"What?"

"That he stays on here a while."

"He can't possibly, Grace. You don't know how ill he is. You couldn't look after him alone. We've had dreadful scenes in the flat. It's not safe. He's terribly strong and becomes completely uncontrolled . . ."

"I know," Grace put in mildly, fending off more description. "Oliver's explained all that. But there's Carlo, you see, Anna's son. He lives with her down the hill. He'll help with all that side of things, I know he will. Please, Melissa?"

"Well *I* can't stay, Grace. It was murder getting these two days; and Sebastian's got to get back to school."

"I think it's an epic idea." They all turned to Sebastian. "After all, Daddy should do what he likes, shouldn't he?"

Johnny Cochrane left the room.

The bathroom was enormous, stone-floored, dark; a single barred window high in one wall. The bath, thick marble, high-sided, stood on a central plinth with two steps up to it. With both taps gushing there was a rushing, rolling echo about the gauntly grand room. Holding on to Sebastian's arm, Lily guided him to the only chair, so high his feet brushed the floor. He had used the room already, was familiar with it, and that he should let her lead him in this way was an indication of his spent spirits. He sat unmoving.

"Shall I undo your shoes?"

He assented with no word, his mouth knotted in the effort not to cry. Lily knelt, unlaced his baseball boots (no longer pristine) and rose with them coupled in one hand. As she did so Sebastian fell forward, his head on her stomach, arms around her, letting out sobs that melded into the roar of the water. Her hands encompassing his head, warm against her, she said, "What happened, darling? Whatever happened?"

For some time his misery was unrelenting and when at last it did subside he felt about her body, pulled her fine lawn, embroidered blouse from her waistband to his face, blowing his nose and rubbing away the grime and tears. Lily bit on her amusement at his unthinking cheek. "Better now?"

"Yes," he mumbled, fiddling with his buttons and, still listless, he let her do it for him.

Although he allowed her, on rare occasions, to undress him, he had reached the age where he did not like to be seen naked. "You're not looking, are you?" he had sometimes inquired. "No, folding your clothes," she would answer, and would be.

Lily turned the taps off so the only sound left was a magnified drip and the swill from Sebastian's careful movements on entering the water. She lounged across the steps, head on hands, while he bathed out of sight in the depths of the bath.

"So why were you frightened?"

"How do you know I was?" His voice came with catacombic resonance.

"I saw your face when you came in."

"God, I'm obvious."

"No you're not. I just know you, that's all. What happened?"

She thought he was not going to answer, the wait was so long, until he said, "I never felt so blind."

"I don't understand."

He sighed at his task of explanation. "They went so fast, Mummy and Johnny, and there were millions and millions of people, all pushing and shoving and it was like we were walking in tunnels. I couldn't feel any space or air most of the time. I tried to hold on to their hands but we'd be pulled apart, somehow. It was like I imagine a riot to be, only they were happy voices. The thing was I didn't know if I was lost or not. I didn't know if they could see me, but I was sure they couldn't. I think they could, actually, but they didn't say so. We'd sit down in places, but almost right away, just as I was beginning to get used to it, they'd want to be off to look at something else. I was a real drag. Must have been. But I kept thinking that if I got lost the only thing I knew was La Pietà, no village or anything. No telephone number, and I can't even speak a word of Italian. It was all I could think about all day: what would I do if I got lost?"

Lily had straightened, resting with her back against the bath, closed eyes containing the trenchant picture. There was nothing she could say.

She pulled the brass plug, a monstrous belch issued from the drain. "Let's go fishing tomorrow, shall we?"

"Oh wicked, Lily. You bet. Ace." He leapt from the bath, zoomed to the towel rail on the far side of the room, pulled one off and wrapping it around him held a fist aloft, calling with triumph, "Ta . . . raaa" leaving Lily standing, somewhat unnecessarily, towel draped across her hands.

Before dinner, finding no one about, Lily poured herself a drink and went to the stone balustrade. The leftover day dawdled, dwindled, dawdled beyond the hills, flirting with infinity. Across the terrace below were signs of a once-formal garden, a square patch of weeds with ruined paths between, contained within brick walls. One could work on that, bring it to life again. Grace could be happy here if only he would let her. What if they left the truth unsaid, find Carol, move the children . . . Let's Pretend?

Lily was aware of someone approaching from behind, hoped it would be Grace. They had not talked, not really. A hand reached past her and placed a photograph on the balustrade. Without registering the picture Lily turned and saw Melissa. "Hi."

Melissa did not smile and Lily understood she was meant to look at the photograph. Although the image was blurred and aslant Lily saw quite clearly herself and Oliver. He was gripping her hands against him; her thigh between his legs. Their heads were out of shot but it was evident from the posture that her head rested on his chest. It was Sebastian's picture, and it said it all.

"How long have you had this?" Lily raised the photograph closer.

"Since Esther brought the whole lot round. That's why she did it. She saw this, the obvious, and wanted me to know. Didn't say anything, just put it on top of the pile."

"Why didn't you . . ." What? Why didn't she what? "You never said."

"I never saw you. You were never round anymore."

"You're usually out anyway."

"Yes, I know that. I could have killed you at first. It seemed you had taken the ultimate advantage. Then one night he went out of the bedroom, started that fearful pacing, and I couldn't face going to him. I lay there praying for some release for him and for me. Begged God to have pity on us both. Well, then I heard him on the telephone, must have been for a cab; one arrived shortly after. I heard him leave. He'd gone to you, hadn't he? Taken his hell round to you. I had my release. And the price of it.

"I've been trying to let you see that I know ever since yesterday morning at the airport. God, you can be thick sometimes. Please Lily . . ." She touched Lily's arm.

Lily faced her. Melissa dropped the hand, glancing, frowning at it, as though by its own volition it had caused an offense. "Help me to say what I want to."

"But I don't know what it is you're trying to say. I'm sorry

for what I've done. I know it's not good enough, that it's no
excuse, but I couldn't help it . . .''

"The thing is . . . it's . . . well . . . all right. I don't mean I
like it, or want it; but what I've been trying to convey, if only
you'd understand, is that I realize I must accept it. I've relinquished any right to complain . . . Oh Jesus . . ." She spun
away from Lily, one hand held out, palm up, as though upon it
was precariously balanced her rationale. "Just for once I'm trying to be sensitive. Act right. I know I lack. Told you that much
in Yorkshire. Well if he loves you . . . needs you . . . then so
be it. You deserve something back from me, after all. Well let
me do this right . . . please." The last words were muffled in
emotion. She ran across the cyprus walk, away to the left, to
the olive grove.

The voices in the walls came again when they were all in bed,
should have been asleep; but Lily was awake with no dreams to
diffuse the source, confuse the sense: Johnny Cochrane and
Grace were arguing. He was alternately angry, and inveigling;
she now subjugated, now feebly insisting. No wonder she was
tired.

Lily went in search of water.

The passage outside her room was split with a narrow slope
of light coming through the part-open door to Grace's bedroom,
giving a view of her emaciated legs hanging over the side of the
bed partially covered by a lacy something; the right half of
Cochrane's lithely muscular body, head to foot, back to the door
in arrogant nudity before her.

"But it *is* my house, Johno," her tone apologetic.

"That's just the trouble, isn't it? That's what I'm trying to
say . . ."

"And he *is* my brother. He must stay a while if he wants to;
so ill too. Please try to see . . ."

Lily did not wait for more, went into the living-room, found
a bottle of water on the consul table. The doors to the garden
were open and she went to stand on the steps in the release of
veiled air; the garden was colorless, black through gray; lifeless,
a deftly cut cardboard stage, and upon it, no surprise to Lily,
was that brother.

She went and found him struck in an attitude quite new: his
arms high and apart, thrashing, his head low and locked, his
eyes the same, mouth stiffly open.

"How long have you been here?" She placed her arms around

his body, gaining her answer from the terrible cold of it through his pajamas. He could only make a noise in response. Lily reached up to his hands, working each finger to mobility, stroking sense back into his nervous system, saying, "Come on, come on . . ."

He wrenched out an answer. "Trying . . . trying . . . help . . ."

Because his body responded to her loosening, she knew he must have been thus a while and the fit was due to pass. She forced him to walk, all the time rubbing his recalcitrant arm at her side, moving round him to attend to the other. He kept stopping, seizing up. "Keep moving, Oliver, keep moving. You can't rest yet," pushing his legs forward. On he would shuffle until once he came to a more decisive halt. "Come *on* . . . Move . . ." Her voice was low, fierce. But he would not. She saw in the ranting thrust of his right arm there was some purpose: he was reaching for her wrist. Placing it in his grasp she was snatched against him with unintended violence. "Stay . . . here . . . too . . . Lily," he stuttered.

"Oh yes," she said. "I'm staying. Don't worry about that. Come. I said move." And they tortoised on while a zillion unseen creatures percussed the night.

Chapter 27

GRACE WAS LEADING LILY, OLIVER AND SEBASTIAN FROM the bright of day into the stippled light of the olive grove; its shadows not olive green at all, but sage. Ancient, gnarled stone statues stood randomly among the trees: goat-legged men, women in robes, a unicorn. "This way. The stream's at the bottom of the slope here. Not far now." She held Sebastian by the hand while he proudly shouldered the fishing rod he had received from her that morning. "Bought it as soon as I knew you were coming," she had said.

No word from her yet that Oliver could not stay. She was hanging in there, Lily thought, though the price was high: clearly Grace had not slept and there had been tension at breakfast. Johnny Cochrane had been surly with her and yet utterly charming, considerate to the rest, as though displaying the delights that she was to miss by not letting him have his own way.

They heard the rattle of the stream before reaching it; its moisture lustrous in the air around. Sebastian had the measure of the path, let go of Grace and went ahead to the sound. When they reached him only moments later he had already taken off his baseball boots and, trousers rolled, was wading the stream.

"There are deep holes, Sebastian. Do be careful," Grace warned and he pretended not to hear, though he moved with extra caution. He found a boulder midstream and, settling himself upon it, began the business of casting, at the same time removing his attention, sinking into thought. But was it thought at all, Lily wondered, or just a shutting-down such as she had besought from God these past months and never received, not for a second, awake or asleep?

They had come with their lunch in a basket although they were not far from the house, because Oliver wanted to be with Sebastian away from the others. Grace remained a while with them in the lush cool; she lay on the mossy shoulders of the stream saying to Oliver such things as, "Do you remember when we were little, how we used to fish for tiddlers, put them in jars?" then look away quickly as though disconcerted by some more recent memory. And Oliver would counter, "Our tree house, remember that?" drawing her back to the days of more certain contentment. "I do . . . I do. We were a jolly pair, weren't we? Even though I was so much older than you . . . than you . . ." Every wave of memory brought her round, round, setting her back on the shingly shore of today's chosen happiness.

At last she said, "I'll go on back to the house now; see the others, attend to things," looking in that direction as though apprehensive of what awaited her there.

Lily was paddling in the water, her cotton lace petticoats tucked up, cloudlike, about her, the strings of her camisole top undone. She stood, hand to the crown of her straw hat, head back, eyes closed, her face lit by a funnel of sunlight coming down through the trees.

"Oh Lily," Grace called as she rose to depart, "look at you. Aren't you pretty? Just like an Impressionist painting. Do you see what I mean, Oliver?"

"Seurat," he said, contemplating Lily.

"Yes . . . yes. Well, quite. Exactly."

"Grace?" Lily lifted her voice only sufficient to be heard, did not alter her stance, hardly dared to. "Can I stay on after tomorrow, too? Just for a while?"

"You ask? You even ask, my sweet? Don't fall in now. See you later."

The hours of the emerald day eased from morning to afternoon with the intimacy of Scotland renewed. Sebastian caught no fish, but did not mind. He scampered like a fawn among the trees establishing an uncanny familiarity with the place. He played hide and seek with Lily and won. With the rasp of dry leaves underfoot, it was hard to be too still for Sebastian's ears.

They tied the bottle of wine to the bank leaving it to bump and cool in the water; they watched the ants carry off the crusts of dry, unsalted Italian bread, while Sebastian made himself gloves of moss. They joked, asked riddles; they promised, they planned; Oliver too, he was there and theirs, all part of it, until his spirit gradually withdrew as, insidiously, that other took over.

They would have to go back to the villa, but not yet, please not yet while there was still peace and pleasure to be shared. They carried on until they knew they had to return for his sake; so he could be alone to suffer his more deranged contortions.

Sebastian went in front of Oliver and Lily, walking backward and waving. "Goodbye stream, bye-bye boulder. We'll come again, we promise." He stopped, sensing melancholy from the other two. "Don't be low, Dad, Lily. Grace and Johnny'll have us back in the summer holidays. It'll all be here waiting for us." He came forward taking his father's hand, guiding him along the unsatisfactory path. "Come on, this way. Uphill."

Oliver winked back at Lily who came barefoot, her hems wet, bedraggled; lunch basket, hat in hand.

"Bye-bye olives. See you soon." Sebastian sing-songed on, fearing nothing, confident that life would come to pass as they would wish it.

Miraculously dinner that night was enjoyment for all of them; Let's Pretend won the day, they gave in to make-believe for Grace's sake alone. Johnny Cochrane was affectionate and kind to Grace in the way she liked best: she walked into the room in a haze of blue and he said, "Gracie. Fabu-luss. Aren't you a sight for sore eyes, or as my best friend here would say," dropping his arm about Sebastian, "epic. Ace. Brill." Sebastian looked triumphant.

"Really, Johno, really?" Kissing him in relief at being brought in from the cold.

"And Gracie tells me you're staying on too, Lil."

"You don't mind?"

"Not at all, my dear, feel free."

"Can we come back, Johnny, in the summer holidays? I didn't catch a fish today and I'm sure I could."

"Come back all you like, sonny, home from home, eh?"

"I told you, Daddy, Lily, didn't I?"

When they had eaten and drunk, become gradually languorous about the table, Johnny Cochrane lounged in his chair, limbs lazily disposed, from time to time lifting Grace's hand to his lips, pausing to study her fingers, rekissing them as though, indeed, they were something wondrous to which he must pay homage. And how it altered Grace: she shone, she teased, she conversed in earnest; luminous now, plumed with his love. And beneath each gesture she made, beneath every superficial expression required by the talk, was another which said: See? See? This is how it *really* is. You didn't believe it, but see. Just see.

Eventually they swapped one kind of stifling heat for another: that of the villa for the vacuum of night. They went to the table beneath the limes. All except Oliver who had gone to his room. He made no issue of retiring and they noticed all at once that he was not there. But Lily had seen; watched him go. Would he decide now not to stay on? Did he feel unneeded once more? Good for nothing but "care"? There was no longer any way of telling from his face or manner.

Grace carried two candles with glass cones, setting them upon the table, making the dark less complete, smudging its edges to disclose the faces of Lily, Angela, Dennis in their complicity of pleasure. Melissa's face was mildly tanned and unusually soft, relaxed; Sebastian beamed round, eager in his relish of the late hour, the wine.

Grace, forearms on the table, was engrossed in a prolonged reassurance to Angela that Larry would be fine in South America, despite no word from him. Johnny Cochrane remained close, perched on the arm of the chair, his hand idling with her hair, at the same time regaling Sebastian with a tale. "When I was a drummer, like, in this club, well, see, there was this massive fight. And there was me . . ." Sebastian was flushed with excitement and concentration.

Melissa said, "Come on, Sebastian, bedtime."

"I knew you were going to say that. Johnny's in the middle of a story, Mummy. *Please*. It *is* our last night."

"OK. OK. I'll go and pack but when I come back for you there'll be no arguments. Understood?"

"Understood. Go on, Johnny." Sebastian touched Cochrane's knee to reinvigorate the story. But somehow, although he did finish it, it was without the same relish in the telling.

Lily chatted with Dennis, and both had agreed they felt too deliciously indolent to move, when Grace said, "Where's Johno?"

"Gone to have a pee," Sebastian answered.

Grace tutted with affectionate exasperation. "He won't bother to go to the house, you know. He does it in the olive grove. Aren't men funny the way they like to pee in the open? Have you ever noticed, Angela?"

"Can't say I have."

When the conversation was lapping once more, Sebastian came to Lily conspiratorially. "Let's go and surprise him."

"Don't be silly, it's pitch dark. It's all right for you, but . . ."

"Oh *please*. Be some fun."

He had got her like that once before, but when? When was that? "OK. If you insist, but if I break my ankle it's all your fault, right?"

"Where are you going?" Grace inquired as she saw them rise.

"To the grove to surprise Johnny," Sebastian said.

"Serves him right." Grace was laughing.

Lily, Sebastian, Angela, Dennis, Grace: they all laughed.

There was moonlight across the cyprus walk; it bathed the villa in parts revealing it as a shy woman with undecided smile; shadows by the grove, deeper, deeper.

"How will you know where he is?"

"Easy, Lily. He'll be crashing about like you are now, and the smell of his cigarettes, that funny kind he's been smoking here."

"That's a common brand. Any prowler might smoke it."

"But not wearing that poofy aftershave too."

"True. Though that's common enough."

Sebastian swung round, hands on hips. "You still don't like him, do you?"

"He's OK, I suppose," she grudged for the sake of harmony.

The olive trees seemed to have grouped more closely, linked branches, afraid in the beamless grove; and Lily despaired of breath in the unrelenting, airtight black of it. The path, inadequate by day, was useless now, though Sebastian swaggered a step ahead of her. "Booby-doop, booby-doop," snapping his fingers.

"Show-off." Lily swiped him.

She footed on as best she could, cussing, grabbing at Sebastian when she tripped.

He turned round and she crashed into him; with his fingers to his lips he said, "Listen. I do admit it's different at night. Do you think it's 'cause there are fewer sounds, and the ones there are important?" He struck a pose of menace, "To do with hunting . . ." his hands strangled his neck, tongue out, ". . . killing," then changed to a pensive note, "Wouldn't it be nice if we could hear all the little birds snoring and burbling in their sleep the way humans do?"

"Will you please stop arsing about, philosophizing, and let's find Johnny and get out of here. I loathe it."

"JOHNNY . . . watch out . . . we're coming to get you . . ."

he sang out in the way they had when hide and seeking that afternoon. But this did not feel the same. Before his echo ceased there was a stilling all about, even the leaves became inert. Sebastian felt behind him for Lily's hand, squeezed it to guide and reassure her. "He's over this way," he breathed.

How? How did he know it?

"Are you sure?"

"Trust me."

He stopped. She stumbled on a few feet when, without warning, Sebastian shouted, "GOTCHA."

Pulverized with shock, she screeched, "Don't *do* that," but could make out Sebastian holding forth a proudly demonstrative hand. "Told you I'd find him . . . Johnny? Lily, can you see him? Right there," pointing specifically to the invisible.

"I can't see a blooming thing. Johnny, where are you?"

They could have drowned in the vessel of silence. Suddenly Sebastian lunged in a rugger tackle, crashing somewhere near with a cry of pain. "Bugger you, Johnny. You moved," he shouted angrily.

"There's no one there, Sebastian," Lily said, with a peculiar sense of being overheard in an error.

"He *was* there, I tell you. I nearly got him. I felt his arm before he moved back. He's still there. You *must* be able to see," pointing again, insisting into invisibility.

Giving up on her eyes, Lily closed them, waited and . . . maybe, yes, there was a vague caloric pulse over there; the merest lingering acridity of nicotine. Nothing she could swear to and yet . . .

"Come on, Johnny. I did find you." Sebastian's voice different, not so brave.

Lily could discern him reaching out with both hands in the manner of the posing, or newly, blind. He was displaying, for once, his disadvantage, wordlessly requesting that it might be considered. "Is it very dark, Lily?" sounding crushed. What did he know about dark? What yardstick could she use?

"Yes. Bloody dark. For Christ's sake, come out, Johnny, if you're there. It's not funny anymore."

Sebastian had moved backward, right against her, but she felt him lean away in a new direction, head focused there. Releasing Lily's protective hand from his shoulder, he stepped out with a laugh, hands lifted, spread in greeting. Humor restored, refreshed, he said, "Mummy. Mummy's there. They both are.

Over there, Lily . . . Mummy?'' Not a sound. "Don't let's play anymore, Mummy, please.''

Oh, for the sight of the sightless.

Moments later: a snap; bated weight on the crisp-leafed mold; a tentative withdrawing. Whoever had been there was gone. They stood, Sebastian and Lily, like shunned petitioners before a blackout door.

As they eased their way back, Sebastian broke from Lily as if no longer able to bear her halting course. She heard a sob, split out of him by the jolt of his run, and was left to find her own way.

Chapter 28

THE NEXT MORNING AT BREAKFAST SEBASTIAN WAS NOT wearing baseball boots.

All assembled, they had been engaged in an uncomfortable quiet caused by Johnny Cochrane's announcement, in response to nothing in particular, "So since Lil and Olly aren't using their seats on the plane, there's room for me. I'm off to London. Gracie's staying. It's all decided."

The amazed eyes that sought clarification from Grace discovered it was no news to her. She was shriveled, dead-beat with confusion and sleeplessness. So long to last night's blooming lady.

No one had aroused Sebastian. He had been left to finish his dreams and dress in peace. There they were, all caught in the hinge of Johnny's lighthearted disclosure and Grace's pain, wondering what on earth to say, when they were given a mutual Godsend of curiosity in a clop and shuffle nearing the room from the passage outside: Sebastian entered in his old, leather, lace-up shoes: a bruise and cut on his face.

Oliver and Grace knew better than to inquire how they were gained; a tumble in the bathroom no doubt; something to do with the stairs.

Sebastian must have registered the change in plan from the talk, said nothing.

"Lots to do in London. Just a little trip to *per-pet-u-ate* my art, what?"

Lily looked at Dennis. Dennis looked away.

Grace gently touched Melissa's hand. "So you really mean you'll try to get him on your show. That would be nice . . ."

264

"Nice? Nice?" Cochrane cawed.

"I mean: an artist needs exposure," adding, "doesn't he?" Her expression begged confirmation that her assumption was right.

"Oh quite."

"Absolutely."

"I know there'll be no problem, Grace, really," Melissa said, breathing a smile at the hand on hers, clearly wishing it was not there.

They gathered outside the villa in the discomfiture of departure. The place that had been so new, unknown two days ago, was now all too known. They were glad to leave. Which, exactly, was the right moment for goodbye? Having said it to one and turned to another, only to be faced with the first again, the departing accidentally kissed those who were leaving too. Every brand of insincere farewell: "See you soon," when they believed they wouldn't; "Thanks for a lovely time," when they weren't so sure. But they embarked: Dennis and Angela in the first car; Melissa, Sebastian, Johnny Cochrane in the second.

"See you in a bit, old boy. I'll ring you tonight and every night," Oliver had said to Sebastian.

"OK, Dad. Brill. Have a lovely rest." Secure in their loving covenant.

Lily had taken him aside too; it was not easy with the crowd of ears. "So. Fine, then Sebastian. OK?" They were the first words to him since last night and simply not enough; but he understood.

"Oh fine, Lily, really. *Honestly.*" His touch to hearten fell to a hug.

Off they went at last. As the second car rolled away in a spat of grit, Grace began to run along beside it, "Johno, Johno," losing pace as it left her behind.

He put out his glossy head. "Yeah? What?"

"I will, Johno. What you want. What we said. I promise I will."

"Atta girl. That's my Gracie." He saluted, drawing back inside; disappearing in the dust and distance.

"I need to go to Florence, dears. You don't mind do you? Back late this afternoon," Grace said almost immediately. She went to the garage where a small BMW and a silver Porsche were parked side by side.

Oliver, hands in pockets, foot lifted to the bumper of the Porsche, said, "Smart."

"I know," Grace answered from the BMW, with the smile of a mother at her child's favorite toy. "Johno's. My present to him. Could you guide me out? I'd hate to scratch it."

When Oliver and Lily reentered the villa it seemed to them to have expanded, relaxed in the way a host does when the peripheral guests have gone and he is left with the ones, or only one, he wanted. There was no sign of others having been there: breakfast cleared, ashtrays emptied, beds changed. Only Sebastian's fishing rod had been displayed prominently in the lower hall, supported horizontally on two hooks.

While the two sat in the long room considering the ebb of these few days, reaching unconsciously for each other's hand, Anna came in with the baseball boots pinched between forefinger and thumb.

"Sebastiano, 'e leava these in been."

"That's all right, Anna. You can throw them away. I think he's grown out of them."

"Good," Oliver grunted.

The day was theirs, Grace had made that clear. Had she done so purposely, guessing at the fissures in their act? They could walk to the penance hill: good for him to move. Must keep moving. They could sit in sun-speckled shade with books: "There's so much I want to read, Lily, and never had the time. Now I've only time."

They did none of that. Lily was the first to go to her room, said nothing. She listened there for the sounds of Oliver entering his; opened the adjoining door and found him standing waiting for her. They made love, and through the fray of it replenished serenity, which had been tapped to a dangerous low.

Glorious to lie between his great big legs, the muscles ravaged, but firm, the skin still brown ("Browned," he said, "by years of Africa. I'll never be really white again"); and to have him between her legs, be annexed to this dying man; the life-giving act giving life to him, flying in the face of clinical fact: we're one now and fighting. We'll live. We'll live: you see if we don't. Expended, we'd become two again, with our limp limbs entangled in an inferior unity and then we'd feel returning the acute separateness of living. Damn it, that was the time we'd start to talk of the very thing we promised not to. It always happened: we talked about death. They say they do: people after loving; that it's a natural corollary. But it made a nonsense of our anthem to life; affixing Amen to its opposite.

Did I lose myself back there? Yes. It happens. Something of me went out to him, did its work and vanished.

Grace did not say why she went to Florence, only lamented she had not had the time to get her hair done.

The first week passed in timeless languor. No one spoke aloud of life back home, but Grace would say to Lily, "He's worse today, isn't he? We won't remind him of London yet," and Oliver would say to Lily, "We won't discuss Cochrane or home in case she rushes back."

It was true that Oliver deteriorated after the others went. Lily's uneasy conviction was that Cochrane's presence had stimulated the mysterious curative of adrenaline; having been pumped by hatred it was now calmed and every day he faded by degrees, his distractions deeper, his contortions more rampant. Still they did not want to leave.

During that time Anna brought her son Carlo to meet Oliver. Until then his work had been running repairs on the villa and surrounding tumbledown buildings. He had only been seen distant and Lily feared a gum-chewing lout; someone with a stereo like Cochrane's friend; someone who would not understand.

When he arrived in the garden, Anna at his side, her customary stomp eased by nervousness and pride, Oliver's arms were manic, up and down they went as though milking a cow twelve foot high. A shocking sight to the unprepared. Despite his body Oliver was perfectly lucid and his voice unaffected.

Anna said, "Signora Grace, I bring Carlo," standing back a step or two with her hands spread toward a stolid, earthy fellow, mid-forties, black hair graying at the temples. This shy, smiling, muscle-bound gentle was the flower and fruit of her life. Grace and Anna believed he could care for Oliver, restrain him, bathe him, be with him whenever the need arose. Lily doubted he could do it. It took a special kind.

"Ciao, Carlo," Oliver greeted with remarkable composure.

Grace and Lily watched to see how he would respond. Was it going to be: "Ciao," fingers in belt, facing away from embarrassment, or, "Giorno," stirring the ground with his foot, resenting being paraded by his adoring mother? No.

"Buon giorno, Dottor Cary." Carlo stepped forward, grasped that right arm mid-pump, held the hand firm in his own.

Few would have dared such an action. It founded a mutual esteem between himself and Oliver, who was referred to thenceforward as "Dottore." Carlo was that special kind.

The narrow room on the far side of Oliver's was prepared for him and there he remained, looking after "Dottor Cary" with earnest diligence and affection.

There was the nightly ritual of ringing Sebastian at seven-thirty. Melissa was rarely in when they called and Sebastian would be alone with the woman who had been employed as housekeeper-cum-nurse for his father. Some nights Oliver could hardly speak; then Lily and Grace would do so for him, relaying Oliver's thoughts and messages jotted down as best he could throughout the day.

When he could form his words Oliver liked to be the last to say goodbye. Replacing the receiver and with something approximating a rubbing of the hands (for his every movement had become imprecise), he would say, "He sounds happy. I'm so glad. A few days more, Lily, eh?"

That hand-rubbing was one of a collection of gestures he tried to make with varying success. It had never been a habit of his as a well man, but now he needed to test himself, prove he could still perform little acts of common body language, watching himself critically as he did so: pointing; linking fingers with upturned palms to explain; thumbs up; thumbs down. He tried these and many more as accessories to his conversation, becoming so absorbed with the doing that sometimes the words teetered off, sense incomplete.

After ringing Sebastian they would continue to sit, trying to be natural: Johnny Cochrane was due to ring at eight or so. It was the "or so" that got them; it could be anything up to an hour; but Grace never gave in and rang herself. "A little held up, I expect."

"Naturally."

"Quite."

In the end he always came through and Grace would emerge from her bedroom having been ensconced there for half an hour, blushing, skittish. "He's very well. Longing to come home. Sends his love," with the shy, lying eyes of one delivering the message which was not spoken but might have been expected.

That regular reassurance was enough for Grace; she even seemed to be relieved of some of her enigmatic burden. She ate a little more, drank a little less, was sleeping too. She would scrutinize her dilapidated nails, shrug and say, "You don't mind, Oliver, do you?" knowing he had a loathing of painted nails anyway. Then she would luxuriate in her sunchair, scanning the hills. "Isn't it all wonderful? Aren't we lucky, Johno and I?," drinking deep the sap of existence.

Oliver and Lily did not understand her mood, but it prevented them from speaking, saying that which had to be said. After all, they were happy too.

Around the twelfth day there was a change of gear: Cochrane did not ring. At the end of the second hour of waiting, Grace said, "I think I'll call."

She was back in no time. "Ansaphone's on."

The next day she fretted; when call-time arrived it was an issue. They waited an hour and a half, a little more. It rang. Grace clacked to the bedroom in her strapless slippers, whereas before there had been a leisurely "Helloooo?" performed in the long room before she retired to privacy.

Lily stood by the drinks tray, keeping still to listen. Making out no words, she heard the sound of Grace's voice, its faltering control.

In order to hear better, Lily went to the door, glancing at Oliver with uncertain shame. He winked approval and, momentarily charmed, diverted, she thought, I do like the way you do that, I'll always remember it, and could not think why she had come to the door at all.

From the doorway Grace's voice could be heard quite clearly. "But I have spoken to them, darling. The day you left I went in person. Told them what I want. It's been telexed through. These things take time, Johno . . . What? . . . Please don't be unkind . . . I know, dear. I know and I love you too . . ."

It was the following night that Oliver called Sebastian at the usual time and had no reply. It disturbed him terribly and he rang every ten minutes thereafter, despite Grace and Lily trying to calm him. During one of those intervals the seconds of which Oliver counted with demented labor, Sebastian rang himself.

He'd been out with a friend, he said, it was all right, everyone knew. Sorry, he didn't mean to upset. Yes, he was happy; summer term was always brill at school; the housekeeper was nice, epic food. Don't worry, Daddy, everything's really ace.

They did agree, however, that from then on Sebastian would call himself, from wherever he was, reversing the charges if he had to, in order that Oliver should not suffer again. Every night thereafter at seven-thirty precisely Sebastian rang.

Grace's calls became increasingly intermittent and brief. She was strapped to anxiety once more, but whatever words Cochrane used on her the effect was to have her remain at La Pietà.

* * *

The three of them were sitting under Grace's favorite olive tree which stood stout like a matron some yards in front of the lisping grove. They were taking tea with the anachronistic elegance Grace enjoyed (damask cloth, silver pot, porcelain cups), when Anna came to the top of the steps, hand raised to brow, waving her knotty arm aloft. "Signorina Leely. Isa telephone for you."

"Coming," she answered, casually walking while in sight of Grace and Oliver; beyond it she was impelled to run.

Lily took the call in the long run.

"Hello. Lily Teape speaking."

"Lily? It's me. Angela."

"Hi. How are you?"

"How am I, you ask? Lily, for goodness' sake, what's going on over there?"

"What do you mean?"

"Have you told Grace yet? This can't continue. If an inspector comes round we could have our license withdrawn or something of the sort. I don't know."

"I don't see why."

"Because you don't just take unknown children off the street. There's nothing to stop Carol from saying we kidnapped them if she was so inclined."

"But she left them, and if she's about why can't you just go up to her? It's not that difficult, surely?"

"It was difficult, Lily, she was elusive, but in any case she's gone now. We haven't seen her for days, and somehow I don't think she'll be back. The point is, I really thought you'd be telling Grace as soon as you were alone. Nearly three weeks have passed and something must be done about them. What's stopping you exactly?"

"I don't know. I think I've been falling under Grace's spell: life's only what you see, don't turn it over and look underneath," adding before Angela could answer, "Oliver's worse," in an oblique hope that she might withdraw her insistence.

"I'm so sorry, dear. It's very hard for you, but you see everything at The Garden is getting out of balance. The Sebastian thing doesn't help either and I called to talk to you about that as much as anything."

"I don't understand."

"Sebastian's become so very violent and belligerent. He's only been here seven days but he's already made the others hate him. He's playing truant at school . . ."

"Where for seven days? And why is it *you* telling me this?"

"Someone's got to know. To help."

"Yes, but why you? What about that housekeeper person, or Melissa? Where's she, anyway?"

"Everywhere, it seems. Her Children Suffering campaign has begun in earnest: posters, radio, television. One hears her, sees her at every turn, but never in the flesh. The 'housekeeper person,' as you call her, left within days of us arriving back. Claimed Sebastian was intolerable. Nothing we could say would persuade her to stay."

"So?"

"Well, so he's *here*."

"Where, Angela, for God's sake?" Don't let this be true.

"At The Garden. Surely you know? Melissa *must* have checked with Grace."

"*You* didn't."

"No, because I understood Melissa had."

"Did Melissa say that?"

"I . . . I can't think, Lily. Not in so many words perhaps, but it was implied, sort of. Don't you ring him every night?"

"He rings us now. Has for a week or so," Lily said; distant, mechanically, facts clearing as she spoke.

"The whole thing's a bigger mess than I thought. The Garden's being misused. It was never intended as this kind of convenience. When Sebastian speaks to his mother every night he's charming, enthusiastic; I eavesdropped purposely one evening; says how much he loves it here. Melissa won't believe he's not thoroughly happy, and I wouldn't in her place. He's terribly convincing. Melissa said it would only be for a week or so, now she wants longer. No time to interview housekeepers or nannies. He's giving all of you the wrong picture and won't talk to any of *us* about why. The poor little boy is very, very disturbed. Lily . . . ?"

"All right, Angela. I'll come home, if I can get a flight, bring Oliver. Maybe Grace too, who can say?" and she thought, I hate you, Johnny Cochrane; you're at the core of it, the one who's distorted our lives. If you weren't a mere human being, and I nothing better, I could find it in me to kill you. Now she understood; it was like Dennis Little had said: one doesn't, one simply doesn't.

She called the airline immediately and with combined disappointment and surprise found they could manage three seats even at such short notice in June: a signal in itself.

She stood at the window with a curtailed view of Grace and
Oliver in repose. It was over now, for all of them. She went
outside, down the steps. When she neared, Grace touched the
empty chair, welcoming, indicating her pleasure in Lily's re-
joining them.

Lily did not sit: she stood before Grace, bending at the waist,
her hands in inverted prayer between her knees. Grace, instantly
alarmed, looked up at Lily, hand to chin, ready for something,
like a regular wrong-doer: what now?

"Grace," in a strong, measured voice, "we have to talk.
There are things you must know." Lily let her eyes slip to Oliver
who was well at that hour. She tried to imply that he need take
no part; and yet had he not done this very thing to her on their
first night at La Pietà, thrown her without warning into the re-
counting of Carol's visit?

Oliver nodded in his practiced way, showing he understood
what she meant by "talk"; that if Lily felt the time had come,
then so be it.

"Yes, Grace," he said, "she's right. We must talk. Let's go
inside. It's cooling out here."

The cooling, in moments, turned to rain. Grace walked
meekly between them to the villa: recreation over, back to the
cell of reality; she knew the time had come.

In the long room Oliver took a straight-backed chair, Lily the
sofa, but Grace remained by the window with her back to them,
silhouetted against the aluminum sky. Her arms were languidly
raised above her as though invisibly tied to a glazing bar, her
head resting against the glass. Neither Oliver nor Lily could
think how to begin now the moment had come; they sat looking
at her, hoping she would turn. She did not, but said, as though
unable to bear any longer the brewing of the unavoidable, the
first lash, "I love him."

"So you know what we want to talk about?" Oliver said.

"I love him," Grace repeated.

Lily resigned herself to take no part until she had to.

"He's a liar, Grace." Oliver's first stroke.

"I love him. I love him." Name, rank and number. Name,
rank and number.

"He's after what he can get out of you, like money."

"He can have it. I've arranged to give him some; make him
independent. A young man has no dignity always saying 'please'
to his elderly wife."

"His words or yours?"

"I love him."

"Do you really believe he cares one jot about you?"

They heard a sibilance; assumed it to be "yes."

"Then why's he over there? Left you here?"

"He's going on Melissa's show this week. She's used her influence to get him interviews, exposure. An artist must have a high profile these days. And he said . . . said I'd be in the way."

"He's left you, Grace. He won't be coming back. He know's the game's up with him and you, even if you don't. If he's ringing still it's a last-ditch hope that you'll give him the money."

"It's not true. None of that."

Lily spoke for the first time.

"He cheated Dennis."

"Johno explained the misunderstanding before he left. I've sent Dennis a check."

"So you stayed here like some pathetic child doing as it's told?" Oliver continued his unrelenting inquisition; his cold professionalism disturbed Lily.

"Not only that . . . No . . . I stayed to be with you, Oliver, because I'm frightened of something I see in your eyes . . . and besides . . ."

"What?"

"It was nice, at first, to rest . . . just to be. Not have to . . ."

"Is he kind to you, Grace?"

"I love him." So they were nearing some truth.

"Is he kind to you?" Oliver repeated.

She brought a hand to her mouth, gnawing at the back of it, shaking her head.

"What does he do, Grace? How has he made you like you are? You're not happy any longer, you're nervy and emotional."

She was crying now and Lily made to go to her but Oliver raised his hand. "Go on, Grace."

"He . . . he laughs at me . . . all the things I try to do to be . . . be young for him . . . brings strangers back who laugh as well."

"And *still* you say you love him."

"I do. I do. You don't understand how it is. I want him. You don't know how he can make a woman feel. You'd *never* understand. He told me you'd say things to turn me against him. On the telephone, he says, Have they talked yet? Told their lies? Turned you? No, darling, I say, and love you regardless. Say

what you have to, I'll still give him the money like I said I would.
He'll believe me then. He's insecure, you see. It comes from
having no one."

Ah.

"That's not true, Grace." Lily gathered herself. "He had
parents who loved him. And more than that . . ." She looked
down at her hands (a lifetime ago, a hot night in Spain, hadn't
she done the same, looked down at her hands?). "Do you remember I told you about the girl who came to my flat looking
for someone? The someone she was looking for was you, Grace.
She wanted you to help her."

Grace began to whisper a word over and over with such moi-
dered repetition that Oliver and Lily looked at each other and
over to the black form of Grace.

"What are you saying, Grace?" Oliver's voice gentler, his
head inclined to hear better.

The whisper stepped up to something louder and they made
out, "Chloë . . . Chloë . . . Chloë . . ." She suddenly turned
round with her hands ensnared in each other as though fearing
their freedom. "Chloë with an umlaut. Hahaha . . ." putting
her head back to retain tears, cliff-top stepping above hysteria.

"I knew at the time, you know, there was more to that. But I
didn't ask. No. No. I knew better than to do that. Do you know
why? Mmmm? It caused Johno to put his arm around me, kiss
my head for you all to see. Then I saw the name in Imogen's
letter, recognized it. But again I didn't ask. Do you want to
know why this time?" snarling the question, "I'll tell you why.
Because after that he took me to our room and made love to me
as never before. Yet *every time* with him is as never before.
Whoever Chloë is, I thought, she makes him show his love for
me. That's when he begged me to give him independence, trust;
he said we have to show trust in each other. And he's right.

"You just won't accept it, will you, that Johno is all I've
searched for? Eighteen years it took me to find him and I won't
let him go. He hasn't left me. Tell me what you like, despise me
or whatever, but my love has settled on him; on cruel, lying,
lovable, vulnerable, dear, dear Johno. I won't explain him. I
can't excuse him. I love him."

"That little piss-arsed con man?"

"Yes, Oliver, that little piss-arsed con man."

She straightened, rigid, turning her face from them to her
shoulder as though preparing for a blow. "Well? So Chloë? Who
is she?"

Oliver said it downright. "So Chloë's his daughter; Damian's his son and wretched Carol the wife he never divorced. She left her children with Lily one night and disappeared. There you have it, Grace. He's not even your husband."

For a long time Grace remained without moving, head still drawn defensively to one side, until she said, "And you put them, those children, in The Garden."

No answer was required. Grace walked with precarious stateliness out of the room.

Oliver and Lily drew close with not a word to say. Ended, it was all ended, but each other for more hours yet. Then Grace reentered.

It must have been to do with the light or the angle at which she was standing, but Lily noticed, for the first time ever, regrowth in Grace's hair, a full whitish quarter inch, glowing somewhat, like a halo between scalp and hair.

"I just thought you ought to know," hands still ensnared, "I love him. Nothing's changed. Marriages, divorces: that's all paper. Feelings remain, they're the real contract." She departed for the last time that day.

It was then Lily told Oliver that she had booked three seats on tomorrow's flight. "Ah," was all he said for a while, then, facing away from her, "dream time's over for all of us."

"I've no choice, Oliver. There's something I have to sort out."

"Of course." But he did not understand. She could feel his belief that she wanted to be free of him. What was there in her life, other than himself, that could demand her so? Only Sebastian, and Lily was thankful he did not remember that.

"And I think Grace will want to go too, don't you?"

"Sure of it."

Still he would not look at her.

She reached toward him. "It's not over. It doesn't have to be over."

"It does, you see. It does."

Nothing to say. And she sensed they were talking about different things.

Johnny Cochrane did not ring at the appointed hour. Sebastian did.

Oliver had been waiting beside the telephone fending off a fit with the lowest of reserved strength. When it finally rang he could hardly speak. Lily answered and passed the receiver to him; she did not mention going home tomorrow, nor did Oliver.

Sebastian did most of the talking and, despite Oliver's tortured responses, it was happy stuff. When the call was concluded Oliver did his routine with the hands: rub, rub. Deep, now, in a cavern of his disability, barely capable of speech, he managed with vocal groping. "He . . . says, 'Life's acely wicked.' New one . . . eh, Lily? Good that." He went to his room.

Lily followed to check he had taken his pills: he had, but that was the prelude to the first of the protracted fits. At eleven that night, exhausted, Lily knocked on Carlo's door and he took her place near Oliver to see he did no damage to himself.

Lily opened the door to Grace's darkened room. "Grace?" There was no answer but a wakeful thrum encouraged her to continue.

"I'm going back to England tomorrow. It's time for Oliver and me to go. I've booked three seats, though, just in case . . . that is just in case you wanted to join us; not be here alone, you know. We'll be leaving first thing."

Remaining without answer, feeling she had been heard, she went to bed and dreamt, of all things, about Lippizaner horses, until she was awoken by Oliver's shout, "LILY, I WANT YOU . . ."

She tumbled through the adjoining door, horses still in her head, to see Carlo supporting Oliver's gyrating body.

"I'm here. It's all right. I'm here," trying to grasp his lunging arm.

"NO CARE."

"I do care. I do, my darling."

"NO SEE: NO CARE: NO HOME. PIETÁ TILL END."

"I've got it," she said. "They won't take you off, Oliver, not into care, if I can help it. And I'll be back to you, my love, as soon as I can."

All his limbs stiffened then and he descended into a long abstraction. Carlo left them and Lily lay in Oliver's bed half-watching, half-dreaming, those Lippizaner horses again.

Chapter 29

THE PLASTIC LUNCH-TRAYS HAD BEEN SERVED AND COL-
lected in the dead-aired aircraft; the pilot was muttering
through the speakers about being over Paris, and Grace
had scarcely spoken.

A few hours previously Lily had been outside the villa waiting
for the taxi, believing, after all, she would be traveling alone,
when Grace appeared, her face bloated, lined as though it had
been immersed in fluid overnight. "Where's Oliver?"

"He asked to stay here, Grace. He's frightened of going into
care. I guessed that, though he never said before. Would it be
all right? For a while anyway, until I can think of another way.
Maybe get another place?"

"My poor, poor Oliver," she murmured, and went away to
see him. On returning she said, "I feel safe to leave him with
Carlo and Anna. Don't you?" wishing for confirmation.

"For a day or so, yes."

"A day or so," Grace repeated. That was the last she had
said.

Grace, head back against the seat, eyes closed, raised her
fourth gin and tonic to her lips.

"What'll you do when you get to London?" was the question
Lily finally selected.

Without a change of position or expression, "I'll go straight
to The Garden, see those children for myself."

"Sebastian's there."

"Where?"

"At The Garden."

Grace lifted her head, disbelieving. "What?"

"Melissa put him there. The housekeeper left and she had no time to interview others. Angela thought Melissa had squared it with you."

"Is Melissa mad? *Out of her mind?* She knows as well as anyone it's not the sort of place for Sebastian. He could be terribly upset by it . . . She had *no* right."

"He *is* terribly upset."

"Does Oliver know?"

"I purposely didn't tell him. I think he'd have gone crazy. I was relieved when he said he wanted to stay behind."

"It's for the best." She reached for Lily's hand, one step to reconciliation. "Oh God, Lily, what madness life is."

Slate-skyed England welcomed them with tepid air, but as the taxi drew up outside The Garden in its leafy street, there was a flourish of sunshine, just to show what could be done.

Mary, the housemother, a warm, fulsome, mouse-colored person, opened the door. "Grace. How wonderful to see you. Angela's here and said there was a chance you'd come."

Angela stood at the back of the narrow hall. "You came then, Grace. There's been the most awful misunderstanding."

Although Grace looked unsteady, shattered, she was showing a determined authority. "There certainly has," and moved on to a back room, leaving Angela to mouth at Lily, "Does she know?" Lily nodded.

The room was a brightly painted playroom, toys about the floor. Grace seated herself in an armchair.

"Tom's collecting the children from their schools," Mary opened. "Now there's Sebastian too, it takes longer."

"And the others?" Grace asked. "They can't be at school."

"Chloë and Damian aren't, no."

That Mary knew there was a personal involvement was plain from her change of delivery; from the outright to something more discreetly comforting. Lily contrived to have Angela look her way, implying the question "Does she know everything?" with a flick of the fingers. Angela emphatically pouted "No."

"They're over there, out in the sandpit. See?" Mary said.

Grace went to the window. Little blonde head, little dark head, lowered in childish industry. "Bring them to me, please." Grace reseated herself.

Angela and Lily stood with their backs to the wall, each retracing how all this had come about. Could they have done better? Could it have been different?

Mary led the two inside, their hands in hers. Neat, clean,

changed children from the ones Lily had briefly succored. "This is Chloë and this is Damian. Are you going to say hello, children? This is Grace." But Chloë's head had swiveled to Lily. Lily looked away.

Grace drew back in her chair as though reviled, while her eyes took stock of their passive features. She began to shake her head, then cupped Damian's face. "So you are then. You really are." (Mary looked inquiringly at Angela who waved her hand to dismiss it.) Grace touched Chloë's spindrift hair. "Look at you," her voice beginning to shake, "aren't you pretty?" Lifting her, holding her close, Grace buried her face in the child's body, with her other arm drawing Damian against her knee.

Bumping, thumping, shouts came from the hall. "They're back," Mary said.

"Hang up coats first, children. How many more times?" they heard her husband call.

A pale-faced girl with black plaits came into the room, stopped, then swooped upon Grace shouting, "Look, everybody. It's Grace at last."

"Imogen, darling." Grace bundled her in with Chloë. Five other children—two boys, three girls, upwards of nine, none older than twelve—collided in the doorway, all making for Grace.

They fêted her, stroked her, plied her with questions and, afloat on the tide of their joy, Grace reached for the large colored carrier bag she had brought with her from Italy. "This is for you . . . and this is for you . . ." handing wrapped presents to each. "Little things I've been collecting for all of you since I've been away."

Chloë watched the pretty parcels being passed in front of her, looking in the bag each time after another had been brought forth. When the presentation was complete she fixed a stare on Grace. Grace stared back some moments, broke into a smile. "And this is for you." A parcel each for Chloë and Damian.

Lily was thinking: they seem happy; the scene can't be so unlike the return of many a traveling mother. But she's not their mother; it's a limited relationship and the children know it without being told. And, yes, the house is very nice: prettier, warmer, cleaner than many a family dwelling. But whatever they did—fancy curtains, private corners, games, good food, fun—they couldn't remove the snuff of authority. Yes, Lily thought, I'd have hated it too. She touched Mary's arm. "Where's Sebastian?"

Drawing her attention from the delightful scene, the reminder caused a closing of despairing eyes. "Honestly, Lily, we really tried. He's not the boy we've had to visit us in the past. And it's not like we don't know how to handle him. Tom and I've dealt with blind and all sorts of handicapped before we came here. It's just not working."

"I know. Don't worry. I'm taking him home."

"He'll be in his room. Top of the stairs on the right."

Lily knocked at the door; no reply. She opened it. Sebastian was standing defensive and suspicious in the center of the room, his head cocked to the door.

"Hi, Sebastian. I've come to take you home."

"No point. There's no one there," he said, showing no surprise.

"Well I'm going to fix that. I've not worked out how, and Daddy's still in Italy, he'll need me back soon, but I'm not leaving you. Not until we've arranged things better."

"I want to stay here."

"No you don't. You're miserable. I've heard what's been going on and I remember what you said about this place. Back in the winter we were sitting on the stairs, remember? You said this place was for children who've got no one, that it . . ."

"Don't say that."

"That's why you're coming with me. You're not one of them. You've got a family, parents who love you. I'm putting some things in your bag now. I'll collect the rest tomorrow. Come on."

He followed her down the stairs but would not enter the playroom.

"Grace," Lily called through the cluster of children, "I'm taking Sebastian home. His home."

"Well I'm coming too, Lily," Grace announced, a chorus of dismay from the children. "I'll be back tomorrow and I'll stay till bedtime." To the adults she said, "I'll spend the day here. Go through things. It's about time."

"I'll drive you," Angela said.

As they pulled away, Lily and Sebastian in the back, Sebastian brought his mouth close to her face whispering, "Is there anyone there? Somewhere down the road?"

"Man walking a dog. Why?"

"No one else? Sure?"

"Sure. Why?"

He withdrew to the corner, averting his face from Lily.

During the journey Grace lapsed back into silence; Angela was to remain unchallenged today. They stopped for Lily to buy food and she thought it was a good omen to find a box of frozen chocolate éclairs. On reaching home, before driving off, Angela counseled Lily in private, "Whatever you do, you stay with Grace."

"She seems all right, though, doesn't she? Strong, in a way."

"Don't be fooled, Lily. I've met it before. Don't leave her alone tonight. I'll be with her all day tomorrow."

Going up in the lift, Lily nudged Sebastian, putting on her Mae West voice, "Her place or yours?" hoping to soften the cold set of his face.

"Don't care."

It was the kind of moment that is helped by a glance thrown to an understanding third person, but Grace was equally detached, staring as unseeing as Sebastian through the concertina gate at sliced floors passing.

Bearing in mind Angela's words, Lily said, "OK, we'll eat up at Grace's."

Neither bothered to answer.

The flat was just the same. Why shouldn't it be? The stinking rubber flooring cloaked the sounds of their entry, reducing it to coy squeaks; Johnny Cochrane's beastly bits throwing their shadows. Nothing would induce Lily to enter her own room; there was nothing there she needed and the figure would be waiting. She went straight to the kitchen; Grace went to the drawing-room where the gin was kept. Sebastian remained, head down, hands in pockets, in the passage.

I'll leave him be, Lily thought, wait till he's eaten; nothing like food to bring him round. They'd talk then. She'd reach him.

Grace came to the kitchen to rummage irritably in cupboards.

"What do you want?" Lily asked.

"Tonic. There's no tonic."

Uninterested, Lily went to the kitchen door to see if Sebastian remained as before. He had moved to the end of the passage, standing quite still, a few steps inside Grace's bedroom, holding on to the door handle.

Lily was about to leave it, call him when supper was ready, but it struck her as an odd thing to do, stand in a doorway.

Grace, about to return to the drawing-room, having found her tonic, also saw Sebastian. She must have thought the same as Lily for she called softly, "Sebastian?"

He did not move.

Grace and Lily moving closer with inexplicable caution, began to hear a chinking and chiming.

"Johno's left a window open," Grace said with a smidgeon of relief, a fond reminiscent smile. "It's the fine chains above the bed. That's what Sebastian's listening to. It's rather nice. They always do that when there's a breeze." Grace went on past Lily, saying to Sebastian. "Don't be frightened, darling, it's only the wind blowing the chains on the bed. Let me past and I'll shut the . . ." She drew up behind him with no further word.

Lily approached. "What's the matter?" easing Grace aside to see on through.

The room was airless, dustily stark in the early evening light penetrating the closed widows, the half-open curtains. Cochrane's clothes sagged in heaps around the floor and on the bed was Johnny Cochrane himself, pumping, groaning for all he was worth, gripped about by female arms and legs.

He jerked his head round to the door, froze in his action, jaw dropping. "Bloody hell . . ."

"What's the matter?" The female voice that went with the arms and legs. Melissa's face emerged from beneath him. "Oh, my God . . . Sebastian . . ."

The following seconds carved themselves immovably in the process of time: four faces in a single attitude of horror, and Sebastian, mouth pulled in over teeth; all his features braided into an unfathomable response.

"Come on, Sebastian, let's get out of here." Lily pulled at him.

He clumped back through the passage, down the stairs; she had to guide him to prevent him from falling. In his own home he went straight to his room, shut the door; Lily went in after him. He had thrown himself on a huge plaid beanbag, legs and arms thrust out like a redundant puppet. Lily knelt next to him, lifting one of his hands, curling the fingers, enclosing it, inert, within her own two hands. She did not try to speak.

When Melissa arrived at the door of Sebastian's room, Lily rose, feeling peculiarly disadvantaged.

"Lily?" she said.

Lily let go his hand, closed the door behind her. They went into the white-walled, green-ferned living-room with the African treasures and the photographs, and quite without warning Lily brimmed with a terrible longing for Oliver.

"Lily," Melissa started straight in, "do you think he understood?"

"He saw."

She regarded Lily with diminishing patience. "For Christ's sake don't play with words at a time like this. Does he understand or doesn't he? Does he know about that sort of thing?"

" 'That sort of thing' is his own expression for it. He saw, I'm telling you; just like he saw you in the olive grove."

"What olive grove?" Melissa flared, turned her back.

Very well, Melissa, Lily thought, as you please. "He can't stay on in The Garden, you know. It's the wrong place for Sebastian."

"I know. Grace just about made that much clear. I had no choice, and Sebastian absolutely agreed, really he did. Angela kept saying things, but I think she was just trying to be difficult . . ."

"She wasn't."

"He *knows* I love him, but I have to work. Especially since Oliver . . ."

"*We* see that, but he's terribly confused. I think he can only see his father's very sick; he's in a home he's always had a dread about, and now you're having an affair with . . ."

Melissa whistled round to face Lily. "And who is his father having an affair with? Tell me that?"

Lily flushed, took steps backward, and almost immediately Melissa said in a level tone, "Please forgive me, it's not easy to hold on all the time. Where is Oliver, anyway? Isn't he with you?"

"No. He wants to stay at La Pietà until . . . I don't know how long."

"But we're paying for his room at the clinic. He's three weeks late already. They won't hold it indefinitely."

"In that case I'd let it go."

"I see."

"Are you in love with him?"

"I take it you *do* mean Johnny?"

"Yes."

Melissa pushed hand in hair, head back, sighed, "Oh God, Lily. In love? In love? Well no. But I've felt so bad, low, inadequate where Oliver's concerned. You've made me feel that. And Johnny's just lifted me, made me feel like a woman again. Sort of whole, desirable. More than in years. Heavens, if you don't know the feeling I can't explain. I've been infatuated, I suppose. I kept thinking this one last time, just once more. It can't hurt. Who'd know? He's live on my show tomorrow. It means such a lot to him. I was going to make that the end, as it were.''

''And now?''

In a manner that implied Lily was short on reason, Melissa said, ''Well we've got to go through with that. Surely you can see? I mean, that's work. But I must make it right with Grace, make her see it wasn't serious. She'd understand, a woman of her experience. Don't you think? Sebastian's harder. I don't know what I'll say to him, but I'll think of something. I'll make him respect me again.''

''You can't give up work, even for a bit.'' A possibility offered as a statement.

''Of course not. And Children Suffering is right on course now. Actually, I've found someone, if only Sebastian will take to her. That's the problem: he drove the other housekeeper out, terrorized her, so she said.'' Melissa uttered a short laugh at the idea.

''I plan on being around a day or two . . .''

''NO,'' Melissa nearly shouted, restrained herself. ''You've got my husband; you're not having my son as well.''

Sebastian came into the room, went straight to the telephone, meticulously counted and dialed.

''Daddy? . . . Hi. How are you? . . . Oh brill, that's cool . . . Me? Fine . . . What was it I said then . . . ? Oh right: acely wicked. Well, life *is* acely wicked. A boy at school always says that . . . Yes, they arrived back this afternoon. She's fine. Grace is fine too. Three more weeks to the end of term. Can't wait . . . Give a hug to Anna from me. Bye. Speak to you tomorrow.''

He was about to leave the room when Melissa called him. He turned and said, ''You go to Yorkshire tomorrow, don't you, your show?''

''Yes dear. Listen, you won't have to go back to The Garden. I know this really nice young woman who's been a friend of mine for ages. She says she'd run the flat for me, cook, drive you around, be there when I can't.''

''Oh,'' indifferent.

''Only if you like her, Sebastian, because if you . . .''

''Lily?'' he interrupted. ''Will you meet me from school tomorrow, it's half day?''

Turning her face from Lily, Melissa crossed her arms, lowered her eyes, allowing a stiff-necked nod.

''OK. I'll be there.''

"Ace." He left them and Melissa said, "Would you mind very much if Sebastian and I were alone now?"

It was as polite a way as any to dismiss her.

Downstairs Johnny Cochrane's voice droned through the bedroom door, and every time Grace entreated she was silenced with further talk from Cochrane lording his brand of reason.

Lily could have remained outside, learn who had the sway of it, but she did not want to hear the method of his lies, or Grace succumbing. She knocked once, opened the door.

Cochrane, barechested in jeans, was holding Grace close to him by the wrists. He was either trying to fend her off or pull her near, there was no way of telling; except Lily guessed which. Wouldn't it always be the same?

Cochrane ceased his talk, yanked his head round to Lily while Grace stayed gazing at him.

"Grace? Do you . . . need me?" A damned silly thing to ask. Need her? Need her? There Grace remained, not answering. She didn't need her, all she needed was Cochrane.

"Enter the prude," Cochrane started. "Always bank on old Lil to stick her nose in. Why don't you bugger off? *Get lost and stay lost*," he yelled.

"Grace?"

Grace was shaking her head at Cochrane as though at something precious broken, but Lily had had her answer.

Chapter 30

THE SINNER'S FLAT HAD THE OVERLAY OF DESUETUDE: IT was filmy and removed, steps behind time. Lily had left it expecting to return in days; instead it had been weeks. The Anna Maria Garthwaite stood dumpy and haughty, offended by dust; the Schiaparelli jacket, disinclined to clown; only the Edwardian butler's livery had the air of expecting no better than to be left and forgotten. "Sorry folks," Lily said, brushing a sleeve, a shoulder, folds. "Didn't mean to desert you." She spent an hour or two cleaning, restoring the collection's faith in her, making her peace with it, chatting all the time. The old food in the fridge had sprung life of its own for company.

There was a knock at the door; Mrs. Gregor, fronted as usual with crossed arms, her barrier against the unbargained-for. "Hello, love," the old inviting neutrality of her worn-out voice.

"Gill. Lovely to see you."

"Thought you'd done a moonlight. Four days, you said."

"Sorry I didn't let you know. I'm going back again as soon as I can, as well."

"I see." And she saw it all. "So you won't be wanting the flat?"

Lily had not thought that far. "Oh I think so. Yes, 'course I do, I've got nowhere else. I won't be here as much, that's all. Why? Do you want it back?"

"Well, it's like this . . ." Now Lily could see there was a purpose behind the visit. "I've got a George."

"What?"

"A George," Mrs. Gregor reiterated, putting up ten fingers.

"I've had two Micks, a Peter, an Adrian and a Chidi, a Shamus, a Duke, would you believe, name not title unfortunately; not to mention umpteen others," these she bundled off with her last three fingers. "Now I've got a George."

"So you've got over the one who lived here. The Sinner who left owing?"

"Thing of the past, dear, thing of the past."

"I'm happy for you. That's great. And you want my flat, right?"

"If you didn't want it, I could move old Mr. Shade up here, giving us more space below."

"Well I do at the moment, I'm afraid."

"No matter. You look done in. Not like you've had a holiday, bar the brown, suits you, that."

"I'm tired, that's all."

"Night then, duck. Don't worry, I'll find another corner for the old Shade." And in the mold of such women, she saved her *coup de grâce* for the stairs by way of a public announcement. "Incidentally, you're two weeks behind with the rent."

Lily released her laughter: there was coziness in Mrs. Gregor's immutable aplomb.

"Keep your hair on. I'll pay you tomorrow."

"Heard that one before, too."

Lily's one pleasure of that day was due last thing; bathed, soothed, preparing for that dissembling which seemed to come so easily to Sebastian, she rang Italy, the yearning for Oliver's voice growing with its imminence. It was their agreed time exactly and it did not ring for long. As she heard the receiver being lifted she pictured Oliver sitting by the telephone as he did for his son every night, and felt ill-served on hearing Anna.

"Pronto, La Pietà," the words spoken low.

"Anna, it's me, Lily. How's everything?"

"Very gooda, Signorina," her voice scratchily whispering.

"Is Oliver there? I'm longing to talk to him."

" 'E sleepa signorina. 'E seeta 'ere after talking Sebastiano: 'e seeta fix, staring, staring, like 'e do, you know. Carlo say, suddenly 'e get upa, go to sofa and sleep. Lika bambino, isa beautiful. So gooda for 'im."

"And he's still on the sofa beside you now?"

"Yais. Carlo stay by, like always."

"You will tell him I rang, won't you? And that I'll call again tomorrow. Goodbye."

Lily pulled the Paisley quilt over herself to glide around the rim of oblivion, with the image of Oliver sleeping peacefully for the first time in weeks. Glad for him, close to him, enfolding him in the reaches of her mind, she slipped, tranquil, into dreamless respite.

Because of such a quiescent closing to that day it was unwarranted to sit up, suddenly and fully awake, called to by a subliminal finger-snap. Lily looked about; the clock read ten past four. Outside old night and very young day were doing something almost too intimate to watch; nothing like the full parade of dawn, dressed up and ready for eyes. Lily stood by her window watching the happening in the sky and knew there was something unnatural about this day; something had emptied out of the world. If she had been told that humanity had moved off elsewhere, forgotten her, she would have said, "Ah, I see, that's it." She surveyed her room, possessions all intact; opened the door; saw the hall, the stairwell in sullen vacancy.

The void was within her; she returned to the window to think. Was it Oliver? That sleep of his: the end? They would have called. Did they know yet? Yes, Carlo would know with his tender observance. Then what? Angela's phrase sprang out so sharp she might have been in the room: "Whatever you do, you stay with Grace. Don't be fooled . . . don't leave her alone tonight."

"She wasn't alone," Lily said aloud. Lord God, after all these years have I got it wrong? So careful, so careful and now look: what had happened between Grace and Cochrane? She should have listened outside the door, it was her part to know; that was the niche she had carved for herself, made it her duty without ever having been asked. And what had she done when that foreknown hour eventually arrived? She had turned her back and left.

Shaking, she dialed Grace's number. Not even the Ansaphone, nothing: it rang, rang, rang. She dressed, raced to her car; it would not start. She coursed down the road, the echoing army of her own running feet dispersing on reaching the main street. Few cars, no taxis, too early for the tube. Walking, running, walking, the day stretched its limbs around her, a shining day that mercilessly confirmed an absence, so sure was Lily that Grace had parceled her unraveled life and "topped herself" as Cochrane had predicted.

She slowed her pace. A cab rattled by and she hailed it. Reason prevailed: why should it be too late? Why so certain?

"Faster, faster if you can," leaning forward in her seat to propel
the vehicle, will it to fly.

Stepping up to the double front doors, the need for haste was
replaced with restraint again. Was she really in such a hurry for
this? Wasn't it just show to make up for having failed Grace?
The building within: the lift, the last flights of shallow marble
stairs, there was nothing in any of that to mitigate her conviction; in fact it was condensed in every particle of the place.

The flat, fitted in its rubber-deadened silence, was much as
she had left it. Through the partly open kitchen door she could
see her own preparations for supper, the eggs broken in a bowl,
packet of bacon cut open. The drawing-room was orderly but
for the wide-open bar.

As she made down the passage with a third-person-singular
consciousness of every breath and action, not once did it occur
to her that she might open that bedroom door and find Grace
and Johnny Cochrane, side by side, sleeping in that hideous bed;
Grace's arm across his shoulder perhaps.

Daylight streamed through the curtains which remained as
they had been the night before. The bed was empty, but Lily
had to stare hard to remove the shale of hallucination: image
upon image of Grace's body, clothed, unclothed; hanged, fallen,
bleeding, stiff. When her eyes accepted reality she remained
convinced she would find Grace dead somewhere because
something had died in this room. What would it be if not Grace?
Johnny Cochranes don't die.

The wardrobe doors, their smoked mirrors smashed, hung
open, bare hangers inside. On the floor was a mass of clothing;
all Grace's, nothing of Cochrane's. Every garment was ripped,
slashed, spewed over with hair dye, squeezed-out tubes, dollops
of cream from a score of pots; smashed ampoules dribbling in
the Zandra Rhodeses, the Jean Muirs and, among them, the
funny little Ossie Clark. There was lacy underwear; stockings;
the ubiquitous strappy sandals, bent back and broken; a fur coat
torn apart; hair pieces shredded; a lady's electric razor; heated
rollers; a face-steamer; all shattered. Every contrivance Grace
had ever used to filibuster time, outwit age, was here, but nowhere was Grace herself.

Lily went to open fully the black wool curtains, assess the
scene, find a clue to what had taken place. She pulled the cord
but one remained draped, hindered by something behind. In
lifting it free, she was confronted with the seated figure of an
unknown, scarecrowed old lady wearing a gray shift, her dingy

pipeclay hair shorn to a quarter inch or less, stubbled this way and that like a worn-out toothbrush.

Bare-footed, pigeon-toed, hands flaccid in lap, she gradually lifted her used-up face to Lily. She looked dispossessed, a refugee, and that was what she was: a refugee from her own life, from Let's Pretend and Make Believe and Happily Ever After.

Lily knelt with her head on the brittle-boned lap and cried. Grace did not move, or lift a hand to comfort. Lily pulled away and saw there were tears too in those vacant, raw-rimmed eyes.

"I shouldn't have left you. I was sure you were dead."

It was a long time before Grace spoke and when she did she reached far to find her voice. "I am."

"What happened? Did Johnny do this to all your lovely things?"

Grace vaguely inclined a negative. "Me . . . I did."

Lily took Grace's hands and did not know them, turned them over in her own: the nails were cut to the quick, softened and peeling, the red varnish smudged away; the skin all over roughened, nearly bleeding. "What have you done?"

No response. On the floor by Grace's feet lay a blue plastic bottle, the charcoal-colored carpet underneath turned pale. In a china bowl nearby was a colorless liquid. Lily smelt it, then Grace's hands. "You've soaked them in bleach. Oh Grace . . ." Lily put her arms about her aunt. "When did he leave you? How long have you been alone?"

Grace's mouth moved several times, as though the answer stalled inside was causing an obstruction. "I made him go." As she screwed her hands into fists, the knuckles began to bleed. She was unaware.

Disbelieving, Lily said, "He didn't want to go and you made him?" Grace allowed one heavy nod. "After all you said in Italy? You knew about the children and that he wasn't your husband. Was seeing him with Melissa so much worse than all of that? With everything else, you must have known he would be unfaithful too?"

Grace faced out of the window, frowning at the sky.

So there it was, Lily thought, Grace would take abuse, ridicule, a foundation of lies; she would even accept his children and that he wasn't her husband. In the end it was ordinary, boring, everyday, trite infidelity that she couldn't take. It was an inexplicably depressing revelation.

"It *was* seeing him with Melissa then? Was it, Grace? *Please* tell me."

Grace was brought to by Lily's agitation. She cranked her face from the window, her neck so frail it was a wonder her head was supported. "No . . . not that . . . expected that much . . . something he said . . ."

"What could he have said to you, to hurt you, that he hadn't said already? I want to understand."

"Not to me he didn't say it."

"About you to someone else?"

"No. It was to you . . . 'Get lost, stay lost . . .' He said it to you." Grace strained her eyes on Lily, reaching out to touch her face with bleeding fingers. "Lost? Lost? She *was* lost. *I* found Lily. And he wanted to lose her again? Get rid of the only good thing that's been in my cheap life? The only one who made it of any value? I knew then that what I'd let him do to me he'd do to all of us, if I let him." Her neck gave up on her head, let it loll to one side, eyes shut, tears forcing through. "My Johno wept . . . my Johno begged . . . my Johno used words I'd used on him to find his pity. He said all the tender things . . . he was *very*, *very* good. I was right, you know, he wasn't going to leave me."

"Then how?"

"By letting him watch me do the thing you feared: do away with myself. He couldn't watch the destruction of Grace Teape, the smashing of her silly little life, all the faking. And do you know why he couldn't? Not because it hurt so, not because he loved me, but because finishing with the flashy clothes, the make-up, the hair, the nails, the miracle creams, all the things he'd derided me for, left a woman that didn't need him anymore. He knew it. He never was a stupid boy."

They sat on without speaking further for so long that the wonder of dawn became a thing of the past; that arcane coupling of night and day had given birth to a perfectly ordinary Wednesday in June.

Grace was the one to end the restorative quiet in which they had remained hand in hand. "You must go back to Oliver."

"What about you?"

"There's to be no more What About You. Get to him quickly, Lily. You need each other."

"I can't leave Sebastian the way he is."

"He's out of The Garden now. Melissa knows she made a mistake."

"There's no saying he won't see off the new housekeeper the way he did the last one . . ."

"Yes there is, because I'll be there. When Melissa's busy there'll always be me. We like each other, Sebastian and I, always have. And if she'll let me, when the holidays come, I'll bring him over to his father. Go on now, Lily, sort your things out and I'll sort mine."

"Only if you're sure you're," Lily hesitated but could think of no better words, "all right?"

"Yes," Grace answered, and there it was, the smile; no entreaty in it, no masking of some other thing, just a smile. "I'm . . . all right."

There you are with your world demolished; you've toiled and failed; trusted and been betrayed, seen the truth and accepted: and those who care are left with nothing to do for you but inquire softly, "All right?"

Lily spent what remained of the morning back in her flat packing her collection and the rest of her possessions.

"Where're you off to, then, duck?"

"Back to where I came from and to Italy. You can put Mr. Shade in there next week if you want."

From Sinner to Shade with a Teape in between; there was poetry in it somewhere, Lily thought.

The task of clearing was still unfinished when she went to collect Sebastian.

Lily was waiting at the steps of Sebastian's school, as she had so often, familiar faces with her. Any minute now Sebastian would appear, her flag of pride would rise: I've come for him. We're together today.

Sebastian came out steady but closed; no radar beam for her whereabouts; no amazement from the others at his dash, for there was none. Reaching the pavement, head down, he called, "Lily, you there."

"Right here."

They walked to the end of the road. "So what do you want to do?" she asked.

"I know exactly what I want to do."

"What?"

"I want to go to the studio."

Hands in pockets, Lily trod an exasperated circle on the spot and bent toward him. "Why, Sebastian, for pity's sake? There's quite another photographer there now. They won't know us and I don't really want to see Esther."

"Not Daddy's studio, Johnny's."

They fell quiet; walked on.

"You know he's left Grace, don't you? Or rather she told him to go?"

" 'Cause of Mummy and him." Not a question.

"Absolutely not. Because of a million other things. Him being a shit is top of the list."

"Is she upset?"

"Destroyed."

He considered this for some time. "I can see him if I like."

"So you still think he's great, right? I thought you'd changed your mind."

"None of your business what I think."

"He probably won't even be there. I expect he's on his way to Yorkshire for the show tonight."

"He will be there 'cause Mummy told me she was collecting him this afternoon. She said it would be the last time alone with him but that you had to end things properly; even when you've made a terrible mistake and a fool of yourself with a person, you have to sort of 'sign off.' It's the right thing to do."

"Well I don't want to go there."

"So don't."

"Jesus, Sebastian, what's the matter with you? I came back only because I discovered you were in The Garden. Are you blaming me for that and everything else too? Aren't we friends anymore? What have I done?"

"Nothing. No one's done anything."

She could not continue without losing her temper so acquiesced. "OK. Look, I'll take you there, but you're with me this afternoon, right? I'll leave you for an hour, you can talk, then I'll be back."

"I want longer."

"So, two hours."

They left it at that. When they came to the shabby garage that was Cochrane's studio. (A. E. GANGE, CRASH REPAIRS), Lily watched Sebastian lifting his feet carefully through the smaller door let into the larger one.

"Johnny? Hi. It's me, Sebastian. Will you let me help you for a bit?"

A ringing of metal on metal, punctuated by the whoof of a welding torch, ceased for Cochrane's voice. "Watcha cock. Well isn't this a turn-up for the book."

Lily walked the few streets to her flat; two hours would be sufficient to complete her packing, tuck up the Anna Maria

Garthwaite, the Schiaparelli, the butler's livery. The Gilbert Adrian she put to one side. That would do for Italy. She lay her old friends down with proper ceremony in linen and mothballs.

That which had taken so long to arrange, make into a home, took no time to dismantle, and she was left with three-quarters of an hour to spare. No way was she going to arrive early; Sebastian would have his two hours. She sat in her shell-backed chair deciding that whatever it took she would find her way back to the real Sebastian by the end of the day. The surly blind boy who had emerged from school this afternoon was not the one with whom she had shared confidences on the stairs; sat beside while he fished the canal; who perched on a boulder in a stream in Italy with philosophic silence; the one whose hand reached secretly for hers in moments of fear. She'd find him again whatever it took.

The street outside Cochrane's studio was crowded. At first Lily thought a market must have sprung up, but shouldering her way through the throng she realized the people were standing, tiptoeing for a view, exchanging exclamations of excited horror. There had been an accident of some sort.

"You can't get through," a stranger informed her as she pressed on. "They've blocked it off, 'specting explosions, they are."

An ambulance siren whined away out of the street; the tops of fire engines and two converging arcs of water showed above the crowd. On drawing nearer Lily found those around less willing to stand aside and let her through.

"What's going on?" she asked of one, who cursed her roundly for shoving.

"It's that garage where that artist chappy hangs out. Gone up like a fireball, it 'as."

Lily thrashed through to the cordon, ducked, ran toward the cage of blackened beams sizzling under the gush of water. The core of the building was a furnace, familiar objects pulsing, darkening, brightening with heat: the table where he kept his mucky array of tools, the domestic corner of sordid kitchen exposed, and central in the garage was a great galvanized tank, twice the height of a man.

"Steady on there, miss, that's far enough."

"Is he out? Is he safe?" she yelled above the roar of the hoses, fire and voices.

"They've just taken him off. Seen worse, he'll be all right, don't worry. Cochrane, right? Sculptor?"

"I mean the boy? There was a blind boy in there too."

The front rafters of the garage moaned and crashed to the ground under the force of water, leaving a spectrum of flame beyond.

The fireman loosened his grip on Lily, focusing his eyes to the blaze with a loathing and awe undiminished by repetition of such sights. "Only got one out, miss. There's no one alive in there."

Screaming, Lily rushed toward what was left of the garage, nearly made it but was tackled by two firemen, brought to the ground and soaked by the splashback of the water. She fought to rise again, with barely coherent shrieks. "He's in there, I tell you . . . He can't see . . . don't let him burn."

"Get her away from here," a bodyless voice rushed on scene, "there's half a dozen more gas cylinders we've just spotted. No saying if they're full or not. Evacuate the street."

With the strength of madness Lily resisted the fireman, monstered by his protective clothing, who was dragging her to the sidelines. From there, pinioned by a policeman, she opened her lungs in an unbroken lacerating cry. Someone slapped her and her vision momentarily blackened. It cleared and, drained of sound, she saw Melissa before her.

"Dear God, Lily, what's happened?"

Lily could not speak. A fireman intervened. "We got the man out, name's Cochrane so the neighbors say, gone to hospital. He's going to be OK. But the young lady says there's a boy in there, blind, she says."

Melissa reeled, hands to head. "It's not possible . . . not possible . . . How long?"

"We've been here best part of half an hour. It's my guess the fire started a good half hour before that."

Melissa snatched Lily's limp arms. "Lily? Lily? Can you hear me? Can you understand what I'm saying? HE'S NOT IN THERE."

"They won't get him out." Lily, dazed, eyes driven to the core of the fire.

"I left Sebastian at home not fifteen minutes ago. He's safe. Hear me? Safe."

The police escorted Lily, wrapped in a blanket, to Sebastian's front door. A brown-haired young woman opened it, unalarmed at the sight of two policemen with a scraggy-haired, dirty-faced girl between them.

"You must be Lily," she said, "Sebastian's cousin."

Lily could not think what the woman meant. In all the years since Sebastian's birth never had he, or she, or anyone put a name to their relationship. Cousins. So that was it.

"We're at the right place then?" the police helped.

"Yes," the young woman said, "I'm Jane, the housekeeper. Melissa Cary's just telephoned, explained what's happened. There's been a misunderstanding."

"Miss Teape here seemed to think there was a blind boy, Sebastian, at the scene of the fire."

"Well he wasn't," she turned her attention to Lily. "He's here and has been for quite a while. Come in and we'll get you dry," encompassing Lily with a kindly ushering arm.

"Quite happy now, miss?" the police inquired before departing.

Happy, Lily thought. Am I quite happy? When was I last quite happy?

"Shock," the police told Jane. "Keep her warm; hot sweet tea, that'll do the trick."

Jane thanked them and closed the door, was about to lead Lily to the sitting-room.

"Where's Sebastian?" Lily asked.

"In his room. He went straight there when he came in. I'm new. But you know that. I met Sebastian this morning at breakfast; took him to school with Melissa. She did say to be careful, tactful with him. I know what he's going through because my father was very ill for a long time too. When he rushed in, slammed his door, I thought it was better to leave him be, not push it."

Comfort and caring were conveyed; beyond that Lily understood nothing. She shuffled to Sebastian's room, went inside, shutting the door behind her.

It was no surprise that Sebastian was not in there. She still believed he was gone in the fire. The blanket fell from her shoulders as she bent mindlessly gathering his clothes thrown all about, going through the motions of a task she had performed for him so often. A shirt, trousers, his favorite heavy-knit sweater; she pressed each one to her face before taking them to the wardrobe, tidying them away. She opened the doors, and low down inside, there amidst the hanging roller skates, flippers, piles of outgrown uniforms and his fishing rod, peered Sebastian's haunted features.

He threw himself against Lily's knees sobbing, "I don't care if they take me away . . . it doesn't matter. I had to, Lily. Someone had to and no one was going to . . . You must see that?" Lily sank, dragging him with her, holding him tight, tight, saying nothing, letting him weep on. "Daddy would've, I know it . . . but I'm frightened now . . . even though someone had to."

She delved for the residue of her strength. "Someone had to what?"

"Get rid of him, out of our lives. He was changing all of us, making us all liars . . . even you, Lily, and Angela. You both lied for him. I know all sorts of things. When I was helping him make the bed for Grace, he used to boast about what he could 'pull off.' He told me how he was going to take back a whole lot of stuff Mr. Little had bought from him. He said, 'A limp-wristed fairy like Dennis won't make a fuss.' Said he wouldn't dare . . . I heard stuff like that and still I thought he was cool . . . and wanted him to think I was cool too. A real dope, I was. He used to say, 'Don't be wet,' when I was frightened of the welding. I just wanted him to think I was big. What a sucker.

"He suckered all of us, then he started making a fool of Mummy too. It was only 'cause she was miserable about Daddy, and Johnny said all kinds of embarrassing things. If Daddy or I said flattering things like he did, she'd have laughed at us. But not at him.

"It was his idea I went into The Garden, made it sound so sensible, that I'd be selfish not to. He just wanted me out of the way so he could work on Mummy, and she let him," his body shuddered with sobs once more, "only 'cause she was unhappy and conned, but she let him, and I got put in The Garden with Johnny's other chucked-off children. Didn't I? DIDN'T I?" he screamed at her, shaking her. "You knew and you never said. Not to me. Not even *to me*. *You knew*. I hated you for that, for hiding his children and helping him . . ."

"It just wasn't like that . . ."

"Wasn't it?" His played-out body slumped. "I suppose I know that now, it's all different. At The Garden I hated everybody . . . except Carol."

"How did you meet her?"

"She came up to me asking about Chloë and Damian. She never knew who I was, thought I was just another in-the-way-child like the rest of them. We got really friendly. I took her to our spot on the canal and she told me about Johnny and how she found you by mistake. That's when they caught me bunking out, late 'n' all. She thinks she'll never get her children back.''

"She can have them any time."

Sebastian was not listening. "He's paid now, hasn't he? He's been paid back for Carol and Chloë and Damian, and Grace and Mummy and Dennis . . . and me, except, oh God, I wish I hadn't, Lily. I'd do anything to change it." He banged his head against Lily's breast. "And they'll take me away, won't they? Won't they?"

"No one'll take you away. Why should they?"

" 'Cause they'll know it was me."

"What was you?"

"The fire. I started it. I killed him." Lily bound him closer, rocking him in silence, listening to his whispered litany, "I had to . . . someone had to . . . I had to . . ."

"What happened?" she finally asked.

Almost inaudibly. "He . . . was working inside a deep tank . . . needed a ladder to get in and out. I pretended I wanted to help . . . the ultimate sucker, he must have thought . . . I got all those greasy rags of his in trails on that oily floor, chatting on like an idiot, passing things he needed into the tank. Then I lit the rags with his lighter, took the ladder away from outside the tank and went. He was still banging on with some story about himself . . . always himself . . . Lily? What'll I do?'' digging his fingers so hard into his eyes that Lily pulled them off. "Lily?" Feeling all over her face now with his fingertips, her forehead, her chin, her mouth. Dropping his hands heavily to her shoulders, he put his head into the cleft of her neck and muffled out, "Help me. I wanted him dead so much, I thought I'd be glad . . . Help me?"

"He's not dead, Sebastian. He's going to be OK."

He freed his face, confronted hers with a knotted brow, gave his cheeks two savage swipes with the back of his hand. "Is that true? Completely OK?"

"The fireman said so. I heard it a couple of times. Really."

"They'll still put me away, won't they, in Borstal?"

"No. Not you. But I'm sure they'll want to question you. Be ready for that."

"So I'll have to tell them."

"Yes, you'll have to tell them you went to 'sign off' like your mother says one should. It's hardly your fault if the place burns down after you go."

"Do you really think?"

Lily took his face in her hands. "You're very brave, Sebastian, I'm proud you're my friend. Guess what?" on a different note. "We're cousins. Ever think of that?"

" 'Course. It's obvious, Veggy Brain."

"Thanks, Jellyfish Features." This time it did not have the uplift, that old tested abuse.

There was a knock at the door; Sebastian clutched at her. "It'll be them. They'll find out . . . and take me . . .''

The door opened. The pinched, gray-capped lady popping her head in was at first unknown. "May I? Not interrupting, I hope." But the voice and manner were quite the same.

"Come in, Grace."

Grace was dressed in flat shoes and knee socks, a straight black skirt with baggy white shirt, sleeves rolled, unsought elegance in the effect.

"Melissa rang me. How are you, Lily?"

"Fine. It was all a misunderstanding. My fault."

"Oh, good then," Grace said with unquestioning finality, eyeing them, proving her knowledge that there was more she might never hear.

"Johnny's in hospital," Lily said.

"Yes, poor boy. Would anyone like a cup of tea?"

It was Lily who went to make the tea. When she returned, kneeing open the door, tray in hands, she was struck by the two faces turned to acknowledge her entry. She knew them, she knew them very well, but how changed. Sebastian's was not the same as five months before, or even three weeks ago. It no longer radiated the indelible belief that life would turn out as they wished. Grace's was scrubbed, unmade-up, frankly revealing her ordeal, but a different brand from other times. This was the ordeal of acceptance and would be done with in time.

"You'll never guess what Sebastian's told me," Grace said, getting up to relieve Lily of the tray. "He's met Carol. They're friends."

"Lily knows. I told her. But she knew all along, didn't she? And never said."

How long would this remain a grievance? Lily was too wasted now to contemplate. She did not speak; there was nothing to say anymore.

"She didn't want to hurt me, Sebastian," Grace supplied. "You can see that, can't you? Now listen," she went on, "we have a task, you and I, to find Carol."

"She's there every day."

"No one but you has seen her lately. Will you talk to her, bring her in, let us help her get on her feet again? Because Lily won't be here to help us, see? She's going back to Daddy; he's staying on at La Pietà."

"What's the time? I'm late for his call . . . Quickly." Sebastian scrabbled to his feet; they followed him through the sitting-room, watched him feeling out the thirteen numbers, then wait, head erect, assembling composure.

"Daddy? Daddy? Hi, it's me. How are you? . . . Good. I'm ace, too, really brill. What? . . . Oh, nothing much. Half day at school, Lily met me. Same old Wednesday, you know."

Epilogue

COMPANION OF MY HEAD, OF MY HEART, I WASN'T ALONE when you were alive; now you're not.

We had nine months and six days of life together from when I returned to La Pietà. I found you in the garden sitting under that tree over there where Grace is, wearing the tattered straw hat I'm wearing now. Your back was to me and your arms were acting some antic charade of their own; you were like a tic-tac man while the rest of your body remained rigid, your mind retaining a private dignity the way it did to the end. I went behind you, covered your eyes, "Guess who?" You said, "Don't leave me again, Lily." I didn't. I tried to share your pain, your unendurable sleeplessness; and I didn't endure, did I? You did, you had no choice. Sleep overcame me. However much we love, we can only go so far with sharing; the rest is first-person-singular.

I wish only the sunsoaked scenes came to mind, and the days when your symptoms vanished so entirely that we were inveigled into mad hope. Sebastian was sometimes there with his medicine of peace and humor (he was so much less frightened than I), Grace too; the new Grace: quiet, disturbingly calm.

We picnicked by the stream, followed the cyprus walk, stayed in the garden with the telescope we bought, pointing it to the hills, voyeurs on infinity.

Still I can't forget the darkness, the dying of my faith, because every answer to our frantic prayers was a new angle on torture. I ask you: if God is benign, how could he cause one of his own creation to be so ridiculous in his agony? Pain him, if He had some ineffable reason; take away his sleep; drive him from sanity. But the pantomime of his limbs, did we have to have that too?

All the time that "otherness," which I first encountered on the train to Scotland, was with us. It took your mind on journeys, long before it took your shell. So far you went, and so deep, that no touch, or voice, or drug could bring you back until it chose to return you. "Where have you been, Oliver? What do you see?" You gave up trying to answer but there was wonder in your eyes. Whatever was with us then, I was in its shadow too, yet remained shut out.

You never lost your faith, did you? Armed with your questions, you went about hunting God for answers. The harder you searched the more absent was He. The cosmic zero. You made forays into his hiding places. We only left La Pietà to visit His houses, dozens of them. Of all the altars at which you ranted I remember the one at Volterra.

Carlo was with us, as he always was; you were too strong for me alone. It was February and Tuscany chafed beneath a monotony of low cloud. There was no one outside the Duomo, the buildings in the pretty Piazza shuttered, observing siesta in winter as in summer. It was a lovely cathedral, so much energy and faith in the building. Had the workmen never been struck as I was? No wives or sons, daughters, parents, no one dear ravaged, so that they downed tools and said, "To hell with your glory."

Carlo and I supported you up the steps. You were talking all the time (did I ever tell you how much I loved your hands, the way your fingers described?). We enclosed you with our strength, ramming down those recalcitrant arms; your legs slowly high-stepping and stamping to walk, walk, walk. Even then you were all to me that is male; there's nothing in my opposite of humankind that you didn't offer me, from the first moment we met to the very last of those fading farewells.

Inside the daylight turned to ash through the alabaster windows, the air leaden with yesterday's Eucharist. I'm sorry, darling, I never did have the same respect as you. You could embrace any belief, see it through to its point. Your respect for the roads of religion carried you with love around the world. There were only two or three people in there; all women, all old, all dressed in black. Why don't we see strutting youngsters mourning? They must be there; they are bereaved too. Well, there's me now.

As soon as we entered you thrust Carlo and me from your sides and staggered forward between the massive columns with your faltering, heavy-footed gait, arms like windmill sails. The

fragments of prayer billowing up when we entered were cut
short by stares when you thundered toward the altar with your
entreaties. No stopping to kneel and cross yourself, no niceties.
Straight to the altar table you went, flailing, flailing, smashing
your fists on to the blood-red brocade, "Dio, Dio, dov'è la tua
pietà ora?" Yes, you may well have wondered where God was
hiding his pity.

You waited, staring up with your head wrenched back, sank
to your knees. I think you only wanted to rise and move away
then, but your wayward arms caught the cloth, dragging it down
along with candlesticks. Outraged, the hallowed stone of the
building amplified the crash and clatter. We went forward to lift
you and a priest with others came rushing from nowhere.

"Vogliate scusarci. È una persona malata," Carlo excused
immediately, and I hoped they would help us to lift you, but no.

"Si, è facile capire che è un uomo malato. Portatelo via, per
piacere." Yes, they said, we see he's sick. But it was spoken
with sarcasm. Take him away, please, examining their fallen
possessions for damage. They thought you were drunk, my love.

That was the last of God's houses you tried. No one home. I
think you sought him in your head after that. I never did understand why you used Italian to address God in those churches, as
though he had a national identity one had to observe.

There was the interminable night Carlo and I sat listening to
you forming the strangest sounds. He thought you were speaking
in tongues. Safe by the fire in the morning when you were allowed your body back for some hours, I asked you about it. I
was leaning by your knees. Do you remember? I do; the feel of
your hand stroking my head. Mornings were often the best.
"Not tongues, Lily," you said, "I was trying to remember
Fulfulde. The Bororo were the ones I loved most in Africa, they
are fine people and that's their language. They wouldn't go to
the towns when the rain didn't come year after year, too proud.
Their suffering was terrible. I never felt closer to God than when
I was with them . . . I think I'm trying to find my way back."

Gone to Africa, the note I never saw. But you did it, the thing
I'd always feared, didn't you?

When my belly began to swell for everyone to see, Grace put
her arm around me. All she said was, "Isn't life strange, and
rich, and good? I'm gladder than you can imagine."

I didn't know how to tell Sebastian. I was sure it would confuse his world further, make even finer ribbons of his loyalty.
When near him I began to hold my body differently so he might

not feel my changing shape. It was a dangerous course, because having our bodies close was as much part of our relationship as words, more perhaps. For a day or two he accepted my repositioning of his hands, guiding them to the less telltale parts of me whenever we sat together watching television or listening to his fancy Sony radio which picked up any country. It strained me and obviously him too, for I was at the top of the stone steps when he ambushed me from behind, arms around my waist, hands purposefully feeling my stomach. It was less than six months grown, but its shape was distinct under the dress I wore. I remained very still.

"Lily?" He said my name with slow accusation.

"What?"

"Your tummy's very hot."

"I know."

"It's a baby, isn't it?"

"Yes. Do you mind?"

"Will it be my brother?"

"Or sister, yes."

He walked to the bottom of the steps nursing the knowledge, then smacked fist in palm, saying to himself, "Wick*ed* . . . a brother. *Ace.*"

"Sebastian?" I called down the steps to his back.

"Speak, O Smelly One."

"It could be a sister."

He turned. "You can teach girls to like fishing, can't you?"

Anna, with her workaday courtesy, simply promoted me from Signorina to Signora.

I often wonder which of our passions, which love-making, began this baby. Grace and Anna tell me it will give me joy and I believe them, but just now my grief overtakes such possibilities. When it makes one of those remote, deep-sea thrusts inside me, even though it is right here, separated from the outside world by mere centimeters, it still seems more likely that my baby exists at the furthest extent of the universe. But it's there, Oliver, our child. One in the eye for death, eh?

You never talked about it, I think because it was too far on the other road, the way in, while you were on the way out; you'd no time to get entangled with new life. But I loved the way you put your hands and your head to where it was cradled in my body.

The day before you died we thought you'd gone blind. Sebastian was back in London, the Easter holiday not begun, and

Grace was with him. It was the afternoon and we'd left you tranquil in one of your rare sleeps. How grateful I was for those; the thanks I gave. And I make out I don't believe? After two hours we heard shouts coming from your room. When we went in you were holding a chair above you, shaking it and saying, "What are you? I can't make it out . . ." You threw it aside, it broke on the floor. You looked into my face and didn't know me. That was loneliness. I knew then what the end would be like. You pressed your palms into your eyes screaming, "I can't see, let me see again." I pulled them away, searched your eyes with my own. You were seeing, but you weren't understanding, no object was known or familiar. You were lost on this earth. "I want light. Dear God, give me light. Ho bisogno di luce," you roared with the terrible force you were capable of.

Carlo and I carried table lamps, standard lamps, torches, and still you begged, "Più luce, più luce, I can't see, Lily."

Anna grasped my arm. "Ginestra, ginestra," she breathed.

"What? What do you mean?"

"You come. Carlo 'e stay with the Dottor."

She took me out on to the hills carrying linen sheets and shears. I had no idea why she'd brought me there away from you, except that she kept saying, "Yais, lighta. We give 'im the beautiful lighta."

High up the penance hill she spread the sheets and bent to work with her shears. Finally I understood.

We amassed mountains of the ginestra, the wild broom that bathed the hills with yellow, tossing the blossom-glowing branches into the sheets and knotting them. We dragged our bundles back to La Pietà. The electric lights were taken away, we filled your room with ginestra, yellow, yellow ginestra; light, dark, gold, fulvous, until the air was incandescent. "Yes," you whispered, "it's better. I see. I understand." You lay down then and resumed that tender sleep in the sequestered glow.

How well you were when you awoke; how well you remained. We even walked, didn't we, slowly down the cyprus way to the folly, where we rested? Do you remember?

Such a fine afternoon, mild, soft; you, quiet by the fire. I'll only be a minute, I said, just a little weeding. You smiled. Then we'll have tea, I said. I wonder what happened when I left? Did you set off on one of those journeys, one of those long absences to which we had become so used? And halfway there did you receive an order, or, of your own volition, did you return to your vanquished body one last time and extinguish the sentinel light?

I know you suffer from our parting too. It can't just be those left behind who feel the pain of separation. But I suspect what hurts you most, what delays you, keeps you near me, as I know you are, is my grief. It pulls you back, won't release you. Almost as if you were saying, "I can't leave you like this." Yet if for a second anything so corporeal as your voice was about me I'd tear my eyes out to hear it again and again. That's how selfish my love is for you. Forgive me. I know you must go, it's what you want.

I'll do the best I can, carry on, you know. I'll look after our people, be there when they need me: Sebastian, Melissa, Grace and our newcomer. The police only questioned Sebastian once about the fire. The garage was uninsured, no money involved, no apparent reason for arson. When they asked him if the place was burning before he left, he said he "did not see." So, you understand, he had his first bitter lesson in welding truth into lie. It hurt him but he's strong and brave, he'll come on through. Melissa is protected by her work. I don't know about Grace. I sometimes wonder whether this different woman is not the one we've always known playing her greatest role, that of realist. I catch her at moments with her eyes set beyond the footlights of our world, seeking, I imagine, a face, hoping a familiar voice will call her, bringing down her sham of acceptance, making everything not like it was, but how she hoped it would be.

"Signora, please you come. Still 'e waita."

"I'm sorry, Anna, I was miles away. Who? Who's waiting?"

"The Cochrane." Another of Anna's conferred titles. Since his departure the previous summer she had only referred to him as "The Cochrane," with its implicit disparagement.

There was a movement at the top of the steps Lily turned, saw no one, only the glass-paned door closing to. She crossed the garden to the villa, pausing once to ensure Grace remained beneath the olive tree. Her arms were raised and held afar, the way the far-sighted do when threading a needle.

As always, Lily was momentarily blinded on entering the shaded long room; only weeks before she would have blundered through it, sightless, not waiting for her eyes to accustom themselves; would have gone to the sofa where he lay. "The teas are a bit dry, the floribundas are holding on and the musks are flourishing, smell delicious. Here's one for you."

This time she waited for the dazzle to die and when it did she still could not see Johnny Cochrane.

" 'Ello, girl." His voice came from the far end of the room. He was standing by the window, the sharper north light behind him obscuring detail; he was no more than a solid shadow.

"What do you want?"

"I want my Gracie."

"She doesn't want you."

"Oh yeah? Says that, does she?"

No, Grace had never said that. "She's not 'your Gracie' anymore. She's different."

"And you're different too. Due any minute, I'd say. What price the prude now, eh? You and old Olly. Guessed as much. You can always rely on an Englishwoman to love a cripple, that's what I say."

"Go away. It's a wasted journey."

"I've been watching the two of you. You digging, her sewing. She never sewed, my little lady."

"Like I say: she's different."

"Not when I talk to her she won't be. Not when I say the things she likes to hear, put her head on my shoulder, touch her hair the way I do. You don't know, Lil, you don't know the half of it, what goes on between man and wife."

It was true, she knew married people were enveloped in an inviolable mystery; whatever was confessed to outsiders, transgressions, faults betrayed, they still belonged to each other in supreme privacy. And Grace had been married to Johnny Cochrane in all but law.

"It's been a year, Johnny. She's forgotten you."

"Oh no she hasn't, and that's why you don't want me to see her. You know she'll come back to me." Cochrane remained a black cut-out at the window, not attempting to move forward. "All I'd have to do is cross this room, down them steps. She wouldn't look up when she heard me coming. She'd think it was you, or that Anna. And all of a sudden there I'd be with my arms around her."

He stepped forward to where he could be seen. Up his neck, over half his face, around the right side of his head lapped unnaturally smooth, poreless skin, snarled in parts with a lifeless purple. There was no feature on the right side that was not disfigured, mocking the handsome left which was as it had always been. "Think she'd have me, Lil? Could I turn her on like in the old days?"

Lily supported herself against the back of the sofa. Cochrane went to settle upon that other one where the tartan rug still lay, folded now, useless. "Don't sit there," she unintentionally shouted, "not there," more gently. "That one's more comfortable," pointing to a stiff-backed armchair. He remained standing. "I never thought it was so . . . bad. Melissa never said."

"Melissa. Melissa. Don't Melissa me. Never came to the hospital, she didn't. I went to see her when I had the bandages off, she wouldn't look at me. Wished me luck but wouldn't look at me."

"Why have you come back?"

"Told you. She loved me, Gracie did, still does, I'll wager. I could make her again, I know it."

Lily could not think what to say, because through all the tears and the mourning, the turmoil of their lives, hadn't she always believed that was true: Grace loved Johnny and probably still did?

"Hello, Johno."

Grace had entered without either hearing. Lily covered her face; on dropping her hand she saw Cochrane was retreating to where the light would hide him.

"No need to hide your poor face, Johno. I've seen it already."

He shrugged. " 'Ello, darling. It's been a while."

Grace placed her hat on the table, approached him so far and stopped. Slight, gray, only the blueness of her eyes animating her face, she looked older than her years and knew it, stood there letting him see until he faced away from her. Which discomforted him more: his sight of her, or her sight of himself?

"So you've come to 'make' me again, have you?"

"Not like that, Gracie. I mean, I wanted to see you again. We had so much going, you and me."

"Did we?" Not cynical, almost asking for illustration, reminders.

"Oh yeah. You know it. There's no one for me but you."

"My poor Johno."

"I'm alone, Gracie, and I'm not good at that. They don't buy my stuff anymore and I haven't got the heart to make new. I stayed away as long as I could, let the old face heal up. But I miss you, girl."

He put a hand toward hers, she did not move from him. "Have me back, darling. Remember how it was? All our good times? We had those, doll. Think of them." He touched her cheek. She stayed very still, stiff. "This isn't you," jutting his chin at her hair. "I can find the Gracie I know." His other hand came to her neck. "She's there waiting for me like she always was." The corners of her mouth trembled.

Whistling came from the garden, closer; it changed to song. "My bonny lies over the ocean, my bonny lies over the sea . . ." up the steps, "My bonny lies over . . ." to the door and in. "Look, folks, two trout. Cool, eh?" Sebastian held the fish aloft before dropping them onto the table, unaware they fell inside Grace's hat. "Who's here, Lily?"

"Grace and . . ."

" 'Ello, son."

"Johnny," Sebastian whispered.

"Right on. What are you doing here? Summer holiday again? Blimey, they do come round, don't they?"

"Half . . . Halfterm. And you?"

Cochrane's now confident hand was over Grace's shoulder, fingers stroking her neck. She was laboring for breath, her eyes shut. "I've come back, old son. Wanderer returned and all that."

"Is it true, Grace?" Sebastian took a step toward his aunt.

Grace was now looking at Cochrane, her hand nearing his disfigured face as though willing herself to touch it. She made no answer.

"Lily?" Sebastian called, fear there. "Is it true then? He's back."

"I don't know," Lily said.

"Since you're here, Sebastian, there's something I want to ask you," Cochrane began. Sebastian drew close to Lily. "That day of the fire when you came to see me . . ."

"What about it?" Hidden by the sofa, Sebastian's hand was feeling for hers.

"See, I've no recollection of you saying goodbye. It's my impression you just walked out. Now why would you do a thing like that?"

" 'Spect you didn't hear me in that tank."

"See, sonny, when I look in the mirror and this Mark II Johnny looks back at me, a voice tells me, 'Little Old Sebastian did that to you.' "

"Did what?"

"Oh, yeah. That's right. You can't see me, can you? Lucky you."

Sebastian pulled at Lily. "Is he different? Is he hurt? You told me he was going to be all right. How's he changed? One of you tell me, *please*. Grace? Grace?" his head down, hands tearing at the air.

Pushing Cochrane's arm from her, Grace crossed the room to
Sebastian, knelt, securing his wrists. "No dear, he's not different. There's nothing there that wasn't there before. It's just that
we can all see it now." She rose. "Time to go, Johno."

"You don't mean that, Gracie. It's you and me, girl, like it
always was since that first night. I was just teasing old Sebastian
here. Wasn't I, son? Always good friends, we were. Weren't
we? Remember the baseball boots? Where've they got to?" indicating the grotesque scarring. "It's this. Am I right? Don't
fancy your Johno anymore."

"Oh, Johno, if it were only that."

"I thought you loved me."

"I did."

"I banked on you, girl. Only waited 'cause I wanted to look
better for my little lady. Christ, Gracie, I've got nothing, nowhere to go, no one to . . ."

"I'm so sorry, Johno." Not cold, but firm.

"Well, then . . ."

"Well then, what?"

"You promised me some money once."

Lily let out a gasp of disgust. Grace was amused. "You're
quite right, I did. And a promise is a promise . . ."

"You *can't*, Grace," Lily exploded.

"But, you see, I have already, in a manner of speaking. Johno,
I've bought your wife a little flat. Something secure for your
children. All in all I thought that was best. She works at The
Garden now if you want to go and find her."

"You're the only one I want. I love you, girl, I always did.
And, like you said, you loved me. Come on, Gracie."

"That lady's long gone, but I tell you what, you can have your
car. Would you like that? It's in the garage."

That evening Sebastian sat at the head of the table in the candlelit
cool of the loggia, Lily and Grace close on either side. Supper
had been cleared. Set before them now was Sebastian's sophisticated radio (a present from Oliver). With its press-button se-
lection Sebastian conjured, listened intent to a multitude of
obscure broadcasts: "This is Polskie Radio Warsaw"; "This is
the voice of the Somali Democratic Republic"; "This is the
overseas service of Radio Maldives broadcasting from Male."

Tonight, however, they were tuned to BBC World Service.
Sebastian had set it, centered it, switched it off to wait, feeling
his watch frequently.

Lily, arm slung over the back of her chair, was viewing the petrol sky. A dog barked far off, another answered near; a woman's voice fired a volley of Italian, a man's in reply; a door slamming, a motorbike starting down the hill: these sounds all collected, muted and boxed in the heat of the night.

"When I'm grown up," Sebastian, head back, contemplated a vision, "I'm going to be a journalist like Mummy. And I'll go all around the world like Daddy used to. Instead of photographing like him, I'll write down everything I see, all the things other people don't." Before Lily and Grace could make any comment, he rushed on, "Hey, hey, it's time to start." Static flacked the air. All three repositioned themselves, shoulders hauled over elbows, heads low to the radio.

A man's voice began: "First in the series *Women of Our Time* . . ."

"It's the one, " Sebastian noisily whispered. "We've got the right one . . ."

"Shhhh."

". . . with us tonight Melissa Cary. There is surely not a household in Britain that has not heard this name, synonymous with compassion and action for sick, handicapped and deprived children.

"In just one year Melissa Cary has raised the sum of seventeen million pounds for the charity she founded herself, Children Suffering. A remarkable achievement.

"Melissa Cary, let's start at the end, shall we? You've had a most strenuous year demonstrating what most of us see as superhuman energy with your hundreds of personal appearances, talks and interviews. What next?"

"Next? Nothing. I'm taking time off to be with my son . . ."

"*Me.* She's talking about *me.*"

". . . we're going fishing . . ."

"It's true. We're going to Norway. Salmon-fishing. Epic, eh?"

"There's been much criticism leveled at you because the money you've raised is for British children alone. Why did you decide that?"

"It's all very well to put your hand in your pocket for long-distance suffering, one does one's bit, pays out and forgets. It's too easy to be blind to what's at our very feet, as it were. I think this year has made us all look and see the deprivation, need, there is right here all about us. If you have no money to give there's always the greater gift: your time. I've given mine, and I will again."

Sebastian moved his hands across the table, felt for Grace's, felt for Lily's, held them tight. "She's really wonderful, isn't she?"

Grace, her head dipped to Sebastian, lifted her eyes to Lily. "Yes, darling, she certainly is."

About the Author

Barbara Neil was born in London. She left school at sixteen to work in the fashion business in London, New York, Paris, and Milan. She now lives and writes on a farm in Wiltshire with her husband and five children. Her first novel was *As We Forgive*.

The
Best Modern Fiction
from
BALLANTINE